FEISTY FELINES
AND OTHER FANTASTICAL FAMILIARS

EXECUTIVE EDITORS
KEVIN J. ANDERSON AND ALLYSON LONGUEIRA

EDITORIAL TEAM
RYAN M. CONNOLLY, EVA ELDRIDGE, BAILEY
FINN, JENN FIR, BRIANNA GARNER, AUDREY
HACKETT, DAKOTA HADLEY, ALEX HALE, MEL
HEATH JOHNSON, R.L. KING, MARK LESLIE,
TAMMY LEWIS, SONIA SANTAELLA, JOSHUA
SMYSER, AND EMILIE THIESSEN

WFP
WORDFIRE PRESS

Feisty Felines and Other Fantastical Familiars
Kevin J. Anderson and Allyson Longueira, Executive Editors

Editorial Team: Ryan Connolly, Eva Eldridge, Bailey Finn, Jenn Fir, Brianna Garner, Audrey Hackett, Dakota Hadley, Alex Hale, Mel Heath Johnson, R.L. King, Mark Leslie, Tammy Lewis, Sonia Santaella, Joshua Smyser, and Emilie Thiessen

EBook ISBN: 978-1-68057-617-7
Trade Paperback ISBN: 978-1-68057-618-4
Hardcover ISBN: 978-1-68057-619-1
Cover images from DepositPhoto by dvargg, Roussanov, banglatipsforyou@gmail.com, and linabudiarti20 | Designed by Allyson Longueira
Vellum layout by C. J. Anaya
Published by WordFire Press, LLC
PO Box 1840 Monument CO 80132
Kevin J. Anderson & Rebecca Moesta, Publishers
WordFire Press Edition 2024
Library of Congress Control Number: 2024933746
Printed in the USA

Join our WordFire Press Readers Group for sneak previews, updates, new projects, and giveaways. Sign up at wordfirepress.com

CONTENTS

Introduction   v

The Dragon's Cat   I
Jody Lynn Nye

So Burn Us Both   15
Lisse Kirk

Trial by Cow   31
Andrew Rucker Jones

Blackwood's Tomb   37
Joseph Floyd

The Ritualist and the Hedge-Wizard   53
Kit Calvert

Beneath the Wings of Night   63
Ngo Binh Anh Khoa

Kitten for Sale   69
Aster Marsh

The Dreamer   71
M. Lalli Lassegard

A Rat, a Root, and a Big Orange Fruit   89
Zach Shephard

Second Life   101
Christina Sng

The Witching Hour Letters   105
Amanda Cecelia Lang & Brittany Noelle

The Familiar's Familiar   123
Maegan Langer

The Cat   141
Sandy White

Some Spider   143
Pines Callahan

Scary, Scary, Skunk   157
Heather Graham

Orphans   173
Matt Beswick

The Last Life of Hilde the Small   185
Jessica Feather

"And Have Never Forgotten"*   197
Mercedes Lackey

Fluffy   215
T. Chandler

Earth, Bonding   233
Kerri J. Roe

Not Common: A Fibonacci Poem   245
Lois T. Bartholomew

The Secret of the Sorceress   247
Alexander Hay

Sink or Swim   265
Rebecca M. Senese

Old Crow   279
Steve Rasnic Tem

Tail-End   289
Lia Wu

Nameless   305
John G. Hartness

Acknowledgments   323
About the Executive Editors   325
If You Enjoyed Feisty Felines   327
Copyright Information   329

INTRODUCTION
FAMILIAR TERRITORY

Animals and magic go together like pen and paper, books and a warm beverage ... writers and cats. We, the editors of this anthology, know that last to be particularly true. We have seven cats between us.

Which is why when our fifth cohort of Publishing graduate students earning their Master of Arts degree at Western Colorado University settled on *Feisty Felines and Other Fantastical Familiars* for their group thesis project, we knew they were on to something.

These fifteen students developed the call for submissions and spent their fall semester wading through the slush pile to find the best familiar stories. And as it turns out, we had not only a clowder of cat stories to choose from but also a plethora of creative familiar stories. So, after careful consideration and much discussion, this anthology holds to its name: about half of the stories are about feline familiars and half are about other animal familiars.

These stories range from light to dark, with several poems threaded through, but all adhere to our most important criterion: that the familiar be the main voice.

The students then arranged the stories, worked with the

authors on copy edits, chose the art for the cover, and assisted in all aspects of production and marketing.

So, thanks to the hard work of these Publishing MA students, and generous funding from Draft2Digital, *Feisty Felines* joins the previous Western Colorado University anthology projects: *Monsters, Movies & Mayhem* (winner of the 2021 Colorado Book Award for Best Anthology); *Unmasked; Gilded Glass;* and *Merciless Mermaids.* Like its predecessors, this book contains an incredible collection of fantastic stories.

We hope you enjoy reading them as much as we all enjoyed working with them. But don't be surprised if once you're done reading this anthology, you find yourself seeking out your own fantastical familiar....

—Kevin J. Anderson and Allyson Longueira
Graduate Program in Creative Writing
Western Colorado University

THE DRAGON'S CAT

JODY LYNN NYE

Warm," said a tiny, high voice somewhere around the armpit under Sochel's left wing. The dragon began to nose through her iridescent pearl-and-coral-colored scales. It wasn't unknown for parasites to nestle in against her hot skin. But they hardly ever *talked*.

She nudged the scales back, searching, but the tickle receded farther away, toward her spine. It annoyed her to be infested. How long had it been since she had given herself a good, cleansing burst of fire? But this felt larger than the usual insects that burrowed down to get away from the chill of her mountainside lair. Sochel kept twisting her long neck until she uncovered a small mat of gray fur. Ah!

She picked it up between thumb and foreclaw. An unexpected tasty morsel. She opened her jaws and extended her long, pink tongue. The bundle struggled, fighting to loosen her grip on it.

"Reeeeow!" it exclaimed, clawing at her paw with minute ivory talons.

It wasn't an insect! It was... a kitten? It had fluffy light gray fur embossed with stripes of darker gray, small round paws, and an isosceles triangle of a ringed gray tail. Its head seemed much too large for its little body. It wasn't scared. Rather, the small creature opened indignant, large green eyes, as though furious to have been pulled away from its warm nest. Sochel was taken aback.

Well, predators didn't normally eat predators. True, they often fought for the same food supply, but this tiny creature couldn't possibly eat enough, maybe in its whole lifetime, to take away a full meal from her. She set it down on the stone floor, just short of the jumbled pile of gold treasure that made up her bed.

Immediately, the tiny beast leaped for her forearm, clambered up, and attempted to burrow its way back under her wing.

"Just a minute, where do you think you're going?" she asked, taking it by the scruff again and lifting it to eye level. The black pupils spread across the green irises, and it blinked beguilingly.

"Warm," it said again.

"You're too young to be out on your own," Sochel said, looking around. "Where's your mother?"

"Yours," the kitten said.

"You're not mine."

"Yes!" As if to prove it, the kitten rubbed its cheek against Sochel's nose. She sniffed, and the intake of air made the kitten wobble in her grasp. It smelled... good. Clean. Familiar, like her own babies of decades past. "*Yours.*"

Sochel fought against the scent. It was making her feel maternal again. "How did you get in here?"

"Dunno." It waved its front feet, and a bubble of light grew between them, and an image formed inside of it. Sochel was so surprised, she nearly dropped the little creature. It had magic. No ordinary cat could manifest an illusion. Was this kitten part dragon?

She peered at the colorful cloud. The little creature was in the middle of it with two, no, three more like it, lying against a smooth wall of striped fur. That must be the mother's belly. Then, the image of the others dropped away as though the kitten had been picked up by the scruff. Light suffused the image, and the next thing she could see was the entrance of her own cavern. She knew it because of the smear of melted gold on the stones at the opening.

"So, your mother left you here," Sochel said. "Well, we need to get you back to her."

But where to begin? Finding one cat out of the thousands or millions in Ombroad must be impossible. Fortunately, she knew someone who was well versed in the impossible.

She tucked the kitten under the scales at the back of her neck. "Come along," she said. "We're going to find your mother."

Sochel spread her wings and arrowed out of the cave into the cold morning air.

"Eeeee!" the kitten sang, its tones piercing her eardrums like a spear. It didn't sound scared. It sounded *thrilled*.

"I don't need a kitten," Sochel complained to Borun, the court wizard who served the queen of Ombroad, the kingdom just over the mountain range from her high cave fastness. His circular stone tower stood high over the capital city, Duranton, and its crenelated roof was large enough for her to land on if she curled up around the flagpole at its center.

Borun looked at her, his blue eyes twinkling over his gold-rimmed half-spectacles, so startling in his dark brown face. She suspected he didn't really need the glass circles, but their presence gave him a look of greater wisdom. They had been friends for nearly a century, and had seen four kings and queens take the throne in that time.

"Obviously, someone, I suspect the mother, believes that you do," he said, chuckling. The kitten had crawled out of Sochel's scales and nestled in between Borun's silvering beard and fluffy knitted scarf. "Friendly little fellow, isn't he?"

"It's a boy, then?"

Borun plucked the small beast from his garments, held it up, and peered under the tail. "Yes, definitely a boy. He did magic, you say?"

"Yes. An illusion. A memory, I think," Sochel said, watching the wizard playing with the kitten. "His mother and the rest of the clutch."

"Litter," Borun corrected her. "Well, I think you can rule out giving him away."

"Why? I can't be forced to adopt him!"

"It's not a matter of being forced. I take it you have never heard of the Cat Distribution System?"

"No!" Sochel lashed her tail into one of the stone crenelations, causing it to shift against the mortar holding it in place, threatening to send it falling over the side of the tower. Borun flicked out the hand not holding the cat, and the stone settled back. Grinding sounds ensued as the cement mended itself. "That sounds like foolish wizard talk."

"It's only that it has proven to be true over and over again. A cat or, in your case, kitten appears in your vicinity, to assuage a need that one of you has. It aids in the balance of power, offers companionship to those who need it, augments or controls magic, and sometimes provides something to care for to those who have forgotten compassion."

"I don't need a cat," Sochel snapped.

"Well, maybe he needs you," Borun said. "Did you ever find out his name? Perhaps there is a clue there. What are you called, son?"

"Merrow," the kitten replied. He leaped from Borun's grasp and snuggled back into the beard and scarf. Purring emerged from the woolly nest. Sochel shook her head.

"You see? He doesn't even know his name."

"I think that is his name," Borun said. He reached into the air. Suddenly, a huge, royal-blue-bound book was in his hand. He thumbed through its pages. "Hmm. Hmm! Well, you have a new friend there whose name is steeped in legend. 'Merrow' means 'defender.' Such a well-named creature would make an excellent familiar, my friend."

"I do not need a defender that is less than bite-sized," Sochel said. "Nor do I require a familiar. My magic is sufficient for my needs. I want only to find his mother and return him to her."

"I believe I can help with that," Borun said. He pulled a chair and a low table out of the air and sat down at it.

"You're a wielder of arcane power. Do you have a cat from her?"

Borun chuckled. "Oh, of course I do! Edriu is in the palace at this moment, keeping an eye on the queen's third son. Prince Harint is four, bound to take over from me one day. Quite a wizard in the making." Borun kept flipping through the pages. "Ah! I found it!"

Sochel peered over his shoulder. "The Cat?"

"No, no, the spell to locate her."

Referring to an ornamented leaf in the big book, Borun waved his hands. "Let us see the Great Cat Mother, O spirits. Find her for the sake of this small one." He gestured toward the kitten. Sparks flew from Merrow's head to Borun's fingers, scorching them red. He shook them with a hiss. "Bless Nature, this one is a powerful familiar!"

Sochel refrained from repeating that she didn't need one. For whatever reason, the wizard didn't believe her, or simply thought that he knew best. That was typical of her old friend. She watched him work.

The blue book vanished, and a rough crystal the size of his head appeared in its place. He set both hands at either side of it, and it illuminated with a deep red light. He reached out to touch the kitten on the head. It rubbed against his finger. He smiled. Beams of the same green as the kitten's eyes shot off from the crystal in a number of directions. One of the fierce lines pierced directly through the dragon's body. She flinched, but it didn't hurt.

"What are those?" Sochel asked.

"Beacons. Traces. They show where the Great Cat Mother is, or where she is going to be. She will be delivering kittens to the places that they ought to be. We want the freshest trail, so you can meet her there." He followed each beam with his finger, then lit upon the one that led to the west. "This is it. She is not there yet, but will be shortly. Out to the west," Borun said, pointing toward the blue shadows of a distant mountain ridge. "Near the Six Cascade Falls. I sense her approach to a warren of caves underneath their cataracts."

The dragon frowned. "That is Ochse's home. He and I do not get along." That was, if anything, an understatement. They had been in a blood feud for almost thirty years. She could hardly recall how it had begun, but incursions upon the villages she had protected had all the earmarks of a cyclops attack: stomped houses, wells kicked in, trees uprooted bodily. Naturally, she had retaliated in kind, tit for tat, and the land between their domains had suffered horribly.

"Well, carry a flag of peace," Borun said, his eyes twinkling again. "It's certainly time you reached out and mended fences. She'll be there in a matter of hours. You must catch her, or I'll have to do the invocation all over again. The Great Cat Mother goes where she must. Time is of the essence, my friend. Do not dally."

"I will not. I can take Merrow there and explain that a mistake was made," Sochel said. "Thank you, good wizard."

"The Great Cat Mother seldom makes mistakes, my friend." Then, Borun looked thoughtful. "Although it's not unknown. I remember... well, never mind. Go. I estimate it's a six-hour flight for you, and you have just about that much time to make your appointment. Fare you both well!"

Sochel gathered up Merrow, removing him wailing in protest from the wizard's mop of curly silver hair. She placed him in a nest of scales behind her right ear, and prepared to spring upward. He carried on squalling. She frowned, bringing her impressive brow ridges to the base of her long snout.

"It would have been less trouble if I had just eaten him."

Borun chuckled. "He would have given you bellyache, my friend! He's meant to be your companion and protector."

"Hmmph!" Sochel couldn't even find the words to retort. She thrust upward into the air and spread her wings.

She flew away with Borun's hearty laughter following her.

The dragon was not looking forward to confronting the one-eyed giant. She had to think of what to say to appease Ochse that would allow her to enter his labyrinth, greet the Great Cat Mother, divest herself of the pesty little kitten, and depart, all without causing another war. Calming words didn't come easily to her. She preferred to fight with fire and magic, and let people give her the space she desired. If Borun hadn't been so insistent that approaching the Cat was vital to the balance of power, she'd have dropped the little beast off on the doorstep of a cottage, and let the villagers within deal with his magic.

The wind began to stir, flicking tiny droplets of rain in her face. She didn't mind a storm, but she worried about the small creature on her head catching cold. She had never thought much about how mammals coped in weather.

Merrow must have been worried, too. He chirruped urgently.

"What is it?" she asked.

"Lightning!" the kitten exclaimed.

"What, in this drizzle?" She glanced at the thin curtain of clouds overhead.

Suddenly, she was surrounded by stabbing bolts of blinding blue-white. The first one jabbed her in the belly. Sochel bellowed in pain. Another carved a gash in her left foreleg. She dodged away from the silver claws. They weren't coming from the clouds! She breathed out a burst of red fire imbued with magic. The red haze swallowed up one bolt after another, but more kept coming, clipping off scales or plunging into her limbs. Sochel fell a dozen yards and caught herself. Opening her wings, she arrowed up toward the clouds. She looked around furiously, trying to determine the source of the lightning.

A form appeared above her, eyes glowing red with fury.

"You stole my cat!"

Sochel backwinged, dipping underneath the figure. Although the being's golden skin had wrinkled and the long tresses of straight hair had gone from black to silver in the decades since she had seen the human, she recognized the enchantress Zindara.

"I didn't!" she exclaimed.

Zindara whirled like a winged seed, shooting up to confront the dragon. Lightning shot from her fingertips.

"You did! I see him right there on your filthy ear! He was promised to me! Give him to me!"

Sochel dodged back and forth, trying to stay away from the hot white points. One took her full in the belly. Out of pure reaction, her wings closed around her body to protect it. She moaned. That was a vicious strike! She could have hit the kitten!

The dragon writhed in pain but flapped her wings hard, putting distance between her and Zindara. She inhaled deeply, and expelled hot golden fire at the enchantress. Zindara's form turned black as onyx. Most of the fire bounced off her, but she doubled over as some of it scorched her. The darkness faded, and her small face contorted in anger.

She threw more lightning at Sochel, in every color of the spectrum. The pale green burned like acid, the orange struck her with the force of boulders, and the sickly purple made her feel ill on contact. That was the most insidious. Even as Sochel fought back, sending every spell she knew at her foe, her muscles started to weaken. Her wings couldn't hold enough air to keep her aloft. She began to fall. Zindara crowed with triumph.

"Bad!" Merrow shrieked. "Up!"

Limbs of brilliant green, the same color as the kitten's eyes, appeared in the air. Some of them molded themselves around the dragon's body. Others warded off the onslaught of jagged arrows, though not perfectly. Some arrows zipped through the defenses and struck the dragon. Merrow leaped out onto the farthest emerald green bar and hissed at the enchantress.

"Such spirit!" Zindara exclaimed. She whirled close and seized Merrow in mid-air.

"Give him back!" Sochel shouted. Somehow, she found the strength within herself to break free and winged after the human.

"No! You intercepted my delivery from the Great Cat Mother!" Zindara called over her shoulder. "All is right now."

"No! He's… he's mine!" Sochel surprised herself. She realized she did like the lively little fellow. The enchantress had no right to take him.

Zindara, with hardly a backward glance, flicked a dismissive hand over her shoulder. The supporting green limbs vanished, and pink, fleshy bonds of magic wound around Sochel like a serpent.

Her wings pinioned, and she plummeted toward the ground. She landed with a tremendous THUD. The pink snake tied her down, stitching itself through the turf to hold her.

Zindara sailed down after her, her red eyes gleeful.

"You see what happens when you steal from me?" she asked. She threw Merrow up in the air and a transparent globe of power surrounded him. "Now, my little beauty, we'll go back to my home, and we will make beautiful magic together!"

Merrow fought and raked at the transparent bubble with his tiny talons, but couldn't get a clawhold. Sochel threw all the magic she still had at it, striving to break him free, but the pink snake tightened on her, squeezing her chest. The harder she fought, the fiercer its grip.

"Leave off," Zindara warned her. "It'll strangle you if you struggle. In an hour or two, or ten, it'll dissolve. I advise you not to follow me."

Sochel gritted her teeth. With all her strength, she wrenched one limb free. She had to save Merrow. Though she started to lose feeling in her other limbs, she stretched out the claw and swiped at the enchantress.

Smack! A flat hand of golden fire slapped her paw to the ground. Sochel bellowed.

"I told you not to! Why don't you listen to me?"

Suddenly, a bolt of green fire blasted down from the sky and knocked Zindara out of the air. Merrow hissed and fizzed inside his floating bubble.

Her hair smoking, Zindara sat up. She grasped the bubble and took a good look at the kitten.

"By the Storm King, this *isn't* my cat! Looks just like him, though." She turned to Sochel, who was nearly strangling, and waved a hand. The bonds loosened. Sochel prepared to breathe fire, but Zindara's snap caused the fire to go out. "Who is this one, and where is my kitten?"

Sochel gasped in a deep breath, and all her fury came raging back. "I don't know! I never asked for a protector or a familiar! I have no idea why I have him, or where your cat is. I'm trying to bring Merrow back to the Great Cat Mother. I have no need for a familiar. I brought him to Borun to get an explanation. He told me that I had to ask the Great Cat Mother. I was to meet her in Ochse's cave. I only had a short time to get there, and you delayed me! I don't know whether I have enough time now."

Zindara's mouth gaped in astonishment. She waved a hand, and the pink snake dissolved into insubstantial smoke.

"Undersea Goddess, I'll have a piece of my mind to give the Great Cat Mother myself! We'd best be on our way."

"We?" Sochel asked, prying herself off the greensward. She shook her wings, dislodging clods of earth.

"Yes, of course, *we!* Give me a ride to Ochse's so I can talk to the Great Cat Mother myself."

"Walk," Sochel said, turning her back on the enchantress. She pounced on the bubble, which popped with a sound like shattering crystal. Merrow crooned and leaped onto the dragon's snout. "My mission doesn't include you."

"Now, don't be like that," Zindara said, with a persuasive smile. She laid a hand on Sochel's wing joint. "This has all been a misunderstanding. I didn't mean to…"

"…To snatch me out of the sky, bombard me with lightning bolts, and squeeze me in a web?" Sochel glared.

Zindara shrugged. "Oh, well, that. Look, you want to give back the wrong kitten, and I want the one that should have been delivered to me." She fluttered her eyelashes. "I'll owe you a favor. You can always use a favor from a powerful friend."

"Well… all right," Sochel said, grudgingly. "Hop on. But don't touch the kitten again."

"Agreed."

Night had begun to draw her cloak over the earth by the time Sochel set down at the rough-hewn pillars that marked the entrance to the warren of twisting corridors and chambers Ochse had occupied for centuries. Putrid stench hovered in the air as she and Zindara crept in. The enchantress lit the way with a globe of golden light. Ochse usually lived alone, but once in a while other terrifying creatures huddled within—until the cyclops drove them away, or ate them, as the gnawed bones in every corner attested. A few hundred yards in, the main corridor split into two. Sochel's keen ears picked up voices to the left.

"She might still be here," she said, turning. Zindara followed her.

"No! No!" a hoarse voice echoed in the distance. Sochel frowned. It sounded like Ochse, but he had never trembled like that in her experience. "Get it away from me! Please!"

She traced the voice, going deeper and deeper into the labyrinth than she ever had before. He must be in distress, but what could frighten a cyclops?

"This way," she whispered. "Be ready!"

Zindara nodded, and prepared a handful of golden fire. Merrow perched behind the curve of Sochel's right nostril, leaning forward like a ship's figurehead.

The sound grew louder and louder until they knew they must be nearly upon it. Sochel hesitated in the darkness before a well-lit doorway, then plunged into the room.

There, plastered against the far wall, was Ochse, standing on a stone shelf ten feet up. He looked as if he had been trying to claw his way through the stone.

"No, please! Leave me alone! Go away! Please!"

His booming voice all but drowned out the tiniest of noises: a mew. A plaintive mew. A cry from the smallest of gray-striped kittens, looking up at the giant with curious eyes. He was almost a twin to Merrow except that his eyes were golden. The whole cavern trembled with the giant's fear.

Ochse stared at the intrusion, and his single orb widened. He begged Sochel and Zindara: "For the love of the Stone Spirits, take that thing away from me!"

"Well, there he is!" Zindara said, pouncing on the kitten and scooping him up. The little beast rolled over in her hands, purring like an earthquake. "Yes, you're all that I was promised, and more! What a cute little thing you are. What's your name?"

"Prem," the kitten said, nuzzling her fingers.

Ochse stood with his back to the wall, looking from enchantress to dragon to kitten with open horror.

Sochel tried not to laugh at her erstwhile rival. "Are you... are you scared of *cats*?"

The giant nodded, his expression sheepish. "Aye," Ochse said. Now that the creature was under control, he climbed down from the shelf and pulled his rough-spun tunic down over his trousers and patted it. "I don't know what that crazy big feline was trying to do, but she said he was to be delivered here. Nary a word more!"

"She's not here?" Zindara asked.

"Nay, gone this hour or more," Ochse said. "No notion why she came or why she went."

"She knew we would come here," Sochel said, with sudden enlightenment.

"Cats move in mysterious ways," Zindara said, trying to keep Prem from burrowing into her hair. "We'll get him out of here at once, Ochse. You can owe us each a favor for saving you from this fierce little tiger." She shared a look of amusement with Sochel. "And we'll keep your secret. My promise on it."

"Agreed," Sochel said. "Mine, too."

Very grudgingly, the cyclops nodded.

"Brother!"

Merrow emerged from Sochel's nose and trilled at the new kitten. It trilled back, and Merrow leaped down to greet his sibling. The cyclops's single eye nearly rolled out of his head, looking from one kitten to the other. But he held his wits about him.

"Do ye want refreshment?" he asked. He gestured to the table near the wall. A couple of large, meaty bones lay on its surface. Sochel's stomach turned at the rotting smell they gave off. He was trying to be hospitable, though she could tell that all he really wanted was for them to take the tumbling kittens out of his home.

"Thank you, no," she said, very politely. She hesitated, and remembered Borun's words. "Ochse, we haven't been on the best of terms. I won't say we haven't had our disagreements, but I want to call a halt to them. Let there be peace be between us."

"Aye," Ochse said, and let out a gusty sigh. "I agree. Peace. Just get those terrible beasts out of here!"

Sochel smiled, showing all her teeth. "Gladly."

SHE TOOK A DEEP, GRATEFUL BREATH OF FRESH, FRAGRANT AIR as they emerged from the stinking cavern. Night had fallen by then. The two kittens raced around them, up into the air under their own power, zooming over Sochel's back and through the silver tresses that brushed against Zindara's long skirts.

"Well, that was an unexpected bonus after a strange day," Sochel said. "I never thought I'd exchange civil words with Ochse ever again!"

"All is well," Zindara said, clapping her hands. "You've mended fences. I have my kitten, and a fine fellow he is. Now, you can take me home, then you can return to Borun and have him descry the next place the Great Cat Mother will be."

"Why?" Sochel asked, startled out of her thoughts. Zindara regarded her with a curious look.

"Why? So you can give this scamp back and have him delivered to where he ought to be, since you don't need a familiar."

Merrow paused in his game with Prem. He looked up at Sochel. His big green eyes widened wistfully. He had, after all, tried to save her from Zindara with powerful spells, almost as strong as one she could summon. Who knew what he could become when he grew up? The Great Cat Mother thought she should have him. And he was a charming little creature, with quite a good purr.

"Well..." Sochel said, her heart brimming over with resignation... and joy. "Maybe I do."

ABOUT THE AUTHOR

Jody Lynn Nye lists her main career activity as "spoiling cats." When not engaged upon this worthy occupation, she writes fantasy and science fiction books and short stories.

Since 1987 she has published over 50 books and more than 200 short stories, most of it with a humorous bent. She has also collaborated with Anne McCaffrey, Robert Lynn Asprin, Piers Anthony, and other notable writers of the fantasy and science fiction and fantasy genre.

Jody has taught in numerous writing workshops and participated on hundreds of panels at science-fiction conventions. She runs the two-day writers' workshop at DragonCon. Jody is the Coordinating Judge of the Writers of the Future. She is also a member of the Cat Writers' Association, which promotes fiction about felines.

Jody lives in the northwest suburbs of Atlanta, with her husband Bill Fawcett, and three feline overlords, Athena, Minx, and Marmalade.

SO BURN US BOTH

LISSE KIRK

There is already ice in the mud, tiny crystals that bite through the delicate skin of my toes, stabs of warning.

Do you feel it? That sense of danger in the air, subtler and sharper even than the needles of ice? The sun is barely up, but something is already wrong with the day.

Humans carry their purpose with them when they go to carry out a task. Sometimes they're bored with the job before they even begin it; that purpose is to hurry through it, or else to ignore it, choosing not to care. Humans are very good at the latter…

As are you, I sometimes think.

I worry about you.

A team of men come into sight, bearing axes. Not an unusual sight, but I feel my skin tighten and my fur begin to stand on end.

Sometimes, humans laugh as they go about certain tasks together—like cutting wood. It can be a great pleasure for them to work at tasks that will bring warmth to their families. Sometimes they find satisfaction in doing a job properly; a well-honed axe blade sinks deeply into a tree with each swing. Firewood is a need they all share. Even you, my beloved witch, need firewood. It is simple work. Clean work.

It is strange for there to be shame amongst woodcutters,

Mother, but that is what I see now. Four men go out to the woods together, leaving the town behind. The autumn dawn is pale and cold and their breath makes great plumes that should make them laugh…

They do not laugh.

They are silent.

They seem ashamed. Furtive. They avoid looking toward our home as they pass us by.

This is the last farm before the endless forest. You have grown a beautiful garden, lovely in all seasons, your pride and joy over all the years I have known you, all of my lives.

They should look at it.

People often come just to look.

These men do not.

The ice in the mud is too cold. Pain radiates up through my too-thin body. My coat is not as thick as it once was. My muscles are not as strong. Leaping onto a fencepost is harder than it was, but thankfully the wood is old and soft and my claws, at least, are still sharp.

Sunlight reaches me up there, although it is not yet touching the ground. It warms me through my black fur. I sit atop the post and curl my tail around my paws, watching the men walk by until there is nothing left to see.

What shame can there be in cutting wood? Why is there warning in the air this morning? I remain very still, listening — not just to the world, but to the currents moving through it.

There should be some hint of what tomorrow might bring…

The sun rises higher and brings no answers. Birds sing, but very few of them; most have already fled these northern lands. The sky believes this winter will be one of its finest accomplishments. I tried weeks ago to warn you of this, that we should flee like so many birds do every year, yet here we are.

Ice in the mud.

Shame in the eyes of woodcutters. Furtiveness in their walk.

Needles of warning.

AFTER THE COLD, IT FEELS SWELTERING INSIDE OUR HOME.

You did not always keep the cabin so warm.

I am pleased by the heat—it seeps into my bones as I sit as close to the fire as I dare—but you have changed. You usually want to stockpile wood, to use it sparingly, especially on these first cold days. You like to "get used to the cold" and adjust by adding layers of wool over your body until the wool doesn't help you enough anymore and you tire of breaking ice in the water pitcher.

Do you think I don't know this of you? Nearly eighty-one years together, you and I. Don't you know it has always been me? Don't you suspect?

Don't you know I worry about you when things change?

My meowing makes you smile, but there is something in your smile that angers me. Your eyes seem distant somehow, like you're smiling at something that isn't here. Well, *I* am here. Stop smiling like that. Is it because my voice is as old and worn as this body?

Or do you know something I do not?

This will be my last life with you, Mother. Don't you know *that*, at least?

You never answer my questions.

You rarely accept my gifts.

I meow at you, somewhat more pointedly.

"Hush, Oliver. You worry too much."

The sound of your voice is sunlight in my heart, even if I know you don't really understand me. Or if you do, you don't let on. I want to be annoyed with you, but your old trick always works and you employ it now, as you place breakfast down before me:

Cream, with all that remains of last night's bread and fish...

And an egg?

You're spoiling me.

Shouldn't you eat that egg? Daisy won't lay them much longer this winter, and she may be too old to lay again when spring comes.

I look up, licking my lips, and mew at you.

"Don't worry about me, Ollie. I find I'm not very hungry today."

Well. If you're sure.

I eat.

It is hard to eat and purr at the same time once one is no longer a kitten, but your knobby hand is still the best touch I've ever known. Never once have you struck me or hurt me. How many animals are so lucky? Time has bent your fingers and weakened my bones, and yet here we are, loving each other as we always have...

As we always will.

Why aren't you eating anything?

Or even sipping tea?

I finish my breakfast and begin grooming—I still have standards, after all—but you are still not eating. Aren't you hungry? Or... maybe you feel those little needles pricking their warning through the fabric of the day after all.

Explain them to me, Mother. Please. Explain this quiet dread sitting halfway up my spine. Explain.

But you do not explain.

You pick up your favorite teacup and smile sadly, tears suddenly bright in your faded eyes.

"My hand looked beautiful when I held this once, Oliver. And now look."

Your hand is still beautiful. Everything that you are is beautiful. My eyesight may be slowly failing, but I can still see that.

"What a beautiful cup." Your thumb caresses the worn blue porcelain delicately as you whisper. "They won't have it."

Have what?

The bone china?

Why would anyone take your teacup?

"I don't want—I don't want anyone else to drink out of it. It won't mean the same thing to them. I don't want them to have it!"

You suddenly hurl the cup into the fireplace where it shatters with a horrible noise. I am up on the table, back and tail arched, my fur all on end, hissing, before I fully understand what has happened.

You…

You *broke* it.

You love that possession!

Why?

Why would you do this?

You pick me up. My tiny heart is beating too fast against your hand. You hold me against your chest and I can feel that your heart is beating hard and fast, too. Your grip is too tight and I want to squirm away, but you're crying.

Sweet Mother. Why are you crying? Why? Are you sad that you shattered your own cup? You didn't have to do that. Who would take it from you?

THE WOODCUTTERS GO BACK AND FORTH SEVERAL TIMES. THEY always avert their eyes. You pretend not to notice them and they pretend your house does not exist, and I pretend there is not a terror growing in my heart with every passing hour.

Everything you can burn, you burn. One precious thing at a time, even the knitting needles your mate made for you from the very walnut tree that later took her life. How can you burn those?

What you cannot burn, you break if you can, or else hurl out into the yard for the cow and the pig to walk over, to stomp into the mud.

Won't we need those things?

Weren't they important for your life?

Why are you using so much wood, Mother? I do not like the woodcutters, but you're going to need to buy from them soon if you don't stop….

Stop!

That sweater keeps you alive when you go outside in winter!

Stop!

The smoke is awful!

What are you doing?

Why are you doing this?

But you ignore me. All this time together, all these lives, how can you ignore me now? How? Why? Have I done something wrong?

I'm sorry, Mother. Whatever it was, I'm sorry. Just stop! Please? Please stop.

Stop destroying yourself!

AT LEAST YOU DO NOT BURN YOUR SPELL COMPONENTS. AS YOU settle in to a working, I try to settle too, but I am still on edge.

Slowly, my nerves calm as I see what you are making.

The poppet is a work of art.

You've always had a hand for them, but there's something about this one that stands out, almost humming with power. Maybe it's because every stitch costs your gnarled hands so much pain. Maybe it's because the tears do not stop falling all the time you sew.

Maybe it's because you have destroyed nearly everything else you own, and the power of all that destruction flows into the poppet.

This is all you have left; you can devote your whole self to making this poppet. Is that what you are doing? I hope so. Either way, I am proud of you.

The young, black-hearted fools of the village have so often been cruel to you. I heard every name they called you. I felt every stone they threw. These people are so self-righteous. They believe such foolish things and believe them so ardently that even a cat such as I must be embarrassed to look at them.

This is better, Mother. It is better that you make this poppet. Whose face will you put upon it? Whose name will you stitch into it? The vain young man who leads the cruelty?

It is better that you do not hurt yourself anymore.

Hurt them, if you must hurt someone.

You have never deserved pain at anyone's hands... including my own claws. I am sorry for scratching you the time you tried to take a goldfinch out of my mouth. But even when you did that, you were gentle. You were always gentle. Your kind soul, your loving heart, your gentle nature. These are the reasons I was sent to you, the reasons the earth chose you as one of her Blessed, the reason the moon smiled upon you when you were young, when you and your mate laughed and danced and spun, skirts flowing out, hair unbraided.

Before the walnut tree.

She was so slender, even the weakest branch would have held her. But they didn't use the weakest branch, did they?

How could you forgive them?

I still don't understand that.

They have done you so much harm. Keep working on that poppet. Let at least one of them finally pay for all of this.

When I see that you are turning the poppet into the village leader, I purr in satisfaction. Yes. This is as it should be. He leads their folly. Let him lead their loss.

THERE ARE VERY FEW NOISES FROM THE VILLAGE. THE AUTUMN air is almost warm now, the day at its peak. No wind, nothing to stir the trees. Everything is still—

And so I hear the noises, and the silences between them.

I do not hear any cries from children. I do not hear the striking of hammers, the creaking of wheels.

Is no work being done in the village?

For a while, I heard the hollow impacts of firewood being tossed, all the wood the men brought back this morning, but now there is nothing. A dog barks and is quickly hushed. A horse whinnies. A child calls out and is scolded, worse than the dog.

People are waiting for something, quiet as animals who sense they are in danger.

What does this mean?

I sit on the porch, tail tapping lightly against the broom leaning by the door; there is a pumpkin in my spot, just as there always is this time of year, or else my perfect tail would not touch the broom.

Pumpkins usually give me joy. I like their shapes and smells, like the energy they contain, and something about their texture is particularly nice to bite and claw on occasion, but I am not in the mood for these things right now. Something is too wrong, even if the day is peaceful and beautiful—something to do with that quiet in the village.

If you won't investigate it, Mother, I will.

I stand and stretch and, to show that I am not spiteful even if I am irritable, I rub my cheek against the pumpkin's curled stem. It really is a lovely texture and I could enjoy scratching my face against it all day—but I can't linger. I have a mission.

You are the only one whose words I can understand unless people are speaking about you. Normally this means that a walk through the village is like walking past kittens babbling their nonsense, but not so today.

Today, everyone is speaking of you.

Speaking of you—and fearing. Children are being held tightly. Dogs are on alert. Geese are not roaming. The other cats all refuse to meet my gaze, although that last is not necessarily new; they've always sensed that I wasn't like them. Housecats and familiars do not fraternize.

But people do. They are fraternizing now, most gathering in an aimless sort of way, as if they all want something but are afraid to admit it.

"Always was different," one human says of you. It has the air of justification.

"You know, we just couldn't get through to her."

"It's a mercy, really. At her age."

"And we have to think of the children."

"Yes, yes. We must always think of the children."

"Still," a woman says with mock empathy, doing such a poor acting job that I want to sink my fangs into her chest and chew until I discover if there was ever a heart in there, "it does seem like a terribly painful way to die."

Die?

My pupils go huge.

A growl rises in my chest but I choke it down. If anyone spots me hiding under the baker's wagon, they'll throw stones at me.

"It is nothing compared to the pain she will face in Hell," another man says. The leader. Ah, yes. The poppet was a wonderful likeness. Look how his neck juts out in the front, sharper than anyone's.

"We must do the right thing," he continues. "We must protect ourselves. It will all be over quickly and then the village will be at peace."

"Now, who is going to help me fetch her?"

The leader moves aside as he speaks, revealing a massive pile of firewood that has been stacked in the town square. The pyre has been built around one tall timber still standing upright.

Firewood.

A painful way to die.

A mercy.

Think of the children.

No.

Are they going to…?

No, no, no, no, no!

I don't wait to see who volunteers to fetch you. I race back to you, running as I have never done before, a streak of blackest lightning on a desperate mission.

"OLIVER. I WONDERED WHERE YOU WERE."

You smile so sadly, but you look beautiful, in your old chair on the porch, the pumpkin beside you gleaming in the golden afternoon sunlight.

You pat your lap, but I couldn't jump up even if I wanted to. That run did something to my body. I can feel the strangest sensation, as if there was firelight within me but it is starting to flicker now—a sensation I know well, the beginning of death. Running took more than my body had left, it seems.

I yowl at you.

"Oliver!"

You reach to grab me and I can't help it. I lash out, my claws tearing right through your papery skin. Blood beads and you yelp and I hiss with everything I have in me.

What are you doing?

This is no time to sit and watch the day go by.

We have to flee!

"Oliver," you sigh. "I know what you want me to do, but don't you see, my darling? I'm too old to run. Where would I go? My life was here."

No.

No!

NO!

I knock over the broom as I clumsily leap onto the pumpkin, uncoordinated in my exhaustion. See the broom? Why have you never heeded the dreams I sent you? You don't have to run, you can *fly*, I can show you how! I'm supposed to show you, I'm supposed to protect you!

"Oliver."

You knew!

You sensed the warnings just as I did and you understood them better and so you fed me all of the breakfast and you ruined everything you owned and now you won't even *try?*

"Stop that yowling," you snap.

I hiss and thrash my tail violently, claws all digging into the pumpkin, releasing its sweet scent. But I stop yowling, as you ordered. My green eyes are fixed on you. I'm not going to forgive you, if that's what you think. You're my family, you're all I have.

You use an old lace handkerchief to dab at the blood, sigh, and look out at your chickens. They're old, too, like us, and barely lay anymore. Does that mean you won't fight for them? Are none of us worth it? You won't *stay* for any of us? For me?

"You don't understand."

No, I don't.

You knew, you had time, and what are you doing now? Sitting and waiting for them? They're going to burn you! Don't you understand?

Where is your poppet? At least take one of those bastards out first. One pin is all it will take. You always used your poppets to *heal*, but you can use them to hurt. Do it, do it now!

"Stop yowling, my love. It's all right. Everything will be all right."

No.

It won't.

You'll be gone.

Nothing will be all right.

Who will feed me?

Who will pet me?

Who will understand me?

Who will I send dreams of magic to?

Whose witchcraft will I bless?

Who will love me when you are gone?

I don't have much time left.

Can't we steal every last minute?

Why can't I weep? It isn't fair that cats can't cry.

I yowl and yowl. Understand me! Agree with me! Come with me! Let's run away and *live*, maybe it's not too late. This doesn't have to be the end. You can save my life if you just let me save yours.

Can't we have more days in the sun, more nights by the fire?

"Oliver. Sweet Oliver."

No. Not sweet Oliver.

If you won't do this, I will.

If we can't have a future, then neither will they.

I dart inside, sniff around, and find the poppet—unfinished, set aside. Your anger didn't last long enough for you to see it through. They're going to do this to you and you won't even fight back?

You healed their injured and their ill. You always had a kind word and a patient ear. If someone needed food, you gave them yours. You were wise, gentle, nurturing, everything a witch is supposed to be—

And they're going to burn you for it.

I won't let this happen silently.

Not unavenged.

If all that is left is spite, so be it.

I run back out, the poppet hanging from my mouth like a dead rat, and stare up at you defiantly.

"Oliver."

Don't use that stern tone with me.

"Oliver, give me that."

You reach. I growl—

And the gate hinges creak. The latch jingles.

They're here.

We're out of time.

Your pupils go wide with horror. Anyone else would probably think you're afraid of the men from the village coming to drag you to the pyre, but I know better. You're afraid of what I will do.

"Get her damned cat," a man shouts, but I'm already gone, racing away.

One last race.

One last errand for my witch.

If you won't avenge yourself, Mother, I will do it for you.

IT DOESN'T TAKE SO VERY LONG TO RUN FROM HOUSE TO house. No one is home. They are all going to watch you die.

I slip into every home, needing no more space than a shadow

or a nightmare, fury and grief summoning more magic than I have ever been able to call on before.

In every house, I lay down in the kitchen, which is the heart of any home, and drop the poppet between my paws. You would need a spell for this, ingredients and words and time to channel your intent and tie threads into the energy of the homes, but I am what I have always been: magic itself. I do not need the trappings. Only the vessel.

Only the will.

The spite.

Flow into the poppet, all you safe and sturdy and oh-so-respectable houses. Become one with it. Tie your fate to it. Winter approaches and I have no mercy for those who possess none themselves.

Hurry.

Hurry.

Yes.

THE VILLAGE SQUARE.

I see her. I run to her.

To my final death.

Nine lives lived.

I will not be born again. Not this time. There is some fear in that, but I will also never die again. This is the last time.

There is comfort in that.

The crowd of dozens seems like thousands. All their hearts are full of hate and every mind closed to reason. How many of them think themselves good people? How many will later claim there was nothing they could do to stop this?

Well, my dear despised townsfolk, let me walk among you with hatred and madness of my own.

The poppet feels heavy and dirty in my mouth. There's a bitter taste to it now. I do not let go. It is so full of magic that it numbs my jaw, but I will never let go.

I feel the threads spun from it, finer than any spider's web. They drag it down, threads connecting it to every home —

Even the one I shared with her.

YOUR PRAYERS FOR MY WITCH'S SOUL ARE ENDING AS I MAKE IT to the small clearing around the pyre.

There she is.

An old woman whose actions were only ever kind, even when she was hurt.

You people have tied her to a stake as if you expect her to run.

Fools.

All of you.

Monsters.

Someone starts forward with a torch, some young husband who thinks too often of the children and believes this intolerance is a lesson worth teaching them.

I dart past him.

He shrieks like a frightened puppy.

People gasp and draw away from me.

A few nimble hops and I am next to my mother. My witch. My friend. My fate.

I sit next to her and look up, my jaw heavy and numb from the poppet, from all of that magic, a thread to every house, a vengeance that will be complete the moment these people decide it to be. No one but I can see those threads. I see them glowing, see their promise. They will not fail me.

My witch's eyes shine brightly. The sun is nearly set. It turns her white hair back to the gold of her youth. She is the most beautiful being, just as she has always been.

"Oliver," she whispers.

There are new tears on her cheeks. Even if she wishes I had escaped, she takes some comfort in my presence now. She always has.

We gaze into each other's eyes for the last time, seeing and knowing and loving all that we can about each other. She is kind and I am cruel, but here we are, at the end, and we are perfect for each other.

The pyre reeks of pitch and kerosene.

The people are overcoming their fear.

They feel strong in their numbers. In their righteousness. They have no idea what their actions will bring down upon them.

The torchbearer moves closer. He is shouting words about my witch, doubtless vile ones, but I choose not to understand them. I sit primly next to her and wrap my tail around my tiny paws. I still have standards. I will not look desperate where you can see me.

I lock eyes with the torchbearer. He looks sickly and sweaty. Pathetic. Afraid.

Do it, you coward.

Burn the woman who is so different from you.

Think of the children.

Yes.

Think of your children. Where will they sleep tonight? Where will any of them find shelter this winter? Your hand shakes as you lower the torch toward the pyre.

It would shake more if you knew.

Flames crackle.

The pyre ignites.

The heat and pain are worse than I thought. They come faster than I imagined.

My witch doesn't move, and neither do I.

We stare you down until a wall of flame and smoke rise between us, sparing us the sight of you.

We rise with that smoke, rise away from our bodies.

My body looks old and frail, too weak for any of the running I did today. I look at it fondly and see the poppet fall free of my fangs—

And begin to burn.

Sparks dance and then the flames take it completely. The

moment they do, every house bursts into flame, fire exploding, blasting out windows, cracking chimneys.

Screams begin.

Cries of despair.

Shouts for water.

Prayers to heaven.

I have no more need to look.

I float freely into the endlessness, content, beside my witch. She is finally flying.

Your homes will burn to ashes tonight and there is nothing you can do to put out those flames.

It was never the witch you mortals needed to fear. It was me. It was always me, the beast who devoted himself to *her*, body, heart, and soul. The cat who mirrors whatever cruelty you give, who knows that *that* is the truth of magic.

The witch's familiar.

Damn you.

Damn you all.

About the Author

Lisse Kirk is a queer author dredged up from the depths of Puget Sound. They enjoy long walks on very cold beaches, finding neat rocks in remote places, and writing first drafts by hand while trying not to spill the inkwell. Although they occasionally write stories about animals, most of their books are focused on LGBTQIA+ characters.

TRIAL BY COW
ANDREW RUCKER JONES

What do cats really *do* for their witches, I ask you? Take my Arwen: she needed the clearing next to her forest cottage mown. The coven expected a tidy homestead and competitive refreshments at her reinstatement hearing. While she ransacked her dusty collection of hand-me-down cake and muffin recipes from when her grandmother headed the coven's knitting club, I grazed the clearing to putting green length. Show me a feline with that endurance and precision, please.

That's not to say Arwen didn't have to do *any*thing about the clearing.

"Stupid bovine," she grunted as she shoveled my pats to a pile at the edge of the forest.

But I knew she didn't mean it. Her re-admittance into the coven depended on a strong bond with me.

Which would never develop if she confined me to the clearing. Arwen had bought me three days previous in a last-ditch effort to procure a suitable familiar and told me if she was on probation, I was too. She wouldn't even name me. If I didn't work out, her next familiar would be a piranha, if I caught her drift.

But she can't have meant it. How would she hoist me into the piranha tank?

While she cleaned up my mess, I discovered she's a monologuer. We share that, even if my monologues tend to be interior, and a feeling of kinship grew in me. At the same time, her monologue disquieted me some, what with its implication of high on-the-job mortality.

She zapped her first familiar in a pique, she said. I can't blame her—it was a snake. Before you think I'm prejudiced, it was past molting and never produced venom (she mistook a corn snake for a copperhead), so it was useless for potion ingredients. The last straw was when the darned thing tipped a whole vial of newt's eyes into the cauldron while hunting a mouse.

Her next familiar was a centipede, and that was an accident. It slept in her boot. The jellyfish from the placement agency was short-lived—she didn't know what it ate. (The agency didn't want her business after that.)

And the Tasmanian devil, well, that was self-defense, pure and simple.

Despite her best intentions, losing four familiars had landed Arwen on probation. Her hearing for re-admittance was today, and here she was, shoveling manure.

I thought maybe her irritation with me was just nerves, so I nuzzled her elbow for encouragement. My timing was a little off. She lost control of the shovel and dropped a pat on her foot. The shovel swished through the air right behind me as I galloped away.

After she had had a chance to cool off, I figured quality time together would strengthen the rapport we had begun to build that morning before the regrettable pat incident. She was baking creepy-crawly muffins when I stuck my head in the window of her cottage. She aimed her wand at the dough and I nuzzled her elbow at the moment she cast a leavening spell. A shock flashed along my body as I channeled power to her, and dough exploded against the back wall where her ingredients balanced on rickety shelves. One collapsed, spilling batwing powder, tadpole jelly, and (expensive!) imported platypus urine into the remaining dough. They ran together in a yellow-green mass threaded with black.

"The guests will be here in an hour!" Arwen cried. She swatted at my head with a broom. "Look, buster, unless you're here to donate an extra tongue or ear, shoo. Stupid, doe-eyed animal." She whacked me once more on my rumpus before I was out of range. "I only picked you because you'd be hard to kill!"

But she couldn't mean that. Butchers were adept at it. Best not to give her further ideas, though.

Greeting the guests fell to me when they arrived at our little soiree. They stroked my flanks and admired my powerful molars. I did a trick for them. You know that moment when a cow goes ice-sculpture still, head straight, eyes unblinking, waiting for time to restart, then that tiny, round ripple runs up its throat to its mouth as it regurgitates the cud, and suddenly the spell snaps, and the cow blinks and works its jaws again? It's a crowd-pleaser. I chewed and nuzzled and mooed until the guests giggled and I harvested jealous looks and hisses from other familiars—all overweening cats, I must note.

By the time Arwen rushed into the clearing, I had the coven wrapped around my silky, twitching ear.

"I hope he hasn't caused problems!" Arwen called as she stumbled our way, eyes on the mounded platter of discolored muffins she carried. I couldn't believe she would serve those things. I wouldn't have ingested them, and I'm a cow.

Madelyn, the head witch, said with a flick of her wrist, "Why, he's downright charming, dear. What's his name?"

Arwen almost dropped the muffins when she glanced up at Madelyn. "He's ... charming?"

Splat! Arwen looked down and cursed. I might have made another mess while entertaining our visitors. She got the shovel and scooped it up.

Madelyn followed, walking as though balancing a book on her head. "What an efficient way to collect maggots and flies!"

Arwen gaped, shovel upside down over the manure pile, flies buzzing around her disheveled flaxen hair and flushed cheeks. "I always got mine from carrion. I ... thought they were higher quality."

"Hogwash!" Madelyn said. "Hogwash really is the best source, but if these are a little weak, use more in your potion."

I nuzzled Arwen's elbow, and she absentmindedly scratched behind my ear. I vowed to make messes as often as she needed. Maybe more often.

Madelyn glided back to the clearing and called the coven to order. Faces grew solemn as Arwen stepped to the center to cast a spell. This was the proof that was in the pudding, or the platypus urine that was in the muffins, as it were. If our bond was weak, her spell would fail, and out she went—no more broom ridesharing, no more group health insurance, no more potluck dinners.

Arwen whispered in the ear she had just scratched behind, "All I can say is 'bulimic piranha.' Don't mess this up, buster."

She can't have meant it, right? The grass sloshed in the first of my four stomachs, and I felt the need to regurgitate more than cud.

Arwen muttered a love incantation and wound up like a baseball pitcher, then leveled her wand at a tree. I nuzzled her elbow encouragingly just as she released the magic. This spell felt like eating thistle, but all over the inside of my skin.

I had never seen a tree hopelessly in love before, and I never want to again.

The tree popped like corn in a kettle as blossoms sprouted along the branches, down the trunk and across the exposed roots until the bark beneath was invisible. Then, in unison, each and every flower released a dusting of pollen. As it would happen, we all stood downwind.

"Oh, my," Madelyn said, wide-eyed, muffin poised halfway to her mouth. And that's all anyone got a chance to say before a pus yellow cloud of sinus trauma encased us.

The witches ran helter-skelter through the clearing, sneezing, coughing, and crying "My eyes!" Tasmanian-devil-strength swearing came from one direction, and I assumed that must be

Arwen. Seems she learned a thing or two from her last familiar before she offed him.

Being a creature of great resilience, I trotted toward the cottage, mooing placidly all the while. The coven took the hint and oriented their scrambling toward my reverberant calls. In short order, I had them all safely inside. Arwen had even rescued the muffins, which she now blew the pollen off of and into the group of suffering witches. Another cry arose, and Arwen lifted the muffins out of harm's way before they could be sneezed upon. As if the muffins could have saved her anymore. She might as well have teargassed the coven.

"I'm so, so sorry! That's never happened to me before. It must be, uh ..." Arwen's glare in my direction was almost as potent as her magic, and I felt the nipping of tiny, razor-sharp teeth at my ankles. Would she add the ignominy of blaming her familiar to the shame of being cast out of her coven? What else could she possibly blame but herself? "It must have been the wand. And the tree. They're the same kind of wood—"

Madelyn sneezed and wiped her crimson eyes. "Such raw power! You two have quite the connection."

I think it's just because I'm big-boned, but I gave Arwen the benefit of the doubt.

"If there are no dissensions ..." Madelyn glanced around, blinking hard. The witches were preoccupied with blowing noses on sleeves, rubbing eyes, and coughing phlegm onto Arwen's freshly swept wood floor, but each found the wherewithal to shake her head. "Arwen, we hereby reinstate you to our coven."

I was pretty sure the tears in Arwen's eyes weren't from pollen as she pressed a muffin into Madelyn's hand and gave her a wobbly smile.

Madelyn bit into the muffin and her eyes widened. She patted her chest with a dainty hand and chewed hurriedly. While I watched for seizures or signs of anaphylactic shock, I wondered if the vote would still stand should the head witch be murdered immediately thereafter. To my surprise, she swallowed and said, "You've been hiding your talents. These are delightfully pungent."

"I can't take all the credit," Arwen said. "My fam—uh, *Buster* helped me there too." She smiled and patted my neck. "I'm twice the witch I was without him."

And *that* she meant.

ABOUT THE AUTHOR

Andrew Rucker Jones was born and raised in Falls Church, Virginia. No muse heralded his birth, and he has not been writing novels since he was in diapers. He received his Bachelor's degree from North Carolina State University in mathematics with minors in computer programming and German. He has always loved reading, so when the time came to choose a new career after twenty years in IT (programmer, system administrator, manager), he decided writing looked like fun. If only it paid.

Andrew's work has been published in venues such as *Dark Matter Magazine*, *The Four Faced Liar*, and *On Spec*.

He now lives in Mannheim, Germany, with his Georgian wife, who actually earns money, their three children, and two cats. No cows.

You can get a weekly dose of the depressing life of a struggling writer on his blog: selfdefeatistnavelgazing.wordpress.com

BLACKWOOD'S TOMB
JOSEPH FLOYD

It had been a quiet morning in the woods north of Brook. The sky was beginning to brighten, though the sun was still well below the horizon. The night creatures were going to sleep. The day creatures were waking up. The nearby brook babbled away, but its consistency added to the stillness. Then came a loud bang from a small cottage hidden in the trees.

In its defense, it had been a fairly melodic bang. It started as a low rumble resembling a heavy drum. There was the tinkling of chimes and broken glass. Multicolored lights flashed in a rhythmic pattern through the basement windows. There was a bleating of brass, and it ended in twelve-bar blues.

Inside the basement was a large cauldron billowing smoke flashing between black, purple, and chartreuse, which gave the dark room a sickly aura. The place smelled of brimstone and elderflowers and vibrated with the last rumbles of the explosion.

Beside the cauldron, sprawled on a very tasteful blue and gold rug, was a young witch. Her face and robes were covered in orange soot. She let out a little moan as her head spun from the blast. Around her were a black cat, a black raven, and a silver and black wolf.

"By the Goddess, she's dead!" the raven squawked.

"She isn't dead," the cat said.

"Alas," the wolf said, voice low and somber. "Death comes for us all."

"She's not dead!" the cat said.

He went up to the witch's head and placed a paw on her forehead. It was hot. He placed an ear to her chest and listened to her rapid heartbeat. He peeled her eyelid open and examined her eye. There were faint blue streaks in the whites that seemed to pulse. The cat scrunched his nose up at the sight.

"Her heartbeat is fairly rapid," he said.

"She's going to die!" the raven said, flapping in distress. "Her heart is going to explode!"

"Alas," the wolf growled. "Though young, the Mistress has reached her end. As summer turns to fall, so too does her life."

"She's not going to die!" the cat snapped. "She's just been stunned by that concoction." He motioned to the cauldron with his tail. "The eyes are a bit concerning, though. Parcival, see if you can get the Mistress upstairs and into bed. Sylvia, grab a damp cloth from the kitchen and put it over her forehead."

"Right away, Figaro!" the raven squawked before taking flight.

"I will be by her side as she faces this battle," the wolf said.

Parcival grabbed the rug and began dragging the witch across the room. Figaro jumped off of her chest and moved to her desk where several books were laid out. He scrambled up as he heard loud thumps from the stairs. He looked and saw that the Mistress's head was bouncing off each step as Parcival pulled her up. He winced, but let it go.

On the desk were several books. One was opened to a potion recipe. Figaro looked it over and compared it to what the Mistress had been mixing. He looked at portion sizes and ingredients. After a few minutes, he nodded in understanding.

"I see," he said.

"What?" squawked Sylvia.

"Ah!" Figaro shouted in surprise. He turned and glared at the raven. "Don't do that!"

"The Mistress is in bed," Sylvia said. "With a damp cloth over her face! I put several just to be safe."

"Good," Figaro said. Then he frowned. "Her face? Not her forehead?"

"Whole face!" Sylvia said happily.

"Can she still breathe?" Figaro asked.

Sylvia's eyes widened in shock before she squawked and darted back up the stairs. She came back down with Parcival as Figaro was pawing through a different book. He would study each page carefully before licking his paw and flipping to the next.

"Figaro," Parcival said. "You have determined the fate of the Mistress and how we may preserve her life's blood for another moon, yes?"

"He knows how to save her life!" cheered Sylvia.

"She's not in danger," Figaro said, a hint of annoyance slipping into his tone before softening. "Not immediately."

Parcival and Sylvia cocked their heads in confusion.

"She used toad's eye," Figaro explained.

Parcival and Sylvia cocked their heads in the other direction.

"She was supposed to use newt's eye, but grabbed the wrong bottle," Figaro said. "Instead of making a flu remedy, she made a poor paralytic. The mixture was bad enough it caused a rebound and inflicted her by mistake."

Parcival and Sylvia looked at Figaro for a few moments. Then they cocked their heads back the other way. Figaro sighed.

"The potion was mixed wrong and now she can't move," he said.

"How long will she be like that?" Sylvia asked.

"That's the tricky part," Figaro said. "It wasn't a proper mixture, so we don't know. It's supposed to last a few hours but could last days. Maybe weeks."

"Weeks!" Sylvia screamed. "She's going to starve!"

"Pity," mused Parcival. "To die of need when the need is plenty."

"We need to crush nuts and feed them to her!" Sylvia said.

"Feed her from our mouths as if she were a pup?" Parcival asked.

"We can't let the Mistress die!" Sylvia hollered.

"Death comes for us all, eventually," Parcival said, closing his eyes in somber contemplation.

"There's a cure," Figaro said, whiskers buried in the book.

"Happy days!" Sylvia shouted.

"We shall halt the reaper's advance and safeguard our Mistress," Parcival growled.

"How do we do it?" Sylvia asked.

"We're in good shape, actually," Figaro said. "We have the hound's tongue, bird's eye, and cat's paw right here."

Sylvia and Parcival both leaned back in horror.

"Not my eyes!" Sylvia said, taking to the air and flying circles around the basement. The hanging talismans and lanterns rattled at the beating of her wings.

"If I must relinquish my tongue for the sake of the Mistress," Parcival said, "let it be done."

"They're plants!" Figaro yelled.

"Oh," wolf and raven said together.

"Hound's tongue and bird's eye are flowers," Figaro explained as he crossed the desk and hopped up to the shelf of jars and boxes containing the witch's potion ingredients. "And cat's paw is a vine. The Mistress collected those last week."

He went from jar to jar, reading each label carefully. He found the first three ingredients and pushed them off the shelf. The glass jars fell to the wooden floor and shattered, spilling dried vegetation and broken glass across the basement.

"Why did you do that?" Parcival asked, dancing back from the jagged shards.

"I see!" Sylvia chirped. "We can't open the jars!"

"Of course," Parcival said. "By breaking the jars, we can now access the valuable plants within." He turned to Figaro with a big grin. "Good idea."

"You're so smart!" Sylvia agreed.

Figaro froze, looking at them with wide, yellow eyes.

"Uh, yeah!" he said. "Of course. All according to plan."

He gave a nervous smile then darted away. Sylvia began picking through the debris while Figaro wove in between the remaining jars and boxes. There was one last ingredient they would need. Figaro began to grow flustered until he found an empty box on the bottom shelf.

"Whiskers," he muttered.

"What's wrong?" Parcival asked.

"We don't have the last ingredient," Figaro said.

"This is bad," Parcival said. "What must be acquired?"

"Grave's root," Figaro said. "It only grows near three-hundred-year-old graves."

"Graves," Parcival said with a derisive snort. "Useless monuments to the dead."

"People leave shiny baubles at graves!" Sylvia said. "I like shiny baubles."

"Trinkets for those without need," Parcival muttered.

"There's a tomb," Figaro said. He had returned to the desk and was pawing through another book. "Deeper in the woods, but not terribly far." He read a few more paragraphs. "A knight is buried there. Sir Blackwood. A holy warrior who fought the last dark lord. At least three-hundred years old."

"So, we need to go to the tomb and find the grave's root!" Sylvia said after lining up the three plants on the workbench next to the cauldron.

"Yes," Figaro said.

"Then let us make ready," Parcival said, puffing his chest up. "The woods can be dangerous to navigate."

"What do you mean?" Figaro asked.

Parcival smirked. "You spend your days within the cottage," he said. "Small wonder you don't know the perils of the woods."

"Is it that bad?" Figaro asked, fur rising down his tail.

"Do you know why we chose to settle here?" Parcival asked.

Figaro shook his head.

"The brook to the south has origins in the land of elves," Parcival said, crouching low. "The wind from the mountain carries the fumes of dwarven forges. The oldest trees have roots that dig deep into the land of demons." He stalked across the room as if he were hunting. "These forces converge and fill the woods with an energy unlike any other. Fantastic if you can tap into that energy like the Mistress can." He reached Figaro and put his nose right against the cat's.

"But that energy also affects those within the woods. Twisting your mind and confusing the senses. Without obvious landmarks you can't rely on your eyes and ears. They will betray you. You might wander the woods forever until you die from exhaustion."

Figaro curled up in fear as Parcival sat up straight.

"But with my nose," he beamed, "I will be able to take us to the tomb. My sense of smell is able to pierce the veil of magic that confuses other travelers. You can count on me to get us through the woods."

TEN MINUTES LATER, THE TRIO WAS WALKING DOWN A WELL-maintained path made of gravel and compacted dirt. Every couple hundred feet was a wooden bench with a small lantern hanging from a pole giving off a soft bluish-white light in the early morning glow. Figaro and Parcival were walking. Sylvia was perched on Parcival's back.

"It's a good thing you knew about this trail leading to the tomb," Figaro said.

"Of course," Sylvia crooned. "I see priests from Brook visiting the tomb several times each month. They all take this trail."

"Huh," Figaro said. "If there's that much travel to the tomb it would make sense for the church to maintain a path. Good eye."

Sylvia puffed up with pride. Figaro looked from her to her steed. Parcival was silent. His head was low, brow furled in irritation. He couldn't keep a low growl from the back of his throat.

"Are you all right?" Figaro asked.

"I am fine," Parcival snapped around a leather sack he held in his jaws.

"I'm sorry you didn't get to lead us through the woods," Figaro said. "I know you were excited about it."

"It's fine," Parcival grumbled.

"We don't have to take the path if you want," Figaro offered.

"The path is the quickest way to the tomb," Parcival said. "And we must not delay."

"Well," Figaro tried, "Maybe the path isn't real? You were saying the woods can be tricky."

"No," Parcival sighed. "It's real. I can smell it."

"Tell you what," Figaro offered. "After we get to the tomb, if we find the grave's root really quick, you can take us back through the woods."

"If I must relinquish my pride for the sake of the Mistress," Parcival grumbled, "let it be done."

"Come on," Figaro said. "I haven't seen you track in years. We'd love to see it. Wouldn't we?" he asked the raven.

"Oh yes!" Sylvia said. "I always love watching you track."

Parcival grumbled again, but Figaro noticed his head resting a little higher and a slight sway to his tail.

After another ten minutes, the path widened into a large, circular clearing. Around the sides were more benches and tables for pilgrims to rest at. A low altar had been built out of stone in the middle of the clearing. It was shaped like a low table with grooves in the shape of the sun, the Goddess's symbol. Sticking out of the middle of the altar was a tall, feathered shaft made of wood. An elaborate glass ornament had been affixed to the very top. Piled around the base were offerings.

Most of the offerings were food and drink. Bottles of wine and ale were lined up in rows along the base. Bread, cheese, and meat were buried in the dirt, though it looked like animals had gotten to most of it. On top of the altar were stacks of smooth river stones. Each was carved with a prayer or proverb.

Across from the altar was the tomb itself. It wasn't quite what Figaro had expected. He was expecting to see a grand building.

Instead, it was just a large, granite slab buried in the ground. Images depicting the knight's life and words in the language of the church were carved into the stone. The most impressive part of the tomb, in his opinion, was the large statue of a knight in full battle dress standing over the tomb. It stood tall with a large two-handed sword gripped in its hands.

"This is it," Sylvia said.

"Huh," Figaro said. "Smaller than I expected."

"Where is the grave's root?" Parcival asked. "You said it grows out of the grave."

"It should," Figaro said as he entered the clearing. "But that's not the grave."

"Then what is it?" Parcival asked.

"It's more like the door." He reached the slab and began looking it over. "A tomb is like a cottage for the dead."

Parcival snorted in disgust as he pawed at some bread that had been dug up but not eaten.

"Food and drink," he scoffed. "Now a cottage. Surely the living have better duties to attend to than to build a life for the dead."

"I don't understand why it's out here," Sylvia said, hopping off the wolf and pecking at the bread. "Don't they have places for the dead in town?"

"According to legend," Figaro said, remembering the book he had read earlier, "Blackwood's greatest foe was the evil wizard Arkatraz who was bent on conquering the world. In their final, greatest fight, Sir Blackwood struck the wizard down."

"Hurray!" Sylvia cheered.

"But the fight did something to him. Inflicted him with some ailment the church couldn't cure. He knew he was going to die, so Blackwood spent the rest of his life designing this tomb at this precise spot."

"An act of utter selfishness," Parcival snorted. "Now how do we enter this tomb?"

"I'm not sure," Figaro admitted. "I assumed there was a doorknob."

Just then, there came a loud crack. Figaro jumped and darted for Parcival, hiding behind his legs. Sylvia took flight and Parcival got low, a growl deep in his throat. They looked for the source of the sound. To their surprise, it was coming from the statue of the stone knight. Its joints gave off an immense grinding noise as it stepped forward, over the tomb, and lifted its sword.

"Halt!" came a deafening voice from the head of the stone knight. "You have come to defile the resting place of Sir Clairmont Blackwood, knight in service of Her Grace. This is heresy of the highest order. No man, woman, or child may cross the threshold of this sacred site. Turn back and pray for forgiveness or face the wrath of the Goddess." The stone knight swung the sword around in a wide arc before raising it up in an aggressive position. "It's your choice."

The trio looked back and forth between each other. Then Figaro stepped forward and raised his paw.

"Um," he said. "I'm a cat."

"What?" the stone knight asked.

"I'm a cat," Figaro said. "He's a wolf. She's a bird."

The stone knight held its position for a moment before lowering its sword. It reached into its belt and pulled out a stone tablet. It traced the tablet as it muttered to itself. "…defile… heresy… no man, woman, or child…." When it was done, it looked up at the trio again. "Well," it said. "Nothing in the rulebook says cats, wolves, and birds can't enter."

It returned the tablet to its belt. Then it reached down and lifted the tomb's door open with one massive stone hand. It stepped around the opening and returned to its position where it went inert once more.

Figaro watched, eyes wide with disbelief. Then he licked his paw and ran it over his face.

"All right," he said. "Let's go."

Sylvia returned to Parcival's back, and the three of them moved toward the now open tomb. The slab had been covering stairs carved out of stone that led into darkness. Parcival gave a sniff and turned his nose up.

"This place is filled with death," he said. "But it's old. Stale."

"Good," Figaro said. "That's what we want. Grave's root needs at least three-hundred years to mature."

They stood at the top of the stairs for a few minutes, looking down into the depths of the earth. Sylvia's feathers were puffed up against the chill. Figaro crouched low at the very edge of the first step. Parcival stood tall, shook his fur, and moved down the stairs. The others followed, staying close to the large wolf.

THE STAIRWELL WOULD HAVE BEEN TIGHT FOR A PERSON. THE stone slabs were wide enough for two, shoulder to shoulder, but the roof was fairly low. A tall man would have to hunch in order not to scrape his head against the ceiling. A funeral procession trying to enter a body here would have had a difficult time getting inside.

The three animals hopped down the steps without an issue.

The stairwell opened into a wide, square room. It was dark, but the sun had risen by this point. Even though clouds blocked most of its rays, enough light filtered down the stairwell and into the room for the trio to see a bit of the tomb. It was as if the stairs were designed to take in as much sunlight as possible.

The walls were made of white, polished stone covered in a layer of dust. Tattered remains of fabric dangling from hooks mounted near the ceiling suggested that tapestries had been hung up when the tomb was built. There was a large, ornate design inlaid on the floor. A mosaic of geometric glass tiles displayed another image of the symbol of the Goddess.

"So much effort and detail," Parcival grumbled. "All to be locked below ground where it will never be seen again."

"Look!" Sylvia said. "Baubles!"

In the back of the room was a collection of silver treasures. Goblets, plates, and coins lined the back wall as offerings to the holy knight. The knight himself was laid to rest in an alcove carved out of the back wall. The trio saw a gaunt body in old, rusty armor on its back with its bony hands gripped around an old, rusty sword. The skin was pulled tight over the bones. Four Dark bulbs grew out of the joints and helmet.

"That's it!" Figaro said.

He zoomed across the tomb and leapt up into the alcove. He looked at the black, dense bulbs. The natural light didn't reach this far into the tomb, making them difficult to identify in the dark. He tried to remember the description he had read in the book as Sylvia and Parcival joined him.

"Are these the grave's roots?" Sylvia asked.

"I think so," Figaro said.

He gripped one in his teeth and gave it a tug. The root didn't budge. It had embedded itself deep in the body's flesh.

"Huh," Sylvia said, hopping to the body's head.

"What is it?" Parcival asked. He put his paws on the lip of the alcove and set the leather sack down.

"The body," she said, pecking at the face. "It's supposed to be centuries old, right?"

"Correct," Parcival said. "Three hundred years old for the grave's root to grow."

"It's in good condition for being so old," Sylvia said. "Flesh doesn't usually last that long."

"It is unnatural, yes," Parcival said. "The work of the divine?"

Figaro gagged and moved away from the bulb. The taste was vile.

"No," he said between dry heaves. "It's mummification. They dried him out so as to preserve the body."

Sylvia tilted her head in confusion. Parcival snorted. "Another pointless gift for the dead," he said. "The spirit of life has gone, yet they work so hard to keep an empty husk."

"Sylvia," Figaro said. "Hold the arm steady."

She hopped over and landed on the wrist. She spread her wings for balance while Figaro gripped the bulb again. After a bit of twisting and pulling, it came loose, the long, thick roots unwrapping from the bones with surprising ease once it got going.

They were dark purple and dripped with a black ichor. Figaro spit it out onto the platform. Sylvia flapped with joy.

"We can save the Mistress!" she cheered.

"Will one be enough?" Parcival asked.

"It should," Figaro said, licking his paw. "But there are three other bulbs. We might as well grab those while we're here. Just in case."

They spent another ten minutes working two more grave's roots out of the body. Each one dripped the same black ichor. Sylvia took the second one and placed them in the leather sack Parcival was holding open.

"Something I don't understand," Sylvia said as they pulled at the final root embedded in the throat.

"What's that?" Figaro asked around the bulb.

"The body was dried out, right?" she asked.

"Uh-huh," Figaro mumbled as he worked the last root free.

"Then why are these so wet?"

Figaro tumbled back as the last root popped free from the body and fell to the ground. It landed with a wet slap, but something was different. Instead of purple roots, it was just one long, silver spike.

Figaro frowned in confusion as he looked at it.

"That's not a root," he said.

The body let out a massive gasp of air. Figaro and Sylvia both jumped and fled from the alcove, hiding behind Parcival, who jumped back, growling. The body clawed at the ceiling of the alcove as if panicked about the tight space. Its armor scraped the stone until the body clawed its way out of the alcove entirely. It fell to the ground, scattering the silver across the floor, and thrashed for a moment. Then it reached up to the lip of the alcove and pulled itself to its feet, gripping the rusty sword in its free hand.

The trio was frozen in shock as the corpse steadied itself. It set the sword in the alcove and adjusted its armor. Then it stretched, arms sticking up as it bent backwards. It let out a groan as the armor squeaked. Then it bent forward and touched its toes, bouncing as if trying to stretch out its back. It stood up straight and twisted at the hip, spying the trio for the first time.

"Ah," it said, voice gravelly with disuse. "I see. You three must have freed me. Thank you."

It grabbed one foot from behind and pulled it to its thigh and held it for a few moments before doing the same with the other.

"Are you okay?" Sylvia asked as it started doing jumping jacks.

"A morning routine is vital to healthy living," it said, armor clanking with each leap. He jumped a few times before he realized something and stopped. "Though, I suppose that's not the right word for it, is it?"

"Are you Sir Blackwood?" Figaro asked.

"Sir?" The body chuckled. "Finally knighted, eh? I suppose he earned that much."

"I don't understand," Figaro said. "You were buried here hundreds of years ago. How are you alive?"

Blackwood smiled with cruel malice.

"Oh," he said with a chuckle. "I'm not alive."

"We need to leave," Parcival said. "Now."

"What is it?" Sylvia asked. "Vampire?"

"Zombie?" Figaro asked.

"Evil," Parcival growled.

"Oh, that's just mean," the body of Blackwood said. "Just because I broke off a piece of my spirit and injected it into Blackwood during our final battle so that I could usurp his body and continue my plans for world conquest when he died, does that make me evil?"

"Yes," the trio said.

"Oh," the corpse said. "Well, I don't need the approval of beasts. Now, if you'll excuse me." He picked up the silver spike that had been lodged in his throat, mulling it over. "Blackwood spent years designing this prison. Now that you've so graciously released me, I will be on my way."

He walked forward. His heavy steel boots clattered as he walked over the mosaic on the floor. He looked up the stairs at the cloudy sky. He let out an evil laugh as he imagined his future.

Then came a loud snarl. Looking down, Parcival stood before him. The wolf's lips were pulled back, teeth out in full display. His snarl was fierce enough to make the corpse stop in its tracks.

"Parcival!" Figaro hissed. "What are you doing?"

"This thing is evil," the wolf said. "I can smell it. If it gets out, who knows what horrors it will wreak upon the land?"

"Oh," said the corpse, "I intend to conquer the world and rule it with an iron fist."

"It is a bringer of death," Parcival said. "All will suffer if it's allowed to walk free. Including the Mistress."

"But Parcival," Sylvia began.

"There's no time," Parcival snapped. "It is our duty to protect the Mistress at all costs." He kicked the sack to the foot of the stairs. "Take the roots and go. I'll hold this thing off as long as I can."

The corpse laughed.

"You think you can stand against me?" it snorted. "I might not have my magic, but I do have the body of the mightiest warrior of his day. I have absorbed all of his skills into myself." He grabbed the sword from the alcove. "Even with this rusty blade and decrepit armor, a single wolf stands no chance against me."

"He's right," Figaro said. "You'll die."

"If I must relinquish my life for the sake of the Mistress," Parcival said, "let it be done."

He crouched, ready to leap. The corpse hefted the sword, ready to strike. Figaro and Sylvia grabbed the leather sack, ready to pull it from the tomb and flee into the forest. As the four of them tensed, ready to move, the clouds parted from the sun. Its light fell over the clearing in front of the tomb. It illuminated the tomb, the altar, and the ornament atop the staff.

As soon as the light hit the glass, a powerful beam of light shot into the tomb. It shot over the trio's heads, landing at the corpse's feet and right in the middle of the large mosaic. The tiles began to vibrate before erupting in a gout of intense, white light.

The corpse let out a scream of pain as the holy light burned into its flesh. Flames popped from the armor's joints. It dropped the sword and stumbled back. It stepped on the scattered coins and tripped, landing back in the alcove where it thrashed in pain as the divine fire burned it from the inside out. After several excruciating moments, the corpse stopped thrashing and became a smoldering pile of ash and armor. The trio froze in shock, not moving until the stink of burnt flesh hit their noses.

"Let's, uh," Figaro began, "let's go."

They watched the smoking alcove a little longer, waiting for the thing to come to life again. It didn't. So, they turned, grabbed the sack, and left the tomb. As they climbed back to the surface, they could hear a familiar voice.

"I'm not trying to defile anything," a young woman was saying. "I'm just looking for my friends."

"Mistress!" the trio shouted in unison.

The wolf, cat, and bird scrambled up the stairs. When they reached the surface, they could see their young witch standing in the clearing opposite the stone statue, which had taken a defensive stance between her and the open tomb.

The trio bolted across the clearing and pounced on the witch. She smiled with relief when she saw them. They collided into her and knocked her to the ground. Parcival gave her face big licks. Sylvia landed on her shoulder and pressed into her neck. Figaro rubbed his head on her chest. She petted them all in turn.

"There you are," she said. "When I woke up, the workshop was a mess, and you guys were gone. I was worried sick."

"The potion wore off on its own?" Figaro asked, ear drooping. "We didn't need to come here at all?"

"You're alive!" chirped Sylvia.

"The reaper was repelled!" whined Parcival.

Figaro's frustration melted into relief, and he just purred.

"Oh guys," the witch said, burying her face in Parcival's fur. "Come on. Let's get out of here."

The trio let her get to her feet. Parcival grabbed the sack and offered it to the witch. She took it and smiled when she looked inside.

"Grave's root!" she exclaimed. "Wow! This is really hard to get. Thank you. All of you."

They left the clearing together, the trio pressing into the witch so as not to lose her again.

As the four of them left the clearing, another cloud drifted across the sky. It floated over the woods and came to rest in front of the sun. The rays blinked away, and the beam of light vanished. After a moment, scraping could be heard from the dark stairs leading down. Suddenly, a blackened hand emerged from the stairs, reaching out in the direction of the witch and her familiars.

Then the tomb door fell back over the stairwell. There was a yowl from within as the fingers got caught by the weight. They twitched before they were yanked back into the tomb. The statue stood over the door it had just dropped back into place.

"No man, woman, or child may cross the threshold," it said as it returned to its position.

ABOUT THE AUTHOR

Joseph Floyd was born in San Diego before moving to the SF Bay Area several months before his fourth birthday. He wrote casually in his childhood, but really got into the craft in high school, having a few pieces published in various school works. He attended Ohlone College pursuing writing as well as theatre, earning an AA in English and appearing in several local theatrical productions, including the world premiere of The Time Machine: Love Among the Eloi, written by Edward Mast and based on the book by HG Wells. Later, Joseph earned a degree in Environmental Studies from CSU East Bay.

THE RITUALIST AND THE HEDGE-WIZARD

KIT CALVERT

The fence split the garden in half; one side paved for ritual circles, the other a cacophony of sunflowers. Palug prowled between posts, stretching out the lengths of his legs, letting the last of the sun catch every inch of coal-black fur, right up to the furred tips of his ears. He knew of his own magnificence, but there were no eyes on him to respect it.

By the time Shallot came jingling through the flowerbeds, it had become dusk. Palug crooked open an eyelid; Shallot leapt up from the earth, and promptly spat out the bundle he carried onto Palug's side of the fence.

Palug eyed this slowly, and then turned the yellowness of his stare to the other cat. "You're late."

"Sorry!" huffed Shallot. "Sorry, sorry. Neil was upset, and it was so warm in his lap. He gets really, really good at stroking when he's sad."

"You're meant to be a familiar. Not a pet."

"I know! I—I am. A familiar, I mean." Shallot sat three fenceposts down from Palug but did not pay him the respect of cowering. "I brought it! The letter."

Palug eyed the envelope on his side of the fence; covered in cat-spit, addressed to one Neil V. Tolliver. "I can see that." He closed his eyes again, but the afternoon sun had died. It was no longer satisfying. "I've planted every piece of correspondence you've brought. Allegra's got a collection on her table in the hallway, next to the little bowl where she puts her keys. But she does nothing. It may be time to consider that our plot isn't working."

"Forgive me," Shallot wheedled. "If only—might I make a suggestion?"

"I suppose you may."

If Palug was not mistaken, Shallot shivered. "Perhaps, when Allegra is busy with her work, you could draw her attention to the letters. Maybe, if you're so inclined ... you could upset the pile."

A moment passed where Palug considered how odd it was for Shallot, in his belled collar, to turn to deceit.

"Just this once, Palug! Just one more. After that, we can try your idea. Though I'm not sure that Neil's ever summoned a witch, before. I don't know if he has any of the components on hand. He's more of a hedge-wizard, and—"

This was why it was so important that the humans collaborated. If Neil had a better-stocked inventory, they wouldn't have had to lower themselves to this idiocy. "Very well," said Palug. "I'll attempt it."

HIS DAWN MISCHIEF WAS EXHAUSTING, BUT ALLEGRA PORED over the manuscript in front of her too closely to notice his efforts. Palug melded into the stamped-gold letters of one of Allegra's tomes. Later, through his doze, he heard the *tchik* of the thirteenth letter addressed to Neil V. Tolliver dropping onto the mat. Then, the sounds of Allegra's bare feet against the rug, the murmured rage, the rustle of paper against paper as envelopes were piled up in his witch's hands. But then—unexpectedly—came the paired clunks of Allegra putting on her boots, and the unlatching of the door, and Palug had to spring out of sleep to not be left behind.

Allegra stood on Neil's doorstep, frowning, either at the sharp yellow of the door, or the jaunty tune that the bell played. As she waited, Palug biffed over one of the ceramic toadstools decorating the grass at the front of the house, for posterity.

Neil was barely dressed. His trousers had a softness to them that suggested he was not expecting company. His jumper was constructed from so many colours of wool that Palug found it hard to look at him. "Allegra, isn't it?"

"Yes." She thrust out the letters to him. Underneath her dark fringe, her pale face remained flat. "Is this you?"

He sifted through the pile, nodding. "Yeah, it is."

"You get so much post. It's exhausting."

Neil scratched the back of his neck, grinning. "I buy a lot of tat from catalogues. A *lot* of garden ornaments. Honestly, you'd be doing me a favour putting these in the recycling."

It was clear that Neil expected Allegra to smile at this, but Palug knew that Allegra did not often smile. Her mouth twisted. "Please endeavour to ensure your... *catalogues*... get delivered to the correct address."

"I will!" he said, as Allegra stormed back down the path. "Thank you very much, Allegra!"

"It failed," said Palug, later, when the afternoon fell again to dusk. "Days spent on this, Shallot, and no progress to speak of."

"I wouldn't be so sure. Neil's *baking*."

In the faint purple light, Palug caught the silhouette of Shallot preening his paws.

"I fail to understand what this might mean for the broadening of their horizons. Allegra needs the plants that Neil grows. She does not need cake."

"We'll see," said Shallot.

Palug had called Shallot there to discuss the witch-summoning they needed Neil to perform. He had planned to give Shallot a list of items to procure, straight from Allegra's books: a protractor, a nub of chalk, the blood of an ancient being, to be spilled in the middle. But Palug considered now that Allegra might not *like* being summoned, especially since she didn't seem to like Neil.

Shallot finished licking his paws. Palug realised that the other cat's hairless frame was fluffier than usual. "Is that a jumper?" he asked.

"I get cold," said Shallot. "Neil bought it for me from one of his catalogues."

Palug found this so revolting that he jumped down from the fence and pattered away.

DESPITE HIS DISGUST, THE NEXT MORNING PALUG NUDGED through a parcel he found on their doorstep. Allegra rolled her eyes at the calligraphic, yellow-inked 'THANK YOU!' on the label and abandoned the cakebox on the corner counter.

Now, she ground down something awful with her mortar-and-pestle, something that sent Palug to the very edge of the room. He flopped atop a book stacked there, absorbing the knowledge within through the pads of his feet. He was so large a cat that she often did not notice the books underneath him; nor was he careless enough to leave fur on the pages.

Everything he understood from the books suggested that Allegra needed balance. Life, to counter the death in her magic. She'd been such a promising student, back at the college. Why else would she have chosen Palug? Then somehow, everything had gone off-course. She'd moved them into a normal terrace house on a normal street, and her study of magic had, for the most part, slipped away.

It had been stupidity to expect that Neil's magic might live up to hers.

"Are you feeling all right, Palug?" asked Allegra. "You look a bit peaky."

He blinked slowly at her, as if to commune that the work she did *reeked*. She came to stand beside him and took a long sniff of the air. "That *man*," she said, throwing down her pestle at the desk, shrugging on one of her many identical black jumpers. "That man doesn't understand how to not encroach on other people's spaces."

And then she left. Palug padded over to the desk and recoiled. It was herbs that Allegra had acquired, foul-smelling leaves that he should've celebrated. But she'd left a sprig in the bowl, and only some of the leaves had been stripped from the stalk.

It wasn't like Allegra to leave a task half-finished.

She'd left the front door ajar. Palug hurried out and found Neil leaning against his doorframe, and Allegra hissing at him. "The fumes from whatever potion you're making is seeping through the wall and is upsetting my familiar. Would you mind moving the cauldron elsewhere in the house?"

Neil's eyebrows rose. "But I'm not making any—" He stopped, understanding. "Oh. *Ohhhhhhhh.*"

Allegra stepped back, pinching the bridge of her nose. "Please. Just tell me you'll move it, and then I can finish my work."

"It's not a potion," said Neil, smiling at her. "It's tea. I made a whole pot, actually. Would you like to come in for a cup?"

To Palug's horror, Neil squatted down and outstretched a palm. Palug shrank back behind Allegra's ankles. "Your familiar is welcome, too."

Neil's kitchen was as sunny as his front door. Palug thought this made sense. No wonder the man couldn't concentrate on actual magic, if he had this much light in the place. He padded around, sniffing at the door that led out to the loudness of the garden, at a curious smell in one of the cupboards. He saw no sign of Shallot.

Allegra lowered herself down stiffly at the kitchen table, her fingers catching the gingham tablecloth. In this room, she too was a stranger. Only that kept Palug from bolting.

"Please, forgive Shallot," said Neil. Palug looked up, then, and finally found the other cat sleeping against a turquoise teapot. "He's so small, he doesn't usually take up much room. Then again, I don't usually have more than one cup going at a time." Neil lifted the teapot, and Shallot stirred. He butted his head into the heel of Neil's palm, purring so loudly he rumbled. "Mind out the way, you utter goblin," said Neil. "You'll get scalded."

Shallot opened his eyes then, and found Palug, cat-smirking at him sitting in the middle of the room. They watched each other while Neil poured tea into Allegra's cup, passed her the mug. "Thank you for shifting," said Neil, scritching behind the velvet curl of Shallot's ear. "Now, can we have some more space?"

Shallot stretched, jumped down, and wandered farther into the house. Palug followed.

"I told you the baking would work," whispered Shallot, when they were out of sight.

"It didn't. And it doesn't need to!"

"What's wrong?"

"Allegra is on the cusp of discovering what she needs on her own. She's meant to be working on it, right now! Neil *distracts* her."

Through the wall, Palug heard Neil say, "Oh, that's nice. I reckon Shallot's showing his friend his best sleeping spot, in the window-seat. It gets ever so much sun there."

Then Allegra's voice came, incredulous: "*Our* familiars are friends?"

"They sit together on the wall, sometimes. Didn't you know?"

"We're visiting your friend," Allegra said, before Palug could argue with her. She'd done something very human to her mouth. It was redder than usual. "Come along."

The next day, Allegra's door-knocker clinked. "I found some notes amongst mine that might be yours," said Neil. "I must say, the way you've drawn these runes is compelling —"

"One moment," said Allegra, and then she lifted her hands behind the closed door; swept the room clean of bloodstains with one graceful motion. "If you wish to discuss my work, I'd prefer it was inside. You never know who might be prying."

And then the day after that: "I brought some seeds, from the garden. I thought it might help that concentration step, in the middle. Am I wrong?"

And, later: "I could carve a rune into the kettle, if you wanted to make your water boil quicker." A pause. "It needn't involve any bodily fluids."

For a handful of days, Palug had been fearful that Allegra would stop her work. But Neil's suggestions seemed to drive her forward. She stayed up until the dawn, sketching at her desk; erasing and re-drawing an inch of ritual circle at a time, until the ghosts of all her past attempts lay there before her.

The sunflowers in the Tolliver garden crumbled to dust. Later, frost began liming the stone slabs, seeping into the cracks. Allegra finished with her sketches and brought them outside in the night chill, shuffling stones and twigs and rosemary around on the patio.

She looked as she had back when Palug was a yearling cat. Focused. Unerring. Even when Neil brought out a steaming mug of tea for her, she did not grow distracted by his lurid pyjamas. Palug was content. If he'd known how to write in human letters, he might have sent a letter to the college, asking for Allegra's studentship to be reinstated. Then they'd move out of the pokey little terrace, and other familiars would look upon his splendor again.

Shallot never paid him enough respect.

Now that Allegra spent most of her time outdoors, it was much easier for Palug to catch up on his reading. Every so often he took in something that might be of use, and if she had listed the item in her apothecary order, he'd bring it next to the circle, batting it across to Allegra so she paid attention to him.

"Do you think she'd like a jumper?" asked Shallot, one day.

"Don't be ridiculous."

But then three nights went past where Palug watched her

move a splinter of amethyst around the circle a millimeter at a time, and he concluded that she might have become stuck.

It took him a longer time than he'd admit to find a book in the stack that might be useful, and then to haul it out to the patio. He dropped it, triumphant, only to find that Allegra was not there at all.

He found her sleeping in a ball on Neil's softest chair, a fleece blanket tucked in around her edges. Her dignity had been entirely robbed from her. As he approached, he took in a small bundle she clutched to her chest, nestled under the blanket. The bundle shifted; and the barest sliver of a pink nose peeked out.

Shallot.

Palug couldn't help himself. He meowed indignantly.

"They both get cold," said Neil, grinning at him. His cheeks were windblown and flushed. Palug regarded the man as if he was an ant. "I've just come back from the market. I picked up a couple of mackerel while I was out. Do you think you might want some?"

Palug meowed again. How *dare* he! Allegra needed to wake up, and keep going—she was on the verge of greatness, and this man did not understand how to not encroach on other people's—

"Ssh. Quiet, or you'll wake her up."

He had not agreed to the mackerel, but still Neil unwrapped the paper, began searching for a dish in the cupboard. "You know, she says you keep bringing her things. Ingredients—components. And the address of the college; a pen, paper."

Neil deposited the mackerel on the floor in front of him, in a dish decorated with a ring of turnips. "She's allowed to be tired. For now, it's enough for her to just... exist. Later, maybe—later, I think Allegra could change the world with her magic. But for now, do you think you could help me convince her that she needs to look after herself, for a bit? That she needs to find some joy in what she does?"

Palug licked the mackerel, and then looked at Allegra, the pale face tucked against pale fleece. He looked at Neil.

"Do you think you could do that?" he said. "For me?"

Palug blinked at him. To his dismay, Neil crouched, and gently scratched behind the furred tips of Palug's ears.

Once he finished eating the mackerel, Palug wandered over to where Allegra slumbered, and pawed at the corner of the blanket. He would not humiliate himself by crawling in next to Shallot. He would wait for his human to awaken, so he could suggest to her a new plan; a plan that took them away from this infernal terrace, and away from this infernal man.

But then Palug settled down. And then, slowly, he fell asleep.

THE WINTER DEEPENED.

Palug woke from a doze to the thunk-thunk of Neil chopping away some of the fence. He replaced his own warmth against Shallot with the corner of fleece, and went to the garden. Allegra knelt and peered at the dry, dusty beds.

"Neil?"

"Yes?"

"I think these might be helped with a concoction of marrow and bonemeal."

"Oh, really?"

"Maybe dentin, if we can get some."

MUCH LATER, THE SUN CAME BACK TO THE GARDEN. NEIL prodded at the yellow crown of one of the new sunflowers, and said, "Allegra, love, I'm not sure I like these as much when they've got teeth."

Allegra came to stand beside him. Palug had watched that morning as they sat on the grass together, Neil weaving daisies into the darkness of her hair. "It adds something," she said, softly. "Ambience."

Palug lounged beside Shallot atop the gate Neil had built for them, and found that he could not disagree.

About the Author

Kit Calvert (she/her) is a speculative fiction writer and scientist, currently based in Edinburgh. Her work is heavily influenced by her Scottish background, with focuses on the trials and tribulations of academia, domestic magics, and celebrating queerness. When she's not writing, she enjoys foraging for treasures in rockpools, painting, and consuming an obscene amount of soup.

To keep up to date with her forthcoming work, visit kitcalvert.com.

BENEATH THE WINGS OF NIGHT

NGO BINH ANH KHOA

A lonesome figure ran along
   A dark and empty street
   With heaving breaths and frantic eyes
   As panic moved her feet.

The girl could hear the taunts and shouts
   That thundered from behind,
   Which pierced the cold night's quietude
   And stabbed her racing mind.

Not used to this strange city's paths,
   She randomly turned right,
   A move that proved most fatal when
   A dead-end blocked her sight.

She turned around and found that it
   Was too late to turn back,
   For at the alley's entrance stood
   Four figures clad in black.

"Come, little girl," she heard one speak,
    And at once, her skin crawled.
    "It's not safe to be out so late.
    We'll take you home," he drawled.

Her back was up against the wall
    As they stalked toward her spot,
    Four predators on a singular prey
    Within an ambush caught.

She would have called for help if she
    Had been born with a voice;
    The best she could make was a string
    Of strangled, meaningless noise.

A calloused, and most callous, hand
    Flew forward forcefully;
    Her eyes were closed, and at that time,
    A caw rang suddenly.

The night air shuddered in its wake,
    And laughter turned to screams;
    Wet noises dwindled to a calm
    Beneath the pale moonbeams.

The young girl dared to take a peek
    And found her chasers dead;
    Their tattered clothes were drenched in blood,
    And each corpse lacked a head.

The trembling girl blinked once, then twice
    As shadowy talons loomed,
    Protruding from the rumbling ground;
    The bodies were consumed.

A third blink brought her eye-to-eye
    With two large orbs of red
    That hovered in the eldritch void
    Expanding overhead.

With shaky hands, the girl then signed
    A question toward the air,
    Night Claw? Her shaky fingers spelled;
    At once, a gale blew there.

When she regained her sight once more,
    Upon the dumpster stood
    A raven staring straight at her
    With eyes the hue of blood.

"The Wordless Witch," the raven spoke,
    "In trouble yet again,
    And I am not the least surprised.
    You, Luna, are a pain!"

A frown contorted her wan face
    As she glared, spitefully.
    The proud familiar, meanwhile, stared
    At her with mocking glee.

Did mother send her pet to spy
    On this mute exile's woe?
    Her fingers, fueled by anger, moved;
    No sorrow she would show.

The raven's eyes then brightly gleamed;
    "Your mother's bound by oath
    To cease all contact with you, child,
    A ruling she does loathe.

But that same ruling, upheld, means
    That you still get to *breathe*
    And not become the Devil's meal!"
    The raven seemed to seethe.

Young Luna was about to make
    Her argument, but then,
    She let her hands drop to her sides.
    Quite long did silence reign.

The moon was swallowed by the clouds;
    The flickering light was dead.
    The minutes tensely passed away
    Till Luna raised her head.

Why are you here? the girl then signed,
    To which the raven spoke.
    "I'm on a break as per my deal
    With mistress," he'd thus croak.

And to the girl's bewildered gaze,
    A mirthful look was shown,
    "We signed a covenant that states
    My weekends are my own.

Henceforth, I'll spend them as I please,
    To which she'll have no say,
    For covenants are absolute,
    Which no witch dares betray.

And since it is a Saturday,
    I'm free to roam the world,
    Away from her intrusive watch,"
    The smug bird told the girl.

"I'm not her eyes or ears right now;
    She can do naught through me.
    Oh, I've not felt such freedom for
    At least a century!"

But if you're free to roam the world,
    Why choose to follow me?
    Young Luna asked after a pause.
    "Pure happenstance!" cried he.

"I have no debt or favor owed
    Toward the likes of you.
    I was just passing through this place
    And chanced upon the view.

So don't expect it all the time,
    For I'm not always near,
    And watch yourself when you go out.
    Try not to die, my dear!"

She processed what the raven said,
    And wild thoughts filled her brain.
    Soon, her eyes widened as she gasped;
    Her hands moved, motions strained.

You used me as a bargaining chip
    To get days off! She signed,
    Vexed by frustration (and respect)
    Toward this bird's wily mind.

The raven cackled in response
    And, flapping his wings, said,
    "A win-win deal for all involved!"
    His thickened shadow spread.

A gust picked up and swept across
 The murky, narrow space,
 And on the dumpster, one lone plume
 Assumed its owner's place.

A stray wind nudged it toward the girl,
 Which she held near her chest;
 It shivered in the stillness and
 Against her heart was pressed.

Her fingers touched her chin and stretched
 Toward the clear moonlight
 Before she left, in shadow cloaked
 Beneath the wings of night.

ABOUT THE AUTHOR

Ngo Binh Anh Khoa is a teacher of English in Ho Chi Minh City, Vietnam. In his free time, he enjoys reading fiction and writing speculative works, some of which have appeared in *Penumbric*, *Star＊Line*, *Weirdbook*, *Spectral Realms*, and other venues and anthologies. He has also received a nomination for a Pushcart Prize along with one for the Rhysling Awards for his poetry. In addition to speculative works, he enjoys writing haiku, some of which have previously won awards and achieved honorable mentions in international contests in the US, Japan, Canada, and elsewhere.

KITTEN FOR SALE

ASTER MARSH

Small black kitten with white eyes and a striped tail available for 100 crowns. Pick-up required. I don't have the option to deliver the kitten to you. You need to come here to my mansion with a big cage, and we will together lure the kitten into it. I will provide the bait. Please, only serious buyers.

Edit: I have gotten a few enthusiastic responses. Thank you. But, after the third person changed his mind after seeing the kitten, I now want to add: The kitten is unusually large and can only be picked up in a BIG cage. He has piercing white eyes and only listens to the name Felice. If this is a problem for you, please don't contact me. Only serious buyers.

Edit 2: NOTE! Don't attempt to pet the kitten before it's inside the cage. If you pet the kitten, I cannot guarantee your safety. Because of this small inconvenience, I have lowered the price to FREE if you pick him up with a large cage.

Edit 3: When you pick up the kitten, bring earplugs or be prepared to block out all unconventional sounds coming from Felice. Some people think the sounds are similar to speech, but as we all know, cats cannot speak. Don't be worried about these sounds and protests against following you home. Felice is only a kitten, nothing else.

Advertisement deleted Friday the 13th of October 2023. *Reason for deletion:* I have decided to keep my kitten, Felice, against my own wishes. During the most recent attempt to get rid of him, I realized there is an unholy bond tying us together. Thank you for showing interest in my ad. I will keep on trying to find a way to break our bond, but until then I'll delete the advertisement.

Best Regards,

Jonathan Fred Ovander.

Account deleted on Tuesday the 17th of October 2023. Reason for termination: Jonathan Fred Ovander has passed away during the night of Friday the 13th of October. A funeral will be held at the All Saints Church in Lund. He will be mourned by his loved ones; among them are his siblings, Edith and Martin, as well as his kitten Felice.

ABOUT THE AUTHOR

Aster Marsh is a former software designer from Sweden who loves fantasy and writes stories in the speculative fiction genre.

THE DREAMER

M. LALLI LASSEGARD

They say that a familiar is created by a resonating of two hearts. If two parties, the witch and the familiar, share a shining of mind, heart, and soul, they will manifest a bond that transcends all magicks. This is truly lovely. Poetic. Cosmic, even. But for the familiar, it usually entails being suddenly whisked away from simple woodland life and deposited before a stranger. It's quite disorienting. And a little ridiculous.

But what do *They* mean our hearts resonated? I was perfectly content with my fruits and leaves, happy to sleep all day and forage all night.

So what? Well, I served a witch for a lifetime. His lifetime. Now I'm left with his loss. *They* never write about what happens once a familiar's witch dies. How was I to prepare for that?

The day I lost my witch was the day I decided to never familiarize myself with magick or witchery again. I simply couldn't bear it. Adika had been my one and only friend. Where I once found delight in the world of magick and witches, I now saw gray.

Other familiars, stronger ones than I, would have found a new witch to serve, but I couldn't. I would instead take a human shape and disguise myself amongst the mundane. Taking a human form isn't so difficult for most of us familiars to do, after all.

Of course, after my witch left me, I needed a change of scenery. The winding roads and scenic getaways of our hometown only reminded me of him, so I uprooted and moved far away.

I chose somewhere cold. Somewhere quiet. A small town with a small population condensed into a respectable grid of shops and apartments. A town where trains ambled through nearly constantly, transporting piney winds and rattling groans. Families of all shapes and kinds scuttled from place to place, all on various schedules and with differing needs. It was the perfect place to drown my melancholy with the hushed presence of others.

Within walking distance of my freshly acquired apartment, there existed a slew of locally owned cafés and bars aplenty, a few different shopping centers, a milkshake parlor, and a bookstore. Most of my first days in the city were spent exploring these places. Just walking, walking, and walking.

Until I got too bored or too tired, I spent my days mentally mapping out the city. By the end of my first week, I could get anywhere I needed with little trouble.

And whenever I returned to the privacy of my flat, I shed my human form. It was terribly burdensome to have to carry myself on two legs all day and, as much as I wanted to integrate myself into the mundane, I much preferred relaxing in my natural form.

She sketched with her right hand but painted with her left. Illuminated only by the brilliant ray of a desk lamp's light, a gaunt woman with bedraggled black hair toiled over her artwork. Hunched as she was over the angled desk, it was difficult to make out her features clearly, but her expression of loving determination was undeniable even so.

This was what she did in her dreams every night. A new painting, from sketch to completion, right hand to left. It was mesmerizing.

The first time I stumbled into one of her dreams, it was by accident. Every subsequent time was by purposeful curiosity until it just became a regular habit. She rarely acknowledged me, and I never tried to interrupt her. I wasn't the most appealing of conversation partners as a four-legged beastie, anyway.

It gets messy when non-witch humans recognize the visitors of their dreams in the wakeful world, so I always took my animal form while in her dreams. Less of a headache.

"Cookie. That's your name. Been thinking 'bout it for a while," she addressed me after ignoring me for a month.

I snorted, taken by surprise.

"Come sit in the light. I'll paint you to commemorate the occasion."

Of course, I complied. The naming of things was well worth commemoration, even if it was done so in a dream.

Once I settled in what I felt was a dignified pose, she started sketching. I felt bashful under her focused observation, but I kept still nevertheless.

After she finished the painting, she presented it to me with a prideful gleam in her eyes. She set it on the floor, leaned up against the desk, and waited expectantly for me to inspect it.

Naturally, I scrutinized the painting from every angle before giving her a nod. The work was immaculate. Whether her eye for detail and steady brushstrokes came from the unreality of a dream or from a reflection of her wakeful abilities, it was clear that she had cultivated quite the artistic skill. I was particularly fond of the way she captured the curve of my snout and the white tips of my ears.

So pleased with this painting was I that I took it back into the wakeful world with me. As soon as I awoke, I hung it on the wall opposite my flat's entryway.

"Oh, sorry!" I opened the door of the apartment building and smacked into the back of a woman smoking outside.

She shrugged and stepped out of my way. Tossed her cigarette aside. Crushed it beneath the toe of her hightop. Turned to me. "S'okay."

I gawked in surprise. It was her! The painter!

"… You the guy that just moved in?" she asked.

"Yeah!" I responded.

"I live in the unit 'neath yours."

"Yeah? Nice to meet you. My name's Vikal."

"Emmi."

She offered a tobacco-stained hand. I shook it while repeating her name over and over in my head, excited to finally learn her name.

"You live alone, yeah? You got any pets?"

"'No."

"No? Huh."

"You?"

"Haven't had a pet in a while," Emmi responded wistfully. "You got a job?"

"No."

"No?"

"I saved up before moving here." That was a stretch to say the least, but I wasn't about to tell a non-witch human I charmed the landlord with a gratuitous pile of leaves that I disguised as cash.

"Huh. What're you gonna do when your savings run out?"

"I haven't thought about that yet."

She flashed me an absolutely bewitching smile. "Wanna work for me?"

"Um … sure?"

EMMI TOLD ME THAT SHE LIVED THE SOLITARY LIFE OF AN OIL painter and that she wasn't of the persuasion to leave her flat often. Said she wasn't fond of being around too many people. Found the world outside overwhelming. Only came out to smoke on the stoop.

She then asked if I would pick up groceries for her at least once a week. Fetch her painting supplies. Grab her parcels from the post. Basically do for her any errands she needed. For payment, of course.

It was hardly a glamorous job. This kind of work was beneath me, but I felt compelled to take her up on the offer anyway. I was curious to know more about the woman outside the dream and I didn't have a better way to make money as a normal human regardless.

I ended up seeing Emmi at least three times a week for this arrangement.

We carried on for about a month, though she never invited me into her home. She greeted me in the doorway instead. Sometimes she would stand there and chat with me, and other times she led me back outside to have a smoke.

WHILE I WAS ENJOYING A BRISK ROMP AROUND THE LOCAL forest, my phone startled me with a jarring ring. A phone call. It took but a moment for me to shift back into my human form and answer. I barely said 'Hey' before Emmi started talking.

"Hiya, Vikal. Could you pick up some reds 'fore Friday?"

"It's a little short notice, Em."

"S'only Wednesday. What else you got going on? Finally got yourself a real job? Made yourself some new friends?" she teased.

"All right, already," I conceded with a chuckle. "What shades of red?"

"I was thinking maybe incarnadine or scarlet. Warm shades, ya know?"

"Think so."

"I'm sure you'll choose nice ones."

"How many do you want?"

"Three total."

"All right. See you Friday?"

"Yep. See ya."

Once she hung up, I immediately shifted back into my natural form. Thanks to the casual nature of our arrangement, I had a lot of free time to frolic around. Surely, I wouldn't be able to play in the woods nearly as often were I to have a human office job! And since I had until Friday, I could spend at least one more night outside before returning to my flat.

With nary a care in the world, I left my clothes and phone in a good hiding spot and snuffled into the brush.

AFTER MY WOODLAND VACATION, I ARRIVED AT EMMI'S FLAT ON Friday, little paper bag of red paints in tow. As promised. She stood in the doorway and regarded me with a charming grin.

"Ya know what, Vikal? I think you're ready for a promotion."

"Yeah? What, from errand boy to delivery boy?"

"Oh hush!" She swiped the bag from my hand with a playful flourish. "How good're you at cooking?"

"I dunno," I answered truthfully. "I don't have any experience."

"Can you read directions 'n follow 'em?"

"Probably, yeah."

"C'mon, then. Got a recipe for you already." She shrugged the door open with her shoulder and ushered me inside.

It was the first time she had invited me into her home. I could hardly contain my excitement! Maybe I'd get to see the desk where she painted in the wakeful world! Maybe I'd get to see one of her paintings! Maybe I'd get to see her paint!

After a moment of gawking at her back, I followed Emmi into her flat and gawked instead at her domain.

Leafy plants hoarded the space of nearly every flat surface, and far too many stained-glass lamps hung brightly from hooks in the ceiling. The walls were cluttered by an assortment of paintings, all of various sizes and colors, that seemingly shimmered under the foliage and technicolor lamps. Opulent rugs lined the floor, buried under a strikingly bizarre mixture of rococo and mid-century modern furniture. Squeezed in next to plants and peeking out from under all of the furniture was a vast number of books. It was overwhelming. Surreal. Beautiful.

It reminded me a bit of Adika's equally cluttered laboratory, and I felt my heart ache at the comparison.

"Kitchen's not much." An understatement. Contrary to the rest of the apartment, the kitchen was stark, clean, and completely free of clutter.

"It's fine," I responded.

Emmi then showed me where all the utensils were. Where the ingredients were. How to turn on the finicky stove. I nodded along politely and tried to peer into the adjacent room where I thought I saw the corner of what might've been her desk.

"Shout if you need anything," She called over her shoulder as she made her way out of the kitchen.

"All right." I forced myself to focus on the task at hand.

Despite Emmi's explanations and the recipe's instructions, I thought it would be much easier if I heated the ingredients with my magick rather than use the stove. Thermomancy was child's play for me, and that's all cooking seemed to require. Heat some things up and mix them onto a plate. Easy.

As it turns out, cooking requires a bit more than thermomancy to pull off elegantly. The meal was, according to Emmi, serviceable but in dire need of flavor.

"S'okay. You'll do better next time, I'm sure of it."

I shook my head. "There won't be a next time!"

"How ever do ya 'spect to 'ford rent unless you do more work for me? Landlord'll have your hide if you don't come up with the cash, and *I* know how much you get paid." Emmi grinned from behind her messy hair. A thinly veiled threat. Cunning. Bit like a fairy.

"Fine." I bent to her baiting. "But don't expect me to improve overnight!"

"Course not. Cooking's an art. Takes time."

"Why not just have me pick something up for you?"

"I prefer home-cooked meals. Even poorly seasoned ones."

"Why?" I balked.

Emmi tapped a finger to her chin and looked up thoughtfully. "How do I put this ..." Tap. Tap. Tap. "It's cozy. Less lonesome. Really makes a place feel like home."

"How so?"

"Be eating alone if you weren't here. You'd make your delivery, go upstairs, 'n go home. We'd both be lonesome then."

"I suppose you're right." I realized again how much I missed Adika. Since Adika's passing, I'd eaten every meal alone. It was lonely. *I* was lonely.

"Hard to be 'lone sometimes, isn't it?"

Why did witches have shorter lifespans than their familiars? It really *was* hard. I sighed.

"S'all right. You just come 'round here, let's say, Mondays, Wednesdays, 'n Fridays to cook. Ya get paid. Ya don't have to be alone. I don't gotta cook. Sound good?"

"Yeah. It does."

"Good." She patted me on the shoulder.

WEEKS LATER, IN ONE OF HER DREAMS, EMMI PAINTED A FIELD of vivid tulips under a deep, starry galaxy. The brilliant reds and oranges of each flower were stark against the velvety blues and misty greens that made up the background. Absolutely stunning.

"C'mere, Cookie. How you like this'n so far?" She beckoned me with a bright grin.

After a nice stretch, I stood from my perch and trotted over to her. She set the painting down at eye-level for me. After glancing over the finer details of it, I nodded my head to show that I liked it.

Emmi chuckled and patted me between the ears. "You like it? You know what I do with these paintings?"

I shook my head.

"I sell them."

As I tilted my head up to look at her, a shrill buzzing invaded my ears. Before I could make sense of it, I was back in the wakeful world, in my apartment, atop the pile of blankets that served as my bed. The buzzing persisted.

It was the door buzzer.

Quickly, I shifted into my human form and pulled on whatever clothes were within reach as I stumbled to the intercom.

Finger jammed onto the button, I slurred, "Yes? Who is it?"

"Is this the Dreamer? It's me. Elias."

"The what? Who?"

"Bah! Just let me in. It's quite chilly out this time of night, you know."

Bewildered, I buzzed Elias in and was practically trampled as soon as I opened the door.

"Oh! Pardon me!" A portly man with yellow eyes and a mop of silver hair stood before me. Elias, I assumed. "You're not what I expected," he said, glancing speculatively around the entryway, no doubt noticing my lack of furnishings.

"I think you're at the wrong apartment," I said as I tried to bar the man from barging further into my barren domicile.

He flicked his eyes up at me, then leaned to the side and peered over my shoulder. "So it would seem, but that painting there ... Would you allow me to see it?"

"No," I said, immediately feeling protective of it.

"Oh, bah! No need to be so stingy!"

"Please," I groaned. "Let's go find who you're looking for."

"I can very well find who I'm looking for on my own, thank you."

"Clearly."

"Oh, you!" the man sputtered. "But you're a familiar, aren't you?"

"You could tell?" My mild annoyance melted into dull surprise. It wasn't unheard of for one familiar to recognize another on intuition, but it wasn't common either.

"You have that smell on you. Magick."

"Do I?"

Elias blinked and looked down (up, actually) his nose at me.

"Why, of course! I'm a cat, you see! Us cats have the keenest sense of smell of any familiar!" To emphasize his point, Elias momentarily released the glamour holding his human illusion and showed a shimmering of his natural self. A regal, silver cat. Long, plush fur. Ember-bright eyes. He returned the illusion promptly. "Now, from one familiar to another, what's it like working for the Dreamer?"

"You're mistaken. I don't currently serve any witch." I frowned.

"No? But ... Oh, bah! Stingy!" Elias tutted, peering around my shoulder again. I tried to step in his way. "What manner of familiar are you? I'm rather *unfamiliar* with the animal in that painting. Could you not allow me to look closer?"

I sighed. "No. Shouldn't you find your Dreamer instead? I'd like to go back to sleep."

"Oh! Fine!" Elias huffed at me but turned back toward the door. "Only because you truly insist!"

The strange man opened the door before me, and to say I was surprised to see Emmi standing on the other side of it would be an understatement. She blinded me with a bedazzling smile. "Hiya, Vikal. Thought I heard ya up 'n about."

"And just who are you?" Elias asked her with a snooty shrug of his shoulder.

"A friend." She responded, unbothered. "Think I know what happened here. Why don't you come with me, Mister Elias. I can get ya where you need to be."

Elias's countenance changed immediately. "Oh? I would greatly appreciate that. This gentleman here has been *less* than helpful!"

"S'no problem," Emmi responded, stifling a giggle.

She spread her arm out in a broad gesture, as if to lead royalty from my apartment, and Elias graciously followed. I closed the door behind them, transformed back into my natural form, and went back to sleep.

IT WAS A WEEK LATER THAT I FOUND THE COURAGE TO BRING UP the strange little invader to Emmi. She was lounging on her sofa, balancing a thin paintbrush on the bridge of her nose. I was cooking dinner in the room adjacent.

"So, did you end up finding who Elias was looking for?"

"Yep."

My eyes shifted away from the boiling pot to glance at her. From where she was sitting, she couldn't see the flickers of flame that danced from my fingertips. "So, how did you know?"

"Know what?"

"How to find who he was looking for. The Dreamer?"

"Lived here a while. S'not the first time I helped anyone out." Out of the corner of my eye, I could see her fine-tuning her balancing act.

"He didn't know who you were, but you knew his name."

"True."

"Yeah …?"

"Yep."

"Do you know that he's, you know, he's …?" I gestured over my shoulder with my wooden spoon. I couldn't bear to say the word *familiar*.

"He's *what*?"

"Nothing. Never mind."

"S'not very polite, talking 'bout folks behind their backs."

"I know. I didn't mean to. Sorry." I dropped the subject to focus on cooking. It was time to stir the noodles. Didn't want them to stick to the bottom of the pot.

"YA KNOW, COOKIE, YOU REMIND ME OF SOMEONE I USED TO know," Emmi said with a faraway sigh. This time, she was painting a glistening koi fish enrobed in a rainbow of glossy colors. It swam through a sky of no particular color, free and whimsical. "She didn't talk much neither."

I blinked slowly in response and snorted.

"If you're worried 'bout breaking my concentration, don't be."
I nodded.

"This is a dream. I'm not gonna be surprised none if ya start speaking. Go 'head and sprout some wings while you're at it!"
I nodded again.

Emmi smirked mischievously. She shook her brush at me and scattered droplets of purple ink at my feet. "C'mon, then. No need to be shy."

"I'm not shy. I just don't have much to say."

"That so? I'm sure you got plenty to say. Ya just need some help." She turned back to her canvas and hunched over one corner of it. As an afterthought, she mused, "I'll think of something to talk about ..."

"Well, actually," I said, "I do have a question."

"Yeah?"

"Why Cookie?"

"You don't like it?"

"No, it's great. I'm just curious why you chose it."

"Ya look a bit like a cookie. The chocolate kind. With the cream. You know."

Her answer delighted a laugh out of me. "I do."

"Got any other burning questions?"

I thought about it. "Yeah. You told me that you sold your paintings."

"Yep. I do."

"Who do you sell them to?"

"Confidential. Can't be sharing client info, can I?"

I tried not to let the disappointment show in my voice. "I suppose not."

She patted my head. "Ya might find out someday. Never know. Maybe *you'll* become one of my clients! Ha!" Tickled, she unleashed a crow's caw of a laugh. "But I already gave you a freebie, so don't be getting greedy."

"I'm not! I'm just curious. How do you meet your clients?"

"I have my ways," she responded with a cheeky wink.

It was December. Monday. Snowing lightly. I was cooking dinner. Emmi was sprawled out across her sofa, reading. It had only been a few months since I'd met her, and already I spent more time in her apartment than my own. It was comfortable. Cozy. Familiar.

As I garnished the plates with sprigs of rosemary, a knock rattled the door. Emmi was up and immediately there, as if she'd been waiting for it. I leaned over the counter and stretched my neck over the threshold to snoop.

But Emmi soon returned with Elias alongside her, rendering my snooping pointless.

"You're just in time. Vikal's almost done with dinner," she chimed warmly. "Go 'n help him set the table."

I cringed internally, expecting the haughty fellow to argue with her, but he didn't. He marched right up to me and held out an expectant hand, upon which I deposited silverware and napkins. While he set the table, I hastily garnished a third plate.

"You know my matron, Mistress Mercy, wished to visit you this evening, but sent me in her stead. She didn't want to impose," Elias called from the other room.

"S'no imposition," she responded. "Mind another guest, Vikal?"

"Nope." If Emmi didn't mind, neither did I.

"Welcome her in, Elias. Set another place at the table, too. If ya wouldn't mind."

"Of course!" Elias responded gratefully. His hand waved in front of my face as he awaited another set of silverware. I obliged him with a huff and prepared another plate.

Rather than enter through the front door, as I expected, our second guest seemingly walked into the living room from thin air. Emmi was not in the least bit surprised. Nor was Elias. I was the only person that was.

"Hiya, Missy!"

"Darling, it's been so long! I hope I'm not imposing!" Tall as a spire and thin as a twig, Mistress Mercy managed to stand out despite the colorful clutter of her surroundings. She was absolutely drenched in a rich assortment of black robes and golden jewelry and her rose-red hair was greased back so tight against her scalp that it could have been painted on her skull.

"Not at all. Have a seat at the table. The boys've finished setting it up."

"Oh, I couldn't possibly! I'm on the strictest of diets, and I'm afraid my sweet Elias and I can't stay for too long."

"Ya sure?"

"Quite!"

Emmi gave me an apologetic shrug. Elias looked ever-so-slightly disappointed.

"All right, then. What can I do for you, Missy?"

"I was hoping to buy a dream. The most extravagant one you've got."

"That wall there's got some good'ns."

Mistress Mercy scuttled over to peruse the offerings, her jewelry chittering as she moved. "You see, darling, my dearest father is in his final stages. I'm afraid he's not got much longer."

"Sorry to hear that," Emmi responded sincerely.

"I want his final dream to be positively glamorous. He used to be a movie star, you know!"

"Well, try the one there. With the sphinxes. Think he'd fancy a dance with the Egyptian gods?"

"Oh, that would be positively divine!" She directed Elias to pluck the painting from the wall. He was careful enough to avoid knocking over any lamps or plants in the process. "How much do I owe you, dear?"

"S'on the house."

Mistress Mercy burst into tears so suddenly, that even unflappable Emmi jolted in shock. "Thank you, darling! Truly!" She shuffled toward Emmi, jingling all the way, and embraced her.

"Don't worry 'bout it."

"Even still! Oh, I'll be sure to visit again soon! And I expect to hear all about your new familiar when I do!" Mistress Mercy fixed her gaze directly on me.

Emmi waved her off. "Take care now!"

After a little more fawning, Mistress Mercy was gone the same way she came. Elias with her. I was at a loss.

"You're a witch." I snapped.

"That I am."

"You lied to me!" The words flew out before I knew it.

"Did not."

"Why didn't you tell me?"

"You didn't seem ready to tell me 'bout yourself, neither, Vikal. Figured you just needed time."

She was right. I knew that. Still, I felt hurt. Angry. Ashamed. "Since when did you know about me?"

"Doesn't matter none."

"Yes, it does!"

"All right. I'm sorry. Wasn't trying to upset you. You just seemed like you needed a friend more than a witch, and I wanted to be your friend." She spoke gently and didn't flinch at my hollering.

"Why? You painted me! You had me working for you! You used me!"

Silently, Emmi sat on the sofa and patted the cushion next to her. I sat down, still fuming.

"Y'know, I had a familiar once. Mia. A mongoose. Liked to watch me paint."

I nodded hollowly, struggling to process my own feelings.

"She was my favorite thing to paint. She was a good friend. A good familiar."

"Was?"

"She's gone now. Passed away."

"Oh. I'm sorry ..."

Emmi smiled kindly. She wrapped an arm around my shoulders and gave me a tight squeeze. "S'all right. Jus' trying to be honest with ya."

I took a deep breath. "My witch, Adika ... He's gone now, too."

She gave me another squeeze, and I leaned on her in response.

"Look." With the wave of her hand, the glamour of her apartment dissipated. The glittering lamps and lush plants shimmered out of existence, leaving barren gaps in their wake. The rugs faded into dusty, moth-eaten piles. Even the books faded away. Until all that was left was a dull apartment decorated only by Emmi's beautiful paintings.

I gasped.

"It's hard to be alone."

With the spell broken, I was able to see that Emmi had been struggling just as much as I. We understood each other. Rather than on my own behalf, my heart ached on hers. How long had she been alone? I couldn't dare ask.

Instead, I embraced her. Neither of us was alone anymore. We had each other.

I told her everything about Adika. About how he taught me thermomancy and tasseomancy. How terrible he was at astronomy. How great he was at alchemy. How we met. How we parted.

In turn, Emmi told me all about Mia. How she loved painting Mia. How good Mia was at baking. How clever Mia was. How she almost quit painting at Mia's passing.

For the remainder of the night, we shared stories back and forth, reminiscing over our favorite memories.

A FEW MONTHS PASSED BEFORE I WORKED UP THE NERVE TO ask Emmi to be my witch. Naturally, she responded that nothing would make her happier. Said that I worked hard enough to earn the promotion from delivery boy to familiar. Not that my work became any more glamorous. In fact, the work I did for her hardly changed at all. She still had me picking up groceries, fetching her supplies, and cooking dinner.

But that was fine by me. Cooking quickly became one of my favorite tasks. So much did I love cooking, that I had Emmi invite our friends Mistress Mercy and Elias to dinner frequently. Tonight was a special occasion, though. Tonight would be the unveiling of my most delicious of meals, the most excellent of recipes.

"This truly is one of your greatest works, darling! I can see why Vikal treasures it so!" Mistress Mercy cried dramatically from the other room as I dismissed the flames from my fingertips and began setting the plates.

"No doubt!" Polishing the silverware was an afterthought for Elias, who stared at the painting of me with unabashed confusion. "Stunning as always. But what manner of creature *is* it?"

Emmi laughed heartily and brought a bowl of garnished potatoes to the table. "A tapir. Not a very common animal 'round these parts."

"Is that what you are?" Elias turned to me with round eyes. "My! You've quite the snout!"

"And quite the knack for somnimancy, I imagine!" Mistress Mercy chimed with a pleased smile. "Though, I've never seen a tapir in person, myself. I've only read about them."

"Somnimancy is my specialty," I said proudly.

"Which helps me out bunches," Emmi added quickly with a nudge. "But enough chatter. Food's gonna get cold."

"Oh! Of course!" Mistress Mercy jangled from the painting to her seat, which Elias graciously pushed in for her. "Thank you for inviting us to dinner, dear Vikal. My Elias and I were quite delighted to receive a summons from you."

"Happy to have you," I responded, unable to hide my grin. "I've finally perfected this recipe, according to Emmi. So I wanted to commemorate the occasion."

"A fine thing to commemorate." Elias nodded proudly.

"Absolutely!" Mistress Mercy shouted.

Emmi grinned. "Hear, hear."

After everyone settled, I took my place at the head of the table and clapped my hands together. With a flourish, I sent a rainbow of sparks dancing around the room to illuminate us in a cascade of light.

"Well, let's eat!"

ABOUT THE AUTHOR

M. Lalli Lassegard is a polyglot with a penchant for collecting linguistic textbooks. Though his linguistic devotion eats most of his time, he spends what remains of it delving into the depths of obscure musical groups from the 80s. He has a song recommendation for any occasion and will not permit anyone think otherwise. When writing, Lassegard strives towards a minimalist writing style and places specific emphasis on the emotional exploration of characters. He draws inspiration from themes surrounding sociolinguistics, language identity, and social ambiguities. His focus is on the mundane aspects of every day life and how they can be either crushingly oppressive or delightfully surreal. While his work can often delve into grim topics, he tries to weave a sliver of hope into his stories. Above all, he hopes that his writing can resonate with others who may be in need of validation or comfort.

A RAT, A ROOT, AND A BIG ORANGE FRUIT

ZACH SHEPHARD

Clara was just finishing up with the pentagram on the basement floor when I wandered down the stairs. I'd thought that sort of thing was supposed to be drawn in blood, but apparently glue sticks and pink glitter are just as good.

"Hey, Vinnie," she said. "How was your cheese?"

I squeaked a long review she couldn't actually understand, because Clara didn't speak rat. But I think she got the gist of it. (The provolone was, at best, amateurvolone.)

Clara arranged a few last candles around the pentagram. She hung a plant-sprig from the beam above it. I aimed my sniffer in that direction and detected ... mistletoe? Oh, god. Please tell me Clara wasn't summoning a demon just to kiss it. Last time we lost a fortune on mouthwash.

"Wanna be my videographer?" she asked. It wasn't very rewarding work, but then, being a witch's familiar in 2024 wasn't exactly a thrill-ride. The game had really changed once people could just buy all their spell reagents on the internet. I couldn't remember the last time I got to sneak into a shady ramen joint to steal a rare herb from the local noodlemancer. One-click buying was the bane of my existence.

Clara propped her phone against a jar with the camera

pointed at her casting zone. She could have easily started recording on her own, but she was just trying to let me feel useful.

"Okay, Vinnie," she said, grinning under freckled cheeks and curly orange hair as she got into position. "Ready when you are."

I pressed the button with both paws. The first two seconds of the video were an extreme close-up of my stupid nose, twitching. There went my Oscar.

Clara chanted a few words, sprinkled some magic dust on the pentagram, and took a step back. The glittery lines flared to life with a burst of pink flame. When the flash subsided, something smoldered inside the design. We both rushed over to investigate.

A chunky brown blob burbled like hot chili. Clara reached a cautious finger toward it. One of the air bubbles popped right as she got there, spitting a jet of flame about six inches high.

We both yelped and jumped back. Clara aggressively sprayed the blob with a can of whipped cream, which reminded me she still needed to replace the fire extinguisher.

"Welp," she said, as the can sputtered some final words on its dairy deathbed, "that was more explodey than I would've liked. I should've used pandrake root."

I never did understand why a plant with roots shaped like a skillet would have magical properties, but maybe that's why I was just a familiar, and not Chief Summoner of Hot Slop.

Clara checked the jars on her shelves. She had mandrake root (shaped like a person); clandrake root (shaped like *lots* of persons); some fandrake root (shaped like a person waving a giant foam finger at a football game); and even a hamdrake root (which vaguely resembled lunchmeat, but only if you tilted your head and used a lot of imagination). No pandrake, though.

She got on her phone to order some. Her face, lit by the screen in the dim basement, scrunched in annoyance. "What? Why is everyone out of pandrake root?" Her shoulders slumped and she tilted her head back, groaning overdramatically. "Oh well. I have other spells I can work on." She busied herself at her desk.

Clara was able to move on without thinking twice, and

normally I'd have done the same. But how often did I get to help my witch these days? How often did I get to feel useful?

After spending the last few years as a glorified Muppet, I could finally be a *real* familiar again. Daring adventures! Thrilling escapes! Probably a number of felonies I'd never actually be charged for because the justice system isn't equipped to prosecute rodents! It was my time to *shine*.

I scurried up the stairs, leaving Clara with her books and reagents. She didn't need to know where I was going — this would all be better as a surprise.

THE REAL SURPRISE WAS DISCOVERING HOW BAD I WAS AT THIS. I didn't even know where to look for spell reagents anymore. After a few hours of wandering I snuck into an IHOP, but it turns out their pancakes contain no actual pandrake. False advertising.

Figuring I'd need help with this project, I visited the cemetery. It was a brisk, starry, Octobery night. I stuck my nose in the air and followed it like a dowsing rod. The Sniffmaster 6000 took me to a mossy tombstone, atop which stood a raven like a statue, wings spread wide.

"Hey, Lenny," I said.

The raven didn't move. I cleared my throat and said again: "Hey, Len—"

"Boo!" Lenny yelled, flapping her wings at me. Since I was there for a favor, I played along: I grabbed my heart with both hands, did a pirouette, and fell over backwards.

The raven hopped down from her tombstone. "You okay, Vinnie? It was just a gag." She pecked my chest in what must have been the corvid version of CPR. I sat up before she could give me beak-to-mouth, because I've seen how birds feed their kids.

"Hey," I said. "It's been a while. How're things?"

Lenny shrugged. "Kind of boring, honestly. No one explores graveyards around Halloween anymore." She sat against the tombstone and pulled a package of gummy worms from under her wing. She tilted them toward me, but I declined.

"Sorry to hear that," I said. "But, hey—if you're looking for something to do, I could use some help. Clara needs pandrake root, and the internet's all out. I'm trying to find some the old-fashioned way."

Lenny dropped three gummy worms down the hatch. She flicked some sour-dust off her wing. "Sorry, Vinnie. Ever since Kazkabar started ordering his stuff online, I've gotten lazy. When you haven't done anything meaningful for so long, it's hard to care about trying again."

I understood what she meant. Sometimes all you want is a project, right up until it's time to start a project. Then you ask yourself what the point of it all is.

But I wasn't about to give up. I was a familiar, and for the first time in forever, my witch actually needed help. I asked Lenny if Kazkabar might have any pandrake in his mausoleum.

"I could check," she said, "but I doubt it. Kazkabar's a necromancer: it's all bones and organs in there. Even if a recipe called for roots, he'd rather substitute a withered spleen. It's why his soufflés never rise. Too spleeny."

I paced on my hind legs, rubbing my chin with a forepaw. Sometimes pretending I'm a detective helps me think.

"Hey," Lenny said around a beakful of rainbow gummies, "isn't that ritual convention tonight?"

She was right: every October, a bunch of witches and warlocks got together to cast spells around a bonfire they'd poured their magic into. Someone there might have pandrake root.

"Lenny, you're a genius! I'll head straight to the pumpkin patch. Is Kazkabar going to be there?"

"I doubt it. He's been spending all his time building cow-sculptures out of beef jerky. Calls it 'snacksidermy.'" She shrugged. "Necromancers are weird."

"Want to come anyway? Might be nice to get out of the graveyard for a bit."

Lenny sighed, in the way people do right before they admit they're going to skip the gym tonight. "Thanks, but I just don't have it in me these days. I think I'll take a nap." She crinkled the gummy-worm bag into a pillow and lay on her side.

I knew what it was like to get stuck in a rut, so I didn't get on Lenny's case about it. But I vowed to come back later and see if I could help.

It was a long way to the pumpkin patch. I tried hitchhiking to speed things along, but rat thumbs are hard to notice alongside a dark country road. Also, they're attached to rats, which some people find off-putting.

I eventually managed to grasp onto something hanging from the back of a passing pickup. It wasn't a very dignified way to travel, but at least I finally discovered a use for truck nuts.

As the pickup passed my turn, I let go and rolled to a stop. Down the dirt road I could already see the light of the bonfire. The orange glow was a bright contrast against the midnight-blue sky. A little *too* bright, actually. Something seemed wrong.

The screams reached me as I entered the field. I doubled my pace.

Bursting through a wall of grass, I finally got a look at the scene. It was like I'd stepped into a burning war zone: witches and warlocks ran all about, flinging spells at the vines chasing them. Flaming pumpkins fell from the sky, whistling like mortar shells. In the middle of it all was a house-sized jack-o-lantern, spitting fire as it cackled at the stars.

"Down, soldier!" The voice hit me at the same time its speaker did, tackling me to the ground. From under a mound of dark fur, I saw a pumpkin soar overhead and roll past us. It came to a stop and turned our way. A fiery grin spread across its face, full of triangular teeth.

The skunk atop me sprang to her hind feet. She raised a crooked witch's wand to her shoulder like a rifle.

"I'll see you in hell, Jack!" The wand unleashed a flurry of neon-green streaks at the lunging pumpkin. A sound like machine-gun fire filled the night, joined by the skunk's battle cry.

Seeds and orange guts flew everywhere. Our attacker fell into a deflated heap before us.

The skunk stepped forward and gave the pumpkin a bayonet-stab. Seemingly satisfied, she lowered the wand.

I rose and dusted myself off. "That was ... yikes. I mean—thanks."

The skunk lit a cigar in the burning pumpkin wreckage. "You've gotta be careful out there, soldier. This is war!" She puffed the cigar. "Name's Tulip."

I snapped my fingers. "Tulip! I knew I recognized you. We met at the Lughnasadh party."

"Right! You're Clara's familiar. I didn't see her tonight."

"I came alone. What the heck is going on here?"

Tulip looked over the distant battle, flames reflecting in her black eyes. She shook her head at the horrors of war.

"It all started the same as usual. Everyone contributed magic to the bonfire for collective use, then began casting their own spells. Things were going just fine, right until some idiot told Linus he didn't have the chops to summon a pumpkin god.

"The damned fool accepted the challenge, even though no one took him seriously. But Linus dug deep and pulled the spell off. Problem is, he didn't have enough gas left in the tank to bind the monster he summoned, and it didn't take kindly to being dragged out of Hades."

Yikes. And I'd thought things had gone bad when Clara accidentally invented mosquito attractant.

"Everyone banded together and figured out a way to banish the thing, but they lost a vital bag of reagents in the chaos. It's got everything they need to finish their spell. If we can just get to that bag, we can end this damned war."

This wasn't the mission I'd signed up for tonight, but Tulip *had* just saved my life. Maybe I could help.

"I've got a pretty good nose for reagents," I said. "If they're nearby, I could probably find them."

The skunk chuckled around her cigar. "No need to *find* the reagents, kid. We already know where they are. It's getting to them that's the hard part." She gestured toward the giant pumpkin, whose vines flailed overhead like grasping tentacles.

There in the distance, I saw it: a small sack at the base of the pumpkin. As if the gourd-lord were challenging everyone to come and get it.

I could have just left. I could have accepted the night as a loss and gone home, where I'd sit around eating cheese all day, sometimes wanting something to do, but just as often not caring at all.

But I thought of Lenny, and how she was no longer the ravin' raven I'd once known. If I didn't do something, I'd end up just the same.

"I can get to the bag," I said. "Not sure I can drag it back, though."

"There's no need for that. The spell is already cast. All that's left to do is chuck the reagents into the pumpkin's mouth. If we can reach the bag, we can finish the job. But this is no easy mission, soldier. You go out there, you might not come back."

I stood tall and saluted sharply. "I'm with you, Sarge."

Tulip's grin spread, pulling the cigar to one side. "That's the spirit, soldier." She cocked her wand like a shotgun; it even made the sound. "Let's. Get. *Stinky.*"

I was pretty sure that was only a skunk thing, but I got the idea. We charged into the fray.

Other familiars darted around us, dodging pumpkin-mortars and shouting to each other. Tulip's wand ripped new face-holes into attacking jack-o-lanterns. Vines grasped at me from every direction, but I zigged and zagged until they tied themselves in knots. We pressed on.

The great pumpkin-god loomed, spewing fire at witches, who threw spells right back. It had turned so it wasn't quite facing the bag anymore; I found myself wondering just how good peripheral vision was in plants.

"Anita!" Tulip yelled. I followed her gaze to the side, where a witch fended off a half-dozen mini-pumpkins with her broom.

"I have to help my mistress," Tulip said, concern filling her striped face. "She's been without her wand this whole time. But you can do this, soldier. Get to those reagents and finish the job. We'll hold them off!" She ran through the blazing pumpkin patch, screaming over the sound of her own machinewand fire.

I continued gourdward. Now that I was alone, I was able to focus more on stealth. No offense to Tulip, but she was kind of the loudest thing there.

When I was nearly at the cackling pumpkin-god, I hid behind a charred bucket. My fur was singed. My heart raced. It smelled like someone had ruined Thanksgiving dinner by burning every pie in a twelve-mile radius. But despite the hell I'd been through, I was almost at the reagents. I took a deep breath and crept forward.

The pumpkin-god spun with a great rumble, snapping its fiery gaze to me. I froze.

"Well, well, well," it bellowed, the heat of its breath forcing me to shy away. "What have we here? Did you think you could finish their little spell, mouse?"

Oh, no he didn't.

My lips curled back, showing my teeth. "I'm not a mouse. I'm your worst nightmare!" I lunged for the bag.

A flaming vine slammed to the ground in front of me. If I hadn't hit the brakes in time, I'd have lost my head.

I raised my forepaws in surrender. "Or, you know—maybe we could negotiate?" Backpedaling, I tripped over something that hadn't been there before.

I reached for the thing and pulled it up. There in the firelight, the bands of the gummy worm glowed bright lemon-lime. I couldn't help but smile.

"On second thought," I said, "I'm not much of a negotiator myself. Let me refer you to my lawyer."

I pointed to the sky above the pumpkin. When it looked that way, Lenny crop-dusted it with the remains of a gummy-worm package. Sour sugar fell straight into the pumpkin's eye.

"Ow!" it said, tentacle-vines fumbling at its squeezed-shut eye-hole. "It stings, it stings! Oooooh, it stings so *bad*!"

I seized the opportunity and opened the bag. I heaved reagents into the pumpkin's grimacing mouth, one after the other. When I got to the last item, I stopped.

"Oh, come on," I said. "Seriously?"

Pandrake root. Of course.

I looked around. With the pumpkin-god distracted by its pain, the tide was turning in our favor. Maybe we could win even without the banishment spell. Maybe I could just take the pandrake root home. Maybe—

I heard Tulip's battle cry over the din. She didn't sound as okay as I'd hoped. With a heavy sigh, I accepted what had to be done.

Into the fiery maw the pandrake went. A moment later, the pumpkin stopped whining about its eye. It froze like someone who'd just realized, with great horror, that they couldn't possibly make it to a bathroom in time.

There came an unsettling gurgling sound. Everyone stopped what they were doing to stare. The pumpkin turned green.

We all ran as far and fast as we could.

I wish I'd had a chance to look back at the explosion, because it sounded pretty impressive: probably something like the grand finale of a fireworks show, if the fireworks were sticky and smelled awful.

A bunch of us gathered at the edge of the pumpkin patch, watching as stringy, flaming guts drifted down like confetti. I felt a paw clap onto my shoulder.

"You did good, soldier," Tulip said. "And so did your air support."

Lenny landed before us. "Thanks for stopping by the cemetery tonight," she said. "Until you left for your mission, I hadn't realized just how boring it was to watch Kazkabar stitch meat together. I needed this, Vinnie."

"I'm glad you changed your mind. I was a goner without you. Thanks."

"Did you find any pandrake root?"

"Not exactly."

Tulip asked around for me, but no one had any more pandrake. Oh well. At least I'd done something that really mattered that night, which was a big change from my usual routine.

I caught a ride home on a broom, and limped inside under a rising sun.

CLARA WAS CURLED UP IN BLANKETS ON THE COUCH, SCROLLING her phone as she sipped coffee.

"Vinnie!" she said. "Yikes—you don't look so good. Where've you been?"

I took a deep breath, ready to give every detail of my wild night. In the end, all I said was "squeak," because it's the only thing she hears anyway.

"Sounds rough. Hey—I've got something for you. C'mere." She lifted me onto the couch, which was great because I was too beaten up to get there on my own.

Clara turned toward the far end-table and reached for something. She spun back toward me. "Ta-da!" In her hands was a potted plant, with little banana-like bushels hanging from its stems. Except they weren't bananas. They were string cheese.

"It's the spell I was working on yesterday. I was right: pandrake root was the key! Turns out I had some in the freezer I'd forgotten about."

Could I have been upset that I'd gone through hell just because my witch was a little scatterbrained? Sure. But I wasn't. Even if the quest for the pandrake root had been unnecessary, it still dug me out of my funk. Lenny, too. And besides: I now had a plant that *grew string cheese*. How could I be mad?

Clara picked a bushel and set it beside me. I sat back into the couch and started munching, watching whatever she had on the TV. She scratched me between the ears and left with a smile. Life was good.

From the kitchen, Clara's voice: "Aw, man! I'm out of pickles. Oh well." She headed off to the basement.

I gazed through the window at the world outside, where everything was dangerous and chaos reigned supreme. I looked down at the strip of string cheese in my paws. With a heavy breath, I tied it around my head like a Rambo bandana.

My joints protested as I dismounted from the couch. I stood before my rat-flap in the front door.

"Your witch needs you, Vinnie," I said. "Let's. Get. *Pickly.*"

I left the safety of home once more, to face familiar territory.

ABOUT THE AUTHOR

Zach Shephard lives in Enumclaw, Washington, where he occasionally writes fantasy, science fiction, and horror stories. Most of his work is either humorous or dark, with very little middle ground. (If you're reading something of Zach's and haven't at least smiled by the end of the first page, you can safely assume the protagonist is in for a rough time.) He's had stories appear in places like *Fantasy & Science Fiction*, the Unidentified Funny Objects anthology series, and a number of Flame Tree Publishing's gorgeous Gothic Fantasy books.

In his spare time, Zach collects board games and chronic injuries. He exercises as much as he can in order to counteract his sugar addiction, and firmly believes that the five-second rule should not apply to cookies. (Bending over to retrieve a fallen Oreo is like performing half a burpee anyway, so the whole thing is a caloric wash.)

For more of Zach's work, check out www.zachshephard.com.

SECOND LIFE

CHRISTINA SNG

Her eyes watch me
    As I go about my day.

The blinding light
    From that night alarmed her
    Like I'd never seen before.

I thought she had a stroke
    But before I reached her,
    She ran and hid.

In the morning,
    She meowed for food
    As she always did,

Eating every kibble
    As she never did.
    Then she looked at me

Expectantly—
    The hairs on my arms stood.
    This was not my cat.

Yet when the world
    Turned to ashes
    And people turned ravenous,

She stared down every
    Cannibal who showed up
    At our door.

Kept me safe
    While I checked every trap
    And picked every vegetable.

We survived together
    When the world ended
    And when the world restarted.

It has been 1000 years
    Since the light blinded us.

I wonder what dark magic
    Came into our lives that day
    To keep us alive.

She's been more affectionate
    Of late, curling up beside me
    To sleep away the day.

I see glimpses of my cat in her.
   Is she really gone or is she
   Still inside this body?

After all this time,
   I realize
   It no longer matters.

At night,
   She sits by the window
   Watching the sky

Eyes sharp, ears alert and wary.
   I sit beside her,
   Crossbow on my lap.

Whatever comes next,
   We are ready.

ABOUT THE AUTHOR

Christina Sng is the three-time Bram Stoker Award®-winning author of *A Collection of Nightmares* (2017), *A Collection of Dreamscapes* (2020), and *Tortured Willows* (2021). Her poetry, fiction, essays, and art appear in such venues as *Fantastic Stories of the Imagination*, *Interstellar Flight Magazine*, *Penumbric*, *Southwest Review*, and *The Washington Post*, and have received multiple nominations for the Rhysling Awards, the Dwarf Stars, the Pushcart Prize, and honorable mentions in the *Year's Best Fantasy and Horror* and *Best Horror of the Year* anthologies.

Christina is a member of the British Science Fiction

Association, the Horror Writers Association, and vice president of The Science Fiction & Fantasy Poetry Association.

THE WITCHING HOUR LETTERS
AMANDA CECELIA LANG
& BRITTANY NOELLE

October 13, Year 665 Under Our Moons

Greetings Lucius Lightningflaw,

By the mercy of our Moons, may this message reach you and not your Master. When I heard you were taken as Gravedigger Crenkhart's new familiar, my heart sank. I pray your ordeal is not as degrading as the stories suggest. Does that lunatic truly bathe with you coiled around his arm? I shudder for you, Lucius, genuinely.

I realize I'm the last familiar you want to hear from. That is, if you even remember my whiskers among the countless witches you menaced during our mandated re-education.

Our time at the Reformatorium Animalis was never amicable. Our philosophies on lawbreaker justice misaligned like sunlight and moonstone. I accepted my sentence with humility and all the lunar grace I could summon. Yet, as mooncalves in our cocoons —stripped of our natural forms, mere pupae—your psychic tantrums withered us less experienced witches. We were all helpless—none of us desired to be there—yet your ceaseless rants against the Reformatorium's methods made our transformations evermore toxic. Later, as freshly hatched familiars, adjusting to the oddities of our new servile forms, toiling to learn the rituals to please our future masters, you singled me out. Spilled my loyalty potions. Hexed my obedience oaths. Blamed me for every shattered alchemy jar and missing grimoire, though everyone knew you were the most slippery.

Felines and serpents never bond in the wilds—why should we be different, imprisoned as we are in fur and scales? Why would I pay heed to one who tormented me so?

Yet, as tormentors go, Lucius, you are mere moondust amid meteorites.

And I have no one left to ask for aid.

Tonight, in the grim shadow of Dustfell's newly raised dome, I reach out, not to throw insults or berate you for our past divisions. I seek your strength, your cunning. Your insolent schemes condemned you to life as a familiar, and your tricky nature haunted every phase of my reformation. Yet I see now: these same contrary wiles may be the key to an overdue rebellion.

Because I believe you. All your forked-tongue ravings about the noxious, overreaching methods of the Reformatorium Animalis, your accusations of corruption among the High Coven of the Dual Moons.

It's true. All of it.

As the Coven's obedience liaison, I hear things. I see things. Under Prime Mistress Millicent Manor herself, I have access to conversations that would boil your cold blood.

I beg you, Lucius, respond in haste. Swear I can trust you with this vital information.

For I swear, by the revelatory glow of the Mirror Moon, the secrets I harbor could end witchkind.

Blessings upon this dire hour,

Litten Gaunt

October 19, Year 665 Under Our Moons

Greetings Merry Bootlicker,

Have you lost your lackwit mind? Sending messages downriver in enchanted bottles that anyone in Dustfell might discover? Do you aspire to find your boot-breathed head swinging from a rope? You'll notice this message was starsent. A spell forbidden to lowly familiars—but then, so is plotting a rebellion. *If* I agree, all future exchanges must be starsent. Assuming, naturally, that I don't turn you in and collect the bounty on your treasonous skull.

Watching you play poster child for the High Coven's most recent propaganda crusade proved absolutely vomitous—though not surprising. How cozy you looked, the obedient lioness curled at your Mistress's feet, so very liberated without your enchanted collar. Congratulations. You were utterly complicit in raising that despicable containment dome over our realm. You sold out every familiar in Dustfell with that move. *Familiar Freedom Under the Dome*—wasn't that your shiny-eyed slogan? Familiars no longer wear collars and leashes, but they've barred us from the forests, caged our view of the sky, obscured our nourishing moonlights with the dome's radioactive aura. I feel weaker every day.

Proud of yourself?

Frankly, you'll always be that sniveling apple-polisher I so despised at the Reformatorium. You with your spineless roars of *"Yes, Mistresses!"* You think they remedy lawbreakers? The Coven was grooming us to be lifelong slaves. Watching you bow to them, when you could've easily chewed out their throats, caused me every migraine.

Yet, now you approach me with whisperings of a rebellion?

I don't believe you're capable of dissent, no matter how blatantly evil the High Coven continues to behave.

You realize if they catch us, your righteouser-than-thou station as the Mistress's lapcat is over? You've always been a rule-follower. You've never tasted true ruthlessness. They loathe free-thinking witches. How do you suppose I ended up as a lowly sewer snake?

Grand thievery? Pilfered forbidden spells?

Believe that and you're more empty-skulled than I suspected.

Despite the Coven's lofty promises under the new rules of the dome, I still only get one hour a day in witch form. One measly midnight hour to drink wine and paint lusty nudes and seduce street wenches and indulge in being myself. So whatever evil your precious Mistress is brewing up better be apocalyptic. I've got worthier things to do with my witching hour than compose letters to the likes of *you*.

And many thanks for inquiring about my servitude with my new master. It's as rotten as you guessed. I spend all my days wrapped around that odious brute's arm, choking on the cursed stench of moon-starved corpses.

Never yours,

Righteous Thunder

P.S. Destroy this message in a cauldron fire of moonash and salt. And never be so dirt-skulled as to use our true names again! Evermore, I am Righteous Thunder and you are Merry Bootlicker.

October 20

Greetings Thunder,

Yes, I'm a rule follower. But I'm not righteous. Like *yourself*, lest you forget, I've broken rules. Even stooped low enough to cast magics not of our dearest Moons.

I thought those days were behind me. Desperate plotting. Tapping the forbidden elements of earth and air, fire and water.

Ancient powers invoke ancient troubles. Our earliest mentors warned us, didn't they? I was foolish, praying I might call upon earthly forces without earthly consequences. That mistake cost me everything—including the cousin whose crimson-maple fever

I attempted to heal. My only living family, dead because of forces I wrongly invoked.

I accepted my new lot, licking my Mistress's boots, as you say. Repenting for my sins, for losing faith in our beloved moons, for harming my own flesh and blood. And yes, I believed in the dome, silly as you think me. Collarless, extended hours in witch form. Progress toward freedom. The chance at a life worth reforming for. That's all I wanted for us.

Yet with daily deceptions laid bare before me, I can no longer abide Mistress Manor and her coven's manipulations.

Though judging by your vexing tongue, you don't appear interested in assisting me, no matter how dire the circumstances. No matter how many mooncalves will be aborted.

Many thanks, Thunder, for sharing the starsent spell, but I'll find someone more congenial to assist me.

I pray you'll find peace,
Reformed Bootlicker

October 21

Greetings Reformed,

Now don't be so hasty. I dare say you've piqued my intrigue... Mooncalves will be aborted?

You'll be shocked and awed to hear it, but I have a gentle place in my twisted old guts for mooncalves.

Forced transmutations are unconscionable, no matter how dastardly a witch's crimes. The Coven debases us during those eight hideous phases from witch to familiar. It's blatant and diabolical, stringing vulnerable mooncalf cocoons around the Reformatorium's oculus like grim decorations, shaming us before our sacred Moons. The transformation could easily be completed in a heartbeat's minute, yet they draw it out. Naked disembodied spirits, a stew of mind and flesh and magic. I shudder to confess that my month as a mooncalf was the only time in all my 373 years when I've known true terror.

In these matters, I swear by the cryptic light of the Unseen Moon, you can trust me.

Now stun me, what obscenity is the High Coven plotting this time?

Sworn to intrigue,

Thunder

October 22

Greetings Thunder,

I'm relieved you have some heart in this matter. Truthfully, you're not the first "free-thinker" I've attempted to recruit. Familiars who didn't spit in my face were spooked by the secrets I revealed. After hearing the lot of it, one of your old partners in mischief was caught attempting to escape Dustfell with his wench and their infant child. Officially, as you've no doubt heard, they were arrested and returned to the Reformatorium Animalis for further re-education.

What the Coven won't reveal is the sinister way Mistress Manor enacted their punishment. As they bowed to her, acquiescing to their imprisonment but begging for their child's freedom, the Mistress assaulted them with her transmutation curse — all three. No care for the innocence of their child, no hesitation. She melted them into mooncalves right there on the Reformatorium's cold marble floor. Tragic shimmering nightmares — she let them squirm for an entire eve before ordering me to slop them into cocoons. I've never taken part in anything so treacherous, so heartless.

The consequences of my blind faith never felt more deplorable.

Observe the Reformatorium tonight, and you'll find our sky-gazing oculus clotted over with mooncalf cocoons. Since summoning Dustfell's dome, the High Coven has been arresting witches at unprecedented rates for the pettiest infractions. They claim Dustfell has been overrun with hoodlums and sinners.

It is no secret that mooncalf magic powers the dome. They champion it as a self-sustaining system. Freshly cocooned sinners supply the magic to keep us seasoned familiars encaged and under thumb.

Yet, the amount of magic the Coven has been harnessing—it's an unprecedented surplus. After noticing the anomaly, I spent every midnight witching hour risking my neck to uncover the Coven's secret intentions. Most recently, I eavesdropped on a private midnight gathering of the Coven and a handful of Dustfell's witch elite. I overheard their plan for an upcoming ritual, a plan that twisted my darkest suspicions into something infinitely more sinister.

By now, you've heard Dustfell's heralds. Our dual Moons are slowly aligning and, after thirteen years, the Feast of Infinity is upon us again. On that day, for all hours, familiars will be free to walk the realm in full witch form to celebrate our eclipsing Moons. The High Coven has promised to lower the dome at the apex of Infinity, allowing witch and familiar alike to indulge in the nourishing light of the blessed alignment.

A ruse.

The Coven has grown weary of ruling over lesser witches, they view us as tedious. They conspire now to obtain a celestial power unlike any magics our lunar histories have seen.

They call this power *The Grim Dominion*.

At the apex of Infinity, as the Unseen Moon passes faithfully over the Mirror Moon, the dome won't drop as promised. For you see, Thunder, the dome is more than a cage.

It is a conductor.

The Coven has been using it to siphon power from every witch in Dustfell. You've felt your strength waning? That's the Coven, slowly suckling from each of us, bolstering their powers. But little sips are just the beginning of their *Grim Dominion*.

At the Feast, during the apex of Infinity, the dome will ignite upon the realm, an explosive curse that will transmute everyone into mooncalves. Familiar, witch, child—every soul whom the Coven deems inferior will be reduced to writhing puddles. A liquefied mosaic of magic. A vast banquet of pure embryonic powers, there for the taking, reserved for Dustfell's most ravenous elite.

Thunder, the Coven wishes to consume us.

I plan to consume them instead.

If you're willing to help, respond in haste. Our hourglass runs low.

Anxiously faithful,

Reformed

October 23

Reformed,

I marvel at the foul curse of my existence.

Leave it to you, shiny-eyed moonsgazer, to afford us only seven days to drop a centuries-old coven to their knees. My intestines twist in riotous knots. The Coven's malevolence has surpassed even the vilest realms of this cynical snake's imagination. *The Grim Dominion.* I've heard faint underground rumors of this ritual. The scrolls containing it were vanquished to the celestial void—even the Coven's Forbidden Archives held no whisper of it. Grand ambitions of the first witches, a murderous attempt to elevate themselves beyond the height of Moons. If the underground histories bear any truth, the High Coven won't just consume our magic.

They'll cannibalize our very souls.

Yes, they must be stopped, swallowed whole. I'd unhinge my jaw this instant, but what can two sorry familiars do to thwart such an ambitious plot? Words of rebellion sound lofty on the page, but I fear you'll discover in execution they often prove tragically futile.

You've impressed me with your keen calculations and sneaky ears—proved gutsier than I ever would've dreamed. Dare I say it, Reformed, I wish we were raising wine goblets together rather than a rebellion. Here's hoping the plot conspiring within your naively bold skull is worthy of your valor. Make haste, reveal all.

Yours in uprising,

Thunder

October 24

Thunder,

Many thanks for believing in me. And forgive my delay. Please know it took a month of witching hours to craft this mutiny. I triple-checked my calculations against elemental wisdoms hidden in ancient scrolls and believe I've unveiled a counter-spell to *The Feast of the Grim Dominion.*

At your age, surely you recall: the temple now housing the Reformatorium Animalis stands upon a cardinal intersection of ley lines. They've remained untapped for centuries. Under the faithful guidance of our blessed Moons, Dustfell has forfeited earthly magics. Yet, I propose we harness the power of these cardinal lines.

Please understand, I don't approach this task lightly. You should know the truth about me, Thunder. Do you recall, before our year at the Reformatorium, the hazy purple combustion of lightning and unseasonal rain that overtook our December sky?

That was me.

Crimson-maple fever had condemned my only cousin to death. Sticky blood boiled inside her veins. In time, the fever would bubble through her skin and harden like tree sap. Dustfell's wisest healers were dumbstruck—the glowing balm of our Moons failed to penetrate the curse.

Yet, I refused to let her die.

My family possessed an amulet, a forbidden heirloom of

ancient philosophies—a ley stone carved from the intersectional heart of Dustfell's cardinal lines. My elders regarded it as an archaic bobble. But during my studies as a young witch, I'd glanced upon my share of forbidden grimoires. I knew our ancestors once summoned earthly elements to aid their medicines.

I rushed. My cousin was dying. I didn't have time to ponder laws or calculations as I normally would. With a fool's hubris, I performed a hasty, shoddily calculated ritual upon Dustfell's cliffs. I invoked the cardinal corners and floated the ley stone above my writhing cousin.

Earthly elements roused to chaos—just as my mentors had warned.

The ground cracked underfoot, sulfuric fog plumed heavenward. Rain thickened the sky, and branches of blazing lightning crackled around us. Yet, in the misty, electric downpour, the sap marring my cousin's skin began receding, revealing smooth witchkind features. I actually cried with joy, fool that I was.

The spectacle on the cliffside alerted the Coven to my misdeed.

Before the ritual's end, lunar guards seized me and the amulet. Without the ley stone, the storm ceased and my cousin's fever surged. Sticky molten blood bubbled from every pore and hardened into a suffocating shell.

She died because I failed to foresee the consequences of hasty calculations.

Yet, Thunder, I'm certain of my latest calculations. Measured, meticulous, they show the elemental energies within the actual cardinal lines could be exponentially more dynamic—equal to the forces that split the ancient Moon and created our blessed two.

I fear resurrecting this magic is our only hope against the Coven's ever-waxing power.

I also fear such an explosive spectacle of elements will betray us before we can complete our task.

Even so, Thunder, this is my proposition:

On the day of the Feast, we'll station rebel spellcasters around the Reformatorium near the four cardinal corners. One each for Earth, Flame, Water, Wind. Minutes before the apex of Infinity, our spellcasters will catalyze the ley lines. The four elements will converge upon the oculus, forming an unbinding web around the mooncalves and severing the dome's power.

As our Moons align over Dustfell, the dome will dissipate and vanish like smoke, as will the Coven's chance at *Grim Dominion*. Every witch will maintain their true form, and the Coven will be quietly thwarted, forced to wait thirteen years for the next alignment.

I pray you know some "free-thinking" spellcasters who might aid us. We'll need three to stand with you at the cardinal corners. Regretfully, I cannot join you. Mistress Manor requires her lioness by her side at all public ceremonies. I mustn't raise suspicion.

A desperate plot, I admit. Yet, I've included my calculations. This time, I'm certain of them.

Yours, too, in uprising,

Reformed

October 27

Reformed,

If there's one thing I know, it's "free-thinkers." I've enlisted three of the *freest*. Took some blackmailing, but they've agreed to help—*if* I don't share their names with the do-gooder likes of you.

That said, your plan, as it stands, is doomed.

I've reviewed your calculations. Thirteen minutes to unbind the mooncalves and destroy the dome is too long. Those cardinal lines are ancient; tapping them won't just ignite an explosion of wind and rain, earthquakes and lightning. All four spellcasters will light up, too— marked by whirlwinds of our respective elements; we'd have no time to flee. The Coven will nab us faster than falling stars.

Lucky for us, I lied.

During my brief employ as the Coven's midnight advisor, I did indeed liberate a spell from their Forbidden Archives. Namely, *Cloak of Spirit*. More than invisibility—a vanishing of flesh! A spell to become temporary spirits. Magical, yet untouchable. Elemental forces will erupt, but we can continue casting without fret of capture. Once the dome collapses, we'll flee and regain our flesh, nourished beneath our eclipsing Moons.

Though, with my foul fortune, the spirits themselves will likely keep me.

And that's not the only looming consequence. The dome will drop, yet the Coven will still reign and plot against Dustfell. We must end them. Only you, the lioness, can come close. If the Coven has been siphoning magic from witchkind via the dome, there might be a flicker after the dome falls when they're powerless. That's when you must strike.

Teeth, claws, whatever it takes.

We *can* consume them.

Yet, I cannot promise you'll survive unscathed. I loathe the peril such an act will shine upon you.

By the allied light of our Moons, truly, the decision is yours.

Championing for you,

Thunder

P.S. My condolences for your cousin. I'm but a thief and a dastard, yet even I can see the nobility in your attempt to heal her. You've cracked this old snake's cold, cynical heart. Perhaps, if the luck of our rebel Moons shines with us, you'll become a healer in other ways.

October 28

Thunder,

Beneath the eclipsing fate of our Moons, please know, your concern for my well-being has stirred bravery within my anxious heart. Know also, I fear not for the safety of my flesh, but for my shivering soul. The feral nature of my task grieves me. Such violence, such crimes…

I still feel the sticky heat of my cousin's cursed blood upon me —and now to add the bitter taste of the Coven's blood to my teeth? Yet how many souls will meet endless darkness if I fail to act? My obedience aligns with the unsuspecting witches of Dustfell.

Even still, I am grieved.

For the good of witchkind, and under the affinity of our Moons, I must summon my strength and armor my soul.

I accept your guidance, wise friend. Your adjustments are sound.

Blessings, Thunder. Let us prevail.

Reformed

October 29

Reformed,

Never grieve the Coven's blood on your teeth. They'll never grieve *you*. Though *I* might experience a shudder should harm befall you, noble witch. Your cousin was blessed to have you fighting by her side. Her blood is upon the Coven, never upon you. You're wise enough not to forget that again. Never let them dull your magic.

Now, down to it. Before the end of tonight's witching hour, I'll sweep the *Cloak of Spirit* around myself and my fellow spellcasters. We'll become untouchable until the dome falls tomorrow.

The same cannot be said of you. Go in strength, Reformed, yet mind your furry neck. For the glory of our Moons, our Earth, and all witchkind.

Your sincerest friend,

Thunder

October 30

FOOLS!

Did you truly believe starsent messages would mask your rebellion? Every starsent word imprints a residue upon the celestial ether, legible to all wise witches. Did you learn nothing at the Reformatorium Animalis besides your lowly station in this realm? You've failed!

Tonight, our Moons will align only for the deserving. Myself, my coven, my chosen devotees. The dredges of witchkind don't deserve to bathe in the light. You don't deserve your lunar-gifted magics. Scum under my Moons!

Clueless wastes of untapped magic, there for the reaping!

Litten, my dearest slave, your weeks of betrayal weigh upon me. I'd planned to keep you at my feet. My tame, sniveling furball. You've proven yourself an ever so useful pawn. But this won't do. I cannot risk future insolence. As you read this, my lunar guards approach your private chamber. Prepare for a short life as a mooncalf, you contemptuous kitten.

Here's my proposal to *you*, Lucius, dear friend.

Given your history as the High Coven's midnight advisor, I'll spare you.

These many years, I've wondered which spell you stole from our Forbidden Archives, what piece of dusty parchment would return to shadow my Moons. Undo the *Cloak of Spirit*, betray the names of your rebel spellcasters, and I'll restore you to the powerful witch you once were. Free to indulge your every vice. Your wines, your women, your leisure. Even your youth, if you wish to reclaim it.

I know you, Lucius. Better than most. Better than any kitty-cat familiar. I know you miss the life I now offer.

Soon, Dustfell will be a witch's utopia unlike any ever conjured.

Rejoin the elite and every luxury will return to you infinity-fold.

I swear it under the Dual Moons themselves.

Awaiting your answer,

Prime Mistress Millicent Manor

October 30

Greetings Mistress,

You think I'm the breed of snake who'll hand over fellow spellcasters? Who'll betray the earnest dreams of a martyr who sees your Coven for the slimy megalomaniacs you are—a feline with whom I might actually raise a wine goblet? You think I'll kick back on the throne you offer and watch all of Dustfell collapse into twitching puddles of mooncalf soup?

You think right.

Happily. I always find it wisest to invest in one's self.

I did warn poor Litten that these matters rarely end in the rebels' favor.

Under the immunity and prosperity of your Dual Moons oath, I've removed *Cloak of Spirit* and attached the rebel names.

I fear, nasty friend, that it'll be a pleasure feasting beside you.

Devilishly yours,

Lucius Lightningflaw

October 30

Greetings Lucius,

I admire your devious nature. Many thanks for your cooperation. I trust you're already enjoying your full return to witchdom. Enclosed you'll find an invitation to worship at the High Coven's private altar tonight. Wear something classy and bring your appetite.

See you at the feast.

Manor

October 31, Year 665 Under Our Moons

Joyous Greetings Former Prime Mistress!

We're almost disappointed. You proved embarrassingly easy to trap. The look shining upon your holier-than-thou face as you transmuted into mooncalf soup proved exquisite. You melted from arrogant satisfaction, to confusion, to absolute terror. Is your ego still reeling? Are you and the liquid remains of your Coven comfortable in your new cocoons?

Frankly, it's insulting how vastly you underestimated us.

Plotting so brazenly with do-gooder kittens nearby, expecting blind obedience to evil.

More so, an entire archive of forbidden spells, and you think a slippery thief would steal only *one*?

Ley lines and *Cloak of Spirit* played for a splendid decoy. But *Curse of Mirror* proved invaluable. Look at yourself, plotting to transmute witchkind into mooncalves, only to become a mooncalf yourself. Do you appreciate the irony of your own *Grim Dominion* being used against you? We surely do.

On behalf of the entire realm, thank you for the feast.

As for starsent messages, you're right. Only fools would use them to plot a rebellion, staining the ether with evidence as they do. We've known that from the start. How else could we bait you into composing an official confession all your own? Your entire nefarious plan, signed by your hand, legible to every wise witch in Dustfell. Your disgrace will be the only immortal thing about you.

Our crimes saw us condemned for mere years.

As long as our Moons shine, Millicent, you'll *never* escape your cocoon.

We hope it becomes quite "familiar."

Enjoy your reformation. Under our united Moons, we're off to raise goblets in celebration of your downfall.

Cheers,

Litten Gaunt & Lucius Lightningflaw

ABOUT THE AUTHORS

Amanda Cecelia Lang is a horror author and aspiring recluse from Colorado. As a die-hard scary movie nerd, her favorite things are meta-horror, '80s nostalgia, and the rise of a fierce final girl. Her stories haunt the dark corners of many popular podcasts, magazines, and anthologies, including *NoSleep, Cast of Wonders, Tales to Terrify, Uncharted, Dark Matter, Flame Tree's Darkness Beckons,* and *Dread Machine's Mixtape: 1986.* Her short story collection *The Library of Broken Girls* will debut in Spring of 2025. You can stalk her work at amandacecelialang.com—just don't be surprised if she leaps out at you from the shadows.

Brittany Noelle is a mobile spirit, traveling with her family to live on both coasts of the States and across its mid-western plains. Settling in Colorado for school was a natural choice, with the majestic Rocky Mountains on the horizon to inspire fantastical adventures. Her written works focus on the shadows of life, where monsters lurk around every thought. Finding the light within us and in the people around us, that is the adventure of a lifetime. Brittany writes in the evenings and on weekends, all the while sipping tea, munching on cookies, and resisting the lure of her video game library. Brittany has published four novellas in her dark urban fantasy saga A Series of Souls. You can visit her website brittanynoellebooks.com or catch her on Instagram and YouTube @brittanynoellebooks.

THE FAMILIAR'S FAMILIAR
MAEGAN LANGER

The Familiar's Familiar was crowded, as usual. It was late on a Friday, and everyone was there to blow off steam. I hopped down the stone steps into the smoky bar, stepped aside to avoid the emerald viper slithering out, dodging the other feet and paws and claws and hooves, and made my way across the floor to the bar.

I fluttered up onto the only empty stool. Stella, the bartender, slid down the counter toward me. Stella's a hare. Her companion was burned at the stake almost three hundred years ago and they say she hasn't been quite the same since. She never paired with anyone else. Management finally took pity and gave her the job at the Familiar.

"Hey, Gordy. The usual?"

"Yes, please. Thanks, Stel."

I folded my wings on the counter, face to face with a fruit bat hanging upside down from a brass frame they'd installed specially for him.

"'Sup, Rex?" Rex is my best friend. I would have been lost without him when I first got the familiar's call.

The bat peeked at me between his leathery wings. "Gordy! I was starting to think you wouldn't make it, man."

"I know. Kevin wanted to practice late again."

"Is he getting any better?"

"We only burned down three stacks of books, instead of five."

"Damn." Rex shook his head.

Stella returned with our orders. "Strawberries from the garden and pressed wheatgrass for you, Gordy."

I dipped into the low ceramic bowl of golden liquid while Rex speared a strawberry with his claw. "Gotta give him credit," he said around a mouthful of strawberry pulp. He had a habit of getting it all over his face, making it look, ironically, like he'd been drinking blood. "The guy does not give up."

Kevin was young, clumsy, forgetful, but oh so earnest. Apparently one of the most devoted apprentice mages in a century, not that I'd know. This is my first pairing. His mentor, Arwel, is a Master Warlock who, frankly, gives me the creeps.

"I try to be supportive, but I don't know how much I'm helping," I said. "Sometimes I feel like I'm just making things worse."

"Uh oh." Rex was staring past my plume.

I choked on a gulp of wheatgrass. "What?"

"They're here."

Great.

I didn't need to ask who "they" were. I took a moment to gather myself and spun around on my stool. Three large black cats stared down at me, tails twitching. Their green eyes and sleek fur gleamed in the oily lamplight.

"Oh hey, ladies," I said. "How's the coven?"

"Powerful," said Lilith, the largest one.

"Congratulations." I turned back to my bowl.

"Why are you still here, Gordy?" said Lada, the second one. "Your companion's going to flunk out of his apprenticeship any day."

I gritted my beak together. "We're working on it."

"You can't even fly."

I turned to the last one, Lapis. That joke was getting old. "I can fly," I said deliberately. "I prefer not to."

"Yeah," Rex piped in. "Quail are quicker on their feet anyway."

Lilith's eyes narrowed to slits. It took everything I had not to look away from her. Have I mentioned she's also Arwel's familiar? "Not quicker than us," she hissed.

I didn't ask for this. "Quail" is not the first thing that comes to mind when you think of an animal companion for a powerful magic worker. Cats, obviously. Ravens, toads, ferrets, the occasional dachshund. But never in my wildest dreams did I expect to be chosen as a familiar. According to my mother, my seven-generations-removed great-grandmother was the last known quail familiar, and heaven forbid I dishonor the family line by turning down the call. So here I was, facing three giant felines who'd tear me apart for breakfast in any other circumstance.

"That's great advice, Lilith. I'll try to remember that," I said. They didn't move. "Run along, kitties. Your pan of milk is getting cold." Then I turned back to my wheatgrass.

"Are they gone?" I mouthed to Rex.

He nodded. I let out a long breath.

"Hey, Gordy." Stella slid a slip of paper across the counter toward me. "This just came through for you."

"Huh."

"What's wrong?" Rex asked.

I'd left Kevin hunched over his collection of ancient magic tomes while I slunk away to drown my shame in wheatgrass. I figured we could use some space after our latest disastrous practice session.

"I've been 'summoned,'" I said. "He's never called me by sending a note before."

"Seems fishy." Rex wrinkled his little bat nose.

"Agreed."

"We should go check on him. I can fly ahead. Case the joint. I'm not due back until dawn anyway." Rex's Druidess companion was notoriously not a night person.

ARWEL'S GREAT RUINED CASTLE SAT ON THE EDGE OF A CLIFF overlooking a canyon of jagged rocks, because of course it did. Skittering along the rocky path, I craned my neck up at the looming turrets silhouetted against an enormous blue moon. The sight of it always filled me with dread. Arwel had given us a small room on the ground floor. A dungeon, really. But Kevin brushed this off when I pointed it out. He was so excited to apprentice to a Master Warlock he couldn't see that the Warlock didn't even take him seriously.

Rex flitted ahead of me and back, pumping his wings to hover just over my head. I paused to catch my breath.

"Seems pretty dead up there," he said.

"Not completely." I pointed at the highest turret, where a light burned in a single window. "Arwel's awake."

"Be right back." Rex was off again.

I rushed to the heavy oak door that led to our room at the base of the castle. Since I couldn't reach the handle, Kevin had cut a miniature door just for me in the wood at the bottom. No light snuck out from under the door. Everything was eerily quiet. Maybe Kevin had fallen asleep. But then why had he —

"Mayday mayday mayday!" Rex came screeching out of the night in a divebomb. "Abort! I heard Arwel say —"

But I didn't get to hear what Arwel said, because a heavy cloak of blackness descended on us both.

"WE ARE IN SO MUCH TROUBLE," REX MOANED NEARBY.

I opened my eyes. I was lying on my back with my wings askew. I sat up, and the floor moved beneath me. Not a floor. The rotted bottom of a wire cage, swinging from a low ceiling. The only light source was the moon shining through a narrow window. I could tell from the moon's position that we hadn't left Arwel's castle. I was wrong about our room in the basement. *This* was the real dungeon.

"You're awake!" Rex fluttered in another cage hanging next to mine.

I brushed my frazzled plume out of my face. "What happened?"

"I was flying down to warn you, everything went black, and now here we are."

"Gordy?"

We both jumped. A hunched silhouette stirred in the corner of the damp stone floor. The figure threw back its hood, and Kevin peeked at us over his drawn-up knees. A bruise was blooming around his eye and dried blood clung to his split lip. Heavy manacles chafed his wrists, attached to iron chains that bound him to the wall.

"How did you get here?" he said.

"You sent for me. At the bar, so I came back."

"No, I didn't. I gave you the night off after we almost disappeared all my study tomes."

"We've been duped," Rex said.

"What is that infernal squeaking?" Kevin squinted in the dark at the bat. Magic workers can only speak to and understand their own familiars. Don't ask me why that's a thing. I don't make the rules.

"That's Rex, Diana's familiar."

"The Druidess?"

"Yeah. If you didn't summon me— "

"Why is he here with you?"

"I'm just an innocent bystander, trying to help," Rex said.

"What's he saying now?"

"He's my friend and he was trying to help!" I don't fluster easily, but this was getting ridiculous. "Someone wanted to lure me back here. What happened after I left this evening?"

"Not to make this all about me," Rex interjected, "but I really need to be back by dawn. Diana's gonna be so mad...."

"*Rex*," I snapped. "Please."

"Sorry."

"After you left, I must have fallen asleep," Kevin said.

"Because the next thing I knew, the lock on the door was jiggling. Then someone was dragging me out the door. I didn't have time to gather my wits for a defense spell. I just kicked and fought." Kevin could be scrappy when he needed to. "Lot of good that did me," he finished morosely.

"Why would Arwel want to imprison his own apprentice?"

"That's what I tried to tell you," said Rex. "When I flew up to the highest window, it looked like the whole coven was there. I heard Arwel say something about the blue moon and a prophecy and 'It's almost time.'"

"What prophecy?" I asked.

"Beats me," Rex said. "That's when they saw me spying, and I booked it outta there."

Kevin pulled his hood back up and dropped his head onto his knees. He looked like a giant sooty smudge in the low light.

"Hey, Kevin!" I whistled.

"What?" the smudge mumbled.

"You know anything about a blue moon prophecy? Maybe a blurb somewhere in all those books you collect?"

After a moment, Kevin said "Well, yes." He looked up at me again. The bruise was getting bigger. "There's the one about the all-powerful and benevolent companion-familiar team who'll usher in a new era of peace and prosperity, but —"

Rex and I exchanged wide-eyed looks. "Gordy," Rex whispered. "What if it's you?"

"What?" I scoffed. "It's not us. I mean, we're the worst. Sorry, Kevin."

"It's all right. I get it."

"Arwel seems to think it's you," Rex said. "And he's no fool. This must be why the coven kitties like to give you a hard time. They think you're part of the prophecy too." Rex gasped. "I bet they're afraid of you!"

"Please, make it stop," Kevin groaned, massaging his temples. "The squeaking is hurting my head."

I dropped my voice to a fierce whisper. "Rex, there is no way

Kevin and I are part of a prophecy to save the world. This is a cruel joke. Or Arwel's lost his mind."

"See, this is your problem," Rex hissed back. "You have no confidence in yourself."

"Shhh! Both of you," Kevin said. "Someone's coming."

Heavy footfalls right outside the thick oak door. Iron keys jangling. And then the lock clicked open and two heavyset men in identical black hoods stepped inside. Arwel liked to make his henchmen wear matching outfits. I guess it was supposed to be good for company morale or something, but they always looked silly to me.

One of them lumbered over to Kevin to unhook the chains from his wrists. Kevin swayed a little when the henchmen hauled him to his feet. That wasn't good. The other reached up to unhook my cage from the ceiling.

"Rex?" I looked back at Rex's cage.

"I'll just hang out here for now." Rex was trying to seem brave for my benefit, but I could tell he was worried. As the henchmen led/carried Kevin and me out of the dungeon, he squeaked, "Remember to belie—"

But then the massive oak door slammed shut behind us.

KEVIN AND I STOOD IN FRONT OF THE ELDERS OF ARWEL'S coven. At least, that's what I thought was happening. Kevin held my cage against his chest with his arms wrapped around the bars, blocking my view of almost everything. Arwel was speaking nearby.

"...high crimes, the depravity of which have not been seen in an age..." He droned on. The man loved the sound of his own voice.

"Kevin!" I fluttered up and down in the tiny space. "Hey, Kevin! I can't see! What's going on?"

He shifted so the cage's bottom now rested on his palms. We were in a room with a high domed ceiling. Sputtering torches in sconces illuminated dark tapestries decorating the walls. Arwel sat in front of us on a raised dais, his long gray beard perfectly coiffed as always, flanked by two well-robed witches. Their familiars, Lilith, Lada, and Lapis were there too. Lilith was curled around Arwel's shoulder, kneading his velvet collar.

Arwel was reading off the alleged charges. "You are accused of fabricating your application to my apprenticeship, thereby wasting my valuable time, the use of forbidden materials during each trial, thus falsifying the results of your tests, and worst of all, stealing the Tome of Wisdom, source of my most sacred spells, handed down from Master Warlock to Master Warlock since the time of Babylon. How do you plead?"

"Obviously, not guilty. Right, Kevin?" I couldn't see his face, but I felt his hands trembling beneath the cage.

"Uh, that's not—" Kevin began.

"Speak up, boy!" Arwel roared.

Kevin gulped. This time, his voice was stronger. "None of that is true."

"The evidence is unmistakable. You are hereby sentenced to—"

"Kevin, say something!" I fluttered frantically in the cage. Why wasn't he defending us? We may have been a joke as a magical team, but that wasn't a crime.

"Control your familiar, young man!" One of the witches, Lapis's companion, burst out.

"You are hereby sentenced to banishment. You will never be a true mage. Your name will go down in the chronicles of our Order as..."

While Arwel was busy monologuing, I wracked my brain for anything Kevin could say to get us out of this. Then, the solution came. We'd come across it randomly in one of Kevin's books during a practice session.

"Pssst, Kevin!" He glanced down, his eyes flicking between me and Arwel. "Ask for one of those nature trial thingies." His forehead wrinkled. "The one where you go out in the woods and let the trees decide your worthiness or whatever."

Kevin blinked. It clicked.

"...you have brought shame upon this great Order with your..."

"I request a trial of the elements."

Arwel stopped short. Clearly, he wasn't expecting this. Kevin took advantage of the pause. "By the rules of the Order, I'm entitled to an elemental trial."

The coven elders traded glances. Arwel looked ready to murder the next thing that moved. Now Lada's witch spoke. "We cannot deny him, once it's been requested."

Arwel grumbled deep in his throat. I heard a similar sound growing inside Lilith. She looked right at me and all three coven kitties hissed in unison.

"Very well," Arwel said. "The powers that govern and guide our Order will decide your fate."

THE BLACK CLOTH COVERING MY CAGE WAS WHISKED AWAY. One of Arwel's color-coordinated henchmen was unlocking the manacles on Kevin's wrists. Once his hands were free, Kevin pulled the hood off his own head, then bent down to open the door of my cage. At last! I hopped out onto Kevin's open palm and he lifted me to his shoulder.

We'd spent what felt like all night jostling in a rickety wagon. I was starting to wish for the ability to throw up when the jostling blessedly stopped. We'd reached the literal middle of nowhere. The twin henchmen smirked at us as they climbed back into the wagon. One turned back to sneer over his shoulder, "Good luck." Then he snapped the reins across the nag's back and they lumbered away.

"Now what?" I asked.

"'Now what?' This was your idea."

We were in a small clearing surrounded by soft, swaying trees that seemed to be whispering at us. Wait, that couldn't be right. Get a grip, Gordy.

Granite cliffs rose in the distance over the treetops. I heard the ocean crashing against rocks and sea birds screeching at each other far away.

"I was trying to keep us from being executed," I said.

"You mean banished?"

"Whatever." Like Arwel was going to stop at banishment. "Either way, I'm out of the cage and you're out of the manacles. I'm calling that a win."

"Let's hope the elements give us a—" Kevin stopped. I thought I knew why, because I heard it too. That whispering again, from the trees. Beckoning. "I think they're telling us to go that way," Kevin said. He pointed to a path that opened up between the slender trunks.

"Are you sure? We don't even know these trees."

"True, but we're here to be judged by the elements. And they seem...friendly."

I realized he was right. The vibes coming off the strange trees had more of a *"Come sit with us, we have cookies"* feel rather than *"Ha ha! Watch us lead these two chumps to their grisly deaths."*

"Okay, but I'm keeping an eye out." I hopped up into Kevin's curly hair to get a panoramic view in case any giant Celtic boars or rabid wyverns decided to ambush us.

Since I was nervous, I kept talking. "Can you believe Arwel? Making up all that stuff about you?"

The air in the forest was darker and damper. The canopy above blocked the sunlight. Kevin's shoes squelched in the mud. The uneven ground threw off his balance, forcing him to grip the tree trunks to steady himself. I dug my feet into his hair to keep from tumbling off.

"Like anyone would be dumb enough to steal his super-secret book of spells. Right, Kevin?...Kevin?" I leaned over the crown of his head to gauge his expression, but all I could see were his knitted eyebrows. "Seriously?!" I burst out. "You stole Arwel's Babylonian Wisdom Tome?"

Kevin stopped to catch his breath. "'Steal' implies an intent to keep something. I *borrowed* it."

"Oh, geez! Kevin, whyyyy?" I buried my face in my wings.

"I was curious. Unfortunately, it was still in my room when they dragged me out. But I didn't fabricate my apprentice application, and I certainly didn't cheat on any of my tests."

"Did you at least learn anything useful from it?"

Kevin started walking again. The light was getting brighter. We were nearing the far edge of the forest. "Not really," he said. "Mostly just dessert recipes and love potions."

"That would explain Arwel's reputation for a mean baklava."

Kevin snorted. I was pleased, in spite of myself. I'd never made him laugh before.

"He was looking for an excuse to get rid of us, though. Do…" I was embarrassed to even say it out loud. "Do you think it really was because of a prophecy?"

Kevin didn't answer. We'd stepped out into the sunlight. A dozen or so massive standing stones formed a circle in the middle of the clearing. The air was weirdly quiet and still. No sounds of the ocean or seabirds now.

Kevin stepped into the circle, and the power of the place made the tiny feathers on the back of my neck stand up. Something was alive in here. I felt it breathing.

"Can you —"

"Yes, I feel it," he said.

The standing stones were covered in carvings, strange symbols etched into the rock long before the Order was founded.

"Say something," I whispered.

"What am I supposed to say?"

"I don't know. You're the wizard in training." I glanced up at the tops of the stones. They seemed to be watching. Waiting. "It feels…rude not to."

Kevin cleared his throat. "Uh, hello? Anybody there?"

I climbed down to Kevin's shoulder, since it might lend him a little more dignity not to have a quail perched on his head when whatever was listening to us finally responded.

"We could use some help here," he went on. "If you're willing."

"Say please," I hissed into his ear.

"Please. And thank you. In advance."

"Smooth," I said.

There was a soft snapping of twigs behind us. Kevin turned toward the sound. Now we were getting somewhere. But it was Arwel who stepped out from behind one of the far stones, stroking Lilith in his arms.

Kevin blinked. "I don't understand."

The Master Warlock smiled in a way that ruffled my feathers as he ambled toward us. He set the cat on the ground. She rubbed against his legs, purring like a drunk dragon.

"The elements have judged you, boy, and found you wanting."

"But they led us here," Kevin said. I winced. He wasn't getting it.

"Yes," said Arwel. "To me."

The full weight of our situation crashed into me. In trying to protect Kevin, I'd played us right into Arwel's hands. "I'm sorry," I said to Kevin. "This was my idea, and now Arwel has what he wants: you and me, alone, with no witnesses."

Arwel kept talking because of course, he couldn't understand what I was saying. "Now you will meet your fate, in this most sacred place where the elements con—"

"Is this about the prophecy?" Kevin interrupted. "The all-powerful companion-familiar team foretold by the Order's founder?"

Arwel's mouth hung open for a beat, then snapped shut. Score one for Kevin.

"I don't know what stories you've heard, but you're here because you are an absolute failure as a student mage, and your punishment will—"

"So it's the prophecy, then," Kevin said.

"This has nothing to do with—" Arwel sighed, pinching the bridge of his nose. His face was getting red. "Are you finished? May I continue?"

"By all means."

Arwel cleared his throat, regaining momentum. "Before I dole out your just punishment, I wish to speak directly to your familiar."

If I had visible ears, they would have perked up. Was this a trick?

"You are not obligated to share your companion's fate. If you so choose, you may go back to being an ordinary animal. Say the word, and it will be so."

I tried to ignore Kevin's side-eye. Arwel was right about one thing: I never wanted this. I accepted the call under duress. For a moment, I imagined what it would be like, life as a regular quail. Meet a hen. Raise twenty-six chicks the way my parents had done. It felt nice.

But that would mean no more Friday nights at the Familiar's Familiar, laughing it up with Rex. No more putting out the latest accidental fire in Kevin's dungeon room. No, this was where I belonged. Kevin and I may be the worst, but we were the worst together. If we survived this, there was nowhere to go but up. I whispered my answer into Kevin's ear and he stifled a laugh.

"Well?" Arwel demanded.

"He says to tell you he'd rather eat dirt."

At that moment, the energy in the circle shifted. Whatever it was, it was on our side.

Arwel's mouth formed a thin, angry line. "So be it."

A weight crashed into me from behind, knocking me off Kevin's shoulder. I knew right away it had to be Lilith. Stupid of me to lose sight of her. No self-respecting prey animal forgets to mind the predators.

I landed hard in the grass. Lilith crouched a few feet away, wiggling her hindquarters.

"I think I'll order poached quail for dinner," she hissed.

Behind her, Arwel summoned a whirlwind that lifted the fallen leaves into a spiral. He flung it at Kevin with enough force to knock him off his feet.

As if on cue, Lilith pounced. I skittered away. She pounced again, and I managed to stay a few feet ahead of her with my pitiful wings. She was going to take her time, toying with me like, well, like a mouse.

Soon, our demented game of leapfrog had taken us halfway around the circle. Kevin was trying and failing to fend off Arwel's attacks. Bolts of green and blue flames, spouts of erupting earth, more whirlwinds. Arwel far outmatched Kevin in skill, and he knew it, hitting Kevin with all of the elements before he ever got a chance to summon a defense.

Of all the things I hated about Arwel, this bothered me the most: he didn't play fair.

Lilith launched herself at me again. I watched her jump, as if in slow motion, white claws and teeth bared —

I spread my wings. But this time, I kept going. Higher and higher, I pumped my wings and rode the air currents. I was *flying*. For real flying. I landed on the top of the nearest standing stone and looked down at Lilith, a black speck on the ground far below. She clawed at the base, hissing and yowling. She looked furious. It was great.

"Ha!" I yelled. "Here, kitty, kitty! What's that, now? You can't catch me because I can fly? Hey, Kevin! Guess what?"

Oops. In my excitement, I forgot we were both literally fighting for our lives. I was faring much better at the moment. Kevin crouched on the ground, so exhausted he could only hold up his arms to protect himself. Arwel loomed over him, forming a massive, spinning fireball with his hands.

Red Fire. The worst kind.

I did the only thing I could think of: divebomb the bastard right in his stupid, ugly face. I launched myself off the stone, tucking my wings tight against my body.

Arwel saw me coming. He raised his hands and brought me up short with a new whirlwind. I beat my wings to keep from crashing to the ground, darting left, right. Arwel shifted his hands to follow my movements, guiding the whirlwind to hold me back.

While Arwel's back was turned, Kevin was slowly rising to his feet. The raging Red Fire still hovered a few feet off the ground.

Kevin reached out, determination on his face. The fireball changed. Now, it was green.

Arwel turned back. Too late. Kevin uttered an incantation, and the Green Fire dissipated in a flash of molten atmosphere, consuming Arwel in its wake.

And then a blast of hot air knocked me out of the sky.

I WAS LYING ON SOMETHING WARM AND SOFT, BUT ALSO... clammy?

"Gordy?" Kevin said from very far away. I opened my eyes, and his grimy, sooty face filled my vision. What was he so worried about?

"Did I die?" I said.

"No!" Kevin laughed. "Not at all."

For the second time in a day, I sat up and brushed my frazzled plume out of my face. Kevin cradled me in his cupped hands. I gasped as the memories flooded back.

"Kevin! I flew. I flew like a real bird! Did you see me?"

"I did. Gordy, you saved my life."

"Huh." I peeked over Kevin's fingers. The standing stones were still there, like sentinels. "Is Arwel...?"

"Arwel's gone. His familiar took off into the woods."

"Woooow," I breathed. I still felt woozy. "What happened?"

He smiled again. "I think the elements judged us worthy."

IT WAS FRIDAY AGAIN, AND THE FAMILIAR'S FAMILIAR WAS crowded. Rex and I sat at the bar with our usual: wheatgrass for me, bloody strawberries for him. (Obviously, liberating Rex from the castle had been our first order of business. Redecorating was the second.)

The two elder witches skedaddled with their familiars after Arwel's demise. The castle was ours now, mine and Kevin's. We moved out of our dungeon quarters into a spacious tower. Kevin let Arwel's former henchmen stay on as groundskeepers. They swore their undying loyalty when he told them they didn't have to dress alike anymore.

Rex was in the middle of telling me about his companion's response to his late return. "Dude, I swear Diana was *this close* to wearing me as a headband, but when I told her about how you defeated Arwel, she was all, 'What? Those two? Who'd a thought?' Anyway, it was…uh oh."

"What?" I asked.

"She's back."

I swiveled around.

"*You,*" Lilith screeched. "This is your fault." The forest had not been kind. Her once-glossy fur was matted and caked with dirt. One of her incisors was broken. Her twisted whiskers trembled with rage. "I was an apex predator," she wailed. "Now look at me."

She was drawing an audience. The din of the bar hushed as the other familiars—a bearded dragon, several raptors, a miniature horse, guinea pigs, and scores of other rodents—leaned in to watch the show.

"I can't even get a gig as a housecat now, thanks to you. A bird who can't fly."

"Ah, ah." I raised one flight feather like a finger. "I can fly. And you know it."

Lilith screamed, rocked back on her haunches as though readying for attack. Then she stopped. Her eyes bulged and her whole body convulsed as she hacked up a gooey hairball onto the floor.

There was a collective groan. Somebody murmured "That's disgusting." The crowd began to disperse. Lilith slunk away up the stairs and out the door.

"I think I'll miss her," I said.

"Not me," Rex said.

"Yeah, me neither."

"So, how do you feel about fulfilling a prophecy?" Rex asked, delicately plucking a leaf off a strawberry with his claw before shoving it into his mouth.

"I try not to think about it too much. Kinda freaks me out."

"I get that," said Rex. "Beating a Master Warlock's gonna be tough to top."

"Geez, I hope we haven't peaked already." I used my flight feathers to draw random patterns in the last dregs of wheatgrass.

"Nah, I don't think so. You two make a good team. You'll figure it out."

I smiled. We were a good team, Kevin and I. Nowhere to go but up.

ABOUT THE AUTHOR

Maegan Langer has a biology degree from Brigham Young University because she was going to be a vet, once upon a time. Now she's set to complete her MFA in Screenwriting and Genre Fiction at Western Colorado University in 2025. Her short stories have appeared in the Utah Horror Writers Association's anthologies *The Peaks of Madness*, *They Walk Among Us*, and *The Big Book of Things That Go Bump in the Night*. She lives in the foothills with her many familiars: a pair of three-legged rescue dogs, spoiled cats, a few old horses, plus numerous wild deer, squirrels, raccoons, turkeys, the occasional chatty owl, and of course, quail.

Find her on Instagram and the site formerly known as Twitter: @theAwkwardLamb

THE CAT
SANDY WHITE

A PANTOUM

The cat protects me, while I sleep at night.
    A terror seeps into the room to tap my dreams.
    Demons freeze the shadows of my darkest fright.
    Deep forces try to trap my soul from realms unseen.

A terror seeps into the room to tap my dreams.
    The cat curls up to hold a vigil on my bed.
    Deep forces try to trap my soul from realms unseen.
    The cat makes sure—that I don't wake up dead.

The cat curls up to hold a vigil on my bed.
    Staring down each quiet ghost and poltergeist.
    The cat makes sure—that I don't wake up dead.
    I meet each day—wrapped up in the morning light.

Staring down each quiet ghost and poltergeist.
    The cat peeps one eye open for mischievous spirits.
    I meet each day – wrapped up in the morning light.
    Fearful denizens creep back into the infinite.

The cat peeps one eye open for mischievous spirits.
    Demons freeze in shadows of my darkest fright.
    Fearful denizens creep back into the infinite.
    The cat protects me, while I sleep at night.

ABOUT THE AUTHOR

Sandy White completed a MFA in Creative Writing/Poetry from Dominican University of California in 2022. She is a painter with a BFA in Painting from the University of Pennsylvania and the Pennsylvania Academy of the Fine Arts. Her website is sandywhitefinearts.com. She has written poetry all her long life and has lived with cats all her long life.

SOME SPIDER
PINES CALLAHAN

The sun had almost set on a perfectly average day, and she'd trapped a fat horsefly for dinner. Her latest web was broad and strong, anchored by two gumbo limbo trees on the edge of a hardwood hammock. There was a human approaching, but the spider was positive the huffing, red-faced creature would turn before walking into a three-foot-wide web at chest level. She was wrong, and she was foolish enough to stay near the center with her prey near instead of ducking into the peeling, coppery bark of the gumbo limbo. Caught off guard, all she could do was cling for life as the human realized its mistake and devolved into a screaming, flailing mess.

Titanic movement and shrieks like a dying rabbit overwhelmed the spider's senses. Frantic hands chased her across the human's torso, promising violence. Safety lay on the forest floor, but she was too disoriented to tell up from down. She careened across the human's shoulder and onto the rough strap of a tote bag. The human's long, inky hair shook against her, and she fell into the dark canvas recesses. Panicked, she huddled inside a wad of fabric. Eventually, the human stopped its chaotic shaking and seemed to calm. She enjoyed a few seconds of relief before the flustered giant continued its trudge, carrying her away from the remnants of her home.

She could have built another web in the time it took for the human to stop moving. Abruptly, her unwitting chauffeur dropped the bag with a heavy thump, and the spider had no time to reposition. She was lucky, a hardcover book barely missed her back legs. Still discombobulated, she wormed her way across the fabric toward what she assumed was the top of the bag. Light flooded the space. The human grasped the fabric and lifted it free. The spider desperately gripped her hiding place as the fabric was unfolded and laid out over a patch of bare earth, spider-side down. Finally, she was back on solid ground!

Before she could race to safety, something large and heavy landed on top of her with a thud. The barest concavity kept the spider from being crushed. She felt around for a break, but a perfect, cold circle surrounded her. She flattened herself against the ground, feeling the pressure of other objects set on top of the fabric. Much more weight and she'd be crushed into the soil.

The human was speaking rhythmically, voice rising and falling with a quaver. She smelled smoke and iron. There was a crack like thunder and the feel of ozone. The hairs on her legs and body stood on end in alarm.

"Familiar?" The human called. "Hey, are you out there?"

There was a long pause, and the human sighed. "Well, that was a waste of time. I can't believe I snuck out for this ... Nikki's going to think I'm so lame."

The spider felt a nagging sense of discomfort at the human's problems, but her own concerns were more pressing. She was sure she was about to die, and considered what happened after. Would anyone miss her?

She rubbed her mandibles together, perplexed. She'd never considered an afterlife before, or her place in the hearts of other creatures. Examining her own thoughts was novel, too. It was equally terrifying and intriguing. Curiosity battled fear, winning out just as the object pinning her in place lifted. The fabric rose as well, and the spider came face to face with her abductor.

She'd seen humans before in passing, but the details of their features blurred into sameness. This human was different. Her face was memorable, important. Her name was Hannah. Sure as she knew she was a spider, she was certain her fate was intertwined with the teenager's. For the first time in her life, she felt the stirrings of destiny. A spider and a human, accomplishing their wildest dreams together. Surely, Hannah felt it, too.

Hannah did not. She screamed and fell onto her bottom, scrambling backwards. That wasn't right. The spider held her ground and raised a leg, rotating it in the way she'd seen humans greet each other, but the girl was already on her feet and sprinting away.

The spider hadn't experienced feelings for terribly long, and she didn't care for the latest. It sat like lead in her stomach and made her legs sluggish. So much for dreams and companionship, Hannah was scared of her. She looked at herself in the shiny metal button on Hannah's discarded bag. Mottled gold body, silver head, black and gold stripes on her legs. She was large, even for a female—about the size of a duck egg—but not so overgrown as to be upsetting. Confused, the spider crawled inside Hannah's bag. It felt right, and made the heavy feelings more manageable.

She waited hours for Hannah to return, considering her predicament. Sentience. It was overwhelming. The thought of processing her new feelings alone left her twitchy and uncomfortably hollow. Hannah didn't want to help her. Hannah didn't want her around at all. Another wave of unhappy heaviness broke over her as she weighed her options. Giving up and finding peace on her own was the easiest choice, but she dismissed that option with a defiant flick of a leg. She was a spider, strong and adaptable, not some cowardly little millipede.

Determined, she crawled over the book in Hannah's bag, and, delighted to discover her new literacy, read the title. *How to Summon Your Familiar*; Hannah had called for a familiar! The book was too heavy for her to move, so she crawled through the other items in the bag, examining them. Dried herbs, surely what had been smoking. Loose papers. Crystals. The fabric Hannah had laid out, balled and forgotten. A piece of bark with a few drops of Hannah's blood that smelled like ozone and made the spider's leg hair stand on end.

It was early morning when Hannah retrieved her bag. The spider was prepared for rough movement, and managed to survive the entire walk back to Hannah's house unscathed. She stealthed up the shoulder strap to watch her new … whatever Hannah was to her.

The teen was practically connected to an illuminated rectangular square. Her phone, the spider's mind supplied helpfully—another new perk. Hannah's phone almost never left her hand. It was a flashlight in the dark forest, and stayed within arm's length at home. Hannah used it to talk to other people, usually by typing messages back and forth. A few times, she asked questions in a blank bar and got back pages of answers in response.

Sheltered in the girl's room, she climbed down Hannah's back and scurried gingerly across the squishy carpet, hiding herself as Hannah unpacked her bag. The fabric got shoved in a drawer, crystals on a shelf, and *How to Summon Your Familiar* was left on her desk. Hannah didn't stay in her room long. The spider knew she was a high school senior, and classes would be starting soon. When Hannah left, the spider came out of hiding, eager to see what answers she could suss out of Hannah's books.

How to Summon Your Familiar was her first source. She anchored a sticky strand of web silk to the edge of the cover and hopped off the other side. As she'd hoped, the cover flopped open. The introduction was illuminating: this was a book for witches. So the spider's transformation was magical. She turned to chapter one: "Inviting Your Familiar." The spider read quickly, flipping the pages as needed. Eventually, she came to the summoning spell itself. The spell should have called the perfect familiar to Hannah's side where she would place burnt offerings before it, cementing the bond. The heavy object that trapped her must have been the offering plate. Placed before and trapped beneath felt extremely different to the spider, but she knew nothing about magic.

That would need to change. She would need to change. If she was a familiar now, she needed to learn how to help her terrified charge. Communication was the first step, but *How to Summon Your Familiar* focused on a willing human speaking to an equally willing familiar. The spider crawled back to the bookshelf. A spine with a spider on it caught her eyes, nearly hidden on the bottom shelf. *Charlotte's Web*. The cover looked promising, a spider and a girl.

Pulling the book off the shelf took maneuvering and more energy than the spider wanted to exert. She hadn't eaten all day. Luckily, there was a freshly dead cockroach under the bookshelf. The spider dragged it out to eat while she read, holding the pages open with silk.

The story was brilliant. Clearly, Charlotte was Wilbur the pig's familiar. Helpful, useful, and a respected companion. The parts with Fern and Wilbur were sweet, but the human couldn't protect Wilbur. Only Charlotte could, and it gave the spider an idea. She wondered how much effort it would take to form letters within her own web.

Normally, her webs were long spokes used for travel and spirals of sticky, prey-catching silk. Adding deliberate shapes felt unnatural and hindered her normal flow. She nearly got herself stuck on her own handiwork several times as she spun and respun until she could form even letters. It took almost the entire day, but her finished product was undeniably perfect: "Some Spider."

She made sure to weave her web in a corner where light would catch it, desperate to avoid a repeat of their first meeting, and hid behind a lamp to watch the teen's reaction after school. Hannah froze as she walked in the room, immediately drawn to the message in silk. She screamed and tore down the web with frantic swipes.

"What does that mean? Some spider is coming after me? How did this get here?"

Hannah stumbled out of the room in a panic, slamming the

door behind her. Clearly, it had been a while since she'd read *Charlotte's Web*. The spider would have to do better, the message should be harder to misinterpret. "Humble"? No. Maybe "Terrific." Yes, that had clear positive associations.

Since Hannah refused to sleep in her own room, the spider had plenty of time to spin. Her second attempt at word weaving went smoother. The next morning, "Terrific" shone like silver in the sunshine.

"'Terrify?' No!" Hannah gasped as she misread, turning abruptly and hitting her head on the doorframe, knocking herself unconscious.

The spider winced. Web messages were clearly out. *Charlotte's Web* had drastically misled her in terms of human reactions to literate spiders. There had to be a way to communicate without alarming the girl.

"Where's my phone?" Hannah asked, slurring as she came to. She swiped it off the floor, threw herself into the hall, and typed furiously.

That was it! The phone! Hannah used her phone to communicate! The spider would follow her companion's lead, but first she needed to understand how the phone worked.

The spider paid attention to how Hannah operated the device over the next two days. She watched her tap a code in to unlock it, 3396. Sometimes she looked up information, but most of the time she sent messages to Nikki, who only answered half the time. The spider couldn't understand that, she would have given two of her legs for a real conversation with Hannah.

On the third day, Hannah returned to her own bed, and the spider had nocturnal phone access. The spider waited until Hannah was asleep to climb on top and press her feet against the virtual keys. It took hard slaps, but she managed to put in the code. Sending her message merited a little extra consideration— the spider had no phone number. She realized her messages would come from Hannah and go to Hannah. She hoped it wouldn't be confusing, rubbing her mandibles together in concentration and considering her wording.

"Dear Hannah, this is your familiar. I don't want to scare you, I want us to be friends. If I come out, you will scream and try to kill me. That won't do. I need you to be brave. Sincerely, your familiar."

Signing it "your spider" seemed like setting herself up for failure.

The next morning, Hannah checked her texts during breakfast, just like she normally did. Today, however, cereal milk came out of her nose. She looked around incredulously.

"Familiar?" she whispered sheepishly. "Are you there? I'm ... I'm being brave."

The spider watched from the flowers on the kitchen table. Hannah seemed receptive. The spider dropped cautiously onto the table and took a few tentative steps toward Hannah. Maybe the teen would think before she —

"Spider!" Hannah screamed, looking around frantically for what the spider assumed would be a weapon.

She was across the table, onto the floor, and under a cabinet before Hannah's shoe could crush both their dreams. The spider groomed herself to calm down. The situation was ... frustrating. Hannah was frustrated, too. The spider could sense her agitation. She wanted to comfort the girl, almost to the point of revealing herself again.

"Familiar? Where are you? Please, help me. I'm being attacked by spiders. Aren't you supposed to protect me?"

I wish I could, the spider thought to herself.

Hannah picked up her phone, sniffling. "Nikki? Hey, I ... oh, sorry. I just ... no, I understand. I'll see you at school. I lo —"

The spider felt Hannah's wave of sadness and longing. Images of another teenage girl, willowy and all in black, poured into the spider's mind. Goth girls did nothing for the spider, but everything for Hannah. Nikki was her girlfriend, but Hannah was sure her own feelings were much stronger than Nikki's. The spider decided she didn't care for Nikki.

That night, she searched the phone for tips on making friends. Step one almost always involved sharing your name and learning theirs in return. Maybe that was the key. She'd give herself a name to seem more approachable.

Looking for names took up another web's worth of time. Finally, she found what she wanted. She hoped hinting at her nature while remaining friendly might bridge the gap. Her research also suggested finding commonalities with potential friends, talking about interests, and sharing goals. Her next text took ages to plan, but the spider was proud of her work.

"Dear Hannah, this is your familiar. I like eating, and I see you do, too. We have that in common. I'm sorry I upset you. I don't mean to leave you alone, and I am here to protect you as much as I can. This is all hard for me, too. We have that in common, also. I don't know how to be a familiar, I wasn't one until you made me. I didn't even know I *was* at all. You gave me a gift, and I appreciate it. I'm sorry I'm not the sort of creature you wanted, but I hope you can learn to love me anyways. Yours sincerely, Arachne."

She watched Hannah mouth the message, her brows furrowing. "Arachne? Wasn't she the girl who got turned into a ... no. No, no. You're not a ... a spider. There's no way."

Arachne inched forward. Hannah looked frantically around the kitchen. Arachne saw the fear in her eyes and eased back into the shadows. She'd give her time to process.

"I've got to get out of here. I can't deal with this right now!"

Hannah grabbed her backpack and hurried out of the kitchen, leaving her breakfast unfinished. Arachne would need to think up another plan.

Hannah's phone went with her to school, and the computers in the house were too large for Arachne's legs to operate, so she read while Hannah was gone, snacking on a half-crushed moth she found by the kitchen door. She jumped back into *Charlotte's Web* and was impressed by the main character's tenacity. Arachne decided to try one last web, with the clearest message she could conjure: "Helpful."

Hannah tore it down again. "Stop it! My familiar isn't a spider, it can't be! Whatever you are, leave me alone!"

Arachne would have cried if she'd had tear ducts. She'd lost her old life, gained sentience, traveled far from home, and it was all for nothing. Hannah hated her. She could hear the teen weeping, but no one came to investigate. Arachne knew Hannah's mother and father were home, but they didn't seem particularly interested in her life. Arachne wanted more for Hannah, even if she tried to kill her familiar on sight.

There had to be a way to get through to her. Arachne thought about what she knew Hannah liked the most. She couldn't win her over by swimming, or playing volleyball. But she could talk to Hannah's friends. Surely some of them would be pro-spider. Arachne hated to admit it, but Nikki, with her spider-filled wardrobe, would be the perfect person to calm Hannah's fear.

That night, Arachne put aside her dislike and looked up Nikki's number on the phone. She accidentally bumped the call button instead of text, and Nikki's voice filled the kitchen.

"Hello? Hannah?" A pause, and a giggle. "I bet she butt-dialed me again. She's such a mess!"

Another giggle answered her. "Then why don't you dump her? I'm tired of hiding."

"Ugh, I would, but she's just so needy. I feel bad."

"Not bad enough to stop meeting up—"

The line went dead. Arachne puffed up with rage. How dare Nikki be unfaithful! Hannah would be so hurt when she found out! Plans to reveal herself forgotten, Arachne threw herself into a new mission: finding Hannah a better girlfriend.

Arachne had absorbed every second of screen time she'd observed, including Hannah's social media. There was a rainbow flag on her profile, and Arachne realized it let other humans know her mating habits. There were a few girls from school on her profile who did the same, making identifying potential partners easier. She considered ruling out any with cats in their pictures, but knew Hannah wouldn't have the same aversions. Finally, Arachne typed out another text.

"Dear Hannah, I know this isn't going well, but I have a way I can help you. These nice girls all go to your school, maybe you can find them and become girlfriends. Nikki is a bad person. You should eat her. Sincerely yours, Arachne."

The text wasn't well received. "Now you're trying to make me dump my girlfriend? I don't know what you are, but I'm cleansing the hell out of this house as soon as I get home from school!"

She slammed down her phone and hid in the bathroom to get ready. Arachne crawled over to this discarded device. It was time to take matters into her own eight legs. She opened the text thread between Nikki and Hannah.

"Dear Nikki. You are a bad person, and I know you're with another girl. Leave me alone or I'll eat you. Sincerely, Hannah."

There. That would do it. Arachne crawled contentedly into a dark corner to spin a tiny web in hopes of catching a few of the fruit flies buzzing around a bunch of almost overripe bananas. A few minutes later, the phone rang.

"Nikki? Hey, good morning, I ... what are you talking about? Glad what's out in the open? No! You didn't ... oh ... Okay. Yeah. No, I'm fine. Really. Okay, bye."

She hung up the phone, hiccuping and tearful, and stared at the screen. "You broke up with my girlfriend?"

Hannah growled and ran into her room. Arachne raced after her as the girl flopped down heavily on her bed, phone tossed on a pillow. She sobbed wretchedly, and Arachne's heart broke with her. Arachne realized Hannah's problems couldn't be solved as easily as catching a fly in a web. For the first time in her life, Arachne understood she was small. She watched Hannah for a few minutes, then crawled silently onto the phone.

"Dear Hannah, I'm sorry you're sad. It hurts to lose something you care about, but I know you will get through this. You're strong, and you deserve a mate who won't hurt you. Look at those girls I sent you again, you have plenty of options. I think —"

It took Arachne a moment to notice the sudden, heavy silence filling the bedroom. Hannah wasn't crying. She perched on the edge of the bed, watching Arachne with hitching breaths. Arachne tensed, ready to spring away from a hand or shoe, but none came. Hannah studied her, sniffing, and blew out a long breath. She closed her eyes and mouthed something to herself. When she opened them again, she looked calmer.

"Can I see?" she asked, gesturing to the message.

Arachne scuttled away from the phone obligingly, trying to ignore Hannah's flinch. Hannah cocked her head as she scanned the words. "What ... what else were you going to say?"

Arachne gestured towards the phone. Hannah gasped and scooted away, then paused as if she'd realized it wasn't an attack. "Oh, uhm, sorry. Here."

She set it down on the table and slid it toward Arachne, still rigid. Arachne took one deliberate step at a time, trying her hardest not to spook the girl. She climbed back onto the keyboard. Hannah hugged herself and looked slightly green.

"Oh my god, you've been touching my phone so much."

Arachne tried not to take offense. "I think Jenny seems nice. And she likes spiders, she had them on her sweater."

Hannah snorted when she read it, and her shoulders relaxed a little. "Jenny's dating Bailey, and I'm way out of her league. How do you know all these people?"

Explaining a combination of shared mental impressions and rapidly gleaned social savvy seemed too complicated, and she got the impression Hannah wouldn't appreciate her snooping. "Familiar-bond magic."

"Is that how you knew Nikki was cheating on me? Wait, no, that doesn't make sense. I didn't know."

Arachne rubbed her legs together guiltily.

"Are you psychic? Do I have a psychic familiar?"

It was the most positive Hannah had sounded about Arachne, and the spider was sad to disappoint her. She gestured for the phone again. Hannah passed it with a steadier hand. "No. I tried messaging her but called instead. I heard her talking to another girl. She said they were together."

Hannah deflated. "Probably Kristina. They're always hanging out. Nikki told me not to worry about her. Guess that was a lie. I wonder how long she would have kept me in the dark if ... if you hadn't helped me."

Arachne asked for the phone again. Hannah slid it over and leaned in close enough to read the screen without lifting it up. She was inches away from Arachne and didn't flinch. Well, only a little. At least until Arachne moved, then Hannah retreated to the edge of the bed. She caught herself and scooted back a few sheepish inches.

"I like helping you. I'm sorry I scare you, and I'm sorry I don't know any magic."

"I don't really know any magic, either," Hannah said with a sigh. "I grabbed that stupid book because I thought it might actually help me make some changes in my life."

"I tried a book, too. It didn't help." Arachne gestured to the out-of-place novel Hannah hadn't noticed.

"*Charlotte's Web*? Oh no, the webs. I get it now. Honestly, those were horrifying. No offense."

"I'm sorry. I wanted you to understand. I'm 'Some Spider.'"

Hannah didn't speak for a long time. She stared at Arachne for so long the spider considered hiding. "If I could change my shape, I would. I'm sorry this is my body," she typed instead.

"Sorry this is your body?" Hannah whispered, eyes watering again. "No!"

Arachne felt a wave of anger and sadness. The teen stood abruptly, fists balled at her side. Images of Arachne, Hannah, and Nikki bombarded the spider, all tinged with rage and regret. Arachne panicked. She'd failed, Hannah was going to kill her. She bolted for cover.

Hannah gasped and held out a hand. "No, wait!"

Fighting every ounce of self-preservation instinct, Arachne froze.

Hannah took a few deep breaths and uncurled her hands. She moved to sit beside Arachne again, then decided against it. "Look ... it's just that when we first started dating, Nikki said she wasn't sure it would work between us, because I'm fatter than she likes.

She said she was giving me a chance because she liked my personality and I could tutor her in Latin."

Arachne considered finding a venomous cousin to visit Nikki.

"You know, I've lost almost thirty pounds since we got together? And she still cheated on me." Her voice cracked. "I hated eating nothing but protein shakes and low-carb shit all semester. I could have had pizza at Chelsea's sleepover! My mom's cheesecake! Point is, I changed myself to fit someone who didn't want me."

"You don't want me," Arachne typed. "And I can't change what I am. I would."

"No! That's just it! You're a spider. I may not like that, but it's who you are. It's cruel to make you change so I feel comfortable."

"What do we do?"

"I don't know," Hannah admitted, worrying the edge of her shirt. "You terrify me. But you're here. Nothing I've ever done magically has worked, except calling you. I think that means something."

"We could try and be friends."

Hannah made a noise too close to gagging for Arachne's taste. "Sorry. I truly am. You seem really nice; if you went to my school we'd absolutely be friends. This is just a lot."

"You need to stop trying to kill me."

"I can do that, I promise."

"Not even with your shoe?"

"No!"

Arachne scooted closer to her. Hannah's hand was inches away. She slowly raised a leg, hoping to rest it on Hannah's pinky. Beads of sweat rolled down Hannah's face as she sat, trembling. Arachne was millimeters from contact before Hannah jerked her hand away.

"Nope, I'm not there yet. How about a long-distance high five? Er, high foot for you, I guess."

Arachne raised a leg in salute as Hannah mimicked slapping the air. The gesture wasn't her favorite, but Hannah smiled. They sat in companionable silence for a few minutes until Hannah's mother called her down for dinner.

"Coming, Mom!" She left the phone for Arachne. "I'll be back in a little bit. And, uhm, thanks."

Arachne puffed herself up with pride. She'd solved a problem and gotten a thank you from her timid companion. Her thoughts raced. If she was going to keep helping Hannah, she'd need to learn more. She scuttled onto the phone screen.

"Dear Hannah, let's talk about what you like in girls. Also, are you sure you don't want to eat Nikki?"

ABOUT THE AUTHOR

Pines Callahan is a former geriatric psych nurse turned professional native plant nerd. She typically writes dark fantasy and cozy horror, but is happy to pursue any story she finds weird enough. As a Floridian—but not the "Florida Man" kind—her writing is inspired by the vulnerable people and places in Florida, the experience of being queer and neurodivergent in a red state, and how we struggle against a cultural lack of empathy. When she's not writing, Pines is typically tending butterfly gardens, swimming or hiking places she probably shouldn't, or spending time with her family. Her work also appears in the anthology *Escalators to Hell*. You can find Pines on Twitter and Instagram at @Pinesforstories or at pinescallahan.squarespace.com.

SCARY, SCARY, SKUNK
HEATHER GRAHAM

N ever, never tell anyone!"

Connie's father spoke the words with such fierce determination she was afraid for a minute that he was angry with her.

"I understand, I understand!" she assured him. She offered him a weak smile. "I mean, I know that long ago, as in the witches in Salem, Massachusetts, innocents were burned—"

He let out another sound of aggravation that startled her. "History! Don't people ever get history right? In the American colonies, witches were never burned. They were hanged. But you do understand the point. People fear what they don't understand. So-called witches were often just people who had knowledge regarding healing, nothing evil! And like most things in the world, such hysteria was usually caused by greed, land grabs . . . never mind. I digress. You just never, never tell anyone you can *see* things happening to other people."

"Right, Dad. I understand!" she assured him. "Can we see the prairie dog now?"

The local pet shop had been advertising prairie dogs for a few weeks and Connie had wanted one in the worst way. Her old dog, Rocket, had passed away last year, and she had wanted another pet desperately. Most of her friends were "cat people," but she loved dogs, the bigger the better. Still, when she had seen the ads for prairie dogs, she'd been fascinated.

They headed into the pet shop. Birds squawked, puppies yipped, and an occasional "meow" could be heard. The prairie dogs were in a glass container front and center.

Connie's dad told the young man at the entrance that they had come to see the prairie dogs. He'd smiled. "Of course. I'll get the prairie dog handler right now."

"Handler!" Connie's dad exploded. He turned to Connie, shaking his head sadly. "Connie, I am so sorry. No pets that need handlers!"

The young man had been holding something. Something tiny in his hand.

"Oh!" He appeared to be about college age; he was probably realizing he shouldn't have said the world "handler." But he smiled broadly. "Ah, okay. No handler, still, here's a special pet!"

The thing in his hand was a little tiny creature, furry and white. It had pink eyes.

"Albino skunk," he informed them.

"Skunk?" her father repeated skeptically.

"Oh, completely de-scented, of course. I had a skunk when I was little—a regular one, stripe and all—and trust me, a skunk makes a great pet. They do litter training like a cat, and they can be incredibly affectionate."

The tiny little white creature looked at Connie as she looked at it. She saw something in those little pink eyes.

"Dad! I want her, please?" Connie begged.

"A skunk?" he repeated.

"Honestly, she's like a little cat!" the young man told them.

"Oh, honey—" Connie's father began. But he looked at her face and then at the man. "Fine. Um, we need to know what to feed it and we need a litter box and litter. . . ."

Twenty minutes later, they were driving home. Connie held the little creature in her hands. Pink eyes surveyed hers almost as if they shared an intimate secret.

Soon they were home. Connie's dad helped her set up the litter box and fill it with litter. She hurried to the kitchen and fixed her pet what she hoped would be a delicious meal of lettuce, carrots, and apples.

Her dad came in to check on her. She smiled at him. He was, in truth, a great dad. Her mom had passed away six years ago when she'd been eight, and it had been just her dad and her since. And, of course. . . .

Whatever special power it was she possessed, a strange vision of something evil happening to someone who was near her, had come to her through her mother's line. Her father didn't really understand it, but her mother had possessed the same "gift" or "curse," and he had adored Connie's mom and believed in her and in Connie—even while he warned her to keep silent to everyone else. Most of the time, they didn't talk about it or even think about it, unless. . . .

Well, she had managed to warn their neighbors when their kitchen caught fire—and her dad passed that off as a sensitivity to smoke.

"Remember, it's hard enough just to be a teenager!" her dad cautioned her.

Well, it was fun, but it wasn't all that easy. Connie loved her school and her friends, and she was delighted her friends all seemed smitten with her skunk.

Snowy Chloe. That's what she named her. She was pure white —except for her adorable pink eyes. Eyes that always seemed to look at Connie as if she understood every word being said around her, as if they shared a special secret.

And they did.

The first time Connie realized that Chloe had her own strange "gift" was when she was with her best friends, Laura and Jennie, at their local café. They were talking about Damon Richardson, cute as could be, probably the most popular guy in their class.

They were seated at the outside tables because Connie had Chloe with her on the little leash she had gotten for Chloe when she had grown to be the size of a big house cat. Few people ever knew what Chloe was—and if passersby asked her and she told them they usually shook their heads in horror and gasped, "Scary, scary—skunk." She was—scary or not—evidently a pet, and pets had to sit outside unless they were service animals. Since Connie had never heard of a "service skunk," she had never thought to file papers to get her qualified as such.

But that day. . .

"Beyond a doubt!" Jennie said excitedly. "Damon is the best football player in our school. And he's nice! He never let being adored by everyone go to his head."

"Nice, and smart. He's on my debate team next week," Connie told them. "We're tackling hard subjects, too!"

"So, so, smart and perfect and. . . ." Laura said and sighed. "But I hear he is dating Mellyora Kingston, you know, little miss school spirit, the head of our cheerleading squad."

Connie shrugged. Then she grinned and looked back at Laura. "Hey, I hear the second coolest guy in the school asked you to the movies next week. A date!"

"You mean Jared Rodgers," Laura said, nodding happily. "Except . . . my parents are so weird. I mean I'm fourteen! High school next year. Almost grown up! And I don't dare say date." She groaned. "Please, please, you two must go to the movies next week, please, please, so I can say I'm with you."

Connie looked at Jennie, and they grinned at each other. Of course, they would go—they were all best friends, real best friends.

But it was at that moment that Chloe, in Connie's lap began to twitch. Something from that "twitch" seemed to streak through Connie and, as it did so, Connie *felt* it, *saw* it in her mind's eye.

A gunman was moving into the café. He was going to step up behind Damon Richardson, put the gun to his head, and warn the owners that if they didn't turn over all the cash in the place, diners would be eating the kid's brains.

Ah, man! She was an unarmed kid! How could she stop it?

Connie wasn't sure how she knew what Chloe was telling her, and she might have been an idiot, but she leapt up, the skunk in her arms, and rushed into the café. She could see the man, see the scene starting to unfold just as she had seen it in her head.

But Chloe made a strange little noise and jumped from Connie's arms. She turned in skunk defense mode and lifted her tail.

The gunman was in his late twenties or early thirties; he looked rough and strong. His face showed a scraggly growth of whiskers, and his eyes were reddened. Damon had been right ahead of him, just about to order.

The gunman set the nose of his gun against the back of Damon's head and shouted, "All right! Every bit of cash in this place or you'll all be eating this kid's brains, got it?"

Then something happened. Something very strange.

Connie smelled nothing except for a faint and pleasant aroma of lavender.

But the gunman suddenly screamed; the gun slipped from his fingers a second before he fell to the floor. And it wasn't that Connie was any kind of courageous heroine; it was just because the gun had slid in her direction. She plucked it from the floor, and, thankfully, she'd seen enough TV to empty it of ammunition. As she did that, a patrolman suddenly burst in from the street, heading to the fellow on the floor who was starting to come to. He was quickly handcuffed, muttering about being poisoned, about poison coming through the air.

Connie scooped Chloe from the floor, anxious to get out before she got in trouble for bringing the animal into the café. As she straightened, she saw that Damon Richardson was staring at her. Damon was already fifteen and already almost six feet tall. He had sleek dark hair, cut short enough for his athletic career, but allowing for a dashing bit of curve over his forehead. His eyes were an ice blue and they rested on her. She swallowed hard and swirled around quickly, so anxious then to get Chloe out of the café.

Of course, other police were there by then, and no one was allowed to leave. Connie huddled with Chloe, Laura, and Jennie as they waited their turn to talk to the cops. Jennie was scared and a little angry. "We weren't even inside, and they're making us stay!" she moaned. "But you were inside. What happened?"

My skunk seems to have the weird power to emit an aroma that knocks out bad guys and just smells like lavender to others, she thought.

Dear God, she could never say such a thing out loud.

"I was kind of far away," Connie said.

"Why did you jump up and go in there?" Laura asked her.

"I wanted to get something . . . umm, hmm. Weird! Now I don't even remember what!" Connie said.

And it was then that Damon Richardson walked out and headed straight toward her. "I don't know how you did it," he whispered, "but I think you saved my life!"

He smiled at her.

But as he did so, Mrs. Englebert, their English teacher, walked out, too. Connie hadn't even seen her in the café.

"Damon, you stop that, and we should all just be thankful that no-good junkie crashed when he did! Connie, I'll be speaking with your father! I mean, I'm sorry, but I don't know what you were thinking or what Damon was thinking, but this thing with you—it's dangerous to your mental health!"

She stared at Damon, who turned and walked away; his mother and father had arrived, and his mother threw herself in her son's arms, sobbing with relief.

Laura looked at Connie and asked, "What the heck?"

"I have no idea!" Connie told her. But, of course, she did. Chloe was now nestled sweetly in her lap.

Naturally, there was a discussion that centered on the fact that their English teacher could be one hell of a bitch.

"That woman is a virago!" Jennie announced, shaking her head angrily as they watched Mrs. Englebert meet up with her husband, who hugged her warmly. To be fair, Connie had always liked the woman. She was slim, kind of young, Connie thought, maybe in her late twenties, with a pleasant face and auburn hair that was pretty when she let it down—in class she was always primly dressed, and her hair was always tightly tied back. And it was interesting to see the woman's husband hurry to meet her and hold her, as grateful as Damon's dad had been to see that all those who had been in the café were fine.

Eventually, all parents and loved ones arrived for the young people and the adults within were allowed to leave. The whole thing hadn't taken that long, Connie knew—it had just seemed like forever.

And, of course. . .

Mrs. Englebert carried through on her threat and told Connie's father that she seemed to think that his daughter had stopped a junkie from killing her classmate.

"Connie, I have warned you so many times!" he told her. "She seems to think that I must get you regular visits with a psychiatrist and that you need therapy—"

"Dad, I didn't do or say anything that would remotely suggest I had anything to do with the guy who had the gun to Damon's head, I swear!" Connie told him. "And I. . ."

"What did happen?" her father asked.

And she had to explain that Chloe had twitched, and her visions had started and. . .

"You jumped up and rushed in? Connie, you could have been killed!"

"But I wasn't, Dad, and what did you want me to do? Let the guy kill Damon?"

"You just must be careful!" her father warned.

"I am careful, Dad, I promise! But—"

"Either a junkie picked that exact moment for his drugs to kick in, or your skunk is special. And I don't get it. She was de-scented just as she was born so that she could be a pet, so. . ."

Connie shrugged, grimacing at him.

"Or you have an amazingly gifted skunk. But again, Connie, you're my only child, and I love you with everything in me. I don't want a Mrs. Englebert getting you locked up in a mental institution!"

"I know, Dad, I know!" she assured him.

He sighed deeply. "To keep the school and others out of our

lives, I am going to set you up with psychiatric counseling. Now, I want you to—" he began sternly.

"Dad!" she protested. "I'll be my sanest best, I promise!"

And she was. She was sweet, lucid, and charming. And she did just fine. But the strangest thing out of it all was her new relationship with Damon Richardson. He assured her he had no intention of saying anything to anyone but he knew that something about her arrival had saved his life.

And he suddenly wanted to date her. Which was fine—Damon was the rare human being who could become Mr. Popularity and still be caring and kind to others, including school nerds. Connie didn't really fit in with the uber-popular kids or the nerds; she was somewhere in between. She sincerely liked Damon, and she was happy to go with him. She attended football games, cheering him on. They went to movies or they played in a paintball team together. Often, they just stayed at his house or her house, doing homework, streaming movies or shows, or just playing video games . . . relaxing on a couch. When she could, she had Chloe with her. And Damon didn't mind at all.

The only thing that seemed painful was . . . Mrs. Englebert's continued insistence that she needed help.

To make matters worse, she had transferred to the high school.

And remained Connie's teacher, watching her suspiciously day after day.

Still, she was a good student, really good.

And she had Damon.

But it wasn't until just before they had graduated and were seriously considering college options that he stopped her one day as they sat on his parents' sofa in their parlor that he lifted her chin and looked into her eyes, then down at Chloe snuggled comfortably in her lap.

"I know," he said softly.

She had been taught all her life never to tell the truth.

And, of course, he hadn't really said anything. And the years had gone by with nothing happening at all—other than Mrs.

Englebert constantly calling her father to make sure that he was
keeping up with her psychiatric care.

"You know what?" she said, and she tried grinning and
asking, "Everything there is to know about the Roman Empire?"

He gave her a slight smile and shook his head.

"I know about you," he said.

"Um, well, we have been dating—"

"No. There's something special about you. I've seen it. Little
things. Like being right by Dr. Brown when he was about to drop
the decanter in chemistry. And then, hmm, all kinds of little
things! You see them happening before they do. And, you did see
what was about to happen to me; you saved my life."

"Damon, the guy was a junkie. He was a mess, and I hope that
prison has helped him, gotten him clean and into a good program.
The gun slipped out of his fingers—"

"Connie, stop. I know."

She inhaled a deep breath, frowning as she looked at him.
"My grandfather had your very strange ability. I've seen it before.
And I know it's in you."

They had been together now for years! Years, and still. . .

"Oh, my God, please! Damon, you didn't need to date me
because you think that I saved your life. I mean, seriously—"

He interrupted her, laughing. "Connie! I wanted to ask you
out way before—"

"But you were with a cheerleader."

"No, people just thought that we should be together. We were
friends, but . . . you need something to be *with* someone. A spark!
Something that causes the blood to tingle and . . . well, you know!
I liked you before, but you were so serious and I'm sure, because
of people like Mrs. Englebert, that you were determined that no
one else *ever* knew about your ability. And I understand. My
granddad played it that way. But we're going to go to college.
We're going to figure out the best college for both of us—and
Chloe, too, of course!" he added, gently scratching the skunk's
white head.

"I don't think Chloe is that concerned about the academic

offerings," Connie said. "But you've been offered a football scholarship—"

"And you've been offered one in mass media," he reminded her. "Thing is, when we've made it, I'm going to be falling on my knees and begging you to marry me! That means honesty, Connie."

He was so fervent and sincere.

Connie shrugged. "Maybe it's real. Maybe it's not, but. . ."

"You don't need to hide anything from me," Damon said.

She let out her breath and managed to smile.

"Okay. But Damon, not even I know if it's real, if a warning of danger will always come to me, and if. . ."

Her words trailed off. Okay, he understood that she had a strange kind of sight.

But. . .

"If what?"

Honesty. She believed in him. She didn't know how, but he really did care about her. Love her. Looking into his eyes, she knew that it was true. And honesty. Honesty could be everything.

"Okay. Chloe has something, too."

"What?" he asked, frowning.

"Chloe has the ability to knock people out when they're about to hurt someone," Connie explained quickly. "Please don't think I'm crazy. Chloe knocked out the junkie before he could hurt you; he didn't fall because too many drugs kicked in at that moment. She. . ."

"She was de-scented soon after she was born, right? Pet skunks aren't your garden-variety pet, but other people do have them and they're de-scented."

"She was de-scented, yes."

"Then—"

"I don't know. I don't understand any more about Chloe than I do about myself," Connie explained. "But you said the word honesty, and I . . . well, I'm trying to be honest."

She was suddenly afraid. Maybe Damon had spent the last years fooling her. Maybe he was secretly working for Mrs.

Englebert or someone who wanted to see her locked away in a mental institution.

Now that was being paranoid, and still . . .

He was gorgeous. He was a school hero. And she simply wasn't.

She didn't realize that she'd been holding her breath until she let out a long sigh.

Damon took her hand and smiled.

She looked into his eyes and asked softly, "Damon?"

"We're going to need to take very, very special care of Chloe!" he told her.

She smiled, set Chloe carefully on her other side and threw herself into his arms.

They began to kiss, and it started to get a little hot and she realized where they were and drew back suddenly.

"Your folks are home!" she reminded him.

He nodded. "Hmm. Sometime in the next months, we need to convince my folks and your dad that the world has changed, and we're going to share an apartment at college. How hard do you think that's going to be?"

"Damned hard!" she assured him.

And yet. . .

They did. Because Damon was honest and passionate and because, almost unbelievably, her father seemed to trust him. Especially when he produced a ring that had been in his family for years—given to him to give to her with his family's blessing.

It was all remarkable, almost too good to be true. But it was true! It was almost as if they were truly leading a charmed life. Because the next great thing that happened was a new letter that arrived in the mail for Connie—offering her a scholarship at the same state university that had offered Damon his football scholarship.

Finally, along came graduation. The day was long, but exciting. Connie and Damon both received special recognition, and it was wonderful to see the pride it gave their parents. There would be a few hours between the graduation and the massive celebration that was to be held at their high school gym, and Connie was glad.

She'd really wanted Chloe to be at her graduation, but. . .

Hey. She was a skunk. Dogs and cats weren't allowed, either. After all the hoopla, Connie told her dad that she needed to get home. He smiled, understanding.

At home, she cradled her skunk and loved the silly whispered kisses she got from her little white creature. When Damon arrived to pick her up for the school party, he held Chloe, too. Then he grinned. "Hey, it's my car—paid for it with the salary from my after-school job. She is welcome to come with us and hang in the car!"

"Deal! And one of us can check on her now and then—"

"We'll take turns!" Damon said, and she smiled and agreed.

There had been almost two thousand students in their twelfth-grade class, something that happened in big cities, they all knew. But the amount of people just made it even more fun—there had been committees on balloons, on food, on music—and the D.J. was spectacular. And, of course, the teachers were there, too, along with the administration, perhaps celebrating the fact that they were getting rid of certain students—and bemoaning the loss of their good ones.

Connie was still best friends with Laura and Jennie, and it was great to see them and others, all knowing that the rest of their lives, as almost adults, were stretching before them.

A few of the teachers gave speeches. The D.J. was amazing; some of the graduating musicians played and sang and it was really a great party.

Then Jennie noted, "Hmm!"

"Hmm, what?" Connie asked her.

"I'm surprised Mrs. Englebert hasn't given a speech. She's been such a live wire all these years."

"I haven't even seen her, have you?" Connie asked her.

Even as the words left her mouth, a darkness seemed to cover her mind as if storms clouds had blackened out the sun.

And she suddenly saw . . . blood. Rivers and rivers of blood.

Her friends, screaming, falling, bullets soaring through the room like rockets and more and more. . .

Blood.

No, no, no, she'd never seen anything quite so horrible!

But it was coming. And it was coming. . . . .

Here.

She needed Damon and Chloe! But Damon had just headed to the car. She turned; she had to run out to him.

But she was stopped. Mrs. Englebert had arrived. She was blocking Connie's path.

"Hey, glad you're here, nice to see you! Excuse me, I need to get out—" Connie began.

But the woman shook her head sadly, placing her hands on Connie's shoulders. "Oh, honey. All these years. You haven't realized yet that it isn't real? Damon had just been . . . well, playing with you. Of course, I've been paying him, too. You know, his 'after-school job.' That's been for me. And, well, I let you get through high school, but now . . . well, I'm going to have you committed. And there won't be a problem. Not after what you do tonight!"

Connie stared at her. The fear had lived in her all the years she and Damon had been together, not on the surface of her mind, but hidden back in her subconscious. And here was this woman. . . .

"What I'm going to do tonight?" Connie whispered.

Mrs. Englebert was carrying something. A case, a big case. And she suddenly whipped something from it. Connie didn't know much about firearms, but. . .

She'd seen it in her mind's eyes. Bullets . . . blood. And she had to stop it, but. . .

Was it real? Had Damon been working for this woman?

It couldn't be real. She needed Chloe. But this time, Chloe wasn't in her lap! First, the woman aimed the huge gun at her. Then she fired rapidly at the ceiling shouting, "This girl is crazy! Lethal crazy and she has been and no one listened to me and now. . ."

She broke off. People were screaming; they were trying to

rush out. They were tripping over one another and now Mrs. Englebert wasn't aiming at the ceiling anymore, she was forcing Connie in front of her, as if she was the danger, and. . .

She was getting ready to spray the screaming, fleeing students and faculty as they tried to leave the building.

But suddenly a shout rose above the crowd.

"Stop now! While you can!"

Her heart skipped a beat. Damon. But. . .

Had it been true? Had he been playing her? Was he about to come in and help with the spray of bullets and the pools of blood?

A second seemed like an eternity. A second in which people were still screaming and fleeing and tripping over one another and then. . .

Lavender. That scent of lavender filled Connie's nose and. . .

She was suddenly free as Mrs. Englebert crashed to the floor, stone-cold unconscious.

Stunned and frozen, Connie stared at the woman on the floor. But then she saw Damon, cradling Chloe and hurrying over to her. The sound of sirens was already filling the night. . . .

Police rushed in.

Then Connie passed out herself.

THAT NIGHT WAS ENDLESS, OF COURSE. BUT IT DID END, AND IT was Mrs. Englebert who wound up in a prison nuthouse.

Damon and Connie headed off to school, both caring for Snowy Chloe with all their love and devotion. Damon had explained to Connie that it seemed the skunk knew when a vision was coming to her and as soon as she did. . .

She went on the offensive. And he had known from Chloe's behavior that he'd needed to get her close to Connie just as soon as possible.

She was an amazing pet.

She was with them when they graduated from college. And she was a "flower" skunk when the two of them were married.

They decided that Damon wasn't going to play football professionally despite the offers he'd gotten.

Nor was Connie going to work for a media corporation.

They were going to spend a few years with the local police force.

Take classes again, this time in criminology.

And then. . .

They'd form their own business as consultants and investigators. A partnership. . .

Colleen, Damon, and Snowy Chloe, her scary, scary skunk!

ABOUT THE AUTHOR

New York Times and *USA Today* bestselling author Heather Graham majored in theater arts at the University of South Florida. After a stint of several years in dinner theater, back-up vocals, and bartending, she stayed home after the birth of her third child and began to write. Her first book was with Dell, and since then, she has written over two hundred novels and novellas including category, suspense, historical romance, vampire fiction, time travel, occult, sci-fi, young adult, and Christmas family fare. Her fiction has been translated into thirty languages and she has 70 million books in print.

Heather has been honored with awards from booksellers and writers' organizations for excellence in her work, and she is the proud to be a recipient of the Silver Bullet from Thriller Writers and was awarded the prestigious Thriller Master Award in 2016. She is also a recipient of the Lifetime Achievement Award from RWA. Heather has had books selected for the Doubleday Book Club and the Literary Guild, and has been quoted, interviewed, or featured in such publications as The Nation, Redbook, Mystery Book Club, People and USA Today and appeared on many newscasts including Today, Entertainment Tonight, and local television.

Heather loves travel and anything that has to do with the water and is a certified scuba diver. She also loves ballroom dancing. She has hosted events to benefits to aid pediatric children's hospital and 2006 she hosted the first Writers for New Orleans Workshop to benefit the stricken Gulf Region. She is also the founder of "The Slush Pile Players," presenting something that's "almost like entertainment" for various conferences and benefits. Married since high school graduation and the mother of five, her greatest love in life remains her family, but she also believes her career has been an incredible gift, and she is grateful every day to be doing something that she loves so very much for a living.

ORPHANS

MATT BESWICK

ap, tap, tap.

It was the middle of the night, with sunrise still hours away, yet Piry the snow leopard was easily roused by the sound of claws on wood. She sleepily clambered down from her alcove, slunk out into the corridor, and approached the big oak door that led outside.

Tap, tap.

Piry pulled open the door, looking down at the late visitor standing on the grass: short, sleek, with small ears and velvet fur. A river otter with a speckled nose, its eyes faintly lit with purple magic. Another orphan.

"Um," it began. "I think — I think I'm meant to come to you."

"What happened?"

"My witch is..." began the otter, not wanting to say the next word.

"I'm sorry. But I'm glad you're still here," said Piry, in her so-soft voice.

"Yes. I'm still here. I didn't *forget*. I came to you because — — because where else would I go? I can't be a familiar without a witch."

"Shh. You absolutely can," said the snow leopard. "Come in, follow me."

Some hesitation. Familiars always knew about Piry's orphanage, though the big cat had never drawn attention to its existence. Those who passed by the wood and stone buildings knew instinctively: this place was not for them. As for the otter, this suddenly was its place now, and that would take some getting used to.

Piry led the otter through the corridor of the decaying old house, with its broken doors and dusty fittings, and through into the newer chamber beyond. Her heavy paw woke up the light orb planted near the center of the space, filling it with the cozy teal light of her magic, and showing off the large circular room with stones piled up as both walls and curved ceiling. Nests and dens and cubbyholes hugged close to the walls, without consistency. The snow leopard had built this room herself, and its many stones bore the marks and scents of life. Trudging through the house, the otter had been silent and shy, but here it seemed visibly more at ease.

"Are there others?"

"Yes. Shew is a squirrel, and he's asleep up there. Magellan is a bat, and it will be back at dawn. I'm Piry."

The otter nodded along, and then paused in its tracks. Piry smelled its fear, and saw the unease in its purple eyes.

"I don't remember my name," it said.

"That's part of being an orphan familiar, I'm afraid. You may be missing other memories. But don't dwell on that tonight," said the snow leopard. "Just pick somewhere to rest now. Find a better spot tomorrow, if you want. If you need anything at all, and I do mean anything, come find me in the house."

The otter shuddered. "In there? It's a dead place. Why wouldn't you be in here?"

Piry gave a muted hiss, a cat's shorthand for a matter she did not wish to discuss right now, and the otter blanched in response.

"Sleep, if you can. If you can't, you know where I am."

Piry crept away, dulling the light orb as she passed by. With silence, and darkness, and the enormity of its new place in the world, the otter was so, so tired. The nearest spot would do, and it flopped down into straw and the stale scent of rabbit; perhaps the last orphan to have been in that spot. Sleep came easily.

SUNLIGHT SHONE BRIGHTLY THROUGH THE OPEN DOOR OF THE stone chamber, while a soft glow slipped through the cracks in the walls. Happily for the otter, Piry's house was not the only way in and out of its new home. Morning was in full swing: Magellan was fast asleep, and sounds echoed around the room as Shew the red squirrel practiced his magic, chasing a little wisp of light back and forth and trying to keep it from reaching the ground.

"There's something I heard, in the stones," he said. "Some familiars can take days to *forget*, after their witch dies. But if you're still here after a week, then you'll probably stay around all your life."

"Guess you're stuck with me," said the otter, keeping out of Shew's way and watching from its little nest nearby. As the days had passed, it spoke more and more, and the vibrant purple color had come back into its eyes. It really couldn't remember its name, and its memories were indeed patchy, as the snow leopard had warned. Magic would be harder, and take a while, as the otter had to effectively start from scratch—if it even cared to. Surely magic wouldn't be the same without a witch.

In the meantime, there were the other familiars to get to know. Piry seemed rough at first, but was secretly a big, soft kitten who happily soaked up everything the otter had to say. Magellan—or Maggie—was a moody, overwhelming ball of energy when it was awake, and the otter simply couldn't keep up. Then, with his silly charm and his one tufted ear, there was Shew.

"The stones also say you need a name," said the squirrel.

"No they don't."

"No, they don't. But it's true, you do."

"Why? You know who I am. Plenty of orphans never had names."

"They did," said Shew, his tail bobbing, with the wisp of light balanced on his nose. "We'll just start calling you Otter, and if you don't find anything better, that'll be your name."

"Maybe I want to be called Otter."

"Oh, is that right?"

"I don't know. But according to you, I'm not really in a rush, am I? I've got time to work it out."

"Charlie? Cookie? Coffee?"

"How about Shew? Ooh, look at me, I'm such a big mouth."

"Hah. You know you like me."

"I certainly tolerate you," it said, stifling a grin.

"So mean," teased the squirrel, rolling his eyes, red-tinted with magic.

Shew was friendly and chatty, and Otter was cool and sarcastic, and the two got on fiercely well. Piry did not truly understand their appetite for banter, but she did let them get on with it. The otter wondered if any snippets of their own conversation were being drawn into the stones, as it had for the familiars who had lived here before. When Shew said he could hear the stones, he meant it, and Otter was slowly getting used to doing the same. So odd, to be in a place where the walls spoke, and yet it could be comforting as well.

"How old is Piry, anyway?" wondered the otter.

"At least a hundred. Maybe two," said Shew, quickly.

"No, really."

"Why don't you ask her," said the snow leopard, making her presence known. This surprised the squirrel enough to dash up the stone wall above Otter's nest, leaving his magical wisp to land on the soft earth and disappear like a bubble: pop.

"Sorry Piry, I was just thinking aloud," said the otter. "You said you made this place, but some of the stones seem pretty ancient."

"I am pretty ancient. What of it?"

"Just curious. Maggie and Shew told me about themselves,

but you like to listen. And you're probably older than all of us put together. So I bet you must have all the stories."

"Oh, I forget," she said, her word choice making both familiars uneasy. "The stones probably remember more than me."

"Uh huh." Otter wasn't going to push it.

"Perhaps a small tale later, then," said Piry, magnanimously. "But I assume you're not both planning to laze about all day without food."

"You could come with us?" said Shew, who always liked the idea of having a big, friendly predator around when he was foraging.

"You and Otter will be fine," said the snow leopard.

"It's not my name yet."

"Uh huh," said Piry, walking back towards the house.

PIRY'S TALE DIDN'T COME THAT NIGHT, NOR THE NEXT. WEEKS passed, the full moon came and went, and only a sliver was left in the sky as Otter and Shew followed the river back towards home, quite satisfied with another day together. It was a clear night, and there were stars both above and below, twinkling in the air and the water. The squirrel thought this was excellent, and even the otter liked the effect; it made the river seem more magical.

"You should probably head out without me one of these days," said Otter.

"But it's better with you around."

"Yes, but the other squirrels run away from me. Don't you want to say hello?"

"Not funny."

"Aww. Sorry. Too far."

Shew had woken up very early that morning, spooked by a nightmare that he had *forgotten*. Suddenly, he was just a squirrel again, without magic or sapience; the usual fate for most familiars after their witches passed on. Seeing squirrels out and about this evening was too much of a reminder, and so he was glad for Otter's presence encouraging them to keep their distance.

"Still feels odd to just be out and about, taking it easy. Like there's something I'm not doing," said the otter, as they kept moving. "But the memories just aren't there anymore. I don't like that."

"It's how it is," said the squirrel. "We can stop for a bit, if you wanna talk some more before we get back."

"I think I'd like to stop for a bit and not talk much at all," said the otter.

The two huddled close, tucked against the base of a tree. Without the noise of their chatter and movement, the sounds of the outdoors took over. Insects buzzed, and creatures scampered; the river trickled, the wind brushed at plants and leaves. Shew was getting tired and felt safe enough against the otter to fall asleep, bundled up in velvet fur and his own bushy tail.

Otter was much more awake. It was mulling over its past, trying to unwind and let time go by, feigning sleep and counting stars and once again considering what a day might look like for an orphaned otter without a witch. Swimming? Fishing? It hated to admit so, but the gentle nagging was boredom. Shew's affection was sweet, but Otter missed feeling useful.

Both the familiars were roused by newer, louder sounds. Heavy paws. Wind flapping around wings. Recognizable chatter, and the sight of a snow leopard head peeking around the tree, eyes lit by stars.

"Yes, here they are," said Piry.

"Aha!" said the restless Magellan, a brown and black blur flitting through the air, its eyes white with magic.

"Oh. Um. Morning, Maggie," said Otter, nudging Shew awake.

"The earliest of mornings," grinned the bat. "My time."

"Oops. Fell asleep," said Shew, dozily.

For perhaps the first time any of them could remember, the four were out and about together; usually Magellan would be up and awake as everyone else was done for the day. Piry had brought one of her teal-colored orbs, which dutifully followed her around and shared its light.

"But you know, maybe everyone should sleep in the day for a while. Join me at night! Everything's nicer. And I'd have company, most nights it's just me, and—and I can only wake Piry so many times before I know it's too many."

"You can always wake me," said the big cat, distracted and gentle.

"Yes, but it is good that I don't, kitty. I understand."

"Why not join us in the day sometime, instead?" wondered Otter. "You must have managed when you had a witch."

"No clue," it said, flatly, looking away. "Probably I could sleep in the night, even if it's the best time not to. I'll give it a try. But not tonight."

In spite of the bat's boisterous, bubbly energy, witches seemed to be a sore spot for Magellan. Whether it really didn't remember a thing, or only wished that was so, the bat had no love for the subject. Otter sighed.

"Being awake at night, urgh," teased Shew, the squirrel doing his best to turn the page. "I think this is too late. But then, it'd be no fun if we were all the same."

"Right, right. Else we'd all live in the past like Otter here," said Magellan, unkindly.

The otter scowled and was quiet for a few moments, before piping up in an unsteady voice, "I really don't know why you don't like us talking about witches."

Magellan clicked in irritation, and Piry looked sad. Shew looked up at the otter, protectively, but it waved a webbed paw. "It's okay, Shew. I mean, I just don't get it. Even if we don't remember much, Maggie, everyone, you all feel it too, don't you? We used to be more, and now we're less. And that's just how it is, and I do like being with you, I really do. But it's okay to be sad about our losses, isn't it? If I can't share that with you, what can I do?"

The squirrel was nodding, but Magellan was up in the air, shrieking, to drown out what it didn't want to hear.

"I have to, sometimes," said Otter, despite the bat's noises. "Otherwise the ideas just roll around in my head, getting bigger and bigger, until that's all I can think about."

"My friends — Maggie, please be quiet — Magellan!" Piry was practically howling, easily the loudest sound that Otter or Shew had heard from her. It was effective, as the bat went quiet and spiraled down to land. The night was crisp, the air was cold. The silence was uncomfortable.

"Sorry," said Magellan.

"Otter?" asked the snow leopard.

"Hard to be sorry about not bottling stuff up."

"Fine, but I don't think you wanted to upset Maggie."

"No, I didn't. Sorry," it ceded.

With a restless sigh, Piry brought the light orb toward her and curled around it, teal light reflected by her eyes.

"Of course I miss how things were," she said. "Maggie, you can leave if you don't want to hear me talk about it."

After a brief, exhausted pause, the bat replied, "Ehh. Just not my thing. But you've never mentioned it at all, kitty. Not since I got here, forever ago. So I'm curious. So I'll stay."

"Well, you're more than welcome to," she said, quietly. "So here goes. We lived in the house, and afterwards, it was just me. I was completely lost; I had no idea what to do. Every day was the same. And then one day I got really upset, I lashed out, I tore through walls and doors, I broke so many things. That was a shame, but it did force me out of the mental pit I'd ended up in. After that, I built the stone chamber. I said, if orphans can have each other, they won't have to suffer like me. They can move on. Some reached the end of their lives, some left to see the world. Some bonded with other witches — "

"What?" squeaked Shew.

"You can do that?" asked Otter.

"The stones know," mumbled Maggie. "To each their own. No, I can't do it again. Losing a second witch would end me."

"I might bond again one day. But even if I did, my place is here," said Piry, her tail sweeping through the air. "Familiars are finding us at the orphanage all by themselves. I don't know how they know. I can't leave them."

"It's a good place," said Shew, warmly. "You did good, kitty."

Piry meowed without really thinking about it, and then looked mildly embarrassed when others gave her a look. Otter even laughed.

"Yes, well. I'm glad to know you all," said the snow leopard, acting as though she had meant to do that.

"Me too," said Shew.

"Yeah! Even if you don't see much of me. I'm keeping watch, you know," said Magellan.

"I still think you should move out of the house and join us, Piry."

"Probably. But not tonight."

"I'll share space with Otter, and then you'll have plenty of room," said Shew, being silly.

"I'd like that," said Otter, not missing a beat.

The squirrel and the otter looked at each other, bashfully trying to work out what to say and do next. Magellan took that moment to quietly fly up and away, with its night just beginning. Piry smiled, and started back toward their home, getting ahead of the others and waiting for them to follow. Not so far she couldn't see them, but far enough away so as to leave the young familiars their privacy.

It was early morning, a few days later, and Otter was exploring the house. The place still made it feel very uneasy, particularly in the dark, but thankfully the familiar had picked up enough magic to be followed by a ball of light, coating the walls in a flickering purple glow. It looked through corridors, into rooms, behind broken doors. Otter knew the snow leopard's story, and the more it looked, the less happy it felt, each room heavy with sadness, rage, and loss.

Piry was in her alcove, not asleep. Up close, she was a giant of a creature, so much bigger than the otter. Gray, with hints of blue, and blossoming black rosette patterns dotted all over her.

"Otter? That's rare. Is everything okay? Still getting on with Shew?"

"I'm fine. It's been great. Actually, I'm here about you. Are you okay? Haven't seen much of you since, you know. Witches. Maggie. Your story."

"Mm. Glad I was able to share."

"You were really serious about me being able to bond again, with a witch?" One of its burning questions. "I didn't hear much about that in the stones."

The snow leopard hopped down, eyes bright with the purple of Otter's light. "Of course. Visit places where there are witches. Get lucky. Try not to vanish without letting me know."

"And—and you really thought you might want to do that again?"

"Maybe. I'm old, so I'm picky. But it's possible."

Otter took a deep breath, and looked right at the snow leopard, pausing on the other thing it needed to ask.

"But you're not a familiar."

"Oh? Interesting. Go on."

"It sounds silly when I say it, but it's just a hunch. All these little circumstantial things. Your eyes never glow with magic of their own. You're nice, and so warm, but there's a real distance you keep between us. Some of it is the way you sounded, after your story; the way I hear you talk about familiars. Always *they*, *them*. Not *we*, not *us*. Never *you*. That's when I felt you weren't a familiar. But then, what does that mean? What else would you be? That kept me guessing for a few days; you can think, and talk, and you care, and you clearly do have magic. So I think you're a witch, Piry. I think this is your house because it always was your house. Because you were a human witch."

"Clever," said the snow leopard. "Yes, all these things are true. My lies are by omission."

"And your story?"

"True, if incomplete," she said, quietly. "You know most

familiars *forget*. Witches know a few do not, they remain themselves, they go on. But you know, if a familiar dies? Most witches will mourn, treasure their memories, and move on. A few do not. We keep helplessly reaching out for the part of us that isn't there anymore. Me, I went mad, cursed away my humanity, I was forever lost in memories and delusions, striking out at shadows; and then, I came back."

Otter listened, attentively.

"I was called back, really. By you, by all of you, coming to my door. We all knew of orphaned familiars, but who ever heard of a truly orphaned witch? The first orphans who came here lived in the house, but you were right; it's a dead place, a home only for me and my grief. I made the stone room, enchanted its walls with listening spells, made it a home and a living library and a tribute to everyone who finds their way here. So now you know. Very perceptive of you."

Otter nodded. It was quiet and seemed deep in thought, at a time when Piry expected an unending stream of questions. The snow leopard waited patiently.

"I—well, in that case—will you be my witch?" it blurted out.

"Uhhh—" Piry, for all that life had thrown at her so far, looked and sounded out of her depth. Eyes wide, fur bristling.

"Ah—you don't have to answer now. Or even soon. But you could think about it. Could you think about it? I'd like that."

"Are you sure that's what you want, Otter? What about Shew?"

"Shew's fine. Magellan might hate you for a while, or maybe forever, but I think you'd be able to talk it round. I hope so. And I hope we'd be great for each other. But it's a question for you too. It's your secret. Are *you* sure?"

The sun began to rise, with sunlight trickling into the old house. Piry, the old snow leopard witch, listened to the young otter who aspired to become her second familiar. There could be no replacing who and what she had lost, but perhaps this would be good for her; for them both. The seed was planted, and she would think about it.

About the Author

Matt Beswick is an engineer, musician and writer, creating cozy and thoughtful animal stories with a generous helping of warm, friendly optimism. He grew up near the sea in Blackpool, in the UK, went from city to city for study and work, and now lives in London with his partner and friends, plus an ever-growing collection of plush creatures.

Matt is neurodivergent, and enjoys the peace and quiet of stories, whether reading them or writing them. When not at a computer, he's a keen walker and cyclist who likes to explore, plus he's slowly learning how to fly an airplane. He's also met a sleepy skunk, been bowled over by a binturong, and misses having a cat around the house.

Matt's writing is influenced by animals, nature, magic, travel, and identity. For updates and upcoming stories, join his mailing list at: matt.skunks.org.uk

THE LAST LIFE OF
HILDE THE SMALL
JESSICA FEATHER

The spring air carries the promise of summer's warming rays while still clasping the reminder of winter's chilling breeze. You pause, straining your ears, as if to hear the breath of the forest, but a different noise catches your ear. The humblest of beings sits atop a branch, looking plaintively at you with her beady eyes, and sighing. Once she has your attention, she asks if you have a moment to hear her tale. You inform her that you are a traveler who loves nothing more than hearing stories from those you meet on your adventures. So, she begins her tale.

BEING ON YOUR NINTH LIFE CHANGES YOU. YOU NOTICE THE details in things that seemed so unimportant in your first three or five lives: the richness of moss swollen with moisture after a rain and the intricate pattern of veins in the leaf of a Mountain Dogwood. In its richness, it is weighty. Dense. Your first life moves like water. Your final one moves like honey, though it may not taste nearly so sweet.

Pardon me. I am getting ahead of myself. My name is Hilde the Small and I am about to die for the very last time.

There is a common misconception about which beings can

possess nine lives. Ask any simpleton hunting for toadstools in the forest and they will tell you that this gift applies exclusively to cats. However, that is an egregious overgeneralization. The fact is, all witches' familiars have nine lives. Yes, felines are the most common beasts to fill that role. But they are not the only creatures that can become familiars. Many beings have the potential to become a familiar. Take me, for example. I am a familiar and, as you see, I am a mere mayfly.

Do not be so surprised! We mayflies are ancient beings. The first mayfly was born into Earth's waters long before the first dinosaur hatched from its egg. We are much older than *cats*. Aristotle and Pliny the Elder wrote of us in the earliest natural histories ever written. We are often a muse to poets and playwrights. Never act surprised by the things we mayflies can do.

I am grateful to you, friend, for sparing a minute to hear me. A minute is all I have remaining. Let me tell you about my life and, most importantly, about my witch.

MY FIRST LIFE WAS, IN MANY WAYS, MY FAVORITE. LIKE MOST younglings, I was naïve. But the agony of anything embarrassing I did or said in my naïveté is far outweighed by the transcendent experience of becoming a familiar.

It was early spring, only a minute and a half after I emerged as a fully formed imago from my freshwater nursery, when I first saw Lenna. I was flittering about, looking for a mate — as newly minted adult mayflies are wont to do — when I saw her. Lenna was only seven human years old, which is very young for a human, even though it is approximately 105,000 mayfly lifetimes.

She was standing in a small grove of trees, casting a spell to call a familiar to her. There are dozens of iterations of the familiar spell floating around in ancient tombs and on new-age blog posts. The specific version of the spell is not particularly important for its success. What is important is that the caster has a strong will, fiery determination, and something else—an ineffable quality that I have not, in the forty-five combined minutes of my nine lives, found a word for. Lenna was rich in all these qualities.

In medieval times, familiars were believed to be demons adopting the form of common animals. This is not quite true, but it is also not quite *un*true. When a witch casts the familiar spell, her magic calls a lesser devil and a nearby animal to her. There must be perfect alignment between the three entities—like a metaphysical version of harmonic resonance—for the spell to work. Thousands of living beings fell within the circumference of Lenna's spell on that day. Rabbits, box turtles, a sharp-shinned hawk, and a fawn left hiding in the grass by its mother. Yes, even a flea-bitten cat was padding quietly nearby, on the hunt for field mice. Yet, of all the creatures touched by Lenna's powerful spell, I was the one whose essence thrummed in time with hers and with Bel'amme, Lesser Devil of the Fifth Circle. The instant the spell touched me, I was filled with all the arcane knowledge that Bel'amme possessed. The cosmos opened to my tiny insect brain. I suddenly became aware of the existence of tear ducts in some animals and, just as suddenly, I desired them more than anything. I wanted so desperately to weep.

I flew to Lenna. She initially looked past me. Her large, brown eyes darted about eagerly searching for her new animal companion. I flapped my wings frantically, trying to stay in her line of sight. She lifted a hand to shoo me away, but she paused to look at me. At last, she truly saw me, and I watched the understanding light up her eyes. She grinned widely.

Bel'amme appeared in the state of a translucent specter, seemingly as ephemeral as myself. Dozens of jagged horns protruded from the crown of his bald skull. While his right and left eye stared steadily at Lenna, the eye in the middle of his forehead slept, and the one just below his lower lip blinked frantically. The incessant blinking caused large tears to drip down his chin.

"Lenna, you desire to become a witch?" his thin voice formally incanted.

She nodded.

"To help you in your journey, I imbued this being with all my knowledge. She will serve as a guide and companion on your journey. To be your familiar."

She nodded again.

Bel'amme hesitated, the eye on the forehead opened from its slumber to glare scrutinizingly at me. In a less formal tone, he said, "Honestly, I think we could redo the spell. You know, if you want something a little more robust than a mayfly as your familiar."

My wings and heart stopped beating in unison, causing me to nearly drop out of the air. Was I being rejected?

Lenna shook her head, "No, I don't want a different familiar. I want her. She's so cute!"

Lenna accepted me for who I was. What I was. I was so happy, I could have died.

And then I did.

A mayfly's lease on life is brief, after all.

In my second life, I spent my months in the nymph and subimago stages fantasizing about what Lenna and I would do together. With only a few minutes of adult life to look forward to, I wanted to plan my magic lessons precisely. I resolved that she should first master levitation. True, it is normally a second tier spell. But my witch's magic was uncommonly strong, so I was certain she was capable. Day after day, I watched the snatches of sunlight dancing at the surface of the lake and dreamed of finally fulfilling my role. Lenna's companion. Lenna's guide. Lenna's familiar.

I was so eager to be with my pupil again, that I emerged in late March, unable to wait until my namesake month to reach my adult phase. I rushed to her side. Witches and familiars can always sense where each other are. This is particularly convenient for a familiar like me. I might easily have wasted all five minutes of my adult life just looking for her.

As it was, I found her making an impressive mess, splashing about in a pit of mud.

"Lenna!" I called to her.

"Oh, Hilde! You're back!"

"Lenna, I cannot wait to teach you the levitation spell."

"Yay! That sounds fun. But I have to finish making my potion first, okay?"

I admit that I was miffed. I only had five minutes, after all. We would never master the levitation spell if I had to divert my efforts to cover potioncraft as well. However, I reminded myself, making potions is also a valuable skill for a young witch.

"What potion are you making?"

She held a small, metal mixing bowl aloft. Mud. This was no potion. This was only mud, sprinkled with flowers, acorns, feathers, mushrooms, and an assortment of other small items harvested from the forest.

"That's not a potion," I sternly informed her.

"Sure, it is. Help me make it! Help me find beautiful things to add. You can find the tiny things that my human eyes are too big to even see. Tiny beautiful things!"

"Lenna, you know I only have a few minutes, right? Do you really think we should waste our time on this game?"

"It's not a game, it's a potion." She bit her bottom lip and scowled at me.

I shook my head, though I doubt the miniscule motion was even perceptible to her, "Lenna, you have all the raw talent to become one of the greatest witches of your era. Why are you dawdling in the dirt? I could be teaching you how to fly by now."

Her face started turning pink, though I could not tell if it was from embarrassment or anger. She opened her mouth to say something, but I never heard her words. Once again, I was dead.

IN MY THIRD LIFE, I DAWDLED IN THE WATER IN MY NYMPH state for a very long time. Clearly Lenna was not ready to take her magical studies seriously, and I was in no hurry to be asked to make mud potions again. If I gave her a little more time to mature, then maybe next time we would actually make some progress on her magical development.

Nearly three years elapsed before I left the waters. When I reached her, you can imagine how relieved I was to find her with a spell book open before her. She was so engrossed in her studies, she did not notice me at first.

"Hello Lenna," I called out, winning her attention.

"Happy spring, Hilde," she greeted me. "I had a sense you would be here today."

"I'm glad to see you are working on your craft."

"Oh, yes, I'm quite determined to be the greatest witch. I want to make you proud. But… I am having a hard time understanding how to transmogrify this caterpillar into a tea cake."

"Have you already mastered the spells to transmogrify inanimate objects?"

She shook her head.

"Oh Lenna, you headstrong child. You are so eager to power ahead, you fail to grasp that there is an order to these things. Manipulating inanimate objects is how you learn the fundamentals. It is very difficult to change living beings. Even if you were to transform the caterpillar, it is easiest to change it into a butterfly. The butterfly is already written in its DNA. It is in the caterpillar's essence. Changing a living thing into something other than something that is already part of its life history is very difficult, indeed. Only the greatest spellcasters can do such a thing."

"But transforming regular objects is boring. I don't want to waste my time with anything that isn't truly amazing."

"The most important lesson a witch will ever learn is patience."

She rolled her eyes, "That's rich, coming from someone who only lives for five minutes at a time."

We both laughed at this. Once our shared laugh finally tapered off, we spent the remaining three minutes of my third life practicing changing a pencil into a paperweight. She made the paperweight in the shape of a sleeping cat. That was all her idea. I would have never suggested the form of a feline.

EARLY IN MY FOURTH LIFE, AS A NEWLY HATCHED NYMPH, A nasty sturgeon swam up and rudely ate me. It was quite embarrassing. I do not like to dwell on my fourth life.

IN MY FIFTH LIFE, I HELPED LENNA LEARN MID-LEVEL divination techniques. When I returned for my sixth life, she was waiting for me in May on the lakeshore. By then, she was advancing to basic necromancy—very advanced for her age! I have fond memories of both these lives. Lenna was applying herself, and I felt an immense amount of accomplishment. After all, I was mentoring one of the most promising young witches of our century.

I SHUDDER TO RECALL MY SEVENTH LIFE. IT IS PAINFUL TO recount to you, my patient friend. The seventh life is the life that weighs heaviest on my conscience. I fear I will never feel at peace unless I tell someone about my great shame, so I will continue.

I rushed through my water-bound developmental stages and reached my imago state in record time. I rushed to my pupil's side, eager to continue the trend of fruitful studies together. I found her sitting in the very grove of trees where we first met. At the sight, I was overcome with nostalgia. To me, it was only moments ago that she was a young child, casting her first spell in this very place. When I saw her in my seventh lifetime, she was a young woman, growing up so quickly. She was reading her spell book and petting a large black cat that had curled up in her lap.

I called her name, but she did not respond. I flew up to her, once again calling out to her. I knew she felt my presence, yet she continued to ignore me for some time. Thirty seconds of being ignored is agonizing when your entire adult life only lasts five minutes.

At last, she glanced up from her book.

"Oh, hi bug. Is that you? I could hardly hear your squeaky little voice."

The manner of her address unnerved me, but I purposefully ignored it. I hear that teenagers are prone to act this way from time to time.

"Lenna, I am so happy to see you. What do you want to work on today?"

She yawned, "I don't want to work on anything with you today, actually. I don't see why I need the help of an insect to do magic, anyway."

I dropped down to land on a blade of grass, my wings suddenly too weak to hold me aloft. The cat in her lap stretched its front legs, yawning.

"Who is this?"

"Gowdie is my friend. She's a wonderful companion. You know, the best thing about her is she doesn't disappear for years at a time."

"Wait… Are you telling people this *cat* is your familiar?"

"Of course, I am. What am I supposed to tell the other girls in my coven? That my familiar is a bug? That my familiar abandons me for years at a time? That I'm a self-taught witch? It's so embarrassing!"

"I'm sorry I'm such an embarrassment to you!" I screamed as loudly as I could, which was not particularly loud. "You should have let Bel'amme redo the spell when you had the chance!"

"Believe me, I've regretted that decision! Every day this past month, I drew the summoning circle to call that devil back to make him redo the spell. Maybe then Gowdie really could be my familiar."

I was about to reply with a very scathing comment, when I keeled over. Dying is a way of life for us mayflies.

I DID NOT EVEN SEEK LENNA OUT IN MY EIGHTH LIFE. INSTEAD, I searched for Bel'amme. The knowledge of the entrance to hell was gifted to me when I became a familiar, so I was able to fly directly to the unholy gate. Unfortunately, unlike my connection with my witch, I do not have a sense of where my lesser devil resides at all times. Thankfully, the other demons were very accommodating with directions. I only wasted two of my five minutes in finding him.

"Well, if it isn't my miniscule familiar," he called out, amiably, as I flew up to him. "What can I do for you?"

"You can unmake me. Lenna deserves a better familiar. She deserves an owl, a tortoise, or even a cursed feline. Some kind of animal that will not be an embarrassment to her. One that will be there when she needs something."

The devil seemed to consider this a moment before responding, "It is not easy to unmake a familiar, my friend. In fact, it is impossible. But don't fret about Lenna. After your ninth life has passed and you finally reach your final death, she will be able to cast the spell again. You see, it is rare for a witch to outlive her familiar's nine lives. But since you, my delicate beauty, are so short-lived, she will have this chance."

I heaved a deep sigh, and my eighth life left my body in my exhale.

AND SO, FRIEND, THAT IS MY TALE. I DID NOT SEEK LENNA IN this, my ninth and final life. Instead, I am here, awaiting my last death. Soon, my dear witch will be free to recast her spell. She will finally have a familiar worthy of her.

Thank you for hearing my tale and being with me as I approach the end.

You picked up the delicate being when she started her tale, and patiently held her in your palm as she spoke. Shortly after her story ends, she gently expires in your hand. You sit in the grove of trees, gazing pityingly at the delicate mayfly's mortal shell for several minutes. You are lost in your own thoughts—so much so that you do not immediately notice the young woman with a black cat riding on her shoulder. She walks soundlessly towards you, her bare feet treading as silently as though she were, herself, a cat.

"May I please hold Hilde," she asks, extending her cupped hands toward you.

You give her the body of the minibeast.

She whispers an incantation and breathes warm air onto the mayfly on her palm. Hilde lifts herself up, her small form quivering.

"Lenna? How did you..."

The young woman smiles, "My necromancy has improved since our last lesson."

"Oh, Lenna, I know I failed you. I'm sorry. You deserved a familiar who would not abandon you. You deserved a familiar who would not be so harsh on you when you just wanted to make mud potions. I'm dying now, and please know, that I'm happy. I'm glad you can recast the spell and draw a new familiar to your side."

"Hilde, your essence is the one of all the creatures in this forest that resonated with mine. You are the perfect familiar for me. I want no other."

The mayfly's small voice sounds even smaller than before, "You know the necromancy spell is temporary. Even if you want me to continue as your familiar, I am only a mayfly. I cannot live as long as you need. In fact, I shall die again at any moment."

"I have a solution to that. Remember when you taught me

transmogrify? I can transform you into something more long-lived. Then you will be by my side for many years to come."

"Transforming a living thing is a very challenging spell. Particularly if you are changing a living thing into something that is not part of its very essence."

She grins, responding, "Don't worry about that. I'm a very talented witch."

"Okay, my heart is willing. Change me. Just, please, whatever you do, don't make me a cat."

Lenna sets the tiny creature on the leaf of a nearby tree. She removes several small glass jars from a pocket in her dress. Whispering strange words, she takes pinches from each container and flicks the dust over the tiny speck of a creature. For a moment, nothing happens. Hilde's wings begin to droop, and you know that she does not have much time left.

Almost imperceptibly, she starts to shimmer. The shimmering builds, larger and brighter. The power of Lenna's spell is palpable. You feel it pulsing in the air and shaking in the branches of the trees. Slowly, her body morphs. You watch the shifting form until the shimmering fades away. Hilde stands there, on two feet, with elegant wings emerging from her back, shining like a dragonfly's.

"I'm... a fairy?" Hilde gasps.

"When I first met you—I was only seven at the time—you were so beautiful to me. You looked just like the pictures of the fae in my storybooks," Lenna explains.

Hilde takes to her wings, spinning about and giggling delightedly. She lands on Lenna's shoulder, opposite the cat, and kisses her on the cheek. "Now we shall have a long life of magic together," she says.

Gowdie meows, in apparent approval.

"I even learned levitation, the first spell you ever tried to teach me," Lenna flourishes her hand and murmurs a quick phrase. She floats slightly off the ground. "Now we can fly together."

And they do. They float off out of your sight.

You watch them, smiling. Only after you can no longer hear their conspiratorial whispers, do you turn back into your true form. Horns emerge from your skull and your two hidden eyes slowly open. There is no need to continue your human traveler disguise. You, Bel'amme, Lesser Devil of the Fifth Circle, wind your way back home to hell, feeling a rare moment of contentedness. It is refreshing to be proved wrong every century or so. And you were wrong to suggest Lenna recast the spell all those years ago. She has the perfect familiar.

ABOUT THE AUTHOR

Jessica Feather (she/her) followed her love of language until it led her to a BA in Linguistics at the University of Texas. By day, she works as a grant writer for hire. In her free time she creates short pieces of fantasy, horror, and dark comedy. You can find her stories in the Grendel Press anthology 'Uncanny and Unearthly Tales' and in the Deathlock & Hemlock online "cookbook." Jessica lives in Santa Fe, New Mexico, with her husband, dog, cat, and surprisingly tall axolotl.

"AND HAVE NEVER FORGOTTEN"*

MERCEDES LACKEY

T he room Dick was in was probably the most luxurious place he'd ever been in his life. It might have been fabbed in place from native materials, but you'd never have known it. The marble looked and felt like marble, the wood like wood, the leather like leather, the air-handler top-notch and not emitting even a whisper. Everything screamed *expensive*, but in a subtle, tasteful manner. Take this not-quite-a-lounge chair he was on. Not only was the "leather" softer than a kitten's fur, it adjusted itself to him until he was scarcely aware he was sitting in anything at all. There was a faint scent of something fragrant in the air, but so slight he was barely aware of it. *So this is what ambassadors live like. If I'm going to be stuck planetside for a while, I guess there are worse places for it.*

Dick White, the youngest and most junior member of the crew of the Free Trade ship, *Brightwing*, glanced over at the enormous pouf of a velvety cat bed, occupying its very own spot that was surrounded by a low wall that was *just* too tall for a kitten to get over, that currently held the reason for him being planetside in the first place. That reason was a very, very pregnant shipscat named Lady Sundancer of Greenfields, the proud product of BioTech's most masterful genesplicing. Well, that was her official BioTech name. The name she answered to was SKitty, for "Dick White's Kitty." With her was her mate, Lightfoot of Sun Meadow, known as SCat.

Across from him, lounging in her own copy of the chair he was enjoying, was the other main occupant of this proto-embassy, the Sssalisshan Lady Sissesa.

Now ... you could not with truth say that her Ladyship, the Alliance Ambassador-in-waiting to this planet, was a reptile. You could not say that, because reptiles were Terran, and her Ladyship was not from Old Earth. You could not even say that because her species followed the reptilian pattern. Her kind were endothermic, gave live birth, and also happened to have four arms. But she *was* green, and her skin *did* have something like scales, and she *was* hairless, and her head looked like a lizard with surprisingly sweet eyes and a huge cranium. Her planet had been one of the first three spacefaring cultures to form the Alliance, predating humans joining by millennia. They liked to think of themselves as "elder states-beings," and when first contact was made, especially with a young culture that was "non-standard"—as Captain Singh used to say "not upright humaniform bipeds with funny lumps on their heads"—they preferred one of their own to be the first emissaries.

There had been a quaint notion back in the pre-starfaring days that cultures that had not yet attained spaceflight should be off limits and left completely alone to mature their own ways. And long, long, long before humans left the Sol system, that particular idealistic notion had gotten vaporized. Because there are, as Captain Singh also put it, "more assholes in the universe than nice guys," and it turned out that all that "being off limits" meant in the real universe was that while the Council of the Alliance rested in the comfortable certainty that those "off limit" planets really *were* off limits, the criminal, the exploitive, and the outright sociopathic were descending on those planets and having their collective way with them. And when the Alliance got around to checking again, to their horror, they discovered exploitation *at best,* and at worst?

Entire civilizations turned into slave labor, entire planets laid waste.

The rules changed then and there. If sentience was discovered, an embassy was immediately put in place, and the Patrol would make regular fly-bys to make sure there was no chicanery. The rest was all very complicated, involving xenologists and sociologists and a lot of oversight, but the end result, though far from "letting cultures mature on their own," was a lot better than "entire populations carried off as slaves and planets strip mined."

And until now, Dick would have added, "all that is way above my pay grade." But BioTech had mandated that SKitty have another litter—this time with BioTech getting their picks first before Dick and Captain Singh took the rest to Lacu'un as part of their trade agreement—and this was the closest planet with any kind of Alliance presence at the time it was deemed necessary by BioTech for SKitty to come down to a gravity well to have the kittens and raise them until weaning. SKitty would not go without Dick. SCat would not stay without Dick and SKitty. The Captain refused to have kittens on his ship again after the first litter—somehow even gene-spliced BioTech shipscat kittens had but a single brain cell, which was programmed to find the most inaccessible place possible and send the kitten straight into it.

So BioTech had sent one of their junior trainers, along with an experienced cat that had lost his ship, as temporary substitutes for the trio; while early this afternoon Dick and the two cats were picked up by the embassy shuttle and Brightwing headed on to their next waypoint. It was a win for everyone; the trainer got to see what a well-functioning small trader worked like, the cat got a temporary berth with people that very much appreciated their cats, with an option to join the small feline colony on Lacu'un if he chose, once Dick and his pair rejoined the Brightwing.

And meanwhile, Dick was getting a luxury vacation, of sorts. Sissesa was the only non-robotic inhabitant of this embassy at the moment. Her job was to monitor all the information-gathering devices keeping track of the local sentients, help the translator try and work out their language, and wait for them to approach the embassy—which had been established on a patch of waste ground that none of the local tribes seemed to want. They didn't *avoid* it, they just weren't interested in it. Until the natives made the first overtures, and Sissesa established all the groundwork, there would be no need for any other living staff. So all the facilities here were basically his to enjoy whenever he wanted, and the guest suite he had just finished checking out was just as lush as the rest of the embassy. He felt a lot like an imposter, but that wasn't going to keep him from enjoying this respite.

Sissesa was a gracious hostess, and one who was very curious about everything. If nothing else, he'd have gotten plenty of entertainment from her questions.

They had just finished an amazing evening meal—at least, his meal had been amazing, and he presumed the pile of what looked like random weeds topped with strips of raw fish with a drizzling of tar had tasted just as amazing to her. Now they were in the lounge, watching a spectacular sunset at her suggestion. This location's peculiar weather systems meant that clouds always gathered on the horizon when the sun went down, which made for some astonishing shows. The landscape was nothing much: an arid "grassland," with occasional "bushes," and a line of distant hills. The sunset made up for that.

SKitty, of course, was only here because Dick was, having no interest whatsoever in sunsets. There were plush cat beds almost everywhere, and no less than three birthing boxes at strategic places, just in case, but she liked to be where Dick was at this point.

Sissesa followed his gaze and blinked emerald eyes benignly. "Why iss it that your sshipss have catss?" she asked. "I haf neffer been on a sship with a cat."

"That's because you won't have traveled on a small ship that docks planetside rather than at a station," he said, satisfied that SKitty was showing no signs of the restlessness that would signal the impending arrival of the kittens.

"But I haf!" the ambassador objected. "Sshuttless!"

"Shuttles aren't ships," he corrected. "They never leave their planetary system—unless they are aboard a much larger ship. Bigger ships never touch a planet and are unlikely to be invaded by vermin. Their shuttles are never allowed to dock without a vacuum purge, to make sure whatever hitched a ride from the surface is disposed of. And they can afford to do that because they are big enough—they can afford to waste the air. Smaller ships like mine can't afford that many vacuum purges, and after a lot of experimentation, people decided that cats were the best answer to the problem. Enhanced cats, of course, because besides enhanced reflexes, they need to be highly intelligent, actually working members of the crew. And Patrol shipscats like SCat need other enhancements I'm not allowed to talk about."

Sissesa uttered a sound like burbling water that he recognized as a laugh. "Oh yess, military ssecretss. Underssstood. And training, one ssuppossess?"

"Training for military and non-military cats, so they generally aren't placed before they are four or five. Then they get to pick who their handler will be." He smiled a little. "I was auditioned by six different cats before SKitty decided she liked me. SCat, of course, tolerates me for SKitty's sake."

Dick interesting, nice, and SKitty loves him,: came the thought drifting into his mind, with overtones of general discomfort. The discomfort was no surprise, considering how big SKitty was right now; she was going to have a litter of six and they were all big and healthy.

One of the things he did *not* talk about was the fact that SKitty was telepathic with him and her mate, and her mate was a receptive, though not a projective, telepath. But unlike SKitty, he wasn't limited to a couple of minds, but could act as a receptive telepath with just about anything that had thoughts. Telepathy was one of the things the military shipscats were specifically bred for, and the military and Patrol would very much rather no one knew that as a certainty. Speculation, of course, would always be rife, but there was so much else to speculate about the Patrol that telepathic shipscats were far down on the list.

And I am very glad you found me interesting, he thought back at her.

He assumed that Sissesa knew pretty much all of the details of just how SCat had joined SKitty and Brightwing. Her security clearance was somewhere up in the stratosphere. "One would think SSCat would more than merely tolerate you, given all the troubles he brought down upon you," she replied.

He shrugged, since he had no real answer for that—or at least no answer that wouldn't make him sound just a little unhinged. He didn't think that Her Ladyship's people even had the concept of *pets*, much less the intense bond he had with SKitty. Even a couple of his shipmates sometimes gave him a side-eye when he said something that implied SKitty had human-like levels of sentience.

"So, the little I got in the way of a briefing said that this place and the natives aren't really conforming to the usual patterns." He scratched his head, ruefully. "I assume that they figure since I am a guest and not staff, that's all I need to know. So what does that mean, exactly?" he asked, to change the subject before it got too close to things he really should not be revealing to anyone, even someone with a higher clearance than his. SCat jumped up on the lounge beside him and stared at the Ambassador intently.

I'd give a credit to know what her Ladyship is thinking.

Her face wasn't mobile enough to frown, but the frown was in her voice. "Iss sstrange. The nativess are herbivores, but I think thiss iss only because there are so few speciess here, and apparently none worth eating. But that is not what iss sstrange. *There are too few species here!* And they all sseem to have evolved from no more than a handful of ancesstor speciess!" She took a deep breath and gestured to the view outside the panoramic window. SCat cocked his head to one side. "Even the vermin are ssparsse! Thiss planet iss … *worn out.* It sshould not be. The ssoil iss poor. It sshould not be. Thiss sshould be a sstandard habital planet. It isss not old. It iss not young. The moonsss are ssmall, but that sshould make no difference." She shook her head. "Am sstill gathering intel. Alsso, nativess are incuriouss. They came to watch when the embassy wass put up, then went away and haf not come back. They are aware of droness but do not sseem to care about them. Thiss ssuggesstss there iss nothing that preyss upon them. Orderss are to wait for contact from *them,* but it hass been months ... thiss iss a sstrange world."

"It has to be the lack of predators in their evolution," Dick agreed. "They've never had to contend with anything but accidents, illness, old age, and violent acts of nature. With an easy life like that, curiosity becomes an option rather than a drive."

She made a thoughtful sound, as the waves of orange and crimson in the sky turned to scarlet and burgundy, and a deep blue hovered at the top of the window. One of the three tiny moons came into view. "Ah, look. There iss the local tribe —" She opened her fingers over a control in the arm of the lounge, and the window obliged by zooming in on a series of distant figures. SCat sat up straighter and looked as well.

The window also enhanced the view until the natives became something other than silhouettes against the sunset and distant hills. He'd already seen pictures of them in his briefing, but this was his first look at a living one.

The briefing said they had both internal (weaker) skeletons and harder exoskeletons, which were various muted colors and had a matte texture. Like her Ladyship, they were six-limbed, but quadrupedal rather than bipedal. Segmented bodies, segmented arms and legs, heads a round ball with silvery "fish eyes" that probably gave them nearly a 360 degree view of everything around them. Very small mouth with mandibles on either side; if they bit you as hard as they could, it probably wouldn't do much worse than take a shallow divot out of you. His briefing had included vid of one of them eating; it took small, neat, thoughtful bites out of a hollow stem of some plant it held in its "hands." Rather than being repulsed, Dick had found it kind of endearing. Two fingers and a thumb, just a bit like a crab claw.

"They make mussic. They make art — *such* art! But they do not have fire, they make very few tools —"

"They don't need tools," he pointed out the obvious. "Their

exoskeletons mean they don't need clothing. They graze. They don't need fire for anything, except to make their artworks, and if they are having free time to make art, they certainly are not suffering without what we'd consider things that are essential." He scratched his head. "Honestly, your Ladyship, their life sounds like the old myth of the Garden of Eden back on Terra. Maybe they could use medical help for injuries, illness, and old age, or maybe it would be beneficial to them to learn agriculture, but I can't think of anything else they actually *need*." He leaned forward. "You sound frustrated. Is there anything I can do to help?"

Sissesa uttered an actual sigh. "You are correct. I am mostly frustrated. I am presented with a mystery and no clues. But there is something you can do to help, if you do not mind some underground exploring."

He glanced over at SCat, who nodded once at him. *So, SCat thinks this is a good idea? Hmm. Do you plan to help me with this, my void-like friend?*

Once again, SCat nodded.

"It's not my favorite thing, but SCat and I are willing to go spelunking for you. Why?" he replied.

"We disscovered, when we dug down for the embasssy lower levelss, that there are tunnelss everywhere here. Tunnelss, we think, and not cavess, and not ssome other ssort of natural formation like lava tubess. I would invesstigate, but I am not permitted to leave the building except if the nativess come make contact." From the tone of her voice, that irritated her too. "I am a trained xenologist, and I cannot make usse of my expertisse!"

He rubbed the back of his neck and shrugged. "That would irritate me, too. So, what do you want me and SCat to look for? All of us traders get at least a little xenologist training."

She relaxed a trifle. "I wass counting on that. Mosstly, I wanted to know if the tunnels were made by ssome large burrowing creature that we haf not sseen, or if they were cut by handss."

"That's a good reason to go looking," he agreed. "Because if that large burrowing creature comes back again, your lower levels could be in danger. And if they were made by sentients?"

She raised her chin and looked fully into his eyes. "I haf a theory about thiss world, and that might provide more evidence that theory iss right."

"A worthy itch to scratch," he agreed. "SKitty isn't due to have her kittens for another week at the very earliest, so she should be all right—" Now he looked over his shoulder at the queen. "You *will* be all right, won't you?"

SKitty yawned hugely, and nodded, adding in his mind :*Dick and Preeet go hunting. Good exercise. Preeet keep Dick from getting lost.*:

Well, that was certainly true. Her Ladyship had noted the nod, and nodded a little in turn. "In that case, we'll have a look around after breakfast. That will give me a chance to get the fabricator to run up some spelunking gear overnight." Not that he knew what he'd need, but there was an entire database of things the fabbers could handle, and spelunking gear was probably in there somewhere!

And lights. Lots of lights. And radio repeaters. She didn't ask me to, but while I'm down there I might as well turn those tunnels into something less like a vid-game level with lights and reliable comms.

THE ONSITE FABBER IN THE BASEMENT WAS AN ABSOLUTE delight and infused Dick with some serious tech-envy. And under the heading of "It's easier to beg forgiveness than ask permission," Dick just equipped himself and SCat with everything he could think of, including a little self-propelled cart to carry the supplies and set the light/repeater modules automatically so he wouldn't even need to think about it. And yes, weapons. He didn't ask permission, because he knew (for the weapons, at least) Sissena would have objected, because there was no evidence of a threat.

Dick, on the other hand, was not going to assume anything, least of all that "lack of evidence of a threat meant lack of a threat."

So, he and SCat proceeded with caution. SCat, on his own volition, acted as a forward scout. He made a good one, too, since his black coat blended into the shadows, he moved in absolute silence, and his Patrol training had undoubtedly included just this job.

Dick moved slowly and deliberately, rifle held at the ready, just ahead of the cart firing tiny light/repeater modules into the ceiling at regular intervals. From time to time he moved off to one side of the tunnel or the other to examine and vid anything Sissena asked him to examine.

The tunnels were perfectly circular, which was not in itself evidence it had been made by anything intelligent. They discussed the marks on the walls extensively. It was clear that these tunnels —there were other, smaller ones, that branched off, but he was sticking to the main one for now—had been *made*. But the question was, by what? To him, the digging marks looked like a boring machine. But she retorted with examples of boring worms and other creatures that made similar marks—and also made the point that often, the designs of the boring machines he knew had been taken from living species that also bored tunnels.

Two things were certain: one, that if these tunnels were indeed made by something living, he definitely did not want to meet it. And two, he was glad he'd fabbed up a couple of weapons.

As these things went, though, it was singularly dull. The floor was relatively even. Only a faint hint of damp down here, nothing in the way of an odor except that damp stone. No sounds, and it wasn't particularly cold, either. The tunnels appeared to have been cut directly from the local stone—a kind of limestone, the analyzer told him—and if indeed they were artifacts of another civilization, they weren't telling him or the analyzer much of anything.

"There's still not a sign of use down here," he said, leaning down and making sure the body camera he wore picked up the layer of undisturbed dust on everything. There wasn't a lot of dust, probably because the walls and ceiling were almost preternaturally stable, but there was enough to clearly show his tracks, SCat's, and the cart. "Have you ever seen the natives use these things?"

The translator hooked into the comm system smoothed out everything about her speech, so it didn't sound like she was hissing every word. *"They don't have fire, so they have no way to cast light in there,"* she reminded him over the comm. *"There's nothing that is naturally phosphorescent on this world, at least, not around here, and their eyes don't seem to have much in the way of dark-adaptation. They do use the entrances as shelters rather than building shelters themselves, but they never go far in."*

That made him wonder if installing lights down here as he was doing would cause them to actually become curious and move deeper into the tunnels—but at that moment SCat came *tearing* back along the tunnel, grabbed Dick's pants-cuff in his teeth, tugging with all his might.

"What—" Sissena said.

"SCat's found something he wants me to see." The cat looked up as he spoke, nodded, then scrambled a few feet ahead of him, paused, and looked back over his shoulder, clearly saying wordlessly, "What are you waiting for?"

The cart could easily keep up with him at a trot, so trot he did, his rifle at the ready, his helmet light at full, and the light-amplifying visor on his helmet showing him nothing ahead of his light cone except the little cat-shaped IR silhouette that was SCat.

Then SCat made an abrupt right angle turn and shot down a side tunnel. *"I think this one leads to the surface,"* Sissena said, sounding a little alarmed. *"At least, that's the best guess I'm getting from the tracker."*

The tunnel wasn't straight, either; it swerved and curved as if it was avoiding something—

"The rock isn't as good here. Whatever made the tunnel seems to have been trying to avoid the worst spots."

That was when he heard it. A very high, thin, chrr-ing sort of sound. A sound that seemed to *him* to signal distress.

He slowed down to a walk. *Maybe it's local wildlife that got itself lost down here.* And just because that noise sounded to *him* like it came from something in distress, that didn't mean he was right. The problem was, with all the twists and turns, he not only couldn't see what was ahead, it was also impossible to tell how far away that sound was—

And just as he thought that, he rounded a corner, almost stepped on SCat, and the light from his helmet fell fully on something about half his height that erupted into a shrill sound that made his forehead flower with pain before his earpods canceled it. Poor SCat yowled and leapt into his life-pod, which was on the cart with the other supplies. Dick managed to keep his weapon trained on the thing, even though his eyes watered with the pain, until he could finally make out what it was.

One of the natives—or rather, one of their children. A female, by the coloration, or at least the child bearer, because you couldn't make assumptions about these things. She lay awkwardly on the floor of the tunnel, next to a rock fall that blocked it, and one of her spindly, delicate legs was pinned under those rocks.

Her mouthparts vibrated as she produced what was probably a scream of terror. And he couldn't blame her. A giant biped with a shining light in the middle of its head looms up at her from out of the darkness? Even if they weren't plagued with predators, that had to be terrifying.

Immediately he went to his knees so he wasn't towering over her. He concentrated on her face so hard that he was barely aware of a voice yammering in his ears, until the little native ran out of energy or breath or *something*, and the scream faded away.

"*...back here, you fool! Leave it! Leave it alone!*"

"No can do, your Ladyship," he said steadily. "She's trapped, she's hurt, she's a child. She can't get back to her people by herself. If I leave her, she'll die here."

There was a long silence. Presumably Sissena was using the cams to examine the situation. Then there was a sigh. "*I am sending another bot-cart with supplies. I hope your luck continues good, Dick White. If it does, we might end up with commendations instead of a trial.*"

The little creature watched him as he spoke with Sissena with huge, deep blue eyes. Only the eyes of the children were this color; as they grew older, the blue faded gradually to silver. It made their faces look innocent, and vulnerable, at least to him. Now he started talking to her. "Ho there, little one. No need to be afraid. I'm going to try to help you."

But it seemed as if her fear had already evaporated—if indeed it had been fear, and not merely a startle-reaction. She tilted her head to one side and reached out with a tentative left limb.

It was SCat that responded before he could, padding slowly toward her, then rubbing his head against the outstretched claw. Then he looked up at her. "Prrrrreeeeet?" he uttered.

"Prrrrrrrrrrrrt," she chirred back. As far as he could tell, what she said was exactly as long as what SCat had said. Was she trying to imitate him?

Then SCat did something that absolutely astonished him. The cat began doing an entire acrobatic routine.

He pranced on his hind paws, and then balanced on his front. He did backflips. He chased something invisible. He twirled. He spun. And gradually, Dick could literally *see* the child relax, and react to the "show" as most children he'd met would have. Surprise, delight, pleasure. And now, she'd relaxed enough to tell him she was going to trust them.

Xenology later, rescue first. No telling how long she's been down here, so primary need— He reached back to the cart, got his canteen by feel, and unscrewed the cap that formed a cup. The thing about water was that there had yet to be any living thing found that didn't need it, and since it was generally in liquid state when you consumed it, you always used a vessel of some kind once your species achieved sentience. He raised the canteen high enough that she could see the stream of water pouring into the cup. He got an instant reaction—both arms outstretched and finger-claws clicking desperately. Certain now of his reception, he got to his feet, moving slowly, and brought her both the canteen and the cup. She took the cup in both claws, brought it quickly to her mouthparts, and a proboscis uncurled down into the liquid. The water level dropped *fast,* so he took a chance, leaned over (within striking range) and refilled the cup while she drank from it. He remained there, continuing to refill the cup, until she took it away from her mouth with a sigh.

"Your Ladyship?" he said into the mic. "Carbon-based, eats sugar?" Another thing that was a commonality across the known universe was that if a species was carbon-based, it could probably eat sucrose, fructose, and glucose, and would probably enjoy them. That was why part of every Trader's kit was a packet of sugar cubes. And that kit never left Dick's side. There were regular rations suitable to your species in that kit, of course, but only sugar was universal.

"Yes, we analyzed plants they ate and fructose and sucrose were present."

Now feeling secure enough to turn his back on her, he left the canteen within her reach and went to the cart and his kit. He got the sealed bag of sugar and by the time he had turned around, she was holding SCat.

He froze, then relaxed, as he realized SCat was relaxed. And not only was SCat relaxed, so was the child. He sat down in front of her, as close as he could, but still leaving a little space between them. She watched him intently as he opened the bag, showed her a sugar cube, and popped it in his mouth.

Nothing. No sign of interest. No sign she understood what he had done. But based on how much water she'd drunk, he was afraid that she was half-starved, too, and before he tried to free her, he wanted to get some calories in her.

SCat looked up at him, then eeled his way out of the child's arms, walked over, and looked fixedly at the hand that held another sugar cube. He meowed, impatiently.

"She didn't understand *me* eating one, what makes you think she'll understand you?" he demanded. SCat just meowed again; Dick shrugged, and held out the cube. SCat took it delicately in his teeth, then walked over to the cup and dropped it in. Then he tapped the canteen and looked at Dick.

Well ... shoot. She didn't recognize the white thing as food. But she'll recognize the sweet taste when she drinks! Thanks, cat! He made haste to refill the cup, and swirled it around so the sugar dissolved before he handed it to her. She looked at it, not taking it. He moved it toward her, insistently. She sat quite still for longer than he liked, before finally taking the cup and putting it to her mouth. And she literally had a startle reaction when her proboscis touched the sweetness. She sucked it up even faster than she had the plain water and held out the cup for more. He gave her a sugar cube, and to his immense satisfaction, this time she put it in her mouth.

She had eaten nearly half the bag by the time the Ambassador's set of supplies arrived. On top, neatly bundled, were the cut, hollow stems of one of the native plants. As soon as she saw them, the child threw out both hands towards them, making a keening sound. Dick gave her the entire bundle, then examined the tools Sissena had sent him. Combined with what he already had, plus the energy rifle, they'd get the job done.

He planted metering nodes all over the rock pile, so he would know if things started to shift—the child didn't even notice, she was so busy alternating bites of stem with sugar cubes. Satisfied that he'd done what he could to minimize risk, he bent to take off the first rock. As expected, the pile shifted, but in a way he'd anticipated. What he had not anticipated was that the child would drop her food and start that chrrring sound he'd first heard before he even saw her.

Hellfire! He swore, because he certainly hadn't intended to hurt her! But SCat had an answer to that, too. He got back onto what passed for her lap and began purring louder than Dick had ever heard him purr before.

She reached around him and hugged him to her as if she couldn't help herself. But her chirring stopped. And it almost seemed as if she was going into some kind of a trance.

How— Then it hit him. *Of course.* SCat couldn't tell her—or Dick—anything telepathically. But he *could* read their minds. Possibly memories, too. He must have noticed the soporific effect of his purr earlier. "You just keep her steady, my friend," he said aloud. "You're doing great."

He looked ruefully at the rockslide pile and the blocked

passageway, and finally sighed. "Well, that stuff isn't getting any lighter," he said aloud, and went to work.

He'd uncovered the child's leg, straightened it to the best of his ability, and put a cast on it when the characteristic sound of Lady Sissena's claws on stone approached. He was *very* glad to hear her, since he reckoned clearing the blockage was going to take the rifle, both carts and four sets of hands. And she had four all by herself.

He turned to greet her, discovering she had changed into a practical coverall and had one of the house androids with her. "Your Lady—" he began, when she interrupted him.

"Your stupid good luck holds, Dick White," she said, sounding relieved, bemused, and maybe a touch appalled, all at the same time. "My superiors deemed this a permissible First Encounter since the child reacted positively, and we are now performing an official mercy mission and Second Encounter. Let's get to work."

With that many hands they were able to completely free the child in short order and move her onto one of the empty carts. The entire time, SCat's purr kept her drowsy, and he continued to do so even during the noise of three energy rifles delicately cutting into the rock pile and fusing the edges of the tunnel to prevent anything more from coming down.

The end was almost anti-climactic. SCat let her wake up once the tunnel was clear and they were able to get her out. Her cries and calls echoed down the tunnel, and eventually faint cries replied.

Because they were bringing their own light with them, the tribe was able to see them coming, with the cart with the child on it leading the way. And as soon as they did, five or six of them broke from the group and ran for them, making Dick terrified for a moment that one of them would fall and break their neck.

There was a lot of whistling, chirping, and chirring. One old male whose neck was covered in necklaces of elaborately carved beads shoved his way in, examined what they'd done to the child's leg, blew out a puff of breath in what sounded like surprise, and looked exaggeratedly from Sissena to Dick and back.

"Erm, that was me," Dick said, gesturing at his handiwork.

The creature blew out another puff of air, then took a necklace off and put it over Dick's head. The creature looked at the effect for a moment, tweaked the way it lay, and scuttled his way back to the rest of the tribe.

"That's either an honorary doctorate or a medical fee," said the Lady from behind him, her tone making it clear she was only half joking. "But I think your shipscat is about to replace me as Ambassador."

SCat directed his gaze at her from his vantage point in the arms of what Dick thought was probably the closest thing these people had to a leader. And even a blind man could have read *that* look.

Oh, but that would be beneath me....

---

* "Cats were once worshipped as gods, and have never forgotten this fact."

—Terry Pratchett, rephrased.

ABOUT THE AUTHOR

Mercedes Lackey was born in Chicago, Illinois on June 24, 1950. In 1985 her first book was published. In 2022 she received the SFWA Grand Master Award, and also in 2022 she won the Dragon Award for Best Alternate History (*The Silver Bullets of Annie Oakley*). She has to date traditionally published 146 books, in many series, including the Secret World Chronicles, Hunter, Valdemar, Elemental Masters, SERRated Edge, Elvenbane, and Obsidian Mountain series, as well as many standalone books, written solo or in collaboration. She is also featured in WFP's anthology *Merciless Mermaids*.

FLUFFY

T. CHANDLER

F luffy slithered around his young master's teenage shoulders, his coils constantly in motion. His charcoal-black top scales mesmerized the eye with their graceful, effortless slithering. Like shadows woven into a living cape. His reddish-orange belly scales — so bright they almost glowed — stayed tucked beneath the layers of coils.

You might wonder why a highly specialized, magical serpent, bred from five different species of deadly reptile, would bear the name "Fluffy." All we can say is that Simeon was very young when he bonded his familiar, and he'd been hoping for a companion who was a little — er — fluffier.

Fluffy didn't mind. Too much. He'd come to terms with the name, and could finally acknowledge that it was magnitudes easier to say than his personally chosen name: Slitheriest Slitherer Supreme Stalker, Son of Sammy, Son of Sim.

… Fluffy had also been very young when it came to choosing names.

Fluffy and Simeon hid in the bowels of a volcano, surveying a crater of lava from above. The lava monsters below possessed the torsos of four-armed gorillas and the lower bodies of octopi. Their skin looked like a barely cooling lava flow—black, with a spider-webbing of glowing red veins. Three creatures basked in the lava, grunting at each other, but Fluffy knew they would only have to touch Simeon to damage the young wizard.

In the meantime, nobody but Fluffy watched Simeon's back. Fluffy was ready to protect the idiot boy from any ambushes in the labyrinthine volcano. However, the only threat seemed to be the trio of lava monsters.

Well, there was also the girl standing next to Simeon . But the teenage boy wouldn't let Fluffy kill *her*.

Simeon wouldn't even let Fluffy snack on the girl's feline familiar. Which was totally unfair. It's not like the hairy thing was of any use.

Fluffy rolled his slitted eyes. Human boys were completely unreasonable.

"Fluffy, can you take the one on the left?" Simeon whispered.

Fluffy rolled his eyes again. The very question was an insult!

"Bite or sting?" he hissed, his fangs itching in anticipation. The venom coursing through them was lethal, but the toxin in his stinger merely paralyzed victims.

Simeon looked at the human girl and her hairy abomination, which sat primly on the black volcanic rock, licking its snowy paws. "Chelseene, can you capture one? We need one alive to access the chamber, or we'll never get that firestone. And you know what Wizard Torin said."

Something about skinning them alive if they didn't bring back three elemental stones? Fluffy couldn't remember, he hadn't paid much attention to their briefing after the word volcano.

The human girl frowned. "I don't think we can hold one. But Majesty and I can kill the one on the right. You'll take the one in the middle? Won't Fluffy need your help?"

Fluffy laughed.

Simeon locked eyes with Fluffy, and their bond sharpened.

They grinned.

"Fluffy, sting!"

Fluffy uncoiled like a spring from his young master's shoulders, shooting through the air like an arrow. A lethal, venomous arrow.

He struck, wrapping the bulk of his long body around the lava monster's neck. The creature thrashed in surprise, throwing up huge gobs of lava with its writhing tentacles and beating its chest with its four gorilla arms. It tried to bellow, but choked as Fluffy tightened his coils.

If Fluffy were using lethal force, he'd simply tap into one of Simeon's strength charms, then tighten his hold till the lava monster's head popped off. But he was supposed to capture, and that took more skill than killing.

More skill than that girl and her hairy creature apparently had.

Fluffy grinned smugly.

The lava monster grasped at Fluffy's coils, trying to tear the serpent off.

Fluffy whipped his tail around and aimed his stinger at the creature's open mouth. The lava monster's maw gaped wide, gasping for air, an easy target. One, two, three pricks to the tongue in quick succession. The monster, panicking, dove into the lava.

This is a very good strategy—for a lava monster. Most things don't like lava.

Fluffy wasn't most things though.

The intense heat of the molten rock enveloped him as the lava monster dove into its depths. Fluffy, however, had inherited traits from that fire salamander great-grandfather of his. (We don't talk about him much. Fluffy's great-grandfather was quite the black asp of the family.)

His underbelly scales soaked in the heat, flashing. Reddish orange. Brilliant orange. Dazzling white in an instant. The heat metamorphosed in his scales, transforming into energy that flooded through his body, and—more significantly—the magical reserves he and Simeon shared.

He felt the instant Simeon drew on the new energy, casting some sort of water cannon spell up above. Probably trying to immobilize the central lava monster by cooling it? Fluffy wished he could watch the young master show up the human girl and her hairy feline.

Technically, they could blend their consciousnesses, letting them communicate mentally and use each other as a platform for their unique magics, but doing so required one of them to be active while the other was passive. And vulnerable. Dangerously vulnerable. So he *could* blend minds and watch the fight up above, but it was simply too risky.

Besides, Fluffy had his own work to do.

Surprisingly boring work.

The lava monster thrashed in the depths of the volcanic crater, trying to tear Fluffy away from its neck, even as the toxin sapped its strength. All Fluffy had to do was hang on. He could hold his breath for three hours. A boon from his yellow-bellied sea serpent heritage.

The lava monster slowed, then stilled, succumbing to the stinger's toxin.

Fluffy grinned. It was almost embarrassingly easy. Tapping into Simeon's strength charm, he tied his coils around the lava monster's arm. Then, lashing his tail and head powerfully, towed his prize to the surface.

"YOU HAVE NOTHING TO BE EMBARRASSED ABOUT," THE HUMAN girl cooed to Simeon.

Fluffy felt Simeon's emotions crescendo into mortification.

"Most apprentices can't handle such a ferocious lava monster. I know I couldn't have without Majesty." The girl patted his hand, but didn't look at him. Instead, she beamed at the white cat lying curled in a ball at her feet, a fiery red stone the size of a large walnut resting between her paws.

Fluffy glared at Majesty. It would be so easy. One lunge, one sting, and a nice squeeze before one swallow ...

"And we got the firestone, that's all that matters," Chelseene continued.

Simeon groaned. "We only got it because Fluffy took care of my monster as well as his." He stretched the tender new skin on his hand, freshly regrown after a lava ball had melted it off.

Two whole healing crystals drained.

"Yes, we're so lucky Fluffy was there in time," the girl said, a little stiffly.

So how come I don't get to hold the firestone? Fluffy pouted.

Majesty seemed to sense his discontent and pulled the stone closer to her body, purring.

Stupid cat.

"What matters now," Chelseene continued, "is that we have the firestone. We only need two more before we can go home!"

Simeon exhaled a frustrated breath, but nodded. "The icestone next. That one, we should be able to trade for. Then the airstone."

Fluffy looked up sharply. Icestone? Like, frozen water kind of ice? The stuff that was really cold, and not at all warm?

"The icestone is in the world Glacy's capitol, so we'll need to do this quietly." Chelseene said, beckoning Simeon closer to plan.

Fluffy felt warm emotions building in Simeon's core as his leg touched the girl's.

Fluffy wanted to gag. Mammals were so silly. Especially human boys. Fluffy would do almost anything for Simeon. They were better—and more powerful—together, than they were apart. But this ... hormone stuff? Simeon was on his own.

Fluffy tuned them out, until Chelseene spoke his name, snapping him to attention. "I think you should transfigure Fluffy for this trip."

Simeon frowned, nodding. "Cold does slow him down. And I have three transfiguration mushrooms left." He looked down at Fluffy. "How about a nice fur coat to keep you warm, bud?"

Fluffy hissed involuntarily. "Things with fur have *legs*! I'll tap a healing crystal to stay warm."

Simeon winced, and opened his jacket to expose his wide belt. Glowing wire secured charms, crystals, and trinkets to the thick leather. Of the ten crystals, four of them shone with a rainbow prism of inner light, the other six were a smoky gray. "Yeaaah," Simeon said, "I don't think we can do that, bud. A constant drain on our healing power, just so you can keep moving, is a bad idea when we're already low."

The girl put a hand on Simeon's arm. "I have the perfect idea, *and* it'll help us blend in."

A swarm of butterflies exploded in the boy's stomach, and Fluffy felt every shivering wing through their link. He squirmed.

Then, Simeon looked into the girl's eyes. She fluttered her lashes.

A thrill zipped up Simeon's spine, hot and instant.

Lead filled Fluffy's stomach, because he knew, immediately, that his young master would do whatever this female mammal asked of him.

And it would most likely involve legs and fur.

FLUFFY'S CLAWS SKITTERED ON THE ICE. HE TRIED TO CATCH himself as he slipped on the polished ice floor of the throne room's antechamber, but tumbled into a heap of extraneous limbs and fur.

Everything about this body was unnatural.

Well, the tail would have been okay, if they hadn't gone and covered it with so much fluffy hair-fur-itchiness!

Fluffy carefully picked himself up off the cold ground—yes, he could still feel the cold, despite all the mammals' promises! "Legs are inelegant!" he grumbled. "Clumsy! With *my* body I am grace. With *this* body?" He slipped again, and lashed his fluffy black tail.

"I think you look very regal," Chelseene said, a laugh in her voice.

"You do look cool," Simeon consoled. "The coolest cat I've ever seen!"

Fluffy carefully pushed into a seated position, claws fully extended. For ninety-nine minutes now he'd been a black long-haired cat—a *feline!*—slightly larger than a bobcat. Bright red fur, frosted with golden tips, covered his belly clear up to his chin, much like his underbelly scales in his true form.

Majesty smirked at him and leaped easily from the floor to a window valance.

Showoff.

Fluffy arched his back and hissed at her.

At least some things came naturally in this body.

The door opened and a steward spoke in a bored voice. "His Majesty will hear your petition now. Please leave the animals here."

Simeon took a deep breath, flashed a thumbs up at Chelseene, and they walked through the door.

Fluffy cast a bitter look at the smug cat looking down on him from above, her tail twitching. Maybe he could eat her now, while the humans were gone? The trickiest part would be using this absurd body to reach her.

Fluffy dismissed the idea. This body couldn't unhinge its jaws. That would make consumption ... messy. And leave far too much evidence for Simeon to ignore.

So, Fluffy resigned himself to practice activating each unfamiliar muscle group in his body as he waited.

He'd been a cat for one hundred and eleven minutes when yelling broke out on the other side of the door. A moment later, it changed to screaming.

Majesty took a supernaturally massive leap from the top of the valance to the doorway. She extended her claws mid-leap, and as they made contact with the door it exploded into a flurry of snowflakes.

Fluffy's reaction time was just as instant as Majesty's. His execution, however ...

He peeled his face off the ice floor, hissing. He concentrated and ran through Majesty's opening.

The two young wizards ran toward them from the throne room. The girl clutched the icestone in one fist.

Simeon spun around and shot a cloud of gas into the hallway behind them. Fluffy felt a drain on their shared magic pool, and on his reservoir of toxin. A moment later, a man and a woman rounded the corner in pursuit. As soon as they entered the trap, they fell unconscious.

"Chelseene, what are we doing? We were supposed to buy the icestone, not steal it!" Simeon yelled. Fluffy didn't need their bond to feel the panic emanating from his young master. "We'll never escape the palace with the alarm raised!"

The two humans ran past, and Majesty joined them, loping along easily. Fluffy ran too, but every ounce of his concentration was on running. He was glad he'd spent the downtime working on his muscle control—he could actually run!—but he quickly fell behind.

He felt Majesty's magic surge. By the time he realized where the spell was aimed he was too far behind to do anything.

Simeon cried out as his feet froze to the floor in giant blocks of ice. His momentum carried his upper body forward and he bent in half, his palms smacking the floor.

"You're right, Simeon," Chelseene said. "Not all of us can escape." She snapped her fingers, and Simeon's hands froze into matching blocks of ice.

Fluffy yowled in anger, but the break in concentration made him stumble.

Simeon stared up into the girl's face, horrified.

She had the gall to put her hand on his cheek for a moment. "Sorry, Simeon. You're a nice guy. But plans change."

The girl reached into his pocket and pulled something out. No, two somethings. The transfiguration mushrooms!

Fluffy was close now, finally, and he leaped at the girl, launching into the air like a pouncing tiger.

Majesty was ready. She spun her tail and a violent flurry of snowflakes blew him into the wall.

If Fluffy were in his own body, he'd already have one of the traitors wrapped in his coils, and his fangs sinking into the other. In this body ...

Majesty coated him in a sheet of ice as he hit the ground.

The world became a prismatic distortion as the girl and her cat bounded away, leaving Fluffy and Simeon trapped in ice.

"THEY WANTED YOU OUT OF THE WAY!" SIMEON HISSED AS HE held Fluffy up to the bars in their cell. "That's why she wanted me to transfigure you."

"Of course." Fluffy's orangish-red belly fur glowed, radiating intense heat. The metal of the bars glowed red-hot, softening.

"She used me!"

"Absolutely."

Simeon dropped Fluffy and attacked the soft metal with one of his spent healing crystals, warping them to make an opening large enough for the prisoners to slip out. "I'm such an idiot!"

"Yep."

Simeon glared at him.

"Just trying to be agreeable." Without meaning to, Fluffy bent back and licked his shoulder.

Ugh! Fur! Had he really just groomed himself?

Simeon slipped through the bars, and Fluffy followed. "It's not my fault! She had a good point, everybody has cats here. A snake would stand out."

"So do wizards who start blasting the throne room, then openly steal a precious icestone."

Simeon set his mouth in a tight line. He cast a stealth spell and didn't speak again until they stood outside the portal.

They stared for a long moment. Simeon only had to recite an incantation, then give the password for their destination. Wizard

Torin had sent them many places over the years, so they had options. But, really, there was only one option.

"If we go back to Torin empty-handed, we're dead," Simeon said.

Fluffy waited for his young master to work his way through it.

Simeon sighed. "We're going after her."

Not a question.

"We need a plan. We won't be able to use any of our usual strategies with you in this ... state."

"You mean, where I go in and destroy the big dangerous things, and you follow to take the glory?" Fluffy said bitterly.

Simeon deflated, his entire body slumping as though his bones had suddenly turned to jelly. "Yeah," he murmured, "that."

Fluffy felt a mix of smug guilt. Simeon deserved that. But ... the boy was as limp as a lizard baking on a hot stone. He wasn't like Simeon anymore. He was like ... a serpent who'd lost his fangs.

Fluffy moved forward, meaning to slither around the boy's leg in comfort and apology.

Oh, right. No slithering.

Instead, he rubbed his head and body against his master's leg. Then he turned around and did it again.

Without his permission, a low rumbling vibrated through his body.

It wasn't a growl. What was that sound?

"Fluffy, are you purring?"

Purring? How ... strange. It didn't feel natural, but it didn't necessarily feel bad.

Simeon slumped to the ground in a cross-legged position, pulling Fluffy into his lap and hugging him tightly. Tears dripped onto Fluffy's fur, trickling through the hairs until they evaporated against the familiar's hot skin. "I was so stupid, Fluffy. I always get us into trouble, and then you have to save us. I'm sorry!"

Fluffy licked the boy's hand and settled into his purr until the noise vibrated through both their bodies. Soothing. Healing. Bringing them onto the same frequency.

"We are stronger together," Fluffy murmured. "Without your magic, your brains, your strength, I'm nothing but a length of muscle and scales, with pointy bits on each end. Without you, we are not us. I like us. Us is better than you or me."

They sat there for a minute longer, just ... being with each other.

Finally, Simeon sniffed and gave Fluffy one last squeeze. When he stood up, his back was straighter, his shoulders firm, like he'd turned that jelly spine to steel.

"All right. Let's go get those stones. And maybe a little payback."

"This time," Fluffy said, "I get to eat the mammal."

Simeon frowned, looking uncomfortable. "Which one?"

Fluffy only smiled.

FLUFFY CROUCHED ON ONE OF JYAJJY'S PEAKS. WIND, HE decided, was unpleasant to creatures with fur. His black fur rustled every which way, completely at the whim of the torrent around him. Still, despite the discomfort, he didn't move from his tense crouch.

Located on a world with a very active atmosphere, the range was made up of pillars of stone. The monoliths crowded in winding corridors that funneled the wind into roaring rivers of air. Some of the pillars were thick enough to build a city on, others as slender as Simeon's arms. Most fell somewhere in between.

Their heights varied as widely as their diameters, like a forest of stairs that had broken apart into individual steps, then scattered. Twisted trees and long grasses clung to every flattish surface.

Wisps of clouds rushed through the corridors of stone, dappling the landscape with shadows that skewed one's depth perception, making the strange landscape even more treacherous.

Possibly more treacherous than the human girl climbing the pillar a hundred yards off to his left.

More accurately, the girl wasn't climbing. She clung to Majesty's back, who was now as big as a horse.

"She must have used one of my transfiguration mushrooms for giantism," Simeon whispered.

That meant only one mushroom left.

Fluffy narrowed his eyes. They couldn't follow in the traitors' footsteps. Those two had several hours' headstart and had obviously used that time to descend the portal's column before climbing the next one over—the tallest in the range.

Suddenly, Simeon pointed. "There's the airstone! It's in the currents above their column. Fluffy, how do you feel about flying?"

Fluffy didn't often rely on his Paradise Flying Snake heritage, but it was a moot point. "This body can't glide." He flexed his chest muscles, but his cat ribs didn't spread like his snake ribs.

"I mean a different kind of flying."

Ten minutes later, Fluffy watched admiringly as his young master tied the last string onto the frame of a large kite. Simeon had cleverly manipulated a utilitarian tent spell, and canvas stretched tightly across an aluminum frame, a guyline serving as the string.

Fluffy purred with pride. It wasn't easy to alter a constructive spell, but his master had done so in record time.

The kite wouldn't carry a human boy, even with the strong wind currents of the Jyajjy range. But it could certainly handle a cat.

The kite lifted Fluffy high into the air. Vaporous clouds shot around and through him, as though they didn't appreciate the extra traffic in their realm. The air currents buffeted him, his stomach dropping and lurching by turns as he alternated between falling to his death and being torn to shreds by the wind.

But the canvas held. And so did Fluffy. And they rose.

Just in time.

A sweaty Majesty pulled herself up over the top of the pillar, heaving with exertion as Chelseene slid off her back. The human girl stroked the giant cat's fur, probably lying to the feline, telling her she was awesome.

The kite's shadow passed over the pair of traitors, and they saw him.

Fluffy cursed as Majesty crouched, ready to spring. He wasn't ready! He could see the airstone, a mere dozen yards away. But he'd never maneuver into position before—

Majesty jumped.

Fluffy felt a jolt on the kite's line.

A water cannon connected with the giant white cat in mid-air. The raging wind robbed the cannon of most of its force, but there was still enough to knock the cat off course. She swiped at the airstone, missing.

Fluffy looked back to see Simeon: trembling with the effort to anchor Fluffy's kite against the gale, a huge grin on his face.

Fluffy grinned back.

Thanks, partner.

They maneuvered the kite closer to the airstone, a combined effort between Simeon and Fluffy. Even so, the wind was fickle, and they could only get so close before they overshot.

Majesty coiled her haunches below and jumped again. This time, Simeon's water cannon missed. Fluffy, a mere five feet from the stone, jumped as well. He couldn't miss.

But he'd also just lost his anchor to Simeon.

His fangs closed around the airstone, his tongue pressing forward to keep it from going down his throat. He'd never held an elemental stone before, and it definitely didn't feel like a rock.

It was like biting down on a rubber ball, if a rubber ball could spin like a spherical vortex as your teeth sank in, moving air in and out of your lungs so fast that it felt like you hadn't had a drink in a week.

Fluffy felt the discomfort of his suddenly dry mouth, but he was more consumed by the fact that he was falling toward Majesty and Chelseene's column. Fast.

Fluffy plummeted toward the top of the plateau and—

somehow—twisted his body, landing on his furry feet right at the edge.

Huh, maybe there was something to that whole cats-landing-on-their-feet thing.

The dirt thudded as Majesty landed. Fluffy turned to face the two angry female mammals. Alone.

Not alone. Simeon spoke into Fluffy's mind.

Fluffy started. *Simeon, is your body secure?* With Simeon's consciousness blending with Fluffy's they could share senses and use each other to launch their spells, but Simeon's body would be vulnerable.

Safe enough. Duck!

Fluffy fell to his belly, rolling to the side as a giant ice ball blew a crater where he'd been standing. Chunks of earth and ice shattered into the air, wind snatching the shrapnel like it wanted teeth.

Chelseene jumped onto Majesty's back, and the giant cat prowled forward, hackles raised. Chelseene thrust a hand forward, and another ice ball launched at Fluffy.

Simeon pushed a spell through their link, shooting water cannons out of Fluffy's front paws at the incoming ice ball.

Water and ice hit in mid air. The liquid froze on impact, making the projectile larger. Fortunately, it also slowed it, and it crashed before reaching Fluffy.

Fluffy panted heavily. The airstone was drying him out. Simeon felt the distress, and immediately Fluffy's mouth filled with water, miniature water cannons shooting out of his fangs.

Fluffy gulped it down, grateful, then froze.

Majesty's eyes started glowing a fiery red.

She's using the firestone! Simeon yelled.

Twin beams of fire shot out from the cat's glowing orbs, straight at Fluffy.

"Finally!" Fluffy jumped in the air—pulling power from the airstone to boost his jump—and met the death rays with his belly.

Heat shot through him. Instant, glorious, thrilling. The fur on his belly flashed. Reddish-orange. Brilliant orange. Dazzling white. Power filled his magic pool as Fluffy landed next to a shocked Majesty.

"But ... you're not a snake anymore. You're a cat."

He spoke around the airstone. "I'm not a normal cat." Fluffy sat up—regally—exposing his underbelly. His fur wasn't like his scales, glowing white hot. No. Fur was different.

His fur burned with magical fire. White-hot flames licking hungrily. Eager to burn.

Simeon turned Fluffy's belly into a water cannon, tugging on the airstone's energy.

Scalding steam shot out of the fiery fur with all the projecting force that an airstone could provide.

Majesty tried to scramble back, throwing Chelseene clear in the process, but Simeon, clever young master that he was, was the one aiming. And it wasn't at either of them. Instead, the super-heated steam turned the ground beneath Majesty into a boiling crater. Gobs of mud clung to Majesty's white fur, weighing her down as she tried to escape the growing quagmire.

She spun her tail desperately, trying to turn the scalding steam into snowflakes. Instead, her power permeated the mud around her, sealing her into a frozen body cast.

"Majesty!" Chelseene screamed. She shot ice ball after ice ball at Fluffy, but between Simeon's strength charms, the power of the airstone, and their shared senses and spells, they always stayed one leap ahead of her.

"Is that all you can do?" Fluffy laughed. He landed next to Majesty's frozen body and pointed his still burning fur at her head. Simeon cast a powerful retrieval spell and, suddenly, Fluffy cradled the comforting heat of the firestone with his tail. Simeon cast a sticking spell to keep it in place.

"Hand over the icestone! Majesty won't survive a direct hit to the head. Not without a bagful of healing crystals."

Majesty meowed mournfully.

Chelseene stopped, fuming. Then, a worryingly calm mask settled onto her face. She walked to the edge of the precipice and pulled something out of her pocket, holding it over the vast expanse of nothing.

"Free her, or the last mushroom goes to the wind."

Fluffy stared, and Simeon, in his head, stared too.

That was the key back to Fluffy's body. To being himself again. His coils, and gliding ribs, and holding his breath for three hours and no fur or legs and ... and ... being him!

In his head, he felt Simeon's emotions, and — shockingly — they mirrored his own.

Simeon wanted Fluffy back. *Him!* Every scaly inch of him. He wanted Fluffy to feel like himself. To ... be happy.

Go ahead, Fluffy. Back down. Simeon said gently.

"How long did it take you to find this patch of transfiguration mushrooms?" Chelseene taunted. "Four years? And then another three to cure them?"

Without those stones, Fluffy argued, *we can't return to Torin. We'll be outcasts, with an incomplete education. If he's angry enough, he'll change the portal passwords and we'll be stuck here forever. Is that what you want?*

Simeon spoke softly in Fluffy's head. *Is this body what you want? Maybe forever?*

I —

Fluffy couldn't think. Couldn't say the words.

Did he want to stay in this body?

Of course not! He wanted to be himself again. Wanted his scales, retractable fangs, Slithering!

But ... that wasn't what he wanted *most.*

Fluffy spun away from Majesty, toward Chelseene. Simeon's magic automatically aligned with Fluffy's intentions. They pulled power from both the air and firestones, creating a hot spinning vortex of air between Fluffy and Chelseene, pulling the girl toward him with a massive magical suction.

She screamed and encased the transfiguration mushroom in a ball of ice, launching it out into the abyss.

"Couldn't you find a way to unhinge my jaws, just a little?" Fluffy wheedled, stretching his mouth. It would hardly fit around one of giant Majesty's toes.

"Sorry, Bud." Simeon checked Chelseene's bonds, then sighed and walked to the edge of the plateau.

"Hmm." Fluffy glared down at the two traitors. Eat one piece at a time? So messy! Why couldn't mammals just swallow things whole, like civilized creatures? Frustrated, he bounded after Simeon, sitting next to him on the edge of the precipice.

The wind channeled through the columns, carrying wispy clouds, debris, and — somewhere — an ice-covered mushroom.

"I'm sorry," Simeon said softly.

"I'm not." Fluffy licked his paw and rubbed it over his face. Then grimaced, realizing what he was doing.

"Why'd you do it?" Simeon asked.

They both knew why he'd done it. They'd been mind-melded. Fluffy couldn't have hidden it if he'd wanted to.

Still, sometimes it's good to hear these types of things out loud.

Fluffy melded their minds, and spoke. *I want my body. But it's not what I want most. I want us. I like us. And us is better when you're not banished to a desolate world with no chance of living your dreams. I only worry ... that you won't like me ... like this. When I'm not me.*

Simeon chuckled. *Fluffy, you are you. No matter what body you wear. Sure, I love your super-cool scales and your retractable fangs. I love 'Bite or Sting!' I also like it when you have claws and I can snuggle your fluffy fur. I like when you rub against my leg and purr. But none of that is you. You are you! And who you are has nothing to do with how you look.*

Fluffy didn't speak. He didn't un-meld their minds, either. They just sat.

Together.

As an us.

And it was enough.

ABOUT THE AUTHOR

Tiffany Chandler was born and raised in Washington state in a large family, where she learned how to run fast and to tell stories —with six brothers and six sisters, how else do you stay out of trouble?

She studied Literary Analysis at Boise State University and hopes she never stops learning. Tiffany now lives in Idaho with her amazing husband, six children, and two inexplicable cats. She loves to cook, read, and go on adventures with her family.

Over the past few years, Tiffany has published a variety of short fiction, from romance to thriller to science fiction to horror, but her passion lies in fantasy. She has published one novel so far.

EARTH, BONDING
KERRI J. ROE

She snuffled around in the moss and grasses, hoping to find a particularly delectable beetle or a nest of eggs. Perhaps even one of those exceptional small, soft creatures that came on the boats with the New Ones from across the water. Their pink toes and noses, the downy fur, the way their long tails slithered down the throat after the satisfying crunch of their delicate bones between her sharp teeth ... Earth sighed happily just thinking about it. Yes, maybe there would be one of those.

The spring wind ruffled her fur, carrying off bits of her shedding winter coat. She shook herself, the delight of the breeze in her underfur enough to make her pause in her hunt. A scent in the crisp air caught her attention. Ears perking, she looked about for its source.

There, a half morning's journey on a distant hill. Something lean, light in color. It seemed to shimmer, like the glint of water when the sunshine hit a ripple. Earth sniffed. Yes. One of those beings, thin ones on two legs. Not the gigantic blockish ones that smelled of earth and rocks; not the lumpy ones whose scent made her bury her nose in the dirt to rid herself of its stench. One of the Hidden People. They had always been on the island, part shadow and part fable, beings who faded in and out of sight. Of course, every fox knew that being unseen was quite different from being not there. She would smell it even if it chose to hide itself.

Earth closed her eyes and breathed deeply. Winter stars and summer berries danced in her nostrils. Spring streams and autumn leaves. And underneath... She cocked her head, considering. The white brush of her fluffy tail, of which she was particularly proud, wrapped around her feet as she sorted smells. This one had a different scent, something intriguing. Like the dancing sky ribbons dappled with snowflakes. From this distance, she could just distinguish the shape of its pale face from its starry hair. The rest of its body had a green covering—not fur; it didn't move like a second skin, but flowed about its limbs in the wind. Earth catalogued the fragrances arising from the distant creature, assessing for danger. It carried none of the long wood pieces that could fly through the air and pierce the body, leaving a fox gasping and waiting for Hel to lead her to the flowered fields of death. Good.

Maybe she should inspect it more closely.

The sound of paw pads on the rocks interrupted her before she could start off. *He's here!* she thought. It had been a long cold season. Her bones didn't hold the warmth like they used to; she had spent an unfortunate amount of time thinking about curling up next to him in their summer den. Stormrain would understand. Of her eight summers, seven they'd spent here, frisking away the winter cold and raising their kits. She watched the rocks on the rise expectantly.

The ears that popped into view were black, not blue-gray. Not Stormrain then. Her tail lowered in disappointment. She chided herself. Their daughter, Sun, had made it back to the family den; she should be happy. She *was* happy—just a little impatient.

With a little yip, Sun approached her mother and nuzzled her, saying, *Hello, Earth*. The name meant mother-fox-with-kits; it was given to her when she had birthed her first litter, and she held it still. Her daughter's belly was already heavy with her own kits. Sun must have found her mate again as soon as the ice began to melt. It had been some weeks since they'd seen each other.

Soon, more feet padded into the den grounds. Sun's mate, Rakki—an agile, brown-colored fox, and some of the siblings and kits from various litters. Their den was old and large; there would be room for all of them. The youngest of them ran through the tunnels, while others waited to pounce on them when their heads popped out of an opening. Earth made her greetings and watched them with half an eye, waiting for her mate's arrival. Dinner was caught; a dozen furry heads bowed over their meals. They stumbled off, yawning, into piles of sleepy blacks, browns, whites, and grays. Darkness covered the land. The black rocks rivaled the sky, and still Stormrain did not come. It was unlike him.

Come in, get warm, Sun coaxed.

Earth twitched her ear. She would wait out here for him. Besides, it was warmer than it had been all winter, when they lived solitary lives outside the den. Sun sighed and went inside. Earth lay down, the scent of the strange being floating through her nostrils as she dozed.

Several days passed. Sun bore her litter—five new kits. Earth had helped with all of Sun's previous litters, but now the many siblings vied for that place. Earth stepped back and let them. The kits were, after a time, tiring; she could perhaps be content just letting them climb over her and curl up to sleep next to her occasionally.

Rakki sniffed out food and shared it with the others; he was young and his sense of smell still sharp. Earth brought food, too, though she avoided the area where the Hidden One had settled down onto its rump and remained unmoving. Earth was determined to show her skulk she had not outlived her usefulness. She was still a hunter. If Stormrain did not come back, she would not seek out a new mate; she would not have more kits. But she could still provide for the family.

"Earth. Eat." Sun pushed some of the meat Rakki had caught toward her. Earth bent and nibbled at it; it was hard enough for Sun with her father missing and a whole new family to care for. Earth remembered how her own mother had wasted away after her father's death; she must try to eat for Sun's sake, despite how Stormrain's absence poached her appetite.

He would come back.

She kept an ear to the voice of the wind, always watching, waiting. Spring winds became summer breezes that carried avian prattle and river gossip, teasing the nose with scents of arctic thyme and sheep sorrel. The tall, thin being that smelled strange and wonderful was still out there, surrounded by tiny blooms of mountain avens, but it never came closer than the next hill.

Earth decided to investigate.

She approached from downwind, the swirls of scent dancing on the breeze. Silent, stealthy, there was no one as skilled at this as she. Nonetheless, she sensed the being sensing her. She was behind it, its fur hanging long and straight and moon-pale down its back. Strange creatures they were, with fur only on their heads, their faces and paws naked to the weather. They didn't grow a thicker coat for the winter, either. With nearly flat faces, just the narrowest ridge of nose between the eyes and expressive slits for mouths, Earth wondered how they caught and devoured their dinner. Surely those clawless paws and flat-edged teeth were useless. The ears, too, almost flat against their heads, oval with a little point at the tip, immobile, inexpressive. Strange.

Earth paused, one forefoot raised in preparation for retreat. Yet the being sat, still as stone. Even the wind dared not disturb its fur. Earth would have thought it dead, but there was no stench of death cloying in the air. Her ears turned forward, her nose worked to ferret out hidden danger. Finding none, she moved forward cautiously, circling on silent feet over the hardened lava and the new green of the velvet moss.

The being—a female of its kind—breathed in slow, steady breaths. Its only other movement was its eyes as it watched Earth's stuttering progress around in front, then back, then around again. Earth moved closer. Still no movement. The being had a scent of spice about it, something sweet but hot that left its taste on the tongue.

It spoke. "Hello, Friend Fox."

Earth skittered away, looking back over her shoulder. She did not need to know more.

AS THE DAYS PASSED, THE KITS NO LONGER NEEDED THEIR mother's milk. Sun and her mate left them daily to get food. The kits wrestled and tumbled about the old lava, falling into shallow holes and laughing as their littermates scrambled to get back out. They practiced their pouncing. First, a pulling together of the muscles, an expectant tightening of the body into a furry ball. A pause. Then a sudden leap high into the air, landing front-end first, front paws and noses working frantically to get at the treat under the ground—or at their siblings. Their aunts and uncles, the ones not busy with their own litters, watched over them in turns.

Still Stormrain had not returned. Earth, no longer needing to kit-sit, wandered farther and farther to look for him. Neither rock nor leaf knew any news of him. Certainty settled on her like a heavy snow.

He would not be back.

She wondered what it was that had gotten him. Was it the cold? Had he not found enough food? She scoffed at the idea. He was a great hunter; he had never failed to provide for his skulk. It had to be something else.

Stormrain had not been her first choice for a mate. As a young vixen, she had admired a tod with a bright coat and swift feet. But the blue-gray fox with warm eyes ran with her, staying by her side rather than proving he could outpace her. He took her to a new place, and they wrestled on black sand next to endless water that spoke in a rhythmic, washing rumble. He brought her delicate, salty treats encased in hard shells that he broke open to reveal iridescent linings. When the cold water chilled her, he lay down beside her and shared his heat.

By the time they returned to the mossy rocks, she was smitten. They selected a place for their den that looked out over the green and black landscape, where the bright line of the water could be seen in the distance. Seven summers, seven litters of kits, and always, he kept pace with her, frolicked with her, and supplied food for the family. Now most of the kits had moved on to their own dens. Earth was grateful that Sun and her family had bonded so strongly and stayed. They provided a buffer from the chasmal loneliness.

So deep was Earth in her thoughts that she didn't realize she was coming up on the strange being's perch until she was within a few feet. *Stupid*, she thought. A fox should always be vigilant.

Just in front of the being was a delicious pile of meat, tern, from the scent of it. Earth licked her chops. Her stomach contracted, reminding her that, despite her intentions, she had not been eating as she should. It had been a long time since she'd had a shorebird. How had the being come by it? It had not left its spot since the fox family had arrived. She wondered how it ate and how it relieved itself. Perhaps it sat in its own filth. Her nose wrinkled in disgust at the thought.

But no, no scents of that sort met her curious nose. Still the starlight and the spice. And now, the meat.

Earth took a tentative step forward. The being looked into the distance, seemingly unaware of her presence. Keeping an eye on it, the fox took another step. And another. One more step...Earth snatched the meat and ran quickly to the next hill. She stopped and looked back at the being. It had not moved. She settled to her meal, holding the largest piece between her paws and tearing off bits with her pointy teeth, all the while keeping her sight on the strange being. She felt a bit deflated. It was not such a thrill to take a meal without a fight. It barely felt earned. Ah well. The meat was delicious, regardless.

And so the season went. Earth played with the kits, but they grew quickly and soon were about their own games. Sun tried to include Earth; still, there is a hollowness in knowing one is a part of things simply because they *ought* to be rather than because they truly belong.

Earth and Stormrain built this den, digging its tunnels with each new litter. And now, she felt out of place in its passages. The kits ran past her in their hurry to get to their business while she pushed herself against the walls. She could nip at them, probably should, so they would remember to respect their elders and their leaders, but she didn't have the heart. Instead, she shuffled along the paths, doing her best to stay out of the way, a white-tailed shadow in the shadows.

The peculiar being stayed in its place. It laid out offerings of meat and eggs more often than not; Earth told herself that she was simply making it feel useful by taking them. None of the others seemed to notice it or care; they certainly didn't seem interested in the delicious treats. Well, that was all right. Their hunting skills were improving; they had plenty of food each day. She did not need to worry overmuch.

The autumn cold came, and Earth crept into the den more often. Soon they would all leave for their winter wanderings. For the first time, Earth was troubled about the icy season. Without the heat of Stormrain's body, her bones had never fully warmed up this summer.

The being had a bit of swan for her this time. Decadent. The birds were generally too big for Earth's kind to get, so it was only when they could scavenge that they got such a treat. This was altogether different, fresh and juicy and without the taint of far-gone death. She settled down where the food had been laid; she no longer feared that the being would harm her or even touch her without her consent.

This time, it spoke, quietly and calmly. "He's not coming back."

Earth's ears lifted and she cocked her head. She knew not this language, yet she understood just the same. How did it know what was so often in her thoughts?

"One of the New Ones got him. I am sorry to tell you this; I came upon it too late to stop them. He was valiant and brave. He carried this for you." The being set out a small object.

The meat in Earth's throat became a rock as she looked at the pale shape. A shell. He had always brought her a shell from the beach at the beginning of den season. She nudged it with her nose. Yes, she could smell it. Behind the spice of the being, behind the salt of the sea. Just a lingering touch of his scent still on it. She lay on her abdomen and rested her chin on the shell, breathing in all that she had left of him. The knowledge had been there, dark and aching and heavy as obsidian, but she had buried it. Now it bloomed, sharp and painful in her chest. A tear slid down the fur on her nose.

The being remained still as her grief carried her in its current. Wind ruffled Earth's fur. It bore the sound of the kits' yips; she barely heard them. She floated in the night sky. She slipped between the stars. She longed for the nuzzle of his nose, just one more time.

After a time, the being's voice came, soft and direct. "Winter comes. I know how the cold hurts your bones; I can feel it. I know, too, the fear of being useless. I am young for my people, yet that fear is not for elders alone." It took a breath. "For eight years, I have felt you. I have known your movements, known your loves and your losses. We are connected. In my language, we call this *fylgja*. Guardian spirit-creature. My people encouraged me to find you and bond you. I did not want to do that. I did not want to take from you your life and your choice. You had the right to it." It looked at Earth, then at the fox family across the way. "It has been a good life. I am glad I did not take that from you."

Earth watched the being intently. There were whispers among the birds and creatures, stories of animals that shared homes and minds with beings who held mysterious powers. Such animals were never completely alone, bearing the consciousness of themselves and their familiar. They lived, not among their own kind, but with the being who bonded them. Some carried messages; others searched out requested items. All were touched by an enchantment that set them apart from the wild creatures.

She had never believed the tales. Perhaps she had been wrong.

The creature's ice-blue eyes met Earth's black ones. "Your time now runs short. Your mate is gone. Your litters have matured beyond your tutelage. I have seen it; you will not last this winter, or maybe next."

Earth blinked. It was the way of things; death was life completed. She thought of more summers without her loving mate. The ache in her chest expanded. She was not sure she wanted to continue on without Stormrain, a burr in the side of her growing family, increasingly unable to hunt, less and less of a contributor and more and more of a weight around their necks as the seasons wound on. Perhaps it was best that this was her last summer.

"That is but one option." The being smiled, a little turning up of the lips. "Ever have I wanted you to be able to make your own choices. Now I offer you another."

The fox twitched her nose. *Death comes for all; there is no choice in that.*

The being bowed her head slightly. "Wise you are, my friend. But like your people, my people are tied to this land. Its lava flows in our veins; its waters form our tears. These New Ones come with new ways. Their history is storm and battle, blood and angry seas. They profess to desire a quiet life; it will be hard for them to calm the rage in their veins."

So they will destroy themselves. Earth swished her tail. *So be it.* If the New Ones had taken her Stormrain, she had no empathy for them.

"It is not so simple," it answered, shaking its head. "Change is coming whether we will it or no. Our part is to protect the land, and to help and guide those who have good in their hearts."

And the rest?

One shoulder lifted, shifting the fall of moonbeam hair. "It will be as it will be. One cannot make choices for another to any good end."

Head tilted, Earth considered the being's words. She had enjoyed the little mice that came on the ships, but the New Ones had already begun cutting down trees where she liked to roam. They crossed the land on two legs, metal axes hanging on their backs, furs of large animals from other lands wrapped around their shoulders. Their language was gruff and loud. They mated roughly and fought endlessly. They took her kin for fur and for food. Nature harvested nature—did not she and her kits eat the eggs and the birds, and the birds feasted on their carcasses when they were gone? But these New Ones did not keep the balance. They did not leave their dead for the wild creatures to be nourished. They did not soften to the stillness of the land.

Her eyes found their way to the next hill. The kits, now half-grown, played and stalked among the black rock and autumn-red moss. Her eyes traced their movements as she addressed the being.

You said choice. What choice?

"My people live long lives. We move between the shadows, hidden unless we wish to be seen. We speak in the whispers of the wind and dance in the music of the waterfalls. I can offer you this, should you choose to bond with me."

Earth huffed. *I am a fox. I already have that.*

A brook of laughter bubbled up from the being. "Yes, you do." Its eyes turned to the kits as well. "But I can also offer you the chance to look out for *them* for many more generations. *That*, you do not have. And a home that is warm all year long, with an open door. You would come and go as you please."

Sun and her mate were returning with a couple of birds for the kits, who crowded around in hungry anticipation. A pang jolted her heart as she thought about not being here to see this next year.

And in return? What do you ask of me?

"That you share your senses. Your keen hearing and sense of smell. Your silent footsteps—for even we Hidden Ones cannot walk as soundlessly as your kind. Your agility. Your companionship."

Earth swung her head to look back at the being. Hidden One as it was, such creatures were known for both their kindnesses and their trickery. Regardless, even they could not hide deceit from the furred ones. Lies had an acrid smell; they burned the nose. It was being truthful.

She looked back at her family.

She had never considered another life beyond this. Exploring and wandering in the winter, loving and living with Stormrain in the summer—there was only that, and then the sleep of After. The world was changing. At one time, Earth's kind had no enemies in this land. They lived undisturbed, limited only by their own lifelines and the amount of food nature provided each year. Now, there were the New Ones and some of the creatures they brought with them—howlers who looked a little like a fox but grew larger and fiercer. Now the dangers grew, and if the being was right, she would not be there to protect her family.

In her bones, she *knew* the being was right.

I will not participate in anything that harms any of my kind.

"Agreed."

And I will not kill for sport or for gain.

"Nor would I."

Sun had stopped in her tussle with the kits and stood on the hill, looking around. A stillness arrested her momentarily when her eyes caught her mother. Earth reassured her with a couple of gekkering yips. They gazed at each other, the matriarch and her daughter, communicating in turns of ears and tips of heads, a hush of silent communication. Sun watched for a moment, a weighted knowing shadowing her eyes. She dipped her head in sorrowful comprehension. Earth dipped hers in return. In love. In farewell.

Then one of the kits bowled into Sun, and she returned to mothering and wrestling.

Earth padded to the being, her heart at once heavy and unfettered. *It is time.*

The being lifted its hand and placed it on Earth's head. Earth's instinct was to back away, but she held strong. A tingling sensation trickled to the tips of her ears and down her neck, to the tips of her toes and tail. Warmth flooded her limbs. Knowledge of many kinds exploded in her mind, and she felt faint. She could feel the being, sense its matching faintness as a second layer between bone and skin.

I am Kaia, the being's voice spoke inside her head.

I am —was Earth. But I am no longer a fox with kits.
Who would you like to be, Earth-no-longer-with-kits?

The fox looked out at the wide world, with its black rock and blue waters and cloud-sanded skies. She thought of the wind that tousled her fur and the waves that carried the shells her mate had brought her without fail. There was a way of things, an ebb and flow. She felt it in her veins, just as she felt the flow of Kaia's veins now, the lift of the woman's chest with each breath. Life comes and it goes. Hope grows and it fades. But still it remains, in little pieces of sand and drops of rain. In the stars and the spring leaves. One just had to hold on. She would hold on. She would remain.

I would like to be Faith.

ABOUT THE AUTHOR

Kerri J. Roe is a writer of lyrical historical fantasy and darkly humorous speculative fiction, both of which like to shapeshift as novels and short stories. Her pen has a mind of its own and often dabbles in poetry, literary fiction, creative nonfiction, and, when it's feeling especially brave, children's stories. Always learning, Kerri is discovering how to embrace being both socially clumsy and social media awkward. She holds a BA in English and Psychology, an M.Ed. in Counselor Education, and is currently working on her MFA in Creative Writing. Kerri lives with her (very patient) family in Alaska, where she spends her time fangirling over books, eating chocolate, and being enticed by the magic of nature.

NOT COMMON:
A FIBONACCI POEM
LOIS T. BARTHOLOMEW

He
lied.
Called me
a common
snapping turtle. Not
common. I can speak with the witch,
even with no vocal cords. I believed the demon.
Bound for life to the enchantress we speak mind to mind.
She loves my ugly face. I lurk
and listen, to warn
of danger.
Watch out!
Move!
SNAP!

ABOUT THE AUTHOR

A lifelong lover of reading, writing, and books, Lois Thompson Bartholomew earned a BA in English from Brigham Young University and an MA in Publishing from Western Colorado University.

Bartholomew is a member of the Society of Children's Book Writers and Illustrators (SCBWI), and the Raleigh, NC based Triangle Association of Freelancers (TAF).

Houghton Mifflin Harcourt published her Young Adult novel *The White Dove*. In 2021 she revised and republished it through her own company, Penn Creek Press.

Bartholomew served as part of the editorial team for the Western Colorado University anthology *Merciless Mermaids: Tails from the Deep*. For seven years the Barron, WI *News Shield* published her parenting column *Mother Matters*. Other publishing credits include *Wisconsin West Magazine*, *The Friend*, *Highlights for Children*, *The New Era*, and *LDS Living online*.

She is proud to add inclusion in the anthology *Feisty Felines and Other Fantastical Familiars* to her list of publications.

THE SECRET OF THE SORCERESS

ALEXANDER HAY

Crackling with eldritch energy, the Sorceress descended slowly from the sky. Clad in billowing robes, her face half covered with a hood, she was a commanding sight. From above, she cast a contemptuous look at the assembled reavers and, with a simple gesture, vaporized them with a volley of lightning that crackled from her fingers.

Turning to the bedraggled defenders of the citadel, she commanded: "Stand firm!" before sweeping aside yet more of the raiders with a blast of electric rage. Then she summoned a great, black-gray cloud, crackling with thunder, and let it float slowly away from her and toward the enemy lines. Lazily, it drifted over the reavers' heads, emitting blasts of lighting and destroying all in its path.

Inspired, the remaining defenders on the battlements rallied to their posts and began loosing arrows at their foes. Within the citadel itself, unshaven sergeants rallied their troops with bold speeches, and nobles readied themselves for one last fight.

"Open the gates!" the Sorceress cried from the sky, still launching lightning bolts at her foes. "They are at bay! Press the advantage!"

The gates creaked open and the defenders surged forward, swords and bills at the ready. What had once been overwhelming numbers of reavers were now scattered and broken by the Sorceress's spells. With a mighty charge, the defenders smashed into their foes, and routed them in a bloody battle. Soon the defenders stood victorious, cheering the Sorceress as she floated above them, storm and lighting crackling around her.

Then she rose into the sky, and into the clouds, disappearing as suddenly as she came, even as the defenders chanted her name.

No one had noticed that her nose had fallen off, or that a large, grumpy mackerel tabby cat had carried it off in his mouth. His name was Pogglesprog—he hated his name—and he was her familiar. Until, of course, she died.

"WELL, THAT WAS SHIT," POGGLESPROG MUTTERED, AS HE SPAT the nose out onto the stone floor of the Sorceress's inner sanctum. This was atop a tower, which hung off the side of a mountain face in a way that defied both reason and physics. It was cold, but at least the views were spectacular.

"I guess the glue didn't work after all..." Pitchdark said with a voice that was both deep yet strangely scratchy. Pitchdark was a small, sharp-featured demoness the Sorceress had once bound. More a cloud of smoldering volcanic dust than a solid thing, Pitchdark hung around mainly because she liked the view (see above), but also because she was good friends with Pogglesprog, who needed the support now more than ever.

"Thing is," Pitchdark continued, "she's not looking too good." She pointed at the (dead) Sorceress, still floating above the ground, having descended through the porthole window in the tower's roof, but now limp and her head flopped to the side. Her empty eyes told a tale or two. She'd been dead for a month.

It was Pogglesprog who cast all the spells, including those that moved the Sorceress's limbs and lips with unseen hands. It was

Pogglesprog who used magic to both create that inspiring voice, and make it appear to be coming from the corpse itself. And it was Pogglesprog who was now wondering how to stop his late mistress from literally falling to bits. What was a (now-unemployed) familiar to do?

"You could always try sewing it back on" Pitchdark said.

"Unless you haven't noticed," Pogglesprog exclaimed, "I don't have any bleeding fingers! And you haven't the strength to pick anything up, so, pray tell, how are we todo that?"

"Calm down, calm down..." Pitchdark soothed, gesturing gently with her hands. "I can still manage to thread the needle for you." She gestured at the sewing kit she'd been able to scavenge, now lain on the floor nearby.

"I can't do this..." Pogglesprog sighed. "It's too much. All of it. The amateur dramatics. The magic. Me picking up bits of dead human. I—I can't endure it anymore."

Pitchdark shifted over to her friend and rested a small smoky hand on his shoulder.

"You know, in a sense, this is the best thing that's happened to you. I mean, in the sense of a crucible of fire. And I know a lot about fire. You've shown your mettle and full potential. I know it's hard, and you're exhausted. But take heart in what you've done so far. I know you can do it!"

For the briefest moment, Pogglesprog bristled at the compliment. But then he softened.

"Thanks, Pitchdark. I—it means a lot."

"With you in charge, all things are possible," Pitchdark said, and she meant it.

"You're right!" Pogglesprog said, as he looked over at the sewing kit. "Pitchdark, thread the needle. I can do this!" he then declared. Obviously, this meant sewing a nose back on with a needle between his lips, but Pogglesprog now realized it could be done.

"That's the spirit!" Pitchdark said, slamming her smoky fist into her other hand. "Let's do it!"

The Sorceress's corpse just floated, and gawped.

POGGLESPROG'S NEXT MISSION WAS TO SAVE THE PRINCE OF Bronze. This was not as easy as one might think, given that the Prince himself had half-merged, half-turned into a dragon and was eating every hero sent to either rescue or slay him. (No one quite knew which was the best solution.)

But then the Sorceress materialized from a storm cloud in the dragon's lair.

"Save me!" the Prince begged, even as his other mouth—a vast, gaping maw in his half-dragon, half-VIP chest—gorged itself on the flesh of the dead.

"Fear not!" the Sorceress declared. "I will rid you of this terrible curse!"

But the part of the Prince that was a dragon was having none of this, and roared in defiance. It spread its mutated wings and smashed out of the cave, up into the sky above.

The Sorceress flew upward through the new hole to meet her foe above, and battle was joined.

"Most would have fled by now..." the dragon cackled, drowning out the Prince's laments. "Do you not fear death? Are you not afraid of what flies before you?"

"I have neither the time nor the inclination to die," the Sorceress quipped, and fired a volley of lightning.

Despite its bulk, the dragon nimbly dogged the attack and replied with a plume of fire. The Sorceress blocked this with a forcefield, before scouring the dragon with a crackling whip of electricity.

The dragon fell to the ground far below. By the time it came to its senses, the Sorceress had already invoked a mighty lightning blast. The dragon barely had time to howl in rage and defiance before it was vaporized...

...Leaving behind a very ragged, shell-shocked Prince in the middle of a very large crater.

Impassive, the Sorceress hung in the air above him.

"Th—thank you?" the ravaged youth finally managed to say.

"The Queen's Knights will be with you soon, your highness," the Sorceress said, coldly. "I bid you farewell."

"B—but...?" the Prince stammered.

She did not hear him as she rose up into the clouds. True, she was dead, so not able to hear anything. But the distance didn't help either.

Nearby, behind a rocky outcrop, Pogglesprog finally let himself roll over onto the ground in utter exhaustion. This had been a tough one.

"AH, YOU'RE BACK!" PITCHDARK SAID, AS THE CAT TRUDGED into the main atrium. Above them, the dead Sorceress hung in the air, floppy like a puppet without its puppeteer.

"I need a sleep," Pogglesprog yawned.

"And you've earned it, friend," Pitchdark said.

"Yeah, but we've still got to work out what to do about the smell..." Pogglesprog sniffed.

Pitchdark's sense of smell wasn't as keen as Pogglesprog's, what with all the sulfur and soot, but even she could acknowledge there was a growing problem. It wasn't as if the insects weren't enough of an issue.

"We could always use mellification..." Pitchdark suggested, trying to be helpful.

"Yeah, but we'd have to keep pulling her out of a giant jar of honey whenever she's needed." Pogglesprog sighed. "And that would attract wasps."

"I hate wasps..." Pitchdark grimaced.

"Everyone hates wasps," Pogglesprog said. "Even the beings of the OuterDusk hate bleeding wasps. And do you know why?"

"Wasps are bastards," Pitchdark agreed. In a world of upheaval, madness and magic, this was one of the few true constants.

"So, mellification is out of the question," she continued. A shame. The demon had hopes.

"Also, where would we find all that honey?" Pogglesprog muttered, looking up at his dead and increasingly smelly ex-mistress. "There are so many better things one can do with bee secretions...

"And then there's the jar, Pitchdark," Pogglesprog added, shaking his head while absent-mindedly licking his paw. "I don't think they do jars that big."

"None of this is very practical," Pitchdark tutted.

It was at that point that the Sorceress's foot fell off.

AND YET STILL THE SORCERESS WAS NEEDED, WITH OR without her foot. When the Sea Maidens of the West Coast shed their beautiful hair and embraced their inner sharks, it was the Sorceress who drove them off and protected the fisherfolk of Northport.

When the evergreen trees of the High Forest shed tears of sap and begged mercy from the axes of the reavers, it was the Sorceress who came to their aid.

And when the House of Thorns was about to rip itself apart in open battle, it was the Sorceress who descended from the sky and threatened dire consequences if this family feud caused any more bloodshed.

Well, in truth, it was all really Pogglesprog. And while he found the work tiring, he also found himself ever more up to the task, his own magic growing ever more powerful and accomplished. He even learned how to teleport back to the tower. It saved on walking.

"WILL YOU PISS OFF!" POGGLESPROG SUDDENLY exploded. At the flies. The sodding flies. They were buzzing around the Sorceress, and the atrium, with some enthusiasm.

"I do have some good news," Pitchdark said. "I've recruited outside help."

Pogglesprog screeched in horror, his first language briefly surfacing. But he soon remembered how to speak again.

"Outside help? Pitchdark, I value your insight and friendship, but aren't we supposed to be keeping this under our hats?"

"Not to fear, friend..." Pitchdark soothed. "I have carefully vetted our new employee."

"Our new employee?"

"Afternoon, my lovlies!" a slightly old, somewhat wonky voice echoed. "I'm looking forward to my first day in service."

A dumbfounded Pogglesprog looked over his shoulder at the strange, stocky old woman who had just walked in. She looked like a birds' nest had come alive, married a scarecrow, and then exploded in a war.

"Who the buggering hell is this, Pitchdark?" Pogglesprog exclaimed.

"Oh, her name is Mildred. She came highly recommended."

"By whom?"

"The Demonic Grapevine. We do talk still, y'know."

"But she is a mad old bat! I mean, look at her."

Pogglesprog turned apologetically to his new employee.

"Sorry, Ms. Mildred, but you are indeed, strictly speaking, mad, and an old bat."

"Oh, I don't mind." Mildred smiled inanely. "It's not done me any harm yet. I am, in fact, the maddest old bat in my county!"

"How can she help us?" Pogglesprog hissed, turning to Pitchdark.

"Pogglesprog, Mad Old Bats are both reliable and highly versatile. Also, you don't get to her age and not be able to keep a few secrets."

"Bollocks to it all," a resigned Pogglesprog sighed. "So,

Mildred, I'm sure Pitchdark has filled you in on our, ahem, 'problem.'"

"I guess you mean her up there?" Mildred pointed. "The dead one."

"Yes, indeed. The dead one. She reeks of encroaching decay. Any ideas?"

"Well, you could always embalm her," Mildred suggested.

Pogglesprog nearly had a stroke at this point.

"Embalm her?" he roared. "How are we going to convince everyone she's alive if she stinks of formaldehyde? It doesn't smell of perfume, apples, and fairy farts, you know!"

("He's going through a rough time,") Pitchdark whispered to Mildred.

("Ah, the male menopause.") Mildred nodded. She'd seen it all before, though this was her first time with a talking cat.

"Look at the state of her!" the late Sorceress's familiar snarled. "I've used every chronomantic spell in the book, and she's still going manky. Entropy is about to throw a brick through our window and crap on our carpet!"

But while Pitchdark winced, Mildred was instead in deep thought.

"Well, if it's the smell you're worried about, I suggest a few herbal tricks I know. For preserving meat. Also, have you ever considered ice?" she asked.

"That would damage her flesh!" Pogglesprog glowered.

"Ah, but if you treat her with wheat spirits first, you can keep her on ice, as it were, without any freezing," Mildred proposed. "Add my herbs, and she'll last for a lot longer!"

She then pulled out a large, bulging bag out from the many layers of rags she wore.

"Makeup bag," Mildred explained. "I do everyone's, back home. Even the Squire asked me to sort his daughters out for their weddings."

"I guess she does need a bit of...rouge?" a wide-eyed Pogglesprog realized. "Plus foundation."

"Her nails could do with a coat of varnish too," Mildred

added. "Once we've chilled her out and rubbed in the booze and herbs, I mean. Also, where's her right hand gone?"

"RIGHT HAND?" Pogglesprog squeaked. He'd only just noticed.

"Shit," Pitchdark murmured. "I knew that bit was hanging off."

THE LAST OF THE STORM GIANTS STAGGERED MINDLESSLY forward, goaded by huge, bald monsters who were still dwarfed by the living weapon's stature. Before it, a procession of decadent priests in silk and gold, with ritual scars and maddened eyes, guided their God forth to war. Around his feet scurried zealots, true believers, and the lost. Whatever the Storm Giant did not smash with its mighty hands and kicks, it destroyed with tornados, storms, and floods. As the procession drew closer to the capital, it became clear only one group of people could stop them.

They were met on the plains by an alliance of mages, including the Sorceress. A savage battle ensued, as mage, cultist, near-giant, and the Storm Giant itself laid waste to each other. The carnage was horrendous as foes tore each other apart with magic, blades, hammers, and their bare hands. The battlefield was soon soaked with blood of many strange and unusual shades, from red to green to black to gold.

In the end, it was the Sorceress and the Grand Diabolist who managed to stop the Storm Giant, overloading its body with electricity and crackling purple magic and causing the huge being to explode, destroying most of its followers in the process. The rest, realizing their God was dead, fled in terror or gutted themselves on the spot. Of the Mages' Alliance, only a few still drew breath. The Sorceress, of course, didn't breathe at all.

The morning after, the Grand Diabolist walked across the devastated battlefield with the Sorceress. She looked younger, but in truth both were in their autumn years, and the Diabolist remembered their youth, and its promise.

"Please," he begged her. "Let us admit our love for one another. Let us set aside our duties and our calling. Let us live, if only for a while. My heart is heavy, and old. I fear being alone. I know you fear it too. Let us live, and love, at last."

"That part of me is very much withered," the Sorceress appeared to say, her face shadowed by the hood. "Were I to take you up on your kind offer, would you know the passion you have always dreamt of? That sweet young girl died a while ago. All that remains is this austere husk."

"Do not say that, I beg you," the Diabolist cried. "If any part of that young fool remains, please—I beseech you, let me be foolish with you too."

"The fool is gone," the dead Sorceress said, flatly. Gracefully, she rose into the sky. Behind her, the Diabolist fell to his knees and held his head in his hands.

"Fool that I am, that is true," he mourned. "I thought my regrets could be undone. I should not have waited so long. No, I should not ..." The man who had helped slay a God began to weep. Then, still kneeling, he threw his head back, purple energy exploding from his hands, and screamed to the heavens.

"LOVE? SPEAK NOT TO ME ABOUT LOVE! WHAT A DREADFUL CURSE IT IS!" he cried. "A CURSE!"

"This is all getting very strange," said the talking cat, hiding in an illusory shrub nearby.

For a while, little of note happened. With Mildred's help, the Sorceress's corpse was preserved, or at least its decay was slowed down enough for the charade to continue. Pogglesprog continued to learn from the Sorceress's library. And Pitchdark handled the admin.

But then word reached the tower of a new threat. The Spine Baron, they called him, an old knight slain and reanimated only to destroy his master and take his place. Now, he led an army of disciplined, well-armed skeletal minions, slowly but methodically sweeping all aside as they neared the kingdom's borders.

With the surviving mages distracted with other matters, it fell on the Sorceress to stop this threat. Or rather, Pogglesprog.

"WE HAVE A SITUATION," POGGLESPROG MUTTERED AS HE padded into the atrium. "That sodding Spine Baron is on the loose, and we're the poor bastards who have to stop him."

But Pitchdark didn't answer. She was up in the air, busily appraising Mildred's latest handiwork on the late Sorceress.

"Pitchdark?" Pogglesprog called up to the demoness. "Is anything the matter?"

"On the contrary," a stunned Pitchdark managed to say. "See for yourself!" She pulled back the sleeve on the Sorceress's robe, revealing the now reattached hand that had caused them so much trouble before.

"My, Mildred must be a magician in her own right!" Pogglesprog exclaimed. "Look at that suture work! You'd barely know anything was amiss!"

"And she's modified the robes so they hide the Sorceress a little more. But not so much as to attract suspicion ..." Pitchdark said. "She thinks of everything, and—"

"Ah," Pogglesprog said, noticing a problem. "Mildred?"

"Hello, Mr. Pogglesprog!" Mildred called from the kitchen, where she had been drinking elm tea. "Anything the matter?"

"May I ask a question about ... *the new eyes*?"

"Oh, of course," Mildred said, wiping her hands on her dress as she shuffled out of the kitchen and into the main atrium. "What's the matter?"

"Well ..." said Pogglesprog, reluctantly," they're a bit ... anomalous?"

"What do you mean?"

"I mean they are obviously glass eyes. One's bigger than the other. The irises are blatantly different colors. Also, she's now cross-eyed."

"Ah, placeholders," Mildred replied.

"Placeholders?" Pogglesprog gasped.

"Oh yes, Mr. Pogglesprog. I've got a glasssmith from Boarstusk working on the proper replacements, but quality takes time. It might be a week or so. Is that a problem, Mr. Pogglesprog?"

"Err, no, of course not, Mildred," Pogglesprog gulped. "You've done a marvelous job. Please, don't let me interrupt your tea break any longer!"

"Right you are!" Mildred said, returning to the kitchen. "Call me if you need anything!"

"We're going to have to do this on our own, aren't we?" Pitchdark said, nervously.

"Shite," Pogglesprog replied. He knew Pitchdark was right.

THE SPINE BARON LED HIS DEAD TROOPS FORWARD UPON A steed barded in splint, as per the old fashion. This was only fitting. The steed, defleshed, its bones polished and lightly embellished with funerary carvings, dated back to those days.

For his part, the Spine Baron was clad head to foot in a patchwork suit of steel plate, with parts from across the centuries. It was weathered, but clean. At his side, along with his shield, he had an ancient, long, straight sword, pulsing with dirty red power.

Behind the Spine Baron, columns of heavy infantry. Pikemen, crossbowmen, swordsmen. Siege engines. Cavalry. All dead for centuries. All picked clean of flesh by crows, by insects, by the elements, and by time. A relentless army of bone.

Then the Spine Baron halted. A strange sight greeted him on the road ahead.

A small smoke demon, looking rather nervous. And a mackerel tabby cat, looking very, very grumpy.

"You don't have to hang around," Pogglesprog said to his friend.

"Look, I know I'm bricking it, but I won't leave you to face this alone," Pitchdark said.

"Hang on," Pogglesprog whispered. "What's that big, dead bastard doing?"

The Spine Baron had commanded his dead troops to halt with a gesture of his hand. They now stood still and silent, and only the faint wail of the wind was heard. It whistled through the gaps in their bones and armor. Such a sinister tune.

The Spine Baron trotted up to the cat and the smoke demon, stopping a short distance away. He dismounted, leaving behind his shield, took off his sword, knelt down on one knee, and raised an open hand; a gesture of truce.

"What is he up to?" Pogglesprog muttered.

The Spine Baron regarded the pair. Despite the empty sockets of a skull glaring at them, Pogglesprog and Pitchdark felt strangely...calm.

"I have questions," a deep, rasping voice declared.

"And if we care not to answer them?" Pogglesprog sneered.

"I do not demand. Rather, I ask. Humbly."

Pogglesprog frowned. He was ready for a fight, to throw every last spell at these abominations. But all of a sudden, diplomacy seemed the better option.

"Very well," he replied. "Ask away."

"The demon is to go."

"No, she is my confidante. Would you make a friend break their vow?"

"I would not. So then, let me ask my first question. What is your name?"

"Pogglesprog."

The familiar expected cold, callous laughter. Instead, the dead thing before him tipped its head to the side, as if curious.

"Who on earth called you that, Pogglesprog?"

"She did. My former mistress. She found it...amusing. As I was bound to her, I could not reject it."

"Oh, so you are the great Sorceress's familiar," the Spine Baron asked.

"Was."

"She is not here?" the Spine Baron enquired. "And yet you are instead? Has she...died?"

"Let's just say she won't be inconveniencing us with her presence," Pogglesprog sneered.

The Spine Baron made a realization.

"Did you even like her, Master Pogglesprog?" he asked.

"No, she was a total cow," Pogglesprog glowered. "She was cruel, arrogant, contemptuous. Anything to raise a laugh amongst herself and her shitbag social circle. Every failure was my fault. I was kicked, pinched, prodded, and mocked constantly. I was the butt of every joke, the target of every rage."

"And as her familiar, you could not resist?"

Pogglesprog said nothing.

"Well, I mean, her calling you 'Pogglesprog' in the first place was a giveaway," Pitchdark muttered, and the Spine Baron slowly nodded in agreement.

"I was glad when she died," Pogglesprog continued. "I felt nothing but ..." He took a deep breath. "... *happiness* when I saw her corpse. That cruel, big head of hers, transfixed with a crossbow bolt. Those empty, stupid eyes. I never felt so happy as when I knew I was free of her. She deserved it. Everyone saw a hero, but I knew the monster."

"And yet, she still appears to live."

"I operate her corpse, like a puppet, to maintain the illusion that she still lives. Not through choice. But because she is still needed. Or at least, the *idea* of her."

"Should she not be exposed for what she was?" the Spine Baron said.

"Humans," Pogglesprog replied.

"I beg your pardon?"

"Humans. You know. It wasn't enough for people to be saved. They had convinced themselves that they needed her. I mean, not just for what she could do. Or appear to do. But also as a symbol. They wouldn't believe a cat could save them."

"And so you made the best of a dire situation," the Spine Baron said.

"Humans love to be lied to," Pogglesprog said. "But they have to be the right sort of lies."

"The right sort for humans, which isn't saying much," Pitchdark sighed.

The Spine Baron nodded. Then he paused, still as a statue. Pogglesprog realized the dead man was deep in thought.

"I have one question," he then asked. "Why not just bring her back, as one of the undead, like me?"

"I hope you don't mind me saying," Pogglesprog said, "But necromancy has a tendency to deprave and corrupt. And there was always a chance she'd come back with some or all of her faculties intact. The thought of her as a Lich..."

"I take no offense, Master Pogglesprog," the Spine Baron replied. "Indeed, the thing about Undeath is that it either makes you hate the life you no longer have, or see it from a different angle. I am inclined to the latter. I suspect that would not be the case for your mistress."

"Then why attack this kingdom?" Pogglesprog frowned.

"Lacking a pulse does not mean lacking ambition," the Wight Knight shrugged. "I freely admit that this land is as tempting to me as any other would-be conqueror. Yet why do you, with all your cynicism (if I may be so bold), stand so firm in defending it?"

"Humans are craven and foolish," Pogglesprog muttered. "If we cats left them to their own devices, they'd all be dead within a week. 'Twas ever thus."

The Wight Knight nodded. "I must admit to being guilty of that myself, in my mortal life. That is part of the reason why I am as I am, of course."

Pogglesprog nodded. "So, unliving one, are we to fight this day?"

"No," the Spine Baron said. "I freely admit you have amused

me in some ways, and impressed me in others. There is no honor in fighting a good man. Err, I mean, cat. You get my meaning. We will venture elsewhere instead."

The Spine Baron rose to his feet and turned to his host of skeleton warriors. Without a word, they turned 180 degrees and began to slowly march and shamble away. The Spine Baron then summoned his steed, mounted it, and made to follow his army. But before this, he turned to Pogglesprog and addressed him one last time.

"I have enjoyed our discussion today. Perhaps we will continue it some other day? Under the flag of truce, of course."

He bade his steed forward and raised a bony hand of farewell as he galloped forth.

"Farewell, good knight," Pogglesprog said.

"This counts as a victory, I guess?" Pitchblack said.

"Well, no one's died who hasn't died already ..." Pogglesprog replied. "Shall we get back to the tower?"

"What about his horse, though?" Pitchdark said, wide eyed. "Talk about having a 'mare."

BACK AT THE TOWER, MILDRED WAS UP A LADDER, FINISHING off her latest makeover of the dead Sorceress, still floating in her usual place. She looked over her shoulder at Pogglesprog and Pitchdark as they teleported into the atrium.

"Did it go well?" Mildred asked.

"It turned out the undead conqueror was a most reasonable fellow," Pogglesprog reported. "We had a chat and sorted it out. You'd probably like him."

"Well, it's the live ones you've got to be scared of," Mildred said, finishing the last application of blusher to the dead face. "In my experience."

"Very true, Mildred," Pogglesprog said. "All in all, a successful day."

"I've got dinner on," Mildred added.

LATER THAT EVENING, AFTER MILDRED HAD GONE TO BED. (She was an early riser.) Pogglesprog and Pitchdark sat looking up at the dead Sorceress, pondering how it had all unfolded.

"Sooner or later, we've either got to get her stuffed or excarnated," Pogglesprog said. "In the case of the latter, she'll have to start wearing an ornate mask and gloves. Mildred's looking into it already."

"I hate all this," Pitchdark said.

"Yeah, even when she's dead, the bitch is still causing us problems. And this kingdom still needs its heroine, and her magic." Pogglesprog sighed.

"It's a pain, isn't it?" Pitchdark sighed.

"Yep, and that's the human condition for you," Pogglesprog grunted. "All for truth until it gets inconvenient. Then, it's smoke and mirrors."

"The usual bollocks," Pitchdark tutted.

"Speaking of which …" Pogglesprog muttered, before burying his head in his bottom, lathering tongue at the ready. (This was one of the advantages of being a cat.)

Pitchdark shook her head in disdain. "I have such admiration for you. But you still disgust me sometimes."

"Good," Pogglesprog managed to say.

Then the Sorceress's head fell off.

ABOUT THE AUTHOR

Alexander Hay's first cat was Millie. Misgendering aside, Millie was also a total bastard. He would use the author as a climbing frame, which hurt. When he wasn't doing this, he would piss and crap everywhere. He was a victim of society.

Next was Manami, a charismatic diva of a tuxedo cat. She had three legs, leading to the author's wife's grandmother to wonder why there weren't any four legged ones available. Notable for the surprisingly large number of people who could not pronounce her name, she was also a massive catnip stoner and reviewed several heavy metal albums for a web site.

Alexander's current cat is Willow, a petite female ginger tabby, as opposed to most ginger tabbies, who are hulking brutes called Dave. Willow has a nuclear blast furnace metabolism and demands to be fed on a minute by minute basis. They live in North West England.

SINK OR SWIM
REBECCA M. SENESE

The house looked like a typical witch's house. Gray, uneven stone outlining the squat, squarish body. A black tiled peaked roof. Gray stone chimney belching smoke into the late autumn air. Green, creeping vines curled around the foundation and inched up the walls, outlining the tall, narrow windows that peeked into the single-story house. Not that anyone could see inside, with those black curtains pulled tight.

Not the sort of place Golda had ever imagined herself being assigned, but when you were in the lower percentile of the class, you took what they gave you.

And shut up about it. Even when it looked wholly unsuitable.

Besides, no one else in her family had ever gotten this far in Familiar Training. All Golda had to do was survive the nine-month placement, and she would graduate as a real, honest-to-goodness familiar.

Her little heart beat even faster, and she relieved her nerves the way she always did. Rushing in a circle around her bowl, fins waving, tail thrashing.

Just a few circles to burn off some energy, not enough to churn the water to spilling over the top. Then she slowed as the courier approached the door. The thudding of his hand on the wood echoed the pounding of her heart.

The door creaked open. The smell of sage and jasmine wafted out, strong enough for Golda to smell it in her water. A long-fingered, skeletal hand gestured forward.

Golda felt the water in her bowl slosh as the courier thrust her toward the hand. For a moment, she thought he would let go, and she would fall or be forced to try a spell on the fly to catch herself, but the hand thrust forward, clutching the base of her bowl.

Behind her, she heard the pounding footsteps as the courier fled.

Then, even before Golda could turn in her bowl to watch the courier, the hand snatched her inside and slammed the door shut.

The golden light from the afternoon sun disappeared, replaced by a dim glow. Golda managed to make out walls covered in tapestries before a face thrust itself against the side of her bowl.

Huge, dark eyes peered at her, narrowing as they studied her long, goldfish body. The face had a sallow complexion. Dark circles smudged under her eyes. The nose was long and narrow with an almost clichéd hook at the end. Wiry gray hair trailed to her shoulders.

"What the Hecate are you?" the witch asked. Her voice was a deep rumble.

Golda resisted the urge to race around in a circle. This was to be her witch for the next nine months. She had to show that she could be a good familiar.

Focus. She might not be able to speak like other familiars, but she was excellent at telepathy.

I am Golda, apprentice familiar, sent for my placement.

"A goldfish," the witch said. "You gotta be kidding me. How the Hecate can you be a familiar to me?"

I know all the required spell work and can provide all necessary assistance and support.

"Hmph. We'll see about that."

The face pulled away, and Golda felt herself being carried forward. She caught a better look at the room, large with overstuffed furniture, dark wood end tables covered with black knit doilies, and a lamp with dark shades spewing reddish light.

Then, they were in a long hallway of dark wood. A thick floor runner covered the hardwood floor, thicker than it looked, since Golda couldn't hear the tapping of the witch's shoes.

A creaking sounded. Golda caught a glimpse of a tall, narrow door, then a flat surface, a table with some folded fabric tucked at the end.

Wait, not a table. There was another surface just above it and another below.

A shelf.

A shelf with linens on it.

Wait a minute!

Golda raced around in her bowl to face the witch, but she already felt the familiar vibration of her bowl being set down. She caught a glimpse of the side of the witch's face as the closet door swung shut in her face.

A closet! The witch had shoved her into a dark closet.

The only way to burn through the shame was to swim round and round and round in the darkness inside the closet.

IT TOOK SEVERAL HOURS, BUT FINALLY, GOLDA SETTLED herself. Okay, not a great start, but she could prove herself. It was just going to be a challenge, was all. With enough concentration and a full-body spell, Golda would be able to enchant the door to open, even to slam open to get attention.

She gulped in air and shoved it through her gills. Okay, ready now.

She focused.

Before she could even begin the incantation, the door swung open.

The dim light blinded Golda. She shook her head, trying to clear her vision.

A large shadow. No, not a shadow. A shape. With another shake of her head, Golda could see better.

The witch stood in the doorway.

"So you were actually assigned ta me," she said, her voice a low, indignant growl. "Can't think what I did to deserve a damn fish for a training familiar, but here ya are."

Her long, spindly fingers reached forward, and Golda felt herself being lifted out of the closet.

This time, she ended up back in the living room, set on an end table with a view of the front door. Beside her, there was a large, dark purple armchair. An even layer of dust told Golda that either the witch didn't clean very often or this chair was never used.

Sure enough, the witch crossed the living room to settle into a dark red armchair that sat closer to the fireplace against the far wall. She flicked her hands, and a pair of knitting needles rose up from the wicker basket tucked in beside her chair. With a soft clicking sound, the needles began to work as they floated in the air in front of her.

Golda could help with that. She was very good with fine, delicate magic. It was one of her specialties. She wasn't good with the big, flashy, showy magic but excelled at small, fine work.

As the knitting needles continued to work, the witch leaned forward and waved a hand at the fireplace. Deep inside the black cavern, a fire sprang up, sending golden light into the room as the flames flickered along the bottom of a black cauldron.

The witch began selecting small bottles from the tray set on top of the end table beside her.

May I assist you? Golda sent the words to the witch.

The witch didn't even bother to turn toward her but gave a dismissive grunt and shake of the head.

And so began Golda's haphazard apprenticeship.

THINGS DIDN'T IMPROVE MUCH OVER THE NEXT FEW MONTHS. Although she had a better view than being shut in the closet, such a view only showed Golda what she wasn't participating in.

The witch did most of her potion-making in the black cauldron set into the fireplace. Over time, Golda realized that the blackness of the mantle was more from soot than the actual color of the marble.

She continued to offer her assistance to the witch, who continued to ignore her offers, usually with a dismissive grunt. That was if she bothered to acknowledge Golda's presence at all. Fortunately, she set a box of fish food behind the bowl, so Golda could easily spell some to trickle into her bowl at regular intervals. She also knew a strong enough spell to keep her water clean, as the witch showed no inclination to clean it for her.

Really showed no inclination to have anything to do with Golda at all. It appeared that although Golda was officially her apprentice familiar, the witch wasn't going to bother with even the slightest training.

So Golda was going to have to do it herself.

As the witch created her potions, Golda focused on identifying them. She was too far away to see the ingredients the witch tossed into the cauldron, but she could smell each one, the spicy and sweet, the bitter and pungent. She began to discern how they mixed and mingled and, over time, started to learn when they were working and when they weren't. She could almost taste the way the magic sifted through her water as the aromas drifted across the living room.

Then, one afternoon, before she realized it, she sent a suggestion to the witch.

A pinch more eye of newt. The spell is slightly off.

The witch's shoulders jerked. Her head swung around, and for the first time since Golda had arrived, the witch speared her with her dark eyes.

"What did you say?" she snapped.

Golda hovered in her bowl. She wanted to dart away and

swim in circles but stayed hovering. The witch was talking to her, paying attention to her. She had to find a way to take advantage.

Eye of newt, Golda sent. *You need to add a pinch more to counteract the grave's dirt or the spell will sour. It is on the edge of turning.*

The witch frowned, her face wrinkling even more than normal. She stood up and gave a grunt that sounded like dismissal, but Golda noticed how she stood in such a way as to hide the cauldron.

And her arm moved as if she was tossing something into it.

She *had* listened, and she *had* taken Golda's advice.

That was something. Wasn't it?

But nothing changed. If anything, the witch ignored her even more, hardly bothering to grunt an acknowledgment.

Nine months of this. How was Golda going to learn anything? And once it was over, where was she going to find a magic user that would take her as a familiar? It was hard enough being a goldfish, but being one who comes out of the apprenticeship with no improvement or skills lowered her odds to zero.

She had to do something to get the witch to take her seriously.

She stayed awake all night, swimming round and round, trying to figure it out.

Meanwhile, the witch continued making potions and spells during the day, ignoring Golda completely.

As the months passed, Golda started to see the pattern of the witch's work. She spent her days brewing potions that she stoppered into dark brown bottles. Once every few weeks, a courier would come to the door, and the witch would hand over a box of well-packed potions. Then she would start again.

Obviously, she was the supply side of a magic shop somewhere and doing well with it.

Until she wasn't.

One blustery fall day, a loud banging sounded on the door. The witch jolted up from her armchair. The knitting needles clattered to the floor as she turned her attention to the door.

The banging sounded again.

Golda peered at the door. She couldn't see who was behind it but could feel their anger and annoyance. Someone was upset with the witch. She started to send a warning, but the witch gathered her skirts and stomped to the door, muttering under her breath.

She yanked the door open.

A towering man in a navy trenchcoat stood in the doorway. Water dripped from his gray hair and gray beard. Dark, bushy brows were drawn together, creating an angry crease on his forehead.

"Your potions have gone bad," he said. "The whole last two batches have been a mess. I've had numerous complaints of side effects or them not working at all. I'm canceling your contract."

The witch reached out to the man. "Regelius, come in out of the rain and sit. Let's talk about this."

"There's nothing to talk about, Minerva. I've given you enough chances. You've lost your touch, and I'm losing business. It's over."

He turned to go, heading back into the rain when the witch grabbed his arm.

"Please, one more chance, Regelius. The next box will be perfect, and I won't charge you for it. Just give me one more chance."

The man hesitated, glanced back over his shoulder.

"The whole box free?"

The witch nodded. "Yes, the whole box."

"One week," he said. "You supply a box of twenty potions in one week, and all of them work perfectly, or we're done for good."

He stomped off before the witch could respond.

She stood in the doorway for several minutes, letting rain dampen the floor around her. With each passing moment, her shoulders sagged lower.

Finally, she closed the door and shuffled back into the living room, her head bowed. From her vantage point on the end table, Golda could still see the witch's face clearly and noticed the tears in her eyes.

Obviously, creating the potions meant everything to her.

And now she was on the verge of losing it.

The witch shuffled past Golda and dropped into her red armchair. For a moment, she stared into the fireplace and then covered her face with her hands.

Golda swam around her bowl. The thick feelings of dismay coming off the witch buffeted her like waves in the water. She slowed, letting herself drift until she could see the witch again.

Her hands shook as she held them to her face. Golda hadn't noticed that before.

Maybe there was a reason she used magic to work the knitting needles. Not just to make the scarves and hats that lay in a pile beside her chair but trying to train her own magic for fine, delicate work.

The kind of work a trembling hand couldn't do anymore.

The kind needed for exacting potion work.

The kind Golda excelled at.

If only she could convince Minerva the witch to let her try.

Before she could gather her thoughts to send them, the witch stood up and stormed out of the room. Her footsteps stomped off down the hall. A door slammed.

Leaving Golda alone in the living room.

With the cauldron still tucked onto the fire.

Could she? Golda swam in a circle around the bowl, peering at the living room anew. Bags and bottles of all sorts of ingredients were scattered around the room. They were too far for her to read what they were, but she had spent months sensing and smelling the ingredients. She could even tell when the potions had gone sour.

Could there be a way for her to make them or at least make one?

Then she could show Minerva her worth, show the witch that Golda could help.

And together, they could complete all twenty in a week.

All Golda had to do was create one.

And she knew just which one. A healing balm that had a hint

of cinnamon to it. Only a few ingredients that Golda was sure she could tell by taste and smell.

And it was going to take all her magic.

She started to swim around the bowl again, gaining speed. Faster and faster, around and around. The tapestries and furniture blurred into a swirl of color.

The water began to warm, to rise like steam. Golda swam faster, felt herself lift up, riding the waves.

Gathering herself.

She leapt.

She soared into the air, waving her tail as a wave of water arced around her.

Toward the small brown bag tucked beside the knitting needles.

As she dropped closer, she angled a fin into the bag, scooping up a smidge of brown thistles. With a twisting, she yanked her fin up toward the ceiling. The thistles flew into the air.

Nudging the brown flecks, she focused them into the cauldron and let them drop inside before she landed back in her bowl with a splash.

The effort was exhausting. Her tail moved sluggishly; even her fins wavered in the water.

But that was just one ingredient. She had at least three more to go.

She could do it.

She gulped water, flushing it through her gills, filling herself with oxygen. It gave her a boost of energy—enough for another dash around the bowl.

And another leap into the air.

This time, she aimed for a bottle on the end table on the other side of the red armchair. A few drops of the yellowish, sour liquid dribbled into the cauldron before Golda had to land back in the bowl.

Fatigue dragged at her, but she couldn't let it stop her. Halfway through and then the potion could simmer. By that time, the witch would have returned, and she would see what Golda had done.

Would realize how Golda could help her.

Just another two ingredients. Just two more.

Bigger effort this time. Her tail swept strong by pure will—her jump barely cresting the edge of the bowl, but the powder she aimed for was closer, in a shallow bowl on a table beside the fireplace. As she swooped around, she was able to brush a fin over the surface of the bowl and splash it into the cauldron.

Final ingredient.

Her whole body moved sluggishly through the water as she tried to gain some speed for another leap. It wasn't just physical fatigue; she could feel her magic waning as well.

Even if she got this final ingredient, some beige flakes that made her think of bland fish food, without the proper incantations and stirring, the ingredients wouldn't mingle correctly. The healing balm wouldn't work.

Had she miscalculated her ability to do this? She was only a goldfish, only an apprentice familiar. She didn't have her full magical ability.

And if she didn't complete this, didn't gain Minerva's trust and help in her apprenticeship, Golda would never make it, would never become a successful familiar.

She had to do it. She had to show that she could be just as good a familiar as any cat or raven. Better even, because no one expected a goldfish to be a good familiar.

But she would be, oh yes, she would be.

Determination gave her a burst of energy, and she used it to gain momentum around her bowl. The water churned, started to steam.

She leapt.

Soared toward the fireplace and the final ingredient in a bottle on the mantle.

She swung her tail and tipped the bottle just enough to send a flurry of flakes raining down into the cauldron. Then another twist, and she straightened the bottle.

It rocked back and forth. Her fin brushed the side to steady it. The bottle rocked once more.

Then clipped the edge of her fin.

Pain jolted her. She yanked her fin out as the bottle shifted again, then settled. Freed from it, the sharpness of the pain settled into a dull ache, one she would deal with when she reached her bowl.

Oh, no, her bowl!

She was at the wrong angle to swoop back to her bowl, already falling at the end of her arc.

Glimpsing the rug beneath her.

Without water to assist her, she could die on the floor, flopping away before the witch found her and returned her to her bowl.

And an apprentice familiar dying on her watch would only seal her fate along with the ruined potions.

Golda twisted in the air and, with a final burst of energy, rolled over the edge of the cauldron.

And splashed into the middle of the dark potion.

Brownish liquid closed over her head. She could feel the grit scrape along her body. Her fins sent swirls around her as she struggled to swim in the thick mixture.

Already, she could feel it sticking to her, making it hard to move. Even the swish of her great tail felt sluggish.

Had this been a mistake? Was she going to die in the middle of this potion?

Oh, what a fool she'd been to think she could make a potion and help the witch. She was a pathetic excuse for a familiar.

But she didn't want to die in this thick potion, even if she was a complete screwup.

She wiggled hard in the thickness and began to move. She felt the grittiness sliding off her fins, felt the sluggish liquid begin to churn.

And as it churned, the color brightened.

And somehow, Golda felt her fatigue dropping away as she swam.

Round and round, faster and faster.

The liquid swirling around her.

No, not swirling. Stirring.

She was stirring the potion!

Stirring with her full body, using whatever magic she had within, and the potion was responding. The separate ingredients churning and molding into a healing potion that poured energy into her even as she reflected it back.

Golda had done it! She could feel the potion working through her and around her as she swam around the cauldron. A perfect healing potion, powerful and energizing.

"What the hell is going on?"

The witch's shout startled Golda. Her tail smacked down on the surface of the potion and swished right.

Sending a splash of potion into the witch's face as she peered over the edge of the cauldron.

Golda froze, barely moving her fins as the witch sputtered. The gentle waves of the potion buffeted her, and she felt herself sink lower.

Maybe she could sink to the bottom and hide. After this, she knew the witch would never listen.

Minerva shook her head, sending droplets of potion flying. She wiped a finger down her cheek and sniffed at it. She frowned and sniffed again, then tested it on her tongue.

"This is a healing draught," she said.

Golda curled her tail around her body.

I thought I could help with the potions. I am sorry for the mess.

"Sorry? My age spots are already fading." The witch held out her hand, admiring it. She gripped the edge of the cauldron. "I ain't seen such a powerful draught before."

A grin lit her face. "We'll package this up and start on the next one. There's one for de-aging and another for growing, and a few different love potions. Other healing potions that are a little trickier as they heal the spirit as well as the body." The witch tilted her head, raised one of her bushy eyebrows.

"Would ya like to learn 'em?"

Golda stuck her head up from the potion and gaped at the witch. Boy, would she!

Yes, oh yes! I'll be the best apprentice familiar you have ever had.

The witch gave a grunt. "Never much liked training apprentice familiars. All that work, and they go ahead and leave ya." She ran a finger along the edge of the cauldron as she dropped her gaze.

She cleared her throat. "Ya wouldn't consider sticking around after the nine months of your apprenticeship, would ya?" Her voice sounded a little rough, a little shaky.

Minerva was asking her to stay!

Golda felt her heart pounding so hard it shook her own body.

Can I have a bigger bowl and move closer to see the cauldron and ingredients better?

The witch smiled again. "I'll get ya a tank that takes up the whole side of that wall, and you can swim right up to see everything clear and easy."

Golda gave a leap of joy and splashed back into the cauldron. The witch chuckled.

"You'd better get outta there so I can package up this potion, and then we can start on the next. I'll get your bowl, and you can sit right here. We'll work on a love potion next. How does that sound?"

Golda swished her tail and did a final lap around the cauldron.

That sounded just fine.

ABOUT THE AUTHOR

Based in Toronto, Canada, Rebecca M. Senese survives the frigid blasts of winter and boiling steams of summer by weaving words of mystery, horror, science fiction, and fantasy.

She is the author of the fantasy/mystery series, the *Noel Kringle Chronicles*, featuring the son of Santa Claus working as a private detective in Toronto. Her work has appeared in *Holiday Hijinks: Mistletoe Merriment, Happy Holiday Historicals, Whimsical Winter Wonderland, Crazy Christmas Capers, Blaze Ward Presents Special Edition: After the Fall, Cutter's Final Cut 4: Witches; Pulphouse Fiction Magazine, Home for the Howlidays, Unmasked: Tales of Risk and Revelation,* the *Obsessions Anthology, Fiction River: Superpowers, Fiction River: Visions of the Apocalypse, Tesseracts 16: Parnassus Unbound, Ride the Moon, Tesseracts 15: A Case of Quite Curious Tales,* and *Storyteller,* amongst others. Find out more about Rebecca at rebeccasenese.com

OLD CROW
STEVE RASNIC TEM

S leek and dark as the forest night, the crow glided over the Appalachian ridges corrugating southwest Virginia. Wallens, Powell, Cumberland. Those were their human names, but for Old Crow they were Home.

He flew early each morning, before the mountain witch got up, because he didn't want to remind her he had the freedom of the skies, and she did not. She'd tried when she was younger, but on her best days her long skirts barely cleared the ground. Now she'd lost even that. She couldn't keep the right words straight in her mind.

During the first hour after sunrise, the crow chased a rabbit and tormented a stray kitten. He meant them no real harm, and after a few minutes tired of the play. Having lived too long, over a hundred years now, games quickly bored him, as did most everything else. He still felt grateful and loyal because of the witch's gift, but he couldn't remember the last time his long life gave him pleasure.

During the second hour he paid his respects at a crow funeral, of which he'd seen many during his time in the world. They'd gathered around the body and in the surrounding trees, hundreds of them, because it was late summer and more than the usual few families were on the move, to gaze at the broken fledgling on the path. According to rumor a farmer's hunting dog was the cause. The alarm over the danger went out hours ago. But now they watched without noise, and after the appropriate time departed in silence but for the sound of all those flapping wings.

Old Crow felt grateful to be included in the rituals of his kind. In their black eyes he was no longer one of them. He was an outcast, barely tolerated because of his differences, but they still sometimes allowed him in. A century spent with the witch woman, Emer, made him something more than crow, although he hadn't the language to say what.

On his way back to her he spotted an acquaintance, the scrub-jay, far below, hopping and bobbing his blue head about the forest floor. Old Crow dropped out of the sky, rustling his tail feathers as he landed in front of him.

"You can't have my food!" Scrub-Jay scolded.

"I don't want your food."

"Well, you can't have it! It's not here!" But Old Crow had already seen him shove acorns, worms, and seeds under a nearby pile of leaves and bark. Scrub-Jay made several such caches in the area, no doubt a few more than he remembered.

"The woman feeds me well. And I'm quite capable of scavenging for myself." To demonstrate, the crow hopped onto a log, pulled a stiff twig into his beak, and used it to fish a grub out of a deep fissure in the wood. Showing off, he then flipped the grub over to Scrub-Jay, who trapped it beneath a talon.

"Mine now!" the scrub-jay squawked.

Old Crow jumped from the log and fluffed his glistening black mantle. "Enjoy the fruits of my labor."

"There's a possum nearby. We can share."

The crow was genuinely surprised by the offer. "No thank you."

"He's dead now."

The crow knew the possum when he was alive, not that it made any difference. Once dead, friends were food, unless, perhaps, they were crows. But more than once he'd fed on the eggs and nestlings of crows.

"I mean *completely* dead."

"I *know*," Old Crow said sharply. "I know the dead very well. My kind invented death, haven't you heard?" He wasn't sure if this was true. There were stories. But he wanted to say a bold thing and so he did.

"I just thought. Well, the gossip is your woman isn't doing so well. You might need to find another one to live with."

"You shouldn't listen to gossip. Where did you hear this?"

"Around. Just around. They say she wanders."

"She has always wandered. It's how she finds what she needs for her spells and cures."

"They say she writes on trees. They say she speaks to herself."

"When she casts a spell she *is* speaking to herself. Who else would she be speaking to? And she has always written on trees. She has always made her signs."

What Old Crow didn't say was writing on trees kept Emer from getting lost. She once knew the woods as well as she knew the many lines marking her own face, but now the simplest journey could be the cause of endless confusion. She marked the trees between her cabin and the nearest store so many times they were losing their bark. But no one needed to know this.

Three blackbirds landed nearby. The scrub-jay went into a panic, jerking its head in a series of sharp turns. "You can't have my food! You can't have my food!"

The blackbirds tried to talk at once, running around and flapping their wings. Old Crow stared at them. He'd been known to eat a blackbird or three when he thought it necessary.

Emer had fallen in the woods. One of the blackbirds suggested that now she was dead she might make a good meal.

Without a word Old Crow took flight.

THE CROW FIRST MET THE WOMAN WHEN HE WAS YOUNG AND eager to try out everything in his surroundings, no matter the risk. He'd settled down in the middle of the highway to dine on some carrion, an unfortunate squirrel who thought she could outrun the humans' automobiles. In those days, the crow was short enough to duck beneath their metal bellies. He only had to avoid their tires.

He soon became aware of the woman watching him from the side of the road. She looked no better than roadkill herself with her ragged clothes and dirty flesh, but beneath the grime he could see the youthfulness in her face and the sharpness in her eyes. She carried a large sack for gathering treasures—castoffs and trash and roots and seeds—detritus which only the smartest of granny women appreciated their hidden value. "Clever Crow" she called him back then. "Clever Crow," she whispered until in a trance he hopped over, and she added him to the collection in her sack.

He considered himself lucky she didn't eat him or take him apart for some esoteric project or other. Instead, he became her constant companion, surprising since she lived alone and did not enjoy the company of others. Depending on her mood, if uninvited strangers ventured near her cabin she might send them away with stings and rashes and running sores.

But the mountain folk owed her much and hired her often for tonics and charms to protect themselves, spells for the sick and lovelorn. But she would not guarantee spells of attraction and sold them only when she needed food or money. Sometimes she would sell a farmer a special scarecrow, and the crow spread the word those fields were not to be touched.

No one liked or fully trusted her. To these people Emer was the outcast crow. But he stuck with her, and over time Clever Crow became Old Crow as she rewarded him with a long life for his loyalty, replacing his deteriorating parts as needed using spit and cobwebs and singsong words spoken barely above a whisper. As her powers grew, so did his.

He found her sprawled off the path among the phlox, bearberry, and creeping juniper. She'd lost her way again, became tangled in the undergrowth and went down. She sometimes forgot there was food in the cabin and went off foraging on her own. He should have been there.

She was poorly dressed for the cool morning weather. She wore her thin silver nightgown and she'd forgotten her hat and shawl. She lay motionless, staring at the sky, her long gray hair twisted and stiff with briars and sticky weeds.

"Old woman, are you dead?" It came out harsher than he intended, but most things did. His voice had no music in it.

"I don't … know. Am I?" Her eyes did not move when she answered him. Her voice was flat and sounded as if it came from a distant place.

"Get up. You cannot lie here."

"I don't know how."

He had no strength to give her, but he possessed serious power to annoy. He plucked at her shoulders and pecked at her legs until she rolled onto one side, then pulling at her sleeves made her get up on one knee. Further torments drove her to her feet, swinging her arms to swat him.

He floated up and made two barrel rolls overhead to remind her any attempt to catch him would be wasted effort.

"Who are you? Are you my husband?" He was alarmed by the tears on her face. In all those years he never saw her cry. If she were ever married it was before he knew her.

"I'm Old Crow. You used to call me Clever. Do you remember?" The idea of being her husband amused him. What was he to her anyway? She never gave it a word. The crow had always been a bachelor, but he loved the females.

"And my name? What is mine?"

She misplaced many things in the past few years, but this was the first time she lost her name. "Your name is Emer. You have told me it is Irish, but I don't know what that means. You are my oldest friend."

During the next few months, the crow stayed closer to the cabin and discouraged the woman from venturing out. She had plenty of food stored away, but if necessary he could kill a small rabbit or squirrel and drag it inside and leverage it with a stick into the fire. Like most crows, he was good with tools, but all these years in her company made him—what was the word she used? —her *engineer*.

But some days, if she were determined, he could not stop her from going out, either to the small country store, or the cabin of some acquaintance, or some favorite source for bulbs, seeds, or roots. For she was a granny woman, a witch, and although he was special, he was mostly a crow. He always followed her, flying between trees and bushes, perching on the edges of roofs or cliffs along her route, waiting while she completed whatever business she had, and then followed her back, cawing his signals, waking her up, reminding her of the safest way home.

Old Crow did the best he could, but he knew his assistance was not adequate. Some mornings she put her clothing on backwards. Other days she had difficulty dressing at all. He could pick the proper clothes for her and pull her sleeves in the right direction, and sometimes turn a blouse around using talons and beak if she hadn't put her arms in yet, but he couldn't button her up and she tended to fight him over zippers.

She fell asleep most afternoons and he used these breaks to fly, gliding through the air making observations, patrolling for predators, and chasing them away with his harsh warning cries. Once freed from Emer duty, he was available to search for the sights which buoyed him, a lovely spider's web perhaps or a wasp colony's elaborate multichambered nest. These were not treasures to bring home or cache in a secret collection like a gathering of shiny stones or buttons or bits of jewelry. They were valuable primarily as memories, and he filled his aging crow brain with as many of them as possible. Isn't that what wise creatures do, before their inevitable end?

Fall soared into winter, and winter meant not letting the flames in the fireplace go out no matter what. Old Crow couldn't count on Emer remembering how to restart the fire or even wanting to. On freezing afternoons, she slept more, waking up only to take a bit of food from his beak or to accuse him of carrying unwelcome messages out of her troubled dreams.

Eventually the seasons circled to spring again and the rising warmth encouraged her to talk, but what she said often made little sense.

"How are you feeling today?" the crow asked, perched on her mountain of quilts.

"I am dead, sorry bird. Please don't try to wake me."

"You're not dead, Emer, but you have been sleeping for quite a long time."

"Can't you smell me, stupid bird? I stink. I am dead."

"You just haven't been able to wash yourself, old woman, and that's beyond my powers to help. Let me find a nurse somewhere in the hollers, or another granny woman to perform the chores I cannot."

"I am hot and then I'm cold and then I'm hot again."

"See? The dead feel neither cold nor heat."

"What is your name again?"

"You once called me Clever Crow and then Old Crow. These have been my only names."

"Well, shut up Old Crow or whatever your name is and let the dead lie in their well-earned peace." She was silent for a time, but then added, "Just don't leave me by myself."

They had been through this charade a few times before. Periodically over the years Emer decided she was finished. She was dead, and all indications appeared to be this was a fact. She had no pulse. She had no breath. Her skin became discolored, her lips blue. The locals took her to a funeral home, and she'd lie there a few hours, but then in the middle of the night she would forget, or change her mind, climb off the mortician's table and leave. Each time it became Old Crow's job to find them a new place to live where she could start all over under a different last name.

She did this for decades. Sometimes the locals put up a gravestone, anyway, waiting for her body to return. Emer's big secret was she had graves all over the Appalachians, each under a different last name.

BUT NOT THIS TIME. THIS WAS CLEAR IN OLD CROW'S BRAIN. There was no getting up this time, no changing her mind and climbing off the table. As spring sailed into summer Emer ate less and less, until it seemed she was living on air alone, and maybe the smells wafting through the cabin windows. She got out of bed only to go to the bathroom, but he wondered why she bothered since there was so little waste produced.

She slept entire days and most of every night. She became reduced to a speech of single words like wind, and dream, and empty, and crow.

For months, the crow wondered what he would do once his granny woman died. Could he organize a crow funeral, or would that have insulted her? Could he get the other crows in these mountains to come?

Could he stay in her cabin forever? This seemed unlikely, unless her reputation was such no one would want to trespass even after her death. It had been decades upon decades since he'd lived in the wild on his own. Could he do it again?

Old Crow began to notice his own changes. He had always had such sharp vision, able to spot a hint of food on the ground even when flying high in the air. But lately the world was always at dusk, his vision reduced, a time to find a roost and avoid the owls.

Before he met the woman the crow roosted with other crows in the same group of trees near water. There they shuffled and squawked, moving down through the branches as more crows arrived, exchanging gossip before settling down to sleep. Since moving in with the old woman he grabbed sleep whenever he could. She gave him so much to do there was little time for slumber.

Now he could barely keep his eyes open in the middle of the

day. He barely noticed when his tail feathers began to fall out. He could still fly, but badly. He kept bumping into things. When his wings started falling apart, breaking down into cobwebs and bits of bark and leaf and yellowed witch's spit, Old Crow knew his flying days were over. As Emer died, he was losing everything she gave him.

On their last day he hardly noticed when she climbed out of bed. He realized what was happening when she shuffled out the cabin door. He crept slowly behind her, losing feathers and talons, a withered eyeball, along the way.

Halfway through the yard she stopped, her limbs stiffening. She raised her arms toward the sky, and they froze. Old Crow dragged himself up her hardening skin with beak and broken claws, desiccated feathers, and fracturing bones, until in the crook of a branch he was able to rest.

He wondered if they would gather, all his dark crow kin. He wondered if they would grant him their minimal respect.

ABOUT THE AUTHOR

Steve Rasnic Tem is a past winner of the Bram Stoker, World Fantasy, and British Fantasy Awards. His novel *Ubo* (Solaris Books), a finalist for the Bram Stoker Award, is a dark science fictional tale about violence and its origins, featuring such historical viewpoint characters as Jack the Ripper, Stalin, and Heinrich Himmler. He has published over 500 short stories in his 45+ year career. Some of his best are collected in *Thanatrauma* and *Figures Unseen* from Valancourt Books, and in *The Night Doctor & Other Tales* from Macabre Ink. You can visit his home on the web at www.stevetem.com.

TAIL-END

LIA WU

hey had clamped Maverick's tongue.

There were, of course, plenty of other things that the vet techs had done to the poor fox since taking him back, but Hai Nianqing couldn't help but fixate on his tongue. It lolled inelegantly out of the drugged fox's mouth, a pink, fleshy ribbon smushed between white plastic. The clamp was attached to a wire that fed information about his pulse and body temperature to a monitor off in the corner of the room. If Maverick had been awake, he never would have let such an indignity pass without comment.

Nianqing pulled out her phone and took a picture.

"We'll send you home with a bag," the veterinarian who had escorted her back was saying. He was gesturing to a bag of saline that hung above Maverick's prone body. It dripped steadily, pumping the liquid mixture relentlessly into the ever-growing hump between the fox's shoulder blades. A hunchback fox. His divine ancestors would surely gekker relentlessly at the thought.

Nianqing took another picture.

They had forced a tube down his throat in order to sedate him. Intelligent and reasonable on a good day, the fox had not taken the threat of an invasive blood draw and x-ray kindly. When

Nianqing had consented to the procedures over Maverick's loud protestations, he had shot her a look of utter betrayal. She had felt a morsel of unease at the time, wondering if she really was making a big deal out of a simple stomach bug as the fox had argued. Now, however, she *wished* she had been overreacting.

They had come into the waiting room with papers highlighted in vibrant red. They had been sympathetic, but relentless in delivering the diagnosis. *Acute kidney failure*, they had reported. *Maybe a week, maybe a day, maybe a few months*, they had estimated when she asked about his life expectancy. She had imagined the worst immediately, wondering if she would be going home with euthanasia plans in her back pocket. But the word never came up, and they had escorted her into the back room. "To show you what to do next," they had explained.

To show her how to keep Maverick alive. To put his life quite literally into her hands in the form of saline bags, medicated wet cat food, and pills to stimulate his appetite.

She took a picture of the instructions, as if such diligence would increase the effectiveness of each step later on.

Maverick was, as expected, not happy when he finally awoke, stuffed in a cat carrier in the backseat of her car.

"That was utterly unnecessary," he groused, shaking the remnants of the anesthesia from his voice with a low growl.

Nianqing didn't respond. Once they came to a stop at a light, she turned around and took a picture of his grumpy face, making sure to focus on the diamond-shaped patch of white fur on his forehead.

Maverick nipped at her sleeve through the kennel door. "I'm perfectly fine," he insisted.

"*Acute* kidney failure," Nianqing said as she turned back around to a green light. "*Failure*, Mav, as in *not working*. That's not *fine*."

Maverick adjusted in the carrier, his claws clicking against the plastic. "My fiftieth birthday is just around the corner," he said, rather than address the actual issue. "You humans have transplant procedures for things like this, yes? We'll just wait it out. Once I turn fifty, I'll be able to shift and then I'll get a transplant and it will all be fine."

It didn't work like that, not really, and they both knew it. *Hulijing* like Maverick tended to reach the maturity necessary to access shapeshifting around the age of fifty, but it wasn't a magic flipping of a switch on the fox's fiftieth birthday at the stroke of midnight. On top of that, Maverick had been the runt of his litter, always reaching the milestones years behind his siblings. While the others had begun adapting to human speech just a decade after their birth, Maverick had taken another twelve years to do the same. Granny Hai had almost written off the fox as mundane, until he finally started speaking alongside a toddling Nianqing. Taking it as a sign that their companionship was meant to be, Granny Hai had declared the fox to be Nianqing's intended familiar on her fifth birthday.

That had been just over twenty years ago.

That should have been the end of it—for Maverick, at least. He should have accompanied Nianqing through her life, stewarding her through the highs and lows of human life, and bid her goodbye as she died of old age. He should have lived to steward her children, and their children, and generations of children beyond them through their mortal lives, while he cultivated ever closer to immortality. He should have curated a knowledge of the ages, enough knowledge to fill nine tails' worth. He should have walked the earth for one thousand years, observing the whimsies and faults of humanity, before joining his kin among the ranks of celestial foxes bridging life between this world and the heavens.

He should not be struggling to eat and dying of thirst as his organs shut down, having lived only five percent of the life he was meant to live. Somewhere along the way, surely, this meant that Nianqing had failed as a mortal shepherd.

Mother, when Nianqing called her with the news, disagreed.

"I was never sure about that runt as a companion for you," she said. "This is good. Now, you will be able to get a proper familiar. I'll call Paixu."

Paixu—the oldest fox still directly involved in mortal affairs and the one to track the births of spiritual fox kits eligible for human stewardship. Nianqing had only met him once, when he had come to her house to approve the new bond between her and Maverick with an odd look on his ethereally beautiful human face.

Nianqing hung up the phone.

Over the next few days, she came to find that getting a diagnosis was only the beginning of a larger battle. Maverick was too proud, too wild of a spirit to take his declining health seriously. Though they shared the same language, Maverick refused to understand Nianqing's efforts to treat him. He continued to not eat. On the second morning, he stalked out of the kitchen with his nose up in the air, claiming that the medicated canned food the veterinarians had sent home with them was "trash—not worth my time."

In response, Nianqing pulled out the blender. She poured the wet cat food in, along with some bone broth, and pureed the gelatinous mixture. She filled up an oral syringe with the pale, vomit-brown concoction. She pulled a towel from the linen closet. Then, she waited.

Maverick, inordinately curious as only a fox of his ilk could be, came in search of her after a prolonged amount of silence. As he padded back into the kitchen, she swooped upon him, wrapping the towel around him in the mimicry of a swaddle.

"Wh—how *dare* you! Release me!" he protested.

"Sorry, Mav, but this is for your own good," Nianqing replied grimly. She snatched up the syringe from the counter in her right hand, pinned the swaddle between her thigh and left elbow, took hold of his jaw with her left hand, and jammed the syringe into the hinge of his mouth.

"Good my a—*grk*."

Her thumb pressed down on the plunger, forcing two milliliters of cat food puree down Maverick's throat. Forced to either drown or swallow, the fox eventually swallowed the substance.

"*Ugk* — don't you dare — "

Nianqing replaced the syringe in his mouth and depressed the plunger another two milliliters. Then she did it again. Then again.

Then, she pulled back, an empty syringe in her hand and a solemn frown on her face. Maverick watched her, a wild, petulant anger in his eyes and in the set of his snout. They sat in a fragile silence.

"I'm not sorry," Nianqing finally said. "You need to eat."

One of Maverick's paws managed to wriggle free of the towel. He jumped out of her lap with the explosive force of a predator on the hunt. His claws caught her arm as he fled, drawing blood with a vengeance. He did not speak to her for the rest of the day.

The next morning, arm bandaged and desperate to make it to work on time, Nianqing tried a different approach. She brought the bag of saline to Maverick. "This will help you quench your thirst. Your kidneys can't process water anymore."

Maverick watched her suspiciously.

"You're thirsty, aren't you?" Nianqing pushed. "Your stomach will sooner burst with all the water you drink than give you the relief you need."

"What are you going to do with that?" Maverick eventually asked, eyeing the long, thin tube that ran from the saline bag, ending in a needle.

"I'll stick this — ," Nianqing brandished the needle, " — into your back, between your shoulders. Then I'll turn this — ," she pointed at a dial midway along the tube, between the needle and the bag, " — to drip the mixture into you. We'll have to wait a minute or two for enough saline — two hundred and fifty milliliters — to flow into you. Then I'll be done."

Maverick considered this. "Okay," he said. "Let's try."

He stood still on the low coffee table and patiently watched Nianqing hang the bag from the light fixture on the living-room ceiling. He scrunched his snout as Nianqing ran her hand up and down his back, feeling for a patch of loose skin. She pulled this skin up and away from Maverick's spine, creating a taut canvas. She took aim, then pushed the needle in. Maverick remained still.

"Is this okay?" Nianqing asked.

"Fine," Maverick reported consideringly. "Just a pinch."

She nodded. "I'll turn the dial now, then."

The liquid began to drip, first slowly and then rapidly. Maverick tensed. "That's *cold*."

"Sorry. Bear with it," she urged.

Maverick's ears twitched. His tail flicked. Nianqing watched the saline level on the bag gradually fall. Fifty milliliters. Seventy-five.

"How much longer?" he gritted out, a yowl building at the back of his throat.

"Just a bit more," Nianqing lied. But even as she said so, she knew that there wouldn't be a "bit" of anything. The black of the fox's ear tips had disappeared, fully pinned back against his skull. He had begun to pant and chitter on his short, bursting exhales. He braced low on his forepaws, as if to dodge the chill of the liquid coursing into him. His teeth gnashed.

"Yeah, *nope*."

He lurched from the coffee table, the needle pulling from under his skin. The saline continued to gush out, soaking the table where it lay discarded.

"Maverick!" Nianqing scrabbled for the dial, rolling it back down to cut off the flow.

"Not happening!" the fox cried back. He darted into the space between the wall and the TV stand a few feet away. "It's *cold*, there's a *lump* on my back that I can feel *oozing as we speak*, and this is all *stupid and unnecessary*!"

"I'm sorry you feel that way," Nianqing conceded, brandishing the point of the needle at him, "but this is *absolutely* necessary!"

"Is not!"

"Is too!"

"Nuh-uh!"

"Yeah huh!"

Nianqing wondered briefly, hysterically, what her family would think if they were to see her now, a twenty-five year old woman living on her own in a rundown apartment with no feat of magic to her name, no door guard talismans on her threshold, no wealth of knowledge or treasures lining her bare walls, engaging in a screaming match with her dying *immortal* fox guardian under a bald-lightbulb-cum-IV-drip fixture. No amount of joss paper offerings would likely appease the absolute mortification her ancestors were undoubtedly drowning in watching her now.

A week ago, the thought would have made Nianqing laugh. They were *supposed to have time.* Maverick had promised that he would *be there* when she finally graduated. He had promised to finally help her build a life-size, to-scale joss paper *palace* (fit to please their ancestors for *decades*) for Tomb-Sweeping Day so that they could laugh at the awe and horror on their family's faces. He was supposed to be an ass and chase off a revolving door ensemble of girlfriends and boyfriends like a cliché overprotective brother until finally becoming best pals with *her one.* He wasn't, however, supposed *to die.*

Nianqing pulled out her phone and took a picture of Maverick where he had wedged himself against the wall. She pulled the saline bag from the ceiling fan and put the cap back on the needle. "Whatever," she said, suddenly very tired. "We'll try again tomorrow."

"Tomorrow" came in the form of Hai Jianquan and Wanmei.

Sticking to *tradition*, Uncle Jianquan had given his own fox a "proper" name. In appropriate fashion, Wanmei had reached the next stage in his cultivation several years ago, obtaining the ability to shapeshift into a human well before he had reached his fiftieth birthday. Now, bright and early in the morning, Wanmei stood at Uncle Jianquan's side, his amber-gold eyes soft and pitying as he peered down at his littermate. Maverick, Nianqing realized, had lost a lot of weight. He was gaunt, his snout sharper than usual. His fur seemed coarser, too. She waited for Wanmei to pass the judgment she had already passed on herself. She had to have failed, had to have messed up far beyond her meager, barely passable proficiency in spells and talismans could have foretold.

She waited as Uncle Jianquan and Wanmei sat down for tea. She waited as they listened patiently to the veterinarian's diagnosis and prescribed treatments. She waited as they entertained Maverick's complaints on the matter. She waited as they returned to the front door, exchanging their slippers for their shoes.

She waited until it seemed like they would never say a word on the matter. She wasn't sure if she should be relieved or upset by the suspense.

Finally, shoes back on and coat tucked over his arm, Uncle Jianquan said, "You've done well."

Wanmei nodded in agreement.

Nianqing blinked. "What?"

"You've been a very diligent companion in your familiar's final days. I would expect nothing less of this filial niece of mine," Uncle Jianquan clarified with a warm, low chuckle. His eyes crinkled as he smiled and he flashed a grin. He had never gone to get braces, though crooked teeth were notoriously bad in the family. He waved and began jogging down the concrete stairs that would take him back to the ground floor.

"Filial?" Nianqing muttered. "Sure. Filial piety for the win and all." She couldn't have kept the bitterness from her voice even if she tried. What good was *filial piety*? Could it replace Maverick's organs? Could it fast-forward his ascension? Rocket him ahead in progression by a thousand years until death was hopelessly unable to catch up?

Wanmei smiled. He hadn't quite yet perfected the art of sculpting the angles of his chin into the smooth roundness of a human's jaw. "Not everyone reaches immortality," he reminded her. "He had always been behind the rest of us, growing up. No one is surprised."

He said it reassuringly. Nianqing, for a moment, hated him. But his eyes were sad, and the tilt of his smile was shallow. She wondered if he was really speaking to her or himself and nodded. "That doesn't mean it hurts less."

"No," he said softly. "No, it doesn't. Take care of him."

Feeling strangely raw and off-balance, Nianqing took this goodbye from Wanmei as permission to be a little shit. If her uncle's familiar gave her a command, it was only natural that she, the filial niece, obey.

Operation "Bag Fox" was a go.

She had stewed in her defeat as she prepared for bed the night before, plotting and revising her plan of attack. With the morning sun and the unexpected visitors, her plan hadn't felt as corporeal or feasible. Now, however, with grief, frustration, and pettiness warring in her chest, she decided it was worth a shot.

She dug out a cloth bag, one of the larger ones that she used as a reusable grocery bag. It was deep, sturdy, had long handles, and had a rectangular frame that made it easy to set standing up on a flat surface without anything in it. It was a shade of maroon that reminded her of beets, which had caused her to designate it the "vegetable bag" on her trips. Maverick had scoffed at her arbitrary labeling, then been the one to use the term more reliably than even her.

She placed it on the coffee table, fluffed it so that it would remain open with the handles pulled out and hanging neatly on the outside, then sat back on the couch just a couple of feet away. Canine though he might have been by scientific standards, Maverick's instincts were truly feline in the most reliable of ways. Within minutes of placing the bag on the table, Nianqing watched the fox wander over, considering the bag in true "it fits, I sits" fashion. He leapt onto the table, then gingerly hopped into the bag.

Nianqing burst into action. She darted forward, took hold of the bag, yanked it up until the edge of the cloth was taut against the underside of his neck and fully covering his hindquarters, then wrapped the handles into a double knot. There was still enough of an opening on either side of the tied handles to let plenty of Maverick's spine peek through, giving her enough skin to poke with a needle.

Success.

Maverick was unimpressed. He stared her down with a deadened glare. Nianqing, honestly not thinking that she would get this far, stared back. She pulled out her phone and took a picture.

"*Stop* that!" the fox hissed. The bottom edges of the bag bulged and writhed as he felt out the confines of her trap. "Put down your damn phone and *let me out*!"

"I'll let you go shortly," Nianqing reassured. "Just let me play nurse for a minute."

The saline bag found its place on the ceiling fan once more. Maverick again bore the pinch of the needle with ease (though, this time, with a lot more grumbling as well). She turned the dial.

Nothing happened.

The small, cylindrical chamber that fed from the bag to the line (and consequently the needle) showed no signs of movement, where previously it had shown a near instantaneous reaction in the form of a steady dripping liquid. Nianqing began to panic.

Maverick, seeing this, wheedled, "Looks like it's broken. You tried your best. Oh, well. Now—"

Nianqing stepped up on the couch cushion stationed directly beneath the light fixture, wrapped both of her hands around the bag, and squeezed. There was a single drop in the chamber, then another, then several. Then, finally, the dripping gained a rapid and steady rhythm, like normal.

Sullen, Maverick snapped his snout shut. As the mixture flowed into him, he tensed as before. "*Cold,*" he muttered. He wriggled in the bag and arched his spine against the knotted handles, but stayed firmly locked within the cloth. Nianqing watched the level slowly decline, from the large 1 to the black line indicating the halfway mark between 1 and 2. Fifty milliliters. It reached the large 2. One hundred milliliters. A yowl started low in Maverick's chest.

Nianqing looked away from the bag to the contraption she had made. Her lips twitched, then she let a laugh slip through.

"Oh, this is *funny* to you, is it?" Maverick said.

"No," Nianqing said, the corners of her mouth desperately fighting against a smile. "It's just...you're...you're my *hongbao*."

Maverick looked at her, no doubt despairing the final dregs of her sanity leaving her, then glanced down again at the red hue of the bag that held him captive. She saw the realization wash over him. He jerked and started thrashing. "I'll show you *hongbao*!" he snarled. "Lucky money, my ass. See if I get you any this year, you little shit!"

"Little?" Nianqing snipped back. "Who's the one stuffed in a shopping bag? Take your medicine like a good fox and stop acting like a child!"

"You're the one that stuffed me in here!" Maverick shouted back. "You've manhandled me and humiliated me and jabbed me with needles and force-fed me *garbage*. If anyone's the child here, it's *you*!"

"What else am I supposed to do?" Nianqing cried back. A thread of dark, oppressing helplessness was starting to weave its way into her lungs. "What am I supposed to do? Let you die?"

"YES!"

Maverick, startled by his own bark, went still as a statue. The refrigerator buzzed and clicked on the other side of the wall. The little water fountain Maverick had picked out for himself at the store gurgled happily in the corner. Nianqing's teeth clacked as her mouth fell shut. Strangely calm, she checked the bag again. Two hundred milliliters. Close enough.

She rolled down the dial, pulled the needle from Maverick's back, capped it, then tugged at the knot to loosen it. Maverick, quiet and wincing, shoved his way out of the bag and jumped delicately down to the floor.

Distantly, Nianqing thought that she might be angry. The veterinarians had been sympathetic. Mother had been excited. Uncle Jianquan and Wanmei had been accepting. Maverick was…Maverick was…Where was the outrage? Where was the upset? The confusion? She felt like she was living in a foreign world, where up was down and left was right. How was she the only one? *Why* was she the only one? This was a battle they needed to fight, even though they had already lost and everyone was acting as if there was never anything worth fighting against in the first place or had already given up and she was tired and scared and she wasn't ready to lose, not him, not yet, not *ever* —

She choked on a sob. Maverick, stricken, sat, ears pinned back and tail wrapped around his paws.

"Why would you say that?" she said. "*Why would you say that?*"

The fox slunk closer to her in a slow and delicate crawl. "I…" He hopped up onto the couch and leaned heavily into her side. "I've never…" He winced. "I've never really belonged. Not like my littermates. Not like you and your parents and uncles and aunts. I'm a failure of a familiar. You can't cast spells — no, listen to me," he said firmly, sensing Nianqing puff up in protest. "You can't cast spells, and your talismans are just pretty pieces of paper because I can't help you channel spiritual energies. I *barely* learned how to speak and, to be honest, we both know I was never going to learn how to shapeshift into anything worthwhile, if at all. It just — it just *makes sense*."

"What, so because you're not useful to me, you should die?" Nianqing snorted. Her face was already swelling up into an ugly mess of splotchy patches of red and a stuffy nose. "That's not fair."

"Life's not —"

"No, I mean it's not fair *to me*," she said, righteously greedy in her grief. "Who decides what's useful? So I can't cast spells, who cares? I share an apartment with a *talking fox*. I have a friend, my best friend, who knows me and knows how to deal with my shit. I can't use talismans, so what? Neither can Lucille next door or my professor with multiple doctorates and a fancy electric car. Christopher and Amy, who *can* use talismans, are unhappily divorced, convinced the world isn't worth saving — Amy trauma-dumped on the stairs last week, which you missed because you were *sick* — and, and…I don't know what my 'and' was, but you get the point!"

Maverick stayed silent.

Nianqing, words run dry, pulled out her phone. She scrolled to her photo album and started sifting through them. There was a closeup of the pureed cat food in a syringe. There was a snapshot of a bowl of untouched food. There was Maverick scowling at her from behind the TV stand. There was Maverick gazing at her solemnly through the door of the cat carrier. There was Maverick, sedated and limp on the examination table. There was Maverick's back to her as he watched the latest episode of their favorite K-drama, Nianqing facing the camera with a hand over her mouth in a dramatized gasp. There was Maverick, curled on the couch, a paw placed over his eyes to shield from the light as he slept, Nianqing looming over him with a smile as she took a selfie. There was Nianqing by herself, with a glue-on moustache, scarf, and hat, posing in an exaggerated swagger with finger guns. There was—

"I took these for you," she said.

Maverick watched the screen as she continued to scroll through the album, taking in the record of the life she had shared with him over the years.

"I thought that, eventually, it would get hard to remember me, after I, you know, kicked the bucket," she said. "Faces of relatives can really blur together after a while, let alone a few centuries, so I thought I'd make it easy for you to keep me separate from all those descendants later on. So I took these pictures *for you*. But now, I realize that I don't have enough *of you*. How am I supposed to accept that? I don't have enough pictures. I didn't think this was something I had to prepare for."

Maverick was silent, still watching the screen. Finally, he asked, "So, all this time, I wasn't…a burden to you?"

"Never."

"You don't want another—a *better*—familiar?"

"No."

"You want *me*?"

"Yes."

Maverick was quiet again for a moment. Then, he said, "I have a confession to make."

"Am I about to be angry?"

"Probably."

"Am I about to cry more?"

"Maybe? You've already started the water works, though, so I can't take all the credit."

"What is it?"

"You're also probably going to laugh."

"Maverick."

"*Okay*, so you know how us foxes are supposed to grow tails? Collect 'em all, become immortal, all that?"

"Yes…"

"And you know how growing those tails isn't connected to age the same way our other abilities are?"

"You *didn't*."

"Yes, I did *and* no, I didn—hold on, don't hit me! Let me show you!"

Maverick hopped back onto the coffee table, embarrassed and shamefaced. He shimmied his tail and scrunched his snout. Then he moved his tail to the side and gestured with his paw. There, at the base of his tail, was a…nub. It was tiny and naked, as if someone had transplanted half of a rat's tail onto Maverick's backside. It was pitiful and ugly, but also the most amazing thing Nianqing had ever seen.

"You have a second tail."

"I'm *growing* one, yes."

"Two tails."

"Ugly as Li Tieguai and incomplete, but yes."

The rush of hope that swept over Nianqing was intoxicating, all while the indignation lurched up her throat like bile. "Why didn't you say anything?"

"Look at this thing! It's embarrassing."

"But do you know what this means? You've got a spare tail! You have excess life energy to expend! You can *live longer!*"

That was simplifying it a little bit. Tails were more like health potions and semi-powerful antidotes than extra lives in video games—helpful in a pinch, but still not a complete panacea. Romances that told of a *hulijing's* efforts to gift a tail to a mortal lover to extend his or her life still often ended in tragedy, despite everything. Still, it was *time*.

They had time.

Maverick grimaced. "Yes, but at a *cost*. Our tails are knowledge, Nianqing. I worked damn hard to get to where I am. I already checked with Paixu. If I give up a tail, I won't be able to speak. I'll have to start over from the beginning, just a dumb, stupid fox who can't talk with you anymore. I'll be no better than a mundane mutt again."

Nianqing considered this. More importantly, she considered Maverick. He spoke with dread, but also a cautious, wary interest. He watched her closely, as if gauging her response.

"I won't think any less of you," she said, hazarding a guess at his uncertainty. "You'll still be Maverick. You'll still be mine."

Maverick slumped and snuffed out a laugh. "No getting rid of you, huh?"

"Not a chance," Nianqing said. "And no getting rid of *you*, either."

Near the stove, a discarded talisman she had crafted in a pique of madness glowed. Neither noticed. Neither cared.

They had time to figure the rest out later.

ABOUT THE AUTHOR

Editor, publisher, author—oh my! Lia Wu is passionate about a lot of things. She collects degrees like other people collect shinies in Pokémon (she's making her way through a doctorate now… stand by). She has a paper mâché collage of comic books held together by the sheer force of her nerddom on her living room wall. She also, to the ongoing exasperation of her ancestors, can't stand spice. But that didn't stop her from writing a story centered in the spirit and mythology of Chinese tradition and it won't stop her from writing more in the future. How do you social media? Lia doesn't know. Send help. @liawuwriteswords

NAMELESS
JOHN G. HARTNESS

A QUINCY HARKER, DEMON HUNTER SHORT STORY

Quincy, what in all nine Hells is *that?*" asked a tall human with dark hair. He stood in the doorway of my new apartment, asking the skinny human that I'd saved from a nest of vampires about me. While I appreciated being noticed, and took the opportunity to lick my front paw and use that to smooth a tiny bit of ruffled fur over my right ear, I did not at all enjoy being referred to as a "that."

But this human smelled wrong, and there was something odd about his aura, a lot like the monsters I'd just left. I tensed, then leapt up and climbed onto the skinny human's (I guess his name is Quincy) shoulder. If I needed to claw this new person's face off, it would be much better if I had some altitude to start with.

Quincy tipped his arm down, dumping me most unceremoniously to the floor. I swatted his leg. Not hard, just enough to let him know that I did not appreciate being cat-handled in such a way.

"Hello, Uncle," Quincy said, walking over to a set of shelves in the wall and beginning to rattle bottles and glasses around.

"This is...well, I guess I haven't named it yet. It's a cat. It was living in the factory where the vampire nest was, and..."

"And it followed you home? Is that the next line? Oh, please tell me that's the next line!" A very pretty blond...human appeared in the living room of the apartment. She just *appeared*. One moment she wasn't there, and the next minute she was standing right there clapping her hands, dressed in blue jeans and a t-shirt with a blue water droplet on the front and the word NOPE in big letters. She smelled *much* better than the grumpy man. I guess his name was Uncle? But she also wasn't human. Something about her aura looked strange. Brighter than a human, but with none of the black splotches that dotted my new human's aura, and almost covered "Uncle's."

"It did not follow me home, Glory," my human said. "I cleaned it up, and it did follow me to my car, then I just brought it home. Figured worst case we can adopt it out to somebody in the building, and best case...well, best case is I guess we'll never have a mouse problem."

Mouse? There are mice? I sniffed the air. I didn't smell any mice. I cocked my head to listen. I didn't hear mice, and they aren't smart enough to be subtle. It's not fair to tease a cat about mice and then not provide them. I took another swipe at Quincy's ankle to make sure he understood this. He ignored me.

"Quincy, we don't have mice. We pay an exorbitant amount in exterminator fees to not have mice. We don't need a cat, and besides, the building has a no pets policy." I was really starting to dislike this older kinda-human.

"I own the building, Luke," Quincy said. So is the mean sorta-human's name Luke or Uncle? Both? I turned my attention back to that pesky patch of fur on my ear. I suppose humans, or almost-humans, are allowed to have more than one name. I have several, regardless of the fact that Quincy had yet to even ask me what my name was.

"That's right, sweetie, you just ignore those two. They'll go on for hours, but eventually Luke will get his head outta his butt and learn to like you." I turned around, fast, because this was another new voice, and I am *not* used to humans being able to sneak up on me. Even the monsters in the factory where Quincy and I met couldn't sneak up on me. But here was another new person, this one sitting on a barstool with her feet crossed at the ankles, watching the two men argue with a little smile across her face.

She looked older than the others, with dark skin and brown eyes, although something about all three of them told me they were older than they appeared. But they weren't human, and this woman was. "Was" is the important word there, because she wasn't human anymore. Not a live human, anyway. Seeing dead people wasn't new to me, there were ghosts in the factory. Usually because the monsters killed people and drained their blood. But a couple of the factory ghosts had been around before the monsters, from when I first crawled out of the hole in the wall where my mother left us.

The ghost woman looked nice, and her aura was a gentle blue, not the angry red or the sad yellow I'd seen around other ghosts. She had dark hair with a lot of gray in it, so she was obviously lovely, as gray fur is preferable to any other, and she had kind brown eyes and a smile dancing across her face. "So you really *can* see me, eh? Mama used to tell me cats could see haints, but that's not something you can test unless you're a cat." She gestured at herself. "Or a haint, which I reckon I am now. My name's Cassie. It's a pleasure to meet you, kitty."

I went over to her and rubbed up against the legs of the stool. I couldn't rub against her legs to make her feel better, because I just went right through her, but she smiled down at me anyway. She stretched out an arm to pet me, but her fingers went right through my fur. It tickled a little, so I rolled over and showed my belly. She didn't have to wonder if it was a trap or not. I couldn't maul her if I tried. It did take a little bit of the fun out of the belly rub, because half the enjoyment is the game of whether the human is smart enough to remove their hand before I bite. But it was worth it even without the bloodshed. Belly rubs are *good*.

"Luke, the cat stays," Quincy said, and I recognized his tone. This was no longer a matter of discussion. The boss monster used that tone with his minions when he really wanted to drive a point home. It even worked sometimes. Luke was a much more reasonable monster, or almost-human, because he just mumbled something and went over to the refrigerator. "Now, the question is, will you look after him for a few days while Becks and I go to Manteo for a much-needed vacation. Alone. As in, without a new pet. Just me and my fiancée. Sorry to spring this on you, Uncle, but I didn't know I was bringing a cat home from a hunt."

The not-human frowned, but nodded. "Fine. I suppose Glory can assist me in tending to the animal until your return. The cat can stay here for a few days. But then it goes to your apartment."

"Yay!" The blond not-human said, clapping her hands. She walked toward me, but I slunk back, unsure about her. I didn't know what she was, and I didn't know if she thought cats were beautiful, or delicious. One of those things leads to pets and scritches, and the other leads to awfulness. The monsters sometimes tried to drink my blood when they had a bad night hunting, but after a clawed eyeball or two, they learned that I was a dangerous snack.

"It's okay, honey," the ghost said. "That's Glory. She's one of the good ones. A *very* good one, in fact. She's a real angel. From Heaven. She won't hurt you."

I don't know why I trusted the ghost. Dead people hadn't been particularly nice to me up until then, but I trusted her. I let the blond woman pet my head, then she scooped me up and cuddled me to her chest, fingering the gems on my collar and smoothing that patch of fur I was having trouble reaching. I butted my head up against her chin and purred, enjoying the gentle contact. For a moment. Then I squirmed loose and twisted around until I was perched on her shoulder. It's important when working with humans, or creatures that appear human, to establish boundaries early, so she needed to understand that while I would happily ride around the room on her shoulder, I would not be carried like a kitten.

"That's right, you adorable little ball of fuzz," the pretty woman said. "I won't hurt you. But where are my manners? We haven't even told you who these humans are, and you're just supposed to trust us and let us take care of you? That's not right at all."

"*Mmmm-row!*" I said, in complete agreement. I definitely needed some better way to think of them than "skinny human," "blond human," and "not human that smells bad but is probably not terrible."

"That's Luke," she said, pointing toward the dark-haired not-human. I knew this, of course, but it's not like I could interrupt her. "He has a lot of names, but the most famous one is Dracula. He's a vampire, but he's not a bad one."

I froze at her words. I'm a *cat*, and even I'd heard of Dracula. The other vampires talked about him like he was a monster, or worse, a really mean dog. He was the thing they told each other about at night when they drank the yellow bad-smelling stuff and wanted to scare one another. Then I relaxed. If they were scared of Dracula, who I guess was also called Luke, and they were awful, then maybe he was only bad to bad people. After all, Quincy liked him, and I liked Quincy, so I suppose I could trust him. Still, I wasn't quite sure how I felt about being in a room with the monster that the monsters were afraid of. I licked the side of the woman's face, as much to make me feel better as her.

She giggled and pointed to my skinny human. "That's Quincy. Quincy Harker. He's one of the good guys. One of the best, actually. Not that I'd ever tell him that. He hunts down the bad creatures and makes sure they don't hurt people."

He sure hunted down the monsters I'd lived with. Hunted them right to pieces and scattered those pieces all over the factory we'd been living in, as a matter of fact. I liked him for that already, but having the pretty woman tell me he did that kind of thing all the time was a pretty good endorsement. I licked her face again, and she gently pushed my face away.

"Stop that, silly. You'll ruin my makeup." I wouldn't, because she wasn't wearing makeup. I reached up and patted her cheek with one paw.

"Me?" She asked. "You want to know about me? I'm…Glory.

Let's just leave it at that. I'm Harker's Guardian Angel. Whenever he gets in trouble that he can't get out of on his own, I'm there to get him out."

I nuzzled up against her ear and let out a long purr, telling her that I appreciated it. If this Harker human got into trouble worse than the bunch of mean vampires I used to live with, and she was able to get him out of it, then she was probably pretty powerful. And she gave really good chin scritches. I patted her face again, turning my head to look at the ghost sitting at the bar. Glory didn't react, didn't even turn to look at the other woman. I guess humans and sorta-humans can't see things as well as cats. Makes sense. Inferior species and all.

I licked her cheek one more time, then jumped down off her shoulder and walked past the arguing humans into a dark room with the door left open a conveniently cat-sized crack. There was a big bed, but all the sheets were pulled tight and there was nothing interesting to rub on, so I crawled under the bed to explore. It was depressingly clean, without even any interesting threads or scraps of fabric hanging down to amuse myself with. I curled up and went to sleep, far enough away from the edges that if anyone wanted to annoy me, they'd have to crawl all the way under there with me, and I'd have enough warning to leave before I could be molested unawares.

I woke up in need of food and a litter box, not necessarily in that order. My nose told me that both of those things were nearby, so I unfurled myself from the ball I'd slept in and went in search of my necessities. There was a fresh litter box in the small room off the bedroom, with all the hard floors and bright lights, with a dish of food and another of water sitting on the floor nearby. I availed myself of these things and sauntered back out into the living area. Quincy and Glory were gone, and Luke was standing on the balcony, leaning over the railing with his sliding glass door open.

The ghost was sitting on the same stool, staring at Luke's back. Cassie didn't say anything, but it didn't take words to see the sadness rolling off her. She hunched over a little on her stool, rocking back and forth a bit with her arms wrapped around herself. Glowing blue tracks of spectral tears ran down her face as she looked at Luke, staring out over the city, lost in thought. I walked over to where she sat and rubbed against her leg. Well, rubbed *through* her leg, because—ghost. But I thumped into the leg of her stool, and she looked down at me.

"Hello, kitty," she said, then sniffed.

"What's wrong with him? Is he sick?" I asked.

"You can talk?" she asked, shocked out of her grief at the surprise.

"Of course I can talk," I replied. "It's just rare that any of you tall folk are smart enough to listen. You seem a little more intelligent than the rest, so I decided to let you in on my little secret."

"And you know that you're the only one here that I could tell, even if I wanted to, so it was safe," she added, proving once again that animals with gray fur are not only more attractive, but smarter, than other breeds.

"Well, that too," I admitted. "But why is he sad?" I wasn't letting her get away with not explaining things just because I'm a cat. I know we are far more intelligent than humans, but I was willing to stoop to her intellectual level to try to understand why Luke seemed upset.

"He misses me," she said simply. "I miss him, too, and we both regret the things we didn't say to each other while I was alive."

That didn't make any sense to me. "Why didn't you say them?" I asked.

"I thought we had more time. I know it's silly. Look at me. I was old when I died, but even at almost seventy, I thought we had more time. Stupid, considering our line of work, but I looked at how long Luke has been here, and how long Quincy has been running into the fire and coming back out again, and I thought I could put off telling him how I felt until tomorrow. But tomorrow never gets here, does it?"

I started to correct her but paused. She was right. No matter what day it became, it was never tomorrow. I turned my answer into a large yawn and started grooming my tail. Tails are tricky things, especially when you have thick luxuriant fur like I do. They're lovely for balance, and useful for expressing emotion, but they do collect dust. Mine often provides a convenient excuse to clean while I decide exactly what to say next. This was one of those times.

"I suppose it doesn't," I finally replied, getting a nice big chunk of dusty fur pulled from my tail. "But if you can't talk to him, and he can't even see you, why are you still here?"

She gave me a wistful little smile, a tiny upturn of her lips that didn't touch the sadness in her eyes. "I can't let him go without someone to watch him. He needs help, and I can't do it anymore. But I also can't let myself stop looking after him yet."

I understood the sentiment. I didn't like the not-humans... *vampires*, I'd lived with, but after Quincy killed them all, I'd felt a little sad. They were the only family I'd known since my littermates ran away into the wild, and now the vampires were really dead, not just the walking around being mean kind of dead they had been before meeting up with Quincy Harker.

"Would it help if I talked to him? Not like this, of course, but like humans expect me to sound?" I asked. If this was going to be my new family, they would require tending. Even the monsters I'd lived with before appreciated it when I brought them mice and other treats. Only Luke said there were no mice in the building, so I wasn't sure what to bring him.

"Maybe," the ghost said. "Couldn't hurt."

I rubbed in the vicinity of her leg again, letting her know I approved of her idea, and strolled across the living room to sit in the doorway to the balcony. *"Mrowr?"* I said, which really meant "Are you okay?" But I knew he wouldn't understand me.

He did turn around, though, so he wasn't so deeply mired in

sadness that he couldn't respond. That was a good sign. "Hello, cat. Do you need something?"

I sauntered over and twined around his feet, rubbing the corner of my mouth all along his legs, trying to erase the sulfur smell with good, healthy cat scent. It didn't work. It seemed like the smell was part of him, somehow. At least he petted me.

"You're very soft, cat," Luke said. I gave him a little purr, partly to tell him that I was well aware of how luxurious my coat is, and partly to let him know that it was acceptable to continue the compliments and petting. He crouched down and continued stroking my fur, then he lifted me up and wrapped his arms around me. I purred loudly this time, nuzzling my face against his, and he let out a ragged gasp, burying his face in my fur. I smelled the salt as he began to cry, shedding hot tears against my fur, and I clung to his shoulder as he rocked back off his heels to sit down hard on the balcony, nearly collapsing against the iron railing. He sobbed like every bit of his heart was shattered, like his entire life had come unmoored, like he'd lost his best friend, or worse, his cat.

I let him cry. I laid my head on his shoulder and let him weep for a long time, purring softly into his ear to let him know that it would be all right, that he wasn't alone, and that I would take care of him. I could feel a slight chill in the air as Cassie came and sat down beside us, and I felt the tingle as she reached out, her hand passing through both of us as she did her best to comfort him. After many minutes, he sniffled, then raised his face from my fur.

"I'm sorry, cat. I seem to have gotten blood in your fur. I expect we will need to give you a bath." I looked down my side, and sure enough, he had wept blood all over my lovely gray coat. And after Quincy had gotten us both perfectly clean with his magic, too. Well, I appreciated the sentiment, but I was *not* letting an almost-human bathe me, even if we had just enjoyed a moment. I leapt from his arms and sprinted across the balcony, through the living room, and returned to my spot under the bed. If he wanted to bathe me, he was going to have to come get me. I curled up and started cleaning myself, licking the bloody tears away as Luke sat on the balcony laughing almost hysterically at my departure. Humans. Even if you aren't one but look like one, you're probably still insane.

I MUST HAVE FALLEN ASLEEP AFTER MY BATH, BECAUSE WHEN I next woke I could tell it was several hours later. The apartment was quiet, but something felt wrong in the air. It wasn't a smell, because Luke's sulfur scent and the lingering tang of blood in my fur was overpowering. It just seemed like there was something out there that didn't belong. A moment later I heard a slight creak as someone walked across the floor in the living room. They were being sneaky, which meant they didn't belong. Humans aren't very good at stealth, almost laughable in the attempt, but I knew that when they were trying to be quiet, it meant they were doing something they shouldn't be doing. Which are of course the most interesting things humans do, so I crawled out from under the bed to take a look.

I recognized her as soon as I peeked around the doorway of the bedroom. She was one of the monsters from the factory, one of the vampires that had invaded my old home until Quincy came and disposed of them. And she was the worst of the lot. She smelled more of sulfur than the others, and she was mean. She drained all the mice she found, leaving just bloodless husks for me, and whenever the boss vampire would set me out in public places as bait for their hunting trips, she would always threaten to leave me out there all alone. I didn't like living in a factory full of monsters, but I liked the idea of living on the streets even less.

"Where are you, little kitty?" she asked, her voice soft and sweet. She looked younger than most of the other vampires, with long red hair and heavy makeup. "Come out, pussy cat. I know you're in here somewhere." She looked at her phone, turning around in circles holding it in front of herself.

"I know you're here, you little fleabag. I can track your collar, so I know you and the bastard that killed my family are here

NAMELESS • 315

somewhere. Now come out here and show yourself, you little shit!" Her voice lost all its sweetness and she spit venom with her words.

I needed to find Quincy, or Luke, and get them to deal with her. Permanently.

Where was Luke, anyway? It seemed strange that he would just let her wander into his apartment like this. I scanned the room until I saw him, slumped on the couch surrounded by half a dozen empty bottles and reeking of alcohol. He was out cold. I'd seen the other vampires try to get drunk before, and they all finally gave up on it because it took so much alcohol to have any effect. For Luke to drink enough that he didn't even notice this monster coming into his home, he must have been very committed to getting wasted. Maybe I should have let him give me that bath.

I had no idea where Quincy was, and he was the one the vampire was hunting. I didn't know if I could wake Luke from his drunken stupor, and none of these people spoke cat, as far as I could tell. I scanned the room for something to knock over, but everything was too far from the edges of the counter. Inconsiderate, really. How was I supposed to warn them of danger, or poor decorating decisions, if I couldn't knock things onto the floor?

"I can lead you to Quincy, but I'm afraid of what she'll do to Luke while we're gone," said a voice from behind me. I turned to see Cassie standing in the bedroom doorway, her face alternating between angry and sad.

"What do we do?" I asked.

"There you are!" the vampire crowed.

Shit. I forgot about vampire hearing. I had tried to speak softly, but the monster heard me, and now she was walking toward the bedroom. I ducked back under the bed while I formulated a plan.

Could I claw her eyes out? No. Vampires heal too fast for that. She'd just grow them back.

Could I outrun her? Maybe, but there wasn't anywhere to go, and I hadn't quite figured out how to operate a doorknob yet.

Could I fight her? No chance. I tried that when the vampires first moved into the factory, and even the weakest among them almost killed me with one kick. She was one of the stronger monsters, so she could tear me in half without a thought.

She knelt beside the bed and reached an arm under, pawing at the floor as she tried to grab me. I swatted at her hand, leaving a trio of long red scratches down her forearm. She hissed and drew her hand back, then chuckled. "I'm going to enjoy this, kitty. I'm going to rip you limb from limb, then I'm going to kill the prick that killed my family. I'll show him not to mess with the Red Fang Crew."

I didn't bother reminding her that the Red Fang Crew was all dead, and I also avoided pointing out what a stupid name that was. Mostly because I knew she was a lesser species, and thus didn't speak cat, but also because I was scrunching myself up as small as I could go into a corner under the bed so she couldn't reach me. The longer I kept her attention on me, the more time I had to think up a way to wake Luke up and tell him there was a vampire in his apartment. Another vampire, that is.

Her hand brushed the fur on my belly, and I grabbed hold of her fingers with my front paws, drawing her hand toward my mouth and biting down into the soft flesh between her thumb and forefinger. She let out a yowl and drew back a shredded hand. "That's what you get for touching without consent," I said. Of course, all she heard was a growl and a hiss, but it got the point across.

The second she pulled her arm back, I sprang out from under the bed and bolted for the living room. I ran full speed for the couch and leapt up onto Luke's stomach. I hoped my weight would be enough to rouse him, but nothing happened.

"Is this him?" the vampire asked. "Is this the bastard that killed my family? This is going to be fun. Not much of a challenge, with him passed out, but fun. Good kitty, leading me right to him."

I jumped down, knocking over all the bottles onto the carpeted floors. Nothing broke, and there wasn't even enough noise to wake Luke up, so I ran for the kitchen and leapt up onto the counter. Nothing was close to the edge except a cup, and it didn't even break when I shoved it to the floor. Just landed with a hollow *thunk*. I looked back, and the vampire was standing behind the couch, staring down at Luke with a vicious grin on her face. I needed something, anything, that would make enough noise to shake him out of his stupor.

"Up there, kitty," Cassie's voice came from the door to the kitchen, and as I looked, she pointed to the top of the refrigerator, where a jar stuffed with coins and bills sat. "That was the swear jar. I made them all put a dollar in there every time they said a bad word, and Quincy got to where he just put a twenty in every morning and said whatever he wanted. Fine by me. The money was for my grandbaby's college fund anyhow."

The refrigerator was tall, but I could make it. I got a running start, then glanced back through the big open window into the living room, where the monster had pulled a big knife from her belt and held it high over Luke's head. I sprinted along the counter, bunched my legs underneath me, and leapt for the top of the fridge. I cleared the edge easily, shot forward, and slammed my head into the jar full of money.

CRASH! The jar hit the floor and smashed into a million pieces, sending shards of glass, bills, and coins out in a broad spray across the tiles. I hopped onto the counter between the kitchen and living room to see Luke still lying on his back on the couch, but he had a hand raised, and clutched in that fist was the other vampire's wrist.

She still held the knife but couldn't move her arm even a millimeter. "You dare?" he asked, his voice low and dark.

"You DARE?" he repeated, the second word growing into a roar, and now I started to see why he was the monster these vampires saw in their nightmares.

"*YOU DARE?*" He was yelling now, and I watched as he stood and swung her around, his grip never slacking. He just pulled the vampire to and fro like a rag doll, then swung her around, letting her collapse to her knees in front of him, the hand with the knife stretched up above her head.

Luke leaned down into the vampire's face. "Do you know where you are, idiot child?"

The mean vampire didn't say anything, just shook her head.

"Do you know who I am?"

Another head shake.

"What are you doing in my home?"

More silence.

"That was not a rhetorical question, woman. Why are you here?"

"You killed my clan. You murdered the Red Fang Crew." She spat the words, defiance returning to her face. "So now I'm going to kill you."

Luke looked confused for a moment, then realization dawned. "You were one of the nest that Quincy destroyed, weren't you?"

"Who's Quincy?"

"My nephew. He destroyed a nest of vampires last night. He brought a cat home." Luke glanced over at me, and I watched his eyes lock onto the jeweled band around my neck. "Ah, that's how you found us. A tracker in the collar. Clever. What was the scam? You set the helpless kitty out on the road, wait for your quarry to take it home, then follow the signal and murder everyone inside? I did something similar in Prague in the eighteenth century. I used a dog, though, and had to follow by scent. No GPS back then. Well, even though I respect the plot, I cannot abide trespassers."

"I'll just leave. No harm, no foul." She looked truly terrified now. I suppose finding out that your intended prey was actually a more terrifying predator than you could be unsettling.

"I'm afraid there has indeed been harm," Luke said. "You violated my sanctuary. That cannot be allowed to stand."

"That's right!" I yowled from the floor.

"And there's the matter of you and your...Red Fang Crew creating vampires without permission. That also cannot be tolerated." It seemed like he had trouble saying the name of her gang with a straight face, which I could relate to.

"Permission?" the female vampire asked. "Who the fuck do you think is going to give us permission? We're the top of the food chain. We don't *ask*. We take."

"If you were the top of the food chain, your nest would still be alive, and I'd be dead," Luke said. "You are so far down the ladder that you can't even *see* the top of the food chain. I am the epitome of apex predator. I am the stuff nightmares and legends are made of. I am all the things that made you sleep with the light on when you were human, and that haunts your dreams even now. And you? You. Are. Dead." With that, he let go of her arm, grabbed her jaw with one hand and hauled the vampire to her feet. He put his other hand on top of her head, pulled his hands in opposite directions, and spun her head around. A loud *crack* rang out, and the vampire slumped to the floor. Luke grabbed her by the front of her shirt and dragged the body into the bedroom. I followed, curious.

He kept walking into the bathroom and dumped her body into the tub. He noticed me following and said, "She will begin to dissolve rapidly, and it's better if that happens somewhere I can just flush her down the drain. Otherwise, we shall have quite the mess to clean up. More even than you made in the kitchen. Thank you for the alarm, by the way. I would have been very annoyed to wake up with a knife in my chest."

"If you'd woke up at all, you old coot," Cassie said. I turned to see her standing in the doorway behind me with a sad smile on her face. "You did good, kitty."

"Thank you," I said. "I didn't want her to kill him. He doesn't smell nice, but I think he might be."

"Oh, no," Cassie replied. "He's anything but *nice*. He tries to be good, and he can be exceptionally kind, but he's by no means nice. He'll take good care of you, though. Will you do the same for him?"

I sensed there was more to her question, and I felt like this was an important moment, both for me and for the ghost. I glanced over at Luke, and it seemed like time wasn't moving for him, just for me and Cassie. This was *definitely* an important moment. I sat down on my haunches and looked up at her. "He matters, doesn't he?"

"Oh yes," Cassie said. "They all do. Quincy, Luke, Glory, all the others...they're very important. I was never that important, but sometimes important people need the little people to help them do important things. And that can make us important, too. What do you say, kitty? Will you help take care of my family?"

"Yes." I didn't need to say more. After all, when cats say something, we mean it.

"Thank you." She turned and looked at Glory, who was suddenly standing in Luke's bedroom. "I'm ready."

The angel smiled, and a bright white light enveloped her, momentarily blinding me. When it faded, Cassie was gone, just a few blue sparkles hanging in the air to remember her by, and Glory was wearing gleaming sliver armor with wide white wings sprouting from her back. She knelt beside me and stretched out a hand. I leaned in, allowing her to pet me.

"Thank you, Augustus Stormcloud Farrington the Valiant. You'll make a fine addition to the team." She pet me on the head, scratched under my chin, then vanished before I could ask her when she learned to speak cat, and how in the world she knew my name. I'd never told any human, or even anything that looked human, my true name.

Luke stood up, wiped his hands on a towel, and stared down at the dead vampire in his tub. "Well, that will take a few hours to decompose, and in the meantime I should like something to eat. I believe I have a few bags of O-positive in the crisper. Would you like some tuna, kitty? Not that cheap kibble that Quincy left for you, but something befitting a hero."

At the mention of tuna, I began to rethink my concerns about Luke. He might smell bad, and he might not be nice, exactly, but if he was going to provide tuna and clean the litter box, we might be able to make this new partnership work.

ABOUT THE AUTHOR

John G. Hartness is a teller of tales, a righter of wrong, defender of ladies' virtues, and some people call him Maurice, for he speaks of the pompatus of love. He is also the award-winning author of the urban fantasy series The Black Knight Chronicles, the Bubba the Monster Hunter comedic horror series, the Quincy Harker, Demon Hunter dark fantasy series, and many other projects.

In 2016, John teamed up with several other publishing industry professionals to create Falstaff Books, a small press dedicated to publishing the best of genre fiction's "misfit toys." Falstaff Books has since published over 300 titles with authors ranging from first-timers to NY Times bestsellers, with no signs of slowing down any time soon.

In his copious free time John enjoys long walks on the beach, rescuing kittens from trees, and playing *Magic: the Gathering*. John's pronouns are he/him.

Acknowledgments

This anthology was made possible with the generous support of Draft2Digital and Western Colorado University's Graduate Program in Creative Writing.

ABOUT THE EXECUTIVE EDITORS

KEVIN J. ANDERSON has published more than 180 books, 58 of which have been national or international bestsellers. He has written numerous novels in the Star Wars, X-Files, and Dune universes, as well as the unique Clockwork Angels steampunk trilogy with legendary Rush drummer Neil Peart. His original works include the Saga of Seven Suns series, the Wake the Dragon and Terra Incognita fantasy trilogies, and humorous Dan Shamble, Zombie P.I. series and The Dragon Business series.

He has edited numerous anthologies, written comics and games, and the lyrics to two rock CDs. Anderson is the director of the graduate program in Publishing at Western Colorado University.

An award-winning writer, editor, and designer, ALLYSON LONGUEIRA has worked in fiction and nonfiction in multiple media, including newspapers, magazines, and books for twenty years. While a newspaper editor she led her newspaper to three general excellence awards in three consecutive years. After she transitioned to fiction editing. Allyson launchedFiction River Presents published by WMG Publishing, for which she serves as series editor. Allyson is the publisher and CEO of WMG Publishing, Inc.

IF YOU ENJOYED FEISTY FELINES
YOU MAY ALSO LIKE...

Monsters, Movies & Mayhem

Unmasked: Tales of Risk and Revelation

Gilded Glass: Shattered Myths and Fractured Fairy Tales

Merciless Mermaids: Tails from the Deep

www.ingramcontent.com/pod-product-compliance
Lightning Source LLC
Chambersburg PA
CBHW020556120726
47903CB00001B/285